TO LEE,

MY VERY WARM AND PERSONAL
REGARDS.

6-26-99

THE MAHDI

A MILLENNIUM THRILLER

by

MARGO DOCKENDORF

Cypress House

Fort Bragg, California

Cypress House
155 Cypress Street
Fort Bragg, CA 95437
1-800-773-7782
e-mail: publishing@cypresshouse.com
http://www.cypresshouse.com

ISBN No. 1-879384-35-3
Library of Congress Card Catalog No.

Cover design by Rebecca Zimmerman

Images copyright © 1998 PhotoDisc, Inc.

Visit the author's website at: www.granitepress.com

Printed in the U.S.A.
First edition

To my mother, father and sister, with love.
To my dearest friend, Alice,
who has been with me through so very much.
To Rebecca, for all the gifts
she has brought to my life.
And to Ann Kempner Fisher,
my beloved editor,
and the often tempestuous
collaboration that made
this work shine.

THE MAHDI

PART ONE

The most beautiful and most profound emotion we can experience is the sensation of the mystical. It is the sower of all true science. He to whom this emotion is a stranger, who can no longer stand rapt in awe, is as good as dead. The deeply emotional conviction of the presence of a superior reasoning power, which is revealed in the incomprehensive universe, forms my idea of God.

— Albert Einstein

CHAPTER 1

December 31, 1999

Bennett Williams sat uncomfortably amidst the rows of empty seats on the Swissair 747. The vacant cabin reflected just how alone he felt.

He recalled his early catechism lessons. He thought about Judas Iscariot. *Should I kiss Abu on the cheek as I betray him?* The plane taxied down the runway and then lifted its mammoth body off the ground and into the night sky, racing toward its destination in the Middle East. *Shall I call him master? Isn't that how Judas betrayed Jesus to the Romans?* He remembered that Iscariot was Latin for assassin. His stomach tightened in that old, familiar way. He hadn't had any stomach problems in a long time.

"This isn't happening," Williams muttered in disbelief. He stared out the plane's window looking for something surreal that would prove this was all a bad dream. But against the blackness of night all he could make out was his own accusing reflection staring back at him.

His thoughts drifted back to an hour earlier. "From here you'll go to Andrews Air Force Base," the President's Chief of Staff had explained as they walked from the Oval Office down the carpeted corridor of the White House. "Dulles and National are closed."

Williams nodded. "I heard air traffic control across the entire country is down."

"Yeah." Lee Cowles said, shaking his head in disgust. "Hundreds of people have been killed. Planes were colliding everywhere before the system was shut down. That computer virus has caused unbelievable damage." He shot a glance at Williams. "Your friend is something else."

Williams knew Abu was responsible, everyone did. The fact that Williams understood why Abu was doing it was little consolation. Could even the noblest end justify all the suffering and destruction that was occurring with ferocious swiftness? "What else has it gotten into? Defense computers?" Cowles didn't answer. Williams knew his allegiance was suspect. Were they worried what he might pass on to Abu? "What happens when I get to Andrews?"

"There's a Swissair 747 waiting for you."

"Where's it taking me?"

"Geneva. By the time you get there we should have worked out your safe passage to Riyadh."

"Wait a minute," Williams said, stopping Cowles with a tug on his arm. "Are you telling me I'm flying into a war zone in a seven-forty-seven without safe passage?"

"As it now stands, yes."

"That's fucking great!" Williams said in exasperation. "The skies over the Mediterranean are filled with Muslim pilots just aching to shoot off their sidewinders, and you haven't secured the fucking airspace!"

"We're in a war, Mr. Williams!" Cowles exploded. "People are dying by the thousands every day. We're on nuclear alert, and so are the Russians, Chinese, French, British and Israelis. How close Sheik Asghar is to pushing his nuclear button is anyone's guess. Your friend"— Cowles voice was filled with contempt—"has supplied his urban soldiers with Stingers. No one is safe anymore. The president can't even leave the White House!"

Williams had no response. This was the worst it had ever been. Some were saying it was the end. Some were calling it Judgment Day; they said Armageddon had truly come, and proclaimed Abu was the Antichrist. Williams ran a hand through his dark hair, took a deep breath, and began walking towards the exit to the south lawn where the revved helicopter stood waiting.

The Chief of Staff regained his composure. "But, like I said, we're working through the Swiss. They're trying to make the arrangements, but communications are extremely difficult. The virus has infected telephone systems and the recent solar activity has severely disrupted those systems that were working. We're mostly relying on short-wave radio." Williams had heard about the enormous solar flares that were appearing suddenly and throwing off the magnetic field around the planet, making satellites go haywire. Once again, he knew Abu was causing it, the same way he knew Abu had caused the recent earth-quakes and volcanic eruptions around the world. Cowles continued. "Since Sheik Asghar asked for you, we're assuming he'll cooperate. We expect a squadron of Saudi F-15s to meet you en route and take you into Riyadh."

"Where is he?"

"We don't know. He may be in a bunker somewhere; he may be living under a tent in the Saudi desert; apparently he likes to stay mobile. If we knew, we wouldn't need you."

"Do you really expect me to kill him?" Williams asked, stopping at the exit. He was looking outside at the armed Marines in full battle dress behind sandbag bunkers posted to protect the White House.

Cowles stared into Williams' eyes. "We're expecting you to do what you can. Whatever it takes."

Williams shot back, unblinking. "Jesus, don't you remember what happened in Jerusalem? Abu is invulnerable. He cannot be killed." There was stiff silence between the two men. A sardonic smile crossed Williams' face. "You guys still don't have any fucking idea who or what you're really dealing with, do you?" Cowles was impassively silent. "I guarantee that you, the president, the defense establishment, this coun-try—Christ!—every country—the whole human race, has never faced anyone or anything like Abu. Never. Forget everything you've ever been taught about fighting a war. It's a whole new ball game. If you guys don't start getting that, we're all fucked!"

Lee Cowles was getting visibly annoyed again. He took a deep breath to calm himself. "Look Ben, the President knows how close you and Sheik Asghar are . . ."

"Were," Williams corrected him. His tone was adamant yet resigned.

Cowles ignored Williams' comment. "The President knows how personally difficult this is for you and what your chances are of com-ing out alive. Believe me, we wish there was another way. Unfortu-nately, you're our last hope. If you manage somehow to pull this off, you just might bring a quick end to the war. You'll save the world and all Western civilization from a madman." The Chief of Staff paused. "But if you fail . . ."

Cowles had made his point. "If you fail . . ." The words echoed in Williams' head ever since leaving Washington, so much so that they had now become his own.

3

Williams thought of Aimee, and his son Matthew. He now had so much reason to live. Before Aimee and Matthew, he'd never known love. Now he wondered if he'd ever see them again. This is insane, Williams thought. How can I kill Abu? How do you kill a brother? Abu was more than a brother to him, much more. He'd been his best friend, his teacher, even his savior. Without Abu, he'd never have won the Pulitzer Prize, he'd never have been asked to write a book, he'd never have known Aimee, he'd never have had a son. And he'd never have found himself.

President Stanton's angry interrogatory shot back into his mind. "Just where's your allegiance, Williams?" Sitting in the Oval Office with the President of the United States, staring mutely down at the carpet and the immense embroidered eagle that clasped arrows in one claw and an olive branch in the other, and surrounded by all the trappings of power and patriotism, Williams couldn't even answer the President.

Then why was he here? Williams asked himself. What made him agree? Maybe it was simply because Abu had asked for him. For some reason it was vitally important that he see Abu again. "To what will you give your allegiance, Ben Williams?" Abu asked him a long time ago around a campfire in Uganda. He didn't know the answer then either. "That is what you must decide," Abu had told him. And it had taken a long time for him to find out. Now, after so much had happened, he was going back to Abu. He didn't know why; he only knew that it wasn't over.

Williams felt like he'd just made a pact with the devil. But who was the devil? He leaned his head back against the seat and closed his eyes. His thoughts drifted back to a year and a half earlier, that July day in Cairo, when Herschel Strunk, his editor at the *New York Times,* had telephoned and told him he was going to Bhopal, India—to the place where he would first meet Abu 'Ali Asghar. Back then he knew where his allegiance was: It was to himself, and his ambition. There was nothing else.

Williams didn't want to go to Bhopal. Bhopal was crowded and dirty. There wasn't even anything interesting about the place; it was like any other industrial town with factories and rude, belching smoke stacks. The only significant thing that happened there in the last few hundred years was an accident at the Union Carbide chemical plant that released tons of toxic gas into the air and killed thousands. That's what he had been sent to cover, even though it was history already written.

Bennett Williams knew that Bhopal had been a tragedy, but as a renowned war correspondent he was a veteran when it came to witnessing tragedies. Williams viewed going to Bhopal as one of those assignments that reminded him no job was perfect.

"Bhopal!? Why me?" Williams' tone was contentious.

"Because," Strunk answered impatiently, "you're the only one available right now."

"All right. But you owe me, Hersch."

Strunk was conciliatory. "How about the war in the Sudan? Finish up there and I'll send you to the Sudan."

"I'm going to hold you to that," Williams said begrudgingly. "Count on it." He opened his notebook. "So what are you looking for? Why Bhopal?"

"There's more to life than war and destruction, Ben," Strunk said.

"Spare me the fatherly advice," Williams replied. "Just tell me what you want."

"I need a standard follow-up piece. It's been over a decade since the '84 incident; what's going on there these days? Remember, it's our job to keep the public informed."

"Yeah," Williams answered. "I'll be in touch."

Funny, Williams thought looking back, when he hung up the phone in Cairo that day, he had no idea just how much that call would forever change his life.

CHAPTER 2

From the moment he arrived in Bhopal, Williams began hearing stories about Abu—stories about miracles; stories about saintly self-sacrifice, about devotion and compassion. Human interest stuff that readers loved.

When he heard the stories, he knew he'd found his angle. He interviewed nurses and doctors outside clinics and hospitals and even went inside once to talk with one of the patients, one of this Asghar fellow's alleged miracles—a young Muslim Indian named Qadir Shahim.

Williams' curiosity was piqued; the stories had so intrigued him, he decided it was time to find Abu 'Ali Asghar. He caught up with him one day while Abu was ferrying medical supplies from one hospital to another. "Are you Asghar?" Williams asked, walking quickly to keep pace with the long-strided, tall, dark man.

Abu glanced at Williams. "Yes," he said as he kept walking.

"I was told I might find you here," Williams said, weaving and dodging other pedestrians in an attempt to keep up with Abu. "My name is Williams," he said, "H. Bennett Williams. My friends call me Ben. I'm a reporter with the *New York Times.*"

"Yes," Abu said, "I know. I have been expecting you."

"You don't say," Williams tried not to show surprise; his voice conveyed skepticism. "And how's that?"

"I was told," Abu said.

"By whom? Anyone I know?" Williams asked sarcastically.

"Not yet," Abu responded, looking at Williams once again. "But someone who knows you very well."

"Will you introduce me?" Williams requested.

"You may depend on it," Abu answered. "When you ask me again."

"Look," Williams said, changing tacks, "this is a bit awkward. Can we talk?"

"I believe we already are," Abu replied, looking straight ahead again.

"It's rather difficult this way. Do you mind if we stop?" Williams asked.

"It is important that the hospital receives these supplies as soon as possible."

"May I walk with you then?"

"If you choose."

Williams noted the proud yet unpretentious way Abu carried himself; his brisk, purposeful walk. He was decidedly self-assured, to a degree many would find intimidating. He wasn't at all what Williams expected.

Abu was probably younger than he looked, Williams thought. More around his own age of 35, but much taller than Williams, about 6'4", and with the kind of muscular body that made him quite imposing. His robes were Bedouin but he wore a blue silk turban like the Sikhs of northern India. He kept a bejeweled, curved dagger stashed securely at his waist. Abu was swarthy and ruggedly handsome with a thick black beard and dark, disturbing raptor-like eyes that stared out above an aquiline nose.

Abu reminded Williams of a princely warrior. Men like Abu didn't exist in the real world, certainly not among the dirty and crowded back streets of Bhopal.

Williams felt drawn to Abu. Something about him kindled the flame of possibility. There was something there, something that needed uncovering, a story that needed telling.

"I'll wait out here," Williams told Abu when they arrived at the hospital.

"As you wish," Abu said with indifference.

Williams propped himself against a wall near the hospital entrance. He tucked his leather jacket under one arm, a souvenir taken from a downed Russian helicopter pilot, and lit a cigarette. He barely noticed the children scampering around him, begging for money or food as he waited for Abu to come out.

Bennett Williams was a man who prided himself on being able to go anywhere, do anything, sleep in, on or beneath whatever was available, and eat whatever he was given if it meant getting a story. He did not, however, like hospitals. They evoked unpleasant memories. More, they reminded Bennett Williams of someone he detested and no longer wanted to be.

He'd been a sickly child, and spent the better part of his early years in and out of hospitals. None of the scores of doctors had ever been able to figure out exactly what was wrong with him, although there were numerous theories. The absence of a clear diagnosis confirmed his father's assessment that his son was simply weak. "Show some guts, Ben! Act like a man!" Bennett Williams, Sr. had admonished his twelve-year-old son over and over again.

Although his lifestyle was synonymous with excitement and adventure, no one knew that Bennett Williams was simply an addict whose opiate was the rush of adrenaline he experienced whenever he heard the sound of incoming mortar shells or ricocheting bullets. He craved that rush. He needed to feel death tapping on his shoulder. It was the only thing that made him feel alive. Perilous mortality was the razor's edge of Bennett Williams' existence.

His journalistic assignments provided something else, something he coveted with secret intensity. He had always dreamed of winning the Pulitzer Prize. It had become his obsession, his reason for living. It kept him going when the rockets and artillery weren't landing around him; when survival meant eating gruel, when his bed was a hard rock atop a cold, unforgiving mountain. Yet, despite his compulsion, or perhaps because of it, the prize still eluded him.

When Abu didn't appear after a while, Williams became afraid he'd lost him. In spite of his abhorrence of hospitals, he went in to look for him.

No sooner was he through the door than the stench hit him like smelling salts. It was that odor that bothered Williams the most; not the stink of the excrement and vomit, but that ammonia smell that all hospitals had. When Bennett Williams smelled that odor, he was a child again, a helpless, sick, bedridden child. God, how he hated that feeling. It had taken years of effort to overcome it. But he won the fight; he killed that child and buried him long ago. He had developed what his father called "intestinal fortitude."

"Do you know Mr. Asghar?" Williams asked one of the attending staff.

The staff worker pointed to a ward at the end of a long corridor. Williams felt his throat constrict. He started to perspire. His skin grew cold and clammy as he moved down the hall. He heard the deafening sound of sick people moaning and coughing. His stomach tightened.

He felt like he was going to throw up. He was afraid he might pass out. The only thing that kept him from doing so was his greater fear of waking up in one of the beds.

He finally found Abu. He was in the gas ward for victims of the Union Carbide explosion. Abu sat on the edge of a bed holding a small baby. The sight of Abu brought Williams a strange sense of calm, his anxiety began abating. He studied Abu for a moment. The picture of the princely man cradling the tiny, delicate child in his broad, steady hands had a profound impact on Williams. It surprised him; sentiment wasn't part of his emotional repertoire.

Abu spoke to Williams without lifting his eyes from the baby in his arms. "If you seek something to write about, write of this one. He is the story, not me."

"Then tell me about him," Williams coaxed gently.

"He was born only a few weeks ago," Abu said, putting the nipple of a milk bottle to the infant's mouth. "His father is in a ward like this one not far from here. His father will die soon."

"And his mother?" Williams asked.

"Dead," Abu said matter-of-factly. "She died giving birth to him. They never knew each other."

Williams looked down at the baby. "And what are his chances?"

"He will soon die," Abu said. "He has a hole in his heart that is not closing. It is a congenital birth defect caused by his mother's exposure to the gas years ago."

"Is there nothing that can be done?" Williams asked. "Nothing you can do?"

Abu stared directly into Williams' eyes. Williams felt embarrassed, and ashamed. He wasn't sure why. Abu then looked down again at the baby who refused the milk offered to him. "His father will soon be dead," Abu finally replied. "He has no other family to care for him." Abu stared up at Williams. "If something could be done, would you take him? Would you accept the responsibility for his life? Would you raise him as your own until he could care for himself?"

Williams had no response. Abu stood up, placed the child on the bed, and began to visit other patients in the ward, many who knew him. Williams watched from a short distance away. Occasionally, his anxiety surfaced. Then, he'd study Abu and grow calm again. As he stood watching, Williams began to wonder about the patients. They all seemed to share similar afflictions. Who were they? Were they all gas victims? Why were there still so many after so many years?

An hour later, Abu left the hospital with Williams in tow. It was early evening. The long rays of the setting sun reflected off the dust and smog-laden air so that a reddish hue spread across the sky above the city. From the tall minarets of the mosques, Muslim muezzin began calling out in Arabic for the faithful to come to prayer.

"Where are we going?" Williams asked.

"To the Taj-ul-Masjid mosque," Abu answered. "It is time to pray."

"Do you mind if I tag along?" Williams asked.

Abu looked at Williams. "Are you Muslim?" Abu asked.

"No," Williams answered. "Don't go in much for religion. To be honest, I don't even believe in God."

"Then why is it that you wish to go to the mosque?"

"Because that's where you're going. And I still intend to talk with you."

Abu laughed unexpectedly. For the first time he seemed even remotely approachable. "You seem to be an honest man, Mr. Williams," Abu said. "I am beginning to like you. You are forthright about your intentions, and obviously determined to pursue them. Those are rare qualities among men; qualities I value. Do come along then; I am certain you will find it most interesting. If nothing else, it will help you to understand these people, and write about what is happening here."

Abu stopped walking and looked deeply into Williams' eyes again. Williams suddenly felt trapped, as though his feet had become permanently attached to the ground. It was an extraordinary effect, as though Abu was able to reach right inside Williams' brain and grab control. Abu's words riveted into Williams. "If you truly wish to be of service, Mr. Williams, do not limit your focus to the wondrous miracles you have heard about. If miracles are what you want, look around you. Observe these people; how they go about their lives, how they have overcome their hardship and suffering. Find your miracles in them— in the fact that they still live and that more did not die when Union Carbide released forty-two tons of deadly gas into the air. Write about how corporate greed turned this city into a death camp like Auschwitz and Dachau. Tell the world about how those who caused this still hide from their responsibility. If you do that, you will truly be helping these people."

After he finished, Abu stared a moment longer into Williams' eyes, then he turned and started walking toward the mosque. Williams followed quickly after him.

Abu waved to a tall, Sikh Indian standing near the mosque and as they came up to him, Abu said, "This is my friend and companion. He is called Bhaiji Singh."

"My pleasure," Williams said, reaching out to shake the Indian's hand. Williams guessed the man to be in his mid-thirties as well. Bhaiji was dark-skinned and had a thick, black beard. His turban was similar to Abu's, but was blood-red rather than steel-blue. Williams wondered if the color meant anything.

Bhaiji pressed his palms together and bowed to Williams. *"Sat Sri Akal,"* he said. It was the traditional Sikh greeting that meant 'God is Truth.' Williams withdrew his outstretched hand and nodded, slightly embarrassed.

As Williams eyed Bhaiji Singh closely, noting the similarities between Bhaiji and Abu—their physical appearance, their temperament—he began to wonder. He looked more closely at Abu. Was he Muslim or Sikh? Indian or Arab? If he was an Arab, why was he wearing a Sikh turban? Where did he come from?

Williams half-listened to Abu and Bhaiji as they discussed a problem that Bhaiji was having with his car, an old Mercedes-Benz sedan that he took great and loving care of. "Do not worry, my friend. It will be well," Abu said.

"But Abuji, it needs parts that will cost more money than we have." He sighed with resignation. "Perhaps I should rid myself of it. After all, it is simply a material object that is unimportant. My attachment to it is far too great."

"Will it be easier to walk to where we go?" Abu asked.

"Perhaps not, Abuji, but it would present less grief," Bhaiji responded.

"Perhaps," Abu said. "But it certainly would be slower, and far less comfortable." Abu glanced at Williams and then turned back to his friend. "Bhaiji, you remind me of a man my father once told me about—a Bedouin—whose trade required that he travel back and forth across the vast desert of Arabia. But because he had a camel, his journey was made possible for without his camel he would die beneath the sun's scorching rays.

11

"At first, he loved his camel and treated it with respect and appreciation. During the day it was his means of travel, in the cold of night it provided warmth, and in the loneliness of the desert it was his only companion. Yet, over time he began to take the camel for granted, and the relative ease with which it carried him to where he wanted to go. With his need satisfied, he began to think only of his wants and desires. He grew tired of losing precious time at oases while his camel drank and rested. He estimated that if he did not have to stop he could make more trips in less time and increase his personal wealth. He began ignoring the camel's needs. Then, one day, the camel died of thirst and collapsed beneath him. Feeling angry and betrayed, he kicked the dead animal and cursed it. But, as he began walking, he quickly became tired and thirsty himself and died beneath the sun's searing rays." Abu paused again. He glanced at Williams and then back at Bhaiji.

"The Bedouin began to appreciate the important contribution the camel had made to his life, and realized how much he and the camel had depended on one another. He recognized, although much too late, that what the camel had given to him was much greater than what he was asked to give to the camel. That lesson was learned at the cost of his own life. Do you see?"

"Yes, Abuji, I do," Bhaiji answered.

Abu looked at Williams. "For you, Mr. Williams, the story also has meaning. You will not win your Pulitzer Prize until you truly see its relevance to you."

Before Williams could respond, Abu turned back to Bhaiji Singh. "But know this as well, Bhaiji. The result would have been no less unpleasant for the Bedouin had he placed the camel's needs ahead of his own, for then the camel, in a sense, would have ridden upon the man's back. Do you understand."

"Yes, Abuji, I do."

Abu smiled. "As for the money to fix the car," Abu added, "it will be there tomorrow. You will see."

Bhaiji was incredulous. "Can you even manifest money, Abuji? Like the bread in the village?"

Williams ears perked up.

Abu looked at Bhaiji. "Of course, Bhaiji. I will call my mother and she will wire the funds to us." Bhaiji smiled, a little embarrassed. Abu sought to reassure him. "The universe is infinitely more cooperative with one who is clear on his own needs and takes steps to achieve them. You may petition God and God will answer but you may also have to wait until God perceives a need for a response. God sees action more quickly than passive piety. And often, Bhaiji, all that God requires is the first step."

Abu looked at Williams again, who was still ruminating about the Bedouin and the camel, and how it applied to him. He was also wondering how Abu could have known about his particular ambition. He figured it was probably a lucky guess.

"But prayer is very important," Abu said, "and now it is time to speak with God. Do you still wish to join us, Mr. Williams?"

"More than ever," Williams answered.

CHAPTER 3

Abu removed his shoes as he entered the mosque. Hundreds of devout Muslims knelt on the floor while being led in prayer by the mosque's senior Imam.

Abu took a place toward the back of the immense hall. He joined in performing the Salat, the manner of Muslim prayer. Williams and Bhaiji remained at the rear, a short distance from Abu. Williams spotted Qadir Shahim close by, kneeling among the other Muslims.

At the conclusion of prayers, it was time for the Imam to speak to the faithful gathering. The message delivered usually contained a special blend of politics and religion, as well as a discussion of important matters for the community. But that night the Imam informed his devotees that he would not be speaking to them. "There is one among us who is new to our city, but many of you already know him. I found him to be most wise and sincere. He has asked that he be allowed to speak tonight." All heads turned as the elder looked to the back of the room. "Would you honor us, my friend?" the Imam asked Abu.

Abu rose gracefully from his place on the floor and walked to the front of the large room. He stepped onto the raised platform, placed both hands together in front of him and bowed. His deep voice filled the mosque. "In the name of Allah, the Merciful, the Compassionate, my name is Abu 'Ali Asghar."

Qadir Shahim had told Williams he'd never seen the visitor who knelt beside him in the hospital and miraculously cured him, the one who he thought could have been no other than Allah. Williams watched Qadir as Abu spoke. "It was him!" Williams overheard Qadir Shahim proclaim in an exuberant whisper to the man beside him. "It was not Allah! It was him! He is the angel from God that cured me!"

"Shhhhh," the man next to him responded.

Williams watched Qadir as he became mesmerized by Abu's words as though his entire life had led him to this moment.

"I am here to speak to you of justice," Abu intoned. "I am here to speak to you of righteous indignation. I am here to speak to you of equality, and who you are in the eyes of Allah." The huge room was silent.

"I am here to tell you that it is God's desire that you learn the truth of yourselves. It is important for you to know that you and Allah are one: There is no separation, no difference. You were born from the light that is God, and it is through each of you that the light of God shines the brightest.

"That is why I speak to you of justice and righteous indignation, for how is it that another can deny you that which is yours? How can you be any less deserving of dignity, of respect, of meager comforts, than any other? How can it be that you, and millions like you, are forced to live in filth and squalor while the privileged few enjoy opulence and wealth? How is it that each of you must send your small children to the streets to beg for money and food when there are others in the world who spend more than you earn in a year on a fine dinner in Paris, Tokyo and New York?" Murmurs rose up from the audience. Heads nodded in agreement.

Williams couldn't help but notice how compelling Abu's voice was. "The Prophet Muhammad delivered God's message to humanity at a time when greed and selfishness had begun to divide the Arab people. Before that time, those in the tribe shared everything; they knew that the survival of the group depended upon the well-being of everyone. There were no rich, there were no poor. But then, as they prospered, some began to hoard their wealth. They made themselves rich and caused others to be poor. The wealthy grew fat and lazy and ignored the less fortunate. The poor were hungry and homeless. They became resentful and bitter. Those who had once shared a common heritage, a common purpose, became enemies.

"Allah was not pleased that his children should be so divided. So he spoke to the world through his messenger Muhammad. He spoke of justice and equality, and God said it was not proper or just that any should be denied their rightful place as children of Allah. His word became the holy law of the Koran. And through Muhammad, God showed humanity how it could regain its strength and its unity. Allah reminded all people of the importance of meeting the needs of the many over the wants and desires of the few." Again, heads nodded in agreement as some whispered to their neighbors.

"Now, here in Bhopal," Abu said, his voice growing indignant, "thousands lay sick and dying. It is as shocking an example of utter disregard for the well-being of others as may be found upon this planet. Do you know what the explosion of the Union Carbide plant says to the world? It says that the people of Bhopal—the poor of the world—have no value. They are, after all, only peasants, stupid farmers. There are too many of them anyway. And their poverty is their own fault. That is what the incident at Bhopal says to the world." There were angry rumblings in the mosque.

Abu's voice was becoming increasingly outraged. "And I say unto you: Those who are responsible are murderers! They walk free and continue to kill, and they engage in a vast conspiracy to deprive you and everyone like you of what is rightfully yours! The perpetrators of this great injustice have been given a slap on the wrist—they have been merely fined. All they must ever do is pay a paltry sum of money— not their money but money from the corporate accounts of Union Carbide. They will go in their big cars to their big homes, and sit with their families around a big table and gorge themselves on lavish meals. They will not think about the people they killed in Bhopal; they will not tell their wives and children about the people they have killed and maimed, the families they have destroyed.

"But what about you? What about the thousands in the hospitals of Bhopal!? What of your children!? What of the young ones who are crippled and sick, and those who will die before ever knowing the joy that life can bring? What of those of you who must watch your children die? Who is there for you? What you will be given are no more than coins dropped in a beggar's tin. That is all you, the victims of Bhopal, will ever get. It will not even pay your medical bills. It will be all the parents of dead children will have to comfort them. It will be all you have to compensate for your pain and anguish." Abu scanned the faces of his listeners. He made a fist and raised it as though begging for a fight. His voice was angry and demanding. "And so it is I ask you: Where is the justice?"

Abu stared at the audience for a moment. He started pacing from one side of the platform to the other. An angry member of the congregation stood up. "There is no justice!" he shouted. "Not for the poor!" He sat down again.

Another stood up. "Allah will smite them!" he proclaimed. It made

Abu suddenly stop and turn. He looked at the audience in such a way that each would later say he looked directly at them, and into their eyes. "Do not expect a vengeful God to smite those who inflict this suffering upon you with his sword of retribution," Abu admonished. His listeners seemed stunned and confused. "Do not expect the universe to answer your prayers for justice so long as you sit passively accepting all of this as Allah's will! I have told you that you are Allah. You are the eyes, the ears, the hands of Allah. If the sword of justice must be swung, then you must pick it up and heave it with all your might. Allah acts through you. If Allah's will is to be done, you must be the ones to do it! Allah will not send forth the indignation of the universe to help you if you do not care enough to do it yourself." Abu paced on the platform.

He turned and faced the audience again. "Do not expect the politicians to help you. They are in league with those who committed this crime against you, against all humanity. Do not expect those in the West to help you, for they are not even aware of you and are too few in numbers."

A voice called out. "But how, Abu, how do we fight the powerful of the world? How do we compel justice?"

Abu's response was immediate and firm. "By aligning yourself with the power of your soul, the power of God that is within you. By accepting that you are Allah and that you have at your disposal all the power of the universe. By becoming spiritual warriors; the sparrows that encircle the falcon. If you do so, there is no power that can vanquish you. Your body may be destroyed, but each of you are, in truth, forever beings. Each of you have existed since the beginning of the universe, and you will survive when the universe ends. If the energy of your soul was instantly released, one of you alone would dwarf the largest nuclear weapon ever made. You would consume the earth and the sun!" Abu looked at his audience. He put his hands on his waist and appeared disappointed. "But you cannot accept this basic truth because you see yourselves as powerless. As peasants."

Abu's voice became pleading. "Stop being victims! Realize your fear; it is a thief in the night that robs you of your strength in the most clever way: It speaks to you like a friend while it reaches into your soul like a blood-sucking leech. It keeps you tethered to the earth and prevents you from soaring like the eagle upon the currents of life.

17

"But know this," Abu's voice became stern, "It is not anger that I speak of, nor hatred or vengeance. For those are born of fear. I speak of the power of Allah, the undeniable, unalterable power of pure love. Do not hate those who cause you to suffer; do not foster prejudice against them for they too are born from Allah.

"If their fear prevents them from doing justice, do not let anger unfocus you, but stand firm with righteous indignation and certainty of conviction. Know what you will allow and what you will not allow, and take steps upon the path of retribution."

Abu paused and looked out at his audience. "If all those like you were to join together, the world would tremble from the quake of your invincible might. There is nothing: No technology, no weapon of war, that could stop you. Allah would see his will being done and the power of all creation would flow through you like a great and mighty river.

"That is why I have come here; to serve you, to help you learn the truth of yourselves and the strength that you seek. I am Abu 'Ali Asghar." Abu bowed and stepped down from the platform.

One man rose to his feet and began clapping. He was followed by another, and another, until the entire assemblage stood on their feet. *"Allahu Akbhar!* Abu 'Ali Asghar!" they chanted. Abu was suddenly surrounded by Muslims, each wanting to touch him and speak to him. When a particular man approached, Abu looked him in the eye. "You wish to join me?" he asked.

"Yes," answered Qadir Shahim.

"Then we will begin," Abu said, placing one hand upon Qadir's shoulder. Another man approached Abu, possessed of the same look of wonderment and confusion, of conviction without direction. There were seven in all who came forward and bore that look, and Abu bowed to each without speaking.

Abu left the mosque, followed by Bhaiji and the seven men. Williams had stopped to hurriedly make copious notes in the steno pad he always carried with him. He would catch up with Abu later. But, first, he needed to call Herschel Strunk.

CHAPTER 4

Williams wrote the story Strunk had asked him to write. It was sent around the world over the *Times'* news service.

Bhopal—The Legacy of Indifference

by H. Bennett Williams
Special to the New York Times

BHOPAL—Qadir Shahim was twenty-four years old when he moved his young family to Bhopal. His wife's name was Athita. She and their two-year-old son, Fayeen, were Qadir's life.

Qadir operated a forklift at the Union Carbide chemical plant just outside of Bhopal, earning $15.00 a week. He and his small family lived in one of the countless, tiny, dilapidated cardboard homes that sprouted near the factory like weeds around a fertile pond; shanty towns where barefoot children played in roads muddied by open streams of sewage. Lacking electricity and plumbing, Qadir watched his wife cook potatoes and discarded vegetables in a solitary pot over an open fire, always hoping it would be enough.

In the summer of 1984, Athita announced she was carrying their second child. Qadir saw it as a gift from Allah; he believed that working harder and Allah's blessing would bring him salvation. He prayed they would leave that refuge for the forgotten and his children would have a good life.

To earn an additional $2.50 a week, Qadir took a night job washing dishes and sweeping floors at a restaurant. He would awaken before each dawn, pray, and go to work at the Union Carbide plant. He'd return in the evening to his hovel just long enough to eat, sleep for an hour, pray, and then go off to the restaurant. Afterwards, his body aching for rest, Qadir Shahim would stop at the Taj-ul-Masjid mosque and pray once more for guidance and, most of all, strength.

On December 3, 1984, Qadir Shahim left the Taj-ul-Masjid just after midnight. In the quiet of the early morning hours there was only the echo of his footsteps. But, on that night, the quiet was shat-

19

tered by an explosion at the Union Carbide plant that was heard around the world. An instant later, a frantic Qadir ran towards home, but the streets had become a fast-moving river of people, guided only by the surging current. Most grasped their throats, coughing, choking, and vomiting blood. Some fell to the ground and were trampled to death while sirens wailed from the plant.

And then, Qadir's lungs felt on fire and he began to cough. His legs grew heavy. The moving mass pushed him backwards, farther and farther away from his wife and son. He staggered and fell. He felt death reaching out for him. He called out to Athita and Fayeen. He lay face down in the dirt, gasping for air and coughing up blood. Convulsions racked his body. He started moving down a long, dark tunnel. The sirens faded.

But Qadir Shahim didn't die. He woke up in a hospital bed. He cried out for his wife and son. A nurse told him they were dead; killed in the first moments of the explosion. For over a decade, Qadir Shahim remained in a hospital bed—blind and disabled, wracked by violent coughs that spewed blood, surrounded by hundreds of others like him. The enormous ward of gas victims still exists, a vast warehouse of death: A purgatory of sorts where the tortured living await absolution, and permission to escape their anguished mortality. The pungent smell of antiseptic merges with the odor of vomit and excrement, creating a sickening, hybrid stench. Incessant coughing and wheezing echoes off the walls and ceilings until it becomes just so much background noise, punctuated now and then with the sound of human retching.

Amidst these forgotten victims has appeared a living example of compassion and selfless dedication. His name is Abu 'Ali Asghar. He has come to ease the pain and suffering and heal the wounded.

"He feels their torment," one doctor said. "They gain strength from him."

"He changes their soiled bedding and bathes them. He brings them water, and feeds those too weak to feed themselves," a nurse reported. When not in the hospitals, Abu 'Ali Asghar helps the victims' families—consoling them, helping them find food or repairing their homes. And, like a skilled lawyer, he negotiates on their behalf with government bureaucrats who are too slow in providing relief funds.

And there are reports of men and women pulled from the brink of death; patients visited by him whose bodies are suddenly, and miraculously, healed. "They are miracles," insisted one staff worker. "It is the only possible explanation."

Qadir Shahim was one of them. Following the explosion, he became a prisoner in his own body—sentenced for some unknown crime to live a crippled and pointless existence. He listened day after day, year after year, to the pathetic sounds of the injured and dying victims that never stopped coming. His envy of the dead soon became resentment: Why did they deserve to die? Had they been more pious or virtuous? What crime had he committed that was so vile, so unspeakable, so sinful that Allah had forgotten him?

The doctors couldn't answer his questions. For all intents and purposes, they said, he should be dead. Allah, they said, must favor him. But, neither could they explain why he didn't get better, or if he would ever leave that place.

Qadir learned that the explosion was caused by the gross negligence of Union Carbide, who'd ignored internal warnings about storing such large amounts of the toxic chemical at the Bhopal plant. They'd done it just to save money. His anger delivered him from his depression.

Then, one day, Qadir felt a presence near his bed, unlike anything he'd ever felt before. It was as though a glorious light encased him in a revitalizing cocoon, a light felt with the heart. He then knew he'd rise from that bed and live again, a whole man.

Qadir raised himself upon his elbows. "Who is there?" he shouted. He then felt the presence kneel beside him. He thanked Allah that he hadn't gone mad. He felt a gentle hand upon his forehead. Qadir dropped back down to the pillow. He waited in anxious anticipation. Had the angel of death finally come to free him? A soft and soothing voice spoke to him.

"My name is Abu 'Ali Asghar. It is for you, and all like you, that I have come." Qadir then felt a hand upon his chest, and another over his bandaged eyes. There was heat where the hands touched him. A second or two later the presence was gone.

Qadir shot up. "Did you see him?" Qadir shouted out to anyone who might be near.

"See who?" a man from the next bed responded.

"The man who was just here!" Qadir said.

"I saw no one," the man answered apologetically, a spasm of coughing cut him off. "I am blind," he added despondently.

"Did you feel him?" Qadir then tried.

"No," said the man, tired of being questioned. "I felt nothing."

Qadir lowered himself back down. Allah had sent a messenger. It was the only explanation. And then Qadir noticed he could breathe easier and his strength was returning. And then he felt itching from the long-festering wounds around his eyes. Light filtered through the bandages. "Doctor! Doctor!" he called out.

"What is it?" the man from the next bed inquired.

"I can see! I can see!"

"Allahu Akbar," the voice beside him said with reverence.

"Yes, God is Great," Qadir replied.

CHAPTER 5

The telephone rang only once; the person on the other end answered immediately. "Jack Whatley."

"Hello, Jack. It's Bennett Williams," he said into the hotel telephone in Bhopal. "How are things in New Delhi?"

Jack Whatley was a CIA operative posted as a member of the U.S. State Department staff at the American Embassy. "Bennett Williams!" Whatley said. "Where the hell are you?"

"Bhopal," Williams answered.

"For Chrissakes, what are you doing there? Has a war broken out that we don't know about?" Whatley said with a sarcastic laugh.

"I'm covering another anniversary of the Union Carbide explosion. A 'what's-happened-since' story," Williams explained.

"Why you?" Whatley asked. "It's not exactly your cup of tea."

"Don't ask me, Jack. Maybe I pissed off my editor." Williams knew that it was part of Jack Whatley's job to know what the American press was up to in India.

"Lucky you," Whatley said, apparently satisfied for the moment. "So, to what do I owe this rare call from the acclaimed correspondent of the *New York Times?*"

"I need a favor," Williams replied. "And before you start giving me that crap about being a lowly staff worker, think about the stuff I gave you on Iraqi troop movements." Although it had been awhile, Williams knew that the information he had fed to Whatley before the Persian Gulf War had impressed the CIA agent's superiors. Whatley received an important commendation as a result.

"I get your point," Whatley acknowledged. "What is it you want?"

"What does State and/or Langley have on a man named Abu 'Ali Asghar?" Williams asked.

Whatley scribbled Abu's name on a piece of paper. He waited for more. "That's it?" he asked.

"That's it," Williams answered.

"Who is he?" Whatley asked.

"You tell me."

"I'll see what I can find out," Whatley offered. "Where can I reach you?"

"I'll call you—tomorrow." Williams replied.

"Look forward to it." Whatley sounded facetious. "Always a pleasure to help the press."

Williams left his hotel and walked out into the bright morning sunlight. The crowded street was already bustling with activity. He went looking for Bhaiji Singh. After a short walk, he stopped at a mechanic's garage. Williams crouched down to a pair of legs extending out from the bottom of a black Mercedes-Benz. "Excuse me—"

"Yes?" a muffled voice said from beneath the car. Bhaiji pushed himself out. "Ah, Mr. Williams," he said standing up.

"I was wondering if we might talk?" Williams asked.

"Of course," Bhaiji answered, wiping his hands with an oily rag. "Abu said you would be calling upon me."

"Is that so?" Williams asked. "What else did he say?"

"Only that I should tell you whatever it is you wish to know," Bhaiji explained.

Williams was beginning to feel set up. He didn't like that. If there was one thing that irritated him, it was the idea of being used.

"You must understand, Mr. Williams," Bhaiji continued, "Abu knows many things. He is no ordinary man."

"Really?" Williams said. "Buy you a cup of coffee?"

Bhaiji hesitated. "Very well, Mr. Williams. My friend will let me know when the parts I am waiting for finally arrive."

They found a cafe off one of the back streets, sat down at a table and ordered two coffees. "Tell me how you and Abu came to be hitched up together," Williams suggested.

"Hitched up?" Bhaiji asked with a smile. "You Americans have such interesting expressions. You mean like a horse to a wagon?"

"No, not quite," Williams said. "I meant, how did you meet?"

"I know what you meant, Mr. Williams," Bhaiji Singh said. "Americans seem to think that anyone who is not American, particularly darker-skinned people, are ignorant—maybe even a little stupid. I have a university education, Mr. Williams. I have also seen a great deal of

American television and I love American movies, especially Westerns. Perhaps I know more of your culture than you do of mine."

"I'm sure you do. I apologize," Williams said.

Bhaiji nodded and sipped his coffee. "I was working as a hired driver at the airport in New Delhi. One day, I was cleaning the dust off my Mercedes and waiting for a customer when I felt something strange."

Williams looked at Bhaiji curiously. "I do not know how to describe it," he said, looking off into the distance, searching for the words. "I felt a presence, that is all I can say."

"Abu?" Williams inquired.

"Yes."

"Of all the drivers there, why do you suppose he approached you?"

"I once asked him that," Bhaiji replied. "He said it was because I took great care of my automobile. He said that was important, that it would be necessary to have reliable transportation for where we were going. But he also said it was because he recognized me."

"Had you met before?" Williams asked.

"No," Bhaiji answered. "But now I think I was the one he was supposed to choose. I remember our first negotiation. He wanted me to take him and his mother north into Punjab suba. But I did not want to go."

"Why?" Williams asked, suspecting he already knew the answer.

"Because it was dangerous," Bhaiji explained, as though stating the obvious. "People were being killed there every day, which meant we would have to travel the roads at night. I was afraid—I had no wish to die young."

"Did you tell that to Abu?"

"No," Bhaiji said, smiling again. "But he knew. He looked at me and asked 'What does it matter if you die, my friend, if you have never truly lived? And if you have truly lived, what does it matter when you die?' "

Williams sat back in his chair, sipping coffee. Neither man spoke for a moment. "Then what?" Williams finally asked.

"I told him I would go," Bhaiji answered. "Then he said that the risk was real, the danger was imagined—that I could not know what lay ahead and my expectations were from the past." Bhaiji laughed. "I have since learned that everything Abu does is meant to teach. You would do well to keep that in mind, Mr. Williams."

Williams' stomach tightened, as though warning him of something yet to come. "Tell me about the miracle you witnessed—bread in the village."

"We—Abu's mother, Satki Kaur, was also with us—were heading north on the Grand Trunk road out of New Delhi. We came upon a village that had been destroyed by a cyclone and a flood. Everywhere there was debris; the road was lined with small children who stared at us with muddy faces and torn clothes. The parents were busy digging up the bodies of relatives and friends. I remember the faces of the children—scared and hungry. I heard Abu once say that children are closer to God than the rest of us. They remember more. Abu says that as we grow older we move farther away from God and need to be reminded of who and what we truly are." Bhaiji downed the last of his coffee. Williams signaled for two more to be brought to the table.

"Then what?" Williams asked.

"Abu walked through the mud to a little girl; the saddest-looking child of all. Abu crouched down and spoke to her."

"What did he say?"

"I could not hear, but then I saw him reach into his robes and remove a loaf of bread. It was actually kulchua, a very tasty bread made by Sikhs. The child accepted it and then wrapped her arms around Abu. He stood up with the girl in his arms and walked back to the automobile. He asked his mother for the kulchua she had brought for the journey. Satki told him there were only a few small loaves, not nearly enough for all of them."

"And then?"

"Abu looked at her sternly. He said: 'There will be enough.' "

"And was there enough?" Williams asked.

"Yes," Bhaiji answered. "There was exactly as much as was needed."

"Maybe there was more in the bag than you thought," Williams suggested.

"No," Bhaiji answered unequivocally. "I saw the bag. I watched. The bag was not large enough to hold all the bread that Abu gave out."

Williams sat back and studied Bhaiji as the waiter brought over two more coffees. As soon as the waiter left, Williams chose his words very carefully. "Bhaiji, why is Abu here?" Williams finally asked.

Bhaiji Singh stirred his coffee slowly. "Why is he in Bhopal?" Williams nodded. "Because he cares," Bhaiji said, a note of caution in his voice which Williams detected.

Williams hesitated. "You're obviously an intelligent man, Bhaiji. Is that all you think it is?" Williams caught Bhaiji's eye and lowered his voice as though about to share a secret. "What's he up to?"

"I told you, Abu is a teacher," Bhaiji said.

"That speech he gave at the mosque wasn't like any teacher I've ever known," Williams said, sitting back in his seat. "It sounded as though maybe Abu has something more in mind."

"It is obvious to me that you are not a trusting man. Let me tell you something, Ben—I have never met anyone more candid, more truthful than Abu."

"That's commendable," Williams said, trying to sound sincere. "Really it is. But I've seen plenty of contenders, and plenty of pretenders, and I'm pretty good at spotting which is which. If Abu is a pretender, maybe people ought to know about it."

"And you are the one to tell them?" Bhaiji asked.

"Yes," Williams said. "That's my job."

The two men stared at one another.

"It sounds as though you have already made up your mind."

"I just want the truth, Bhaiji, that's all," Williams said, lighting a filtered cigarette. "If Abu is everything you say he is, he'll withstand the scrutiny." Williams stared at Bhaiji a moment. "So, what's Abu here to teach us?"

"Perhaps that is something you must find out for yourself," Bhaiji answered. "As I have found out. There is a reason I am with him. I suspect it is similar to what you are feeling now."

Williams didn't respond.

Bhaiji looked down into his coffee for a moment, as though recalling something. "I remember the day I knew I wanted to remain with Abu and not return to my place at the airport in New Delhi. I was so confused. Abu said to me, 'It is a difficult choice, is it not?' I remember how sympathetic he sounded." Bhaiji smiled. "But I pretended I did not know what he meant. He said he was referring to the choice of allowing one path to end and beginning upon a new one."

"What was your response?" Williams asked.

"I kept pretending I did not know what he meant. We were watching the villagers rebuild their village after the flood."

"He explained that these people rebuilt after every disaster, as they had for centuries, simply because their survival depended upon it. Very much like ants do after their homes are washed away. But the villagers did so with an indomitable spirit and determination, not because it was simply in their genetic makeup. Ants had no choice. We human beings did."

"What was his point?"

"As long as I continued to do something and did not question its purpose, then I was choosing to live like the ant, and I would have the same degree of fulfillment."

"An interesting concept," Williams acknowledged.

"And then, just when I felt I had grasped his meaning, he told me something else: That in all things that I did there was a need, a want, and a desire."

Williams sat waiting, expecting more. "That's it?"

"He said need is born from fear. It is rooted in the instinct to survive. Desire was pure; it was the total absence of fear."

"And 'want'?"

"'Want' is the balanced place between the two."

"I see." Williams was groping.

"He gave me an example: He said you need food to survive, you want food that tastes good, you desire gourmet food. If you are in fear, everything is a threat to survival and the only steps you can take are in furtherance of fear. You remain in need, you merely react, rather than act to gain your wants and desires. You take only the steps that give the illusion of security—you protect yourself against change." Bhaiji stopped and looked at Williams. "Shall I continue?"

"Yes. Please go on."

"Abu then told me what I now understand is the most important element of his teachings."

"What's that?"

"Change is the only constant; the only thing upon which we can truly rely. To live full lives we must embrace change. If we do not, we stop growing."

Williams felt his stomach tighten again. He wasn't particularly fond of change, he'd even become cynical about it. Nothing ever changed, not really. Not even people; especially himself.

"And then Abu told me to look upon the fear that kept me from achieving what I truly wanted and desired."

Williams sat back and thought for awhile. "What if you don't know what you want?"

Bhaiji smiled. "I wondered the same thing. Before I met Abu, I was content to be what I was. But after, I felt only that I should stay with him. But I did not know why, and did not trust myself."

"And?"

"All Abu would say is that want served intention and leads to desire. Desire was passion. He told me what I wanted was to discover who I am so that I could realize my desire. My desire was to live my purpose with joy. He said this I could not do by returning to Delhi and being a hired driver. And he was right."

At that moment, the grease-smudged mechanic appeared in the small cafe. "Bhaiji," he said, approaching the table, "the parts you wanted have come."

"Good!" Bhaiji exclaimed getting up from the table. "Ben, I have work to do."

"Yes, of course. Maybe later we can talk more?" Bhaiji nodded and left. Williams took a long drag on his cigarette and slowly blew out the smoke as he sat back and pondered what Bhaiji had just told him. It was all so unsettling—it made him feel anxious, worried, as though something was about to happen that he wouldn't like.

CHAPTER 6

Bennett Williams understood what Bhaiji felt when he first met Abu. He didn't like it. He felt resentment, even anger, and he didn't know why. What he did know was that he wanted to discover the truth about Abu 'Ali Asghar; to debunk the myth that shrouded the man.

Williams was aware of his feelings but didn't trust them. Feelings were fallible; too easily manipulated. He preferred his intellect; the skepticism of his left brain.

He went back to his hotel to call Strunk. The Indian phone system was notoriously bad—it took forever to make a long distance call and the connection was usually a contest between human voice and phone static.

"Hersch?" Williams had to shout into the phone to be heard when the call finally went through. He'd never liked anyone as much as he liked his boss. Beneath the gruff and demanding exterior, Strunk was surprisingly urbane and literate.

"Williams?" Herschel Strunk yelled back. "Is that you?"

"Yeah," Williams answered.

"Where are you!?" Strunk demanded. "Why aren't you on your way to the Sudan?"

"I think I have something better."

"You don't say." Strunk always made his reporters sell him on an idea so he could gauge their interest. "Let's hear it."

"I want to stay on this Asghar fellow," Williams said. "There's something here."

"Like what?" Strunk asked, still not sold.

"It's hard to explain," Williams said.

"Words are your profession, Ben," Strunk said impatiently. "Try and find a couple."

"He's rather unique," Williams said. "Even extraordinary." Williams

29

knew that sounded pretty lame. "There are reports of miracles," he said almost desperately. The line filled with static.

"Yeah," Strunk shouted, "I noted that in your piece. So? Do you believe them?"

"No. But, he's managed to impress a lot of people around here," Williams answered cautiously. "And he's developed quite a following. He seems to have appeared out of nowhere. I heard a speech he gave at a mosque. He had a thousand Muslims on their feet chanting his name. He's touted as a man of God dedicated to helping the masses— a Mother Theresa type. But I think there's more. That speech was too political."

"There's ten thousand holy men in India, Ben," Strunk yelled. "You can't swing a dead cat without hitting one of them—and many of these holy types have political ambitions. So, why's this guy different?"

"I don't know," Williams answered. "Maybe he's not. I just have a feeling, that's all. There's something here, Hersch; I know it." The phone connection began crackling and hissing. Williams held the receiver away from his ear for a moment.

"When did you start going on feelings?" Strunk didn't mind reporters going on intuition; sometimes it was all there was. He just knew Williams. There was no reply. "Ben—?"

"I'm here, Hersch."

"Be careful. Maybe you're the press agent this guy's looking for. And we don't want the *Times* to become his platform."

"I hear you," Williams said. "The thought's crossed my mind."

"Okay," Strunk said. "I'll authorize a few more days. Is there anything you need on this end?"

"Have research see if there's anything on him. Anything at all."

"All right," Strunk responded. "Give me a call in a day or two."

"Thanks, Hersch." The phone static suddenly subsided and then stopped.

"Maybe you ought to call me from Egypt in two days—I think their phone system is slightly better than India's." Williams laughed as both men hung up the phone.

Williams lay down on the bed and watched the ceiling fan spinning slowly overhead. He thought about the piece he'd written—the story of the sick and dying in Bhopal. It had a human interest slant, but it lacked something more powerful. It lacked true compassion. He had given Strunk what he asked for, but they both knew he was capable of better work.

Williams wondered why he didn't feel compassion these days. Had he become cynical beyond redemption? Was life nothing more than the constant daily struggle for survival he observed around him? Had he spent too much time surrounded by brutality and death?

The ease with which those questions suggested the answers troubled Williams. Something was eluding him.

He thought of Abu's story about the Bedouin and his camel. What could it possibly have to do with his desire to win a Pulitzer Prize? A shudder went through his body. He sat up quickly. "What's happening to me?" he said out loud. The image of the princely warrior filled his mind. 'Abu is a teacher,' Bhaiji had said with such devotion.

That night Williams had terrible dreams. He was back in the Bhopal hospital, walking through the wards of the sick and dying. Hands reached out to touch him, cries of pain assaulted his senses, patients begged him for drinks of water, but all Williams wanted was to get out of there—he ran down corridors and into rooms but couldn't find the hospital's exits. More than once he awoke in a panic. Each time he was drenched in sweat and breathing hard. By morning he was exhausted. A knock on his door forced him out of bed. Bleary-eyed, he opened the door. Bhaiji Singh stood there, smiling.

"Are you all right?" Bhaiji asked with concern. "You look horrible."

"Thanks," Williams grumbled as he went over to the wash basin and began splashing cold water on his face. "What brings you here so early?"

"Abu asked that I stop by," Bhaiji explained, "to invite you to join him. He is with some of the men from the mosque."

Williams wiped his face with a clean towel. He thought of asking Bhaiji what Abu was really up to, but knew he wouldn't find out what he wanted to know from this Indian. "Be with you in a minute," Williams said, hurrying into the bathroom for a quick shave and a change of clothes.

Bhaiji took Williams to the outskirts of the city. The Union Carbide plant could be seen in the distance. Abu was sitting amidst flowers in a field. Around him in a small half-circle were the seven men from the mosque. Abu nodded when he saw Williams approaching

31

but said nothing. Williams and Bhaiji joined the group and Abu began speaking.

"It is time that you learn who you truly are," he said to the men. "It is time for each of you to learn to communicate with your souls directly, and without reliance upon any other for the answers you seek. Everything you need to know is readily available to you, all you need do is ask."

"Ask who?" one of the men inquired, not fully grasping what Abu was telling them.

"Yourself," Abu said in reply.

The men looked at one another in apparent confusion.

"Each of you," Abu said, "has always looked outside yourselves for your identity, without ever realizing that your identity comes from within. You have shaped your identity based upon what you wanted people to see because you believe you are flawed." Abu paused, and looked at each of the men.

Williams felt slightly uncomfortable, as though Abu was revealing some secret about him.

"You have lost contact with who you truly are," Abu went on to say. "But now, each of you, wants to know. It is your soul's desire as well. It has guided you, even when you were unaware that you were being guided. It is your soul speaking to you; it is God. Listen."

Williams scanned the faces of the men. He wondered if they too felt like Abu was talking only about them.

"God's only desire," Abu said, "is to know itself."

"But, Abuji," one of the men interrupted, "how can it be that God does not know itself? How can God know all, and yet not itself?"

"In the beginning," Abu answered, "God existed only as energy, an energy with consciousness that held an infinite array of possibilities: All the stars and galaxies, all the comets and planets, all the living things that were yet to be. And God was all the events that have occurred and that are yet to occur. Time is a concept limited to the three-dimensional world in which we live. God is unfettered by time, just as it is unfettered by physical matter."

"But," Williams interjected, seeking to find inconsistencies in Abu's words, "a moment ago you said 'In the beginning . . . ,' and now you say God is unfettered by time."

"Yes," Abu answered calmly. "For God, there has never been a beginning, and there will never be an end. But in our universe there was a beginning. Our universe has had many lifetimes, Mr. Williams, just as you."

"I still do not understand," another man confessed.

"Human scientists," Abu continued to explain, "have now surmised that the physical universe is ever-changing. What is more, they have come to accept that the universe began with what they now call the 'Big Bang.' It was at that moment that God exploded in its quest to find definition of itself, to know itself just as you now seek to know yourselves. It was at that moment that your souls were created. Your souls, my friends, are part of God."

"And that is what Muslims know as the moment of creation, and the Hindus know as the Outbreath of Brahmin?" Bhaiji asked, in order to help the other men understand better.

"Yes," Abu answered. "Part of the pure energy that exploded outward became physical matter: Planets, and moons, fish in the seas, the plants in the fields, the animals in the forests—and it became you. The human animal evolved over time, in cooperation with the earth, adapting, changing and growing so that your soul could attach itself and observe through you; so that God could know itself.

"But yet," Abu continued, "while part of that energy assumed physical form, part remained pure energy, an energy with consciousness that exists beyond the physical world. That energy is what forms your souls. So each of you exist in the physical world and you also exist in the realm beyond. This three-dimensional world," Abu said, extending his arms outward, "is where your body lives. But your soul lives in the fullness of ten dimensions where the past, the present, and the future exist together in the moment."

"But Abu," Qadir Shahim interrupted, "how does God discover itself through us? What can we teach God?"

"It is not the role of the teacher that you are asked to be," Abu explained. "God does not require knowledge as we define it in these three dimensions. That kind of knowledge is only needed to understand the physical world. No, what God asks of you is simply to be an observer." Abu paused again. The men looked at one another as if to see if they were alone in their confusion.

"God," Abu went on, "seeks to define itself. God asks: 'If I am everything, then what is everything?' "

Williams found Abu's explanation of God and the universe intellectually palatable. It was rational. The idea that God was a distinct personality who sat in heaven running the universe like a king ran an empire, sometimes merciful and sometimes vengeful, seemed patently absurd. For the better part of his life Williams had waffled between agnosticism and atheism, lacking the conviction of either.

"Because God is simply energy, it lacks eyes and ears, and does not have the ability to taste, to feel, to experience the physical world in which you live. That is where you come in; that is why God needs you. You are the observer. You are God's physical agents."

The men murmured amongst themselves. Williams scribbled some notes.

"When God creates," Abu said, regaining the attention of the men, "it does so by combining energies. You see the physical results of the creation; your soul sees the combination of energies that are the creation."

"Combining energies?" one of the men interjected. "But did you not say that God was merely one energy?"

"Yes," Abu answered, "but when God looked upon itself in seeking its separate parts, it became two. It is like you looking in a mirror: You see your reflection and thereby gain an awareness of yourself. And then God wondered what more there was and it became four. And when it sought further definition it exploded—this so-called 'Big Bang.'

"But," Abu said, looking back at the man who had asked, "when God exploded outward in search of itself, it separated into the eight energies that when combined together form God in its totality. It is like the colors of the spectrum: When white light is filtered through a prism, its separate parts can be seen more easily."

Some of the men understood and nodded. Those who did not still wrestled.

"Of those eight energies," Abu explained, "seven are a purity of essence. Your soul, as a splinter of God, is made up of those seven energies. You may think of the eighth as an emptiness, a void which the other seven may fill in varying combinations. That eighth energy is chaos—the transmutation of disorder into order, the organization of disparate elements into something which has definition. It is chaos which God seeks to fill; it is like a bowl into which the ingredients of a cake are poured, and from which arises a new creation."

Abu paused. The men around him were mesmerized by his words, even if they were having difficulty comprehending them. "Your ability to feel, to experience emotion, is the very reason your soul has chosen the human form.

"Your soul may create an event, an experience for you to observe. Whenever you feel an emotion, the seven energies are combined to form a new creation. God has further defined itself. When you feel, you participate in your soul's creation; you help God discover itself."

"But Abu," Williams again interjected, "are you telling us that we are merely puppets of this divine energy, simply steered along a path chosen by our souls? That we have no control over what we do, and how and where we do it?"

"No," Abu quickly answered. "What I seek for you to understand is that you have a relationship with your soul. You are not just your soul, but neither are you simply physical beings. You are a partnership, a union of your body and soul.

"Human beings are most wondrous animals," Abu said. "The brain evolved so you could learn and interpret what you learn."

Williams was feeling slightly uncomfortable again, but it wasn't annoyance or anger. It was something altogether different. He listened more intently as Abu spoke.

"You experience an emotion depending upon your interpretation of an event. Through your emotions, you tell your soul what you will observe. But, while your soul will create according to what you will observe, it is also very stubborn and will create what you are afraid to observe. It will do so no matter how many times you hide from it. It will create it larger and larger so that you can no longer hide from it. Your soul makes no judgments; it feels no pain. It is not bound by morality, or ethics, for those are purely human concepts. Its only concern is helping God know itself. And it can be most persistent.

"But so that you do not see yourselves as puppets, or victims," Abu went on, glancing at Williams, "your soul wants to create out of joy and passion, for those are creations that you will happily observe. It is fear that limits your soul's ability to create. Fear causes denial and results in waste. It forces your soul to create the same thing over and over again until you finally observe it. The greater the fear, the larger the creation must be so that you will see it."

Williams stopped scribbling for a moment. He looked up to see Abu staring directly at him. He looked down at what he'd written. 'The greater the fear, the larger the creation must be.'

Abu went on. "You can choose to create in joy or from fear. If you choose joy and passion, your soul will create most wondrously for you. The entire universe will cooperate with one who is the master of his fear. You will have power beyond your imagination."

"Abuji," Qadir Shahim interrupted, "how do we become the masters of our fear?"

Abu scanned the faces of the men around him. "I will leave you now," he said. "There is work that remains for me in Bhopal. We will talk more later." He looked over at Williams. "Would you care to walk with me?" he asked.

Williams nodded. "Very much," he said.

Abu rose gracefully, effortlessly, as though he was levitating, Williams thought. "For those of you who still have questions," Abu said, "Bhaiji Singh and I have spent many hours talking of these things. Perhaps he can help you to understand." He looked at Williams. "Shall we go?"

"Quite a sermon," Williams said. Abu glanced at him with penetrating eyes but said nothing. Williams wasn't sure how to begin. "Jesus, it's hot," he said, pulling a handkerchief from his pocket and wiping his brow. He noticed that Abu seemed unaffected by the heat.

"It gets much hotter where I am from," Abu said, looking straight ahead.

"Sri Lanka?" Williams asked.

"Yes."

"I've never been there," Williams noted.

"You should go. It is a magnificent place," Abu said with reverence. "Muslims believe it was the original Garden of Eden."

"Is that right?" Williams was genuinely curious.

"It must be," Abu said, "for if any land has fallen from grace it is the place of my birth. There is such bitterness and hatred," Abu said with a deep sadness. "Such brutality."

"I understand your father was murdered there," Williams said, trying to pry into Abu's background.

"Yes," Abu answered matter-of-factly.

"How'd it happen?" Williams asked.

"He was butchered like an animal. He was pulled off a train while he was on his way from Jaffna to Colombo and hacked to pieces with machetes."

"Who did it?"

"Sinhalese Buddhist extremists."

"Why?"

Abu sighed, almost inaudibly. "Because he was close to bringing an end to the centuries old conflict between the Tamils and Sinhalese. He was about to bring peace to his adopted homeland."

"Your father was in politics?" Williams asked.

"Yes," Abu answered. "He was a very successful maker of fine gold jewelry in Jaffna. But politics was his passion. He was highly respected by many and, as a Muslim, he had been asked to mediate between the Hindus and Buddhists. He had worked very hard and a resolution was finally at hand. But there are many in Sri Lanka who do not want peace; they thrive on hatred. There are many like them in this world."

"Are you a man of peace?" Williams asked.

"Yes, of course," Abu replied.

"That speech at the mosque the other night," Williams challenged, "sounded more like a call to revolution—"

"There are many steps in a journey," Abu interrupted. "You must first plow the fields before you can plant the seed. You must first lay a foundation before you can build a house. How can you have peace without justice? How can you have justice without equality?"

"And what makes you think you can accomplish this lofty desire of yours?"

"If I were alone in it," Abu said, "I doubt very much if I would succeed. But it is humanity's desire as well. I am merely a servant, Mr. Williams," Abu added. "I am here to help humanity in its transition. I will be whatever humanity chooses for me to be."

"Transition to what?" Williams asked.

"A greater level of consciousness," Abu answered. "A greater awareness of itself."

"Just like God?" Williams asked.

Abu smiled. "You use your mind most effectively, Mr. Williams. Are you as adept at dealing with your emotions?"

There was an awkward silence between the two men as they continued walking; it made Williams feel anxious, trapped. He was afraid to

37

speak, not knowing where his words would lead him; not wanting to betray his secrets.

And then, as if Abu had read his mind, "You know, Mr. Williams," Abu continued, "the secrets that we carry within us are the things that can harm us the most."

"I don't know what you mean," Williams said. His stomach tightened.

"You will never be strong, Mr. Williams, so long as you continue to judge yourself as weak." Williams shot a glance at Abu. "It is very simple, Mr. Williams," Abu explained. "You have constructed a wall between who you are and who you think you must be. That child you once were is still you, yet you are ashamed of that child. You locked him away in a dark fortress so that no one can see him, touch him— not even you. You present an image for the world to see, but it is a false image." Abu didn't let up. "You stand upon the parapets of your fortress, Mr. Williams, and regard the world around you as hostile. Is it any wonder that you became a journalist? You hide behind the notion of journalistic objectivity. You claim you cannot afford to get involved, but you are simply afraid to become involved. Without involvement, how can you ever hope to understand? Without compassion for yourself, how will you ever feel compassion for others?"

Williams tried to dismiss what Abu was saying but couldn't. He was rendered defenseless by the truth.

"Shall I continue?" Abu asked.

"Yes." Despite his discomfort, Williams felt compelled to hear more. In an odd way, Abu's words were having a liberating effect on him.

Abu paused for a moment. Williams didn't speak but merely scanned the fields surrounding Bhopal. A sudden breeze swept through.

"It is time for you to tear down those walls, Mr. Williams," Abu said breaking the silence. "Until you do so you will remain isolated, disconnected from yourself and the rest of humanity. You will never attain what you want from life. You will never truly live."

"How?" Williams asked. He suddenly felt very tired.

"Begin by seeing how you judge yourself, how those judgments are the walls of your fortress. Are you really as weak as you think you are? Look at all you have accomplished, Mr. Williams. Is that evidence of weakness? Look at how your fear of weakness made you strong, how it enabled you to survive. But, now it is time to move beyond survival."

Williams felt as though his entire life—his past, present and future—had just been thrown up into the air, like a jig-saw puzzle so painstakingly assembled, and then so easily demolished. He stopped in his tracks. "What did you mean when you said you were expecting me," Williams asked. "That you'd been told I was coming? Who told you?"

"Haven't you figured it out?"

Williams didn't answer. He knew what Abu meant; he just couldn't accept it.

"You were led here, Mr. Williams." Abu's voice was calm.

"By whom?" Williams asked, his tone was arrogant. "God?"

"You," Abu answered.

"That's funny. I could've sworn my editor sent me," Williams said with a sarcastic chuckle. "Okay then, tell me why you think I'm here."

"Because you want to change," Abu said. "But, first you must end your isolation and begin involving yourself in your life." They had reached the end of the meadow. Abu turned onto the road and began walking toward Bhopal. "I have much work to do. We will talk again," he called back to Williams, who was standing still, staring after Abu and feeling ever so slightly foolish.

CHAPTER 7

"Hello today, Mr. Williams," the hotel desk clerk said in a clipped Indian accent as Williams collected his room key. "There is message for you." He handed Williams a piece of paper. "New York," the clerk added with solemn respect, as though he was referring to Mecca.

"Thanks," Williams said and headed toward the elevator. The moment he got into his room, Williams grabbed the phone, but instead of calling Strunk in New York, he dialed a number in New Delhi.

"Jack Whatley," the voice answered.

"Jack, it's Bennett Williams."

"Hello Ben," Whatley said. "Listen, I'm glad you called. This Abu 'Ali Asghar you're so interested in—is he in Bhopal?"

"Why? You have something for me?"

"Yeah," Whatley said. "Langley has a file on him."

"No kidding," Williams responded. "Bingo," he muttered under his breath. "What's in it?"

"He's a convicted murderer," Whatley answered.

Williams was stunned. He hadn't imagined anything like that. Not anything remotely like that. "Jesus Christ," he said.

"Yeah," Whatley said, "practically decapitated some punk in East London about fifteen years ago; slit his throat wide open, ear to ear in front of a pub full of witnesses. There was a big trial, front page stuff in the London papers. He was defended by a pretty well-known London barrister, a guy named Muhammad Amani."

"An Arab?" Williams was surprised.

"Yeah," Whatley said, "He was from Sri Lanka, sort of an ambassador-without-portfolio type. He packed some clout in Whitehall."

"Tell me about the trial," Williams said.

"The British government claimed he was a terrorist," Whatley said. "On the day of the murder he was seen coming and going from the Libyan Embassy. That evening, he'd just finished speaking to a group of young Sikh radicals. He was in the company of a woman named Nanaki Kaur."

"Where's she now?" Williams asked.

"Dead. She was killed during the incident."

"Anything else?"

"Yeah. He did a few years in Her Majesty's Prison at Dartmoor. It's a vile place—where they send their worst scum."

"How'd he get out?"

"This part is really interesting. It's confidential; understand that I'm giving you some secret stuff here. It came direct from some friends in the Circus." The Circus was the CIA's name for British Intelligence.

"Got it," Williams said.

"After this, we're even, okay?" Whatley insisted.

"Yeah." They weren't even by a long shot, but Williams just wanted him to get on with it.

"The British government tried to soft pedal it," Whatley explained. "But it seems there was a riot, a big fucking riot. The inmates took over damn near the entire prison. Enormous destruction. Downing Street dispatched a Deputy Home Secretary to handle it and fired the prison superintendent. General elections were close and the whole episode scared the shit out of the government. They weren't about to have another scandal blow up on 'em. And guess who was behind it?"

"Our friend?" Williams said.

"None other," Whatley said. "There was another guy, too. An inmate named Gerald Morton a/k/a Mubambo. A Botswanan. Reports say he was Asghar's right hand man; his chief lieutenant. Pretty interesting, huh?"

"Yeah," Williams said, wondering what was wrong with this picture. "So, how'd he end up here?"

"His old man had some pretty good connections in Sri Lanka, so the Brits took the easy way out; they deported him back to Sri Lanka."

"Anything else?" Williams asked.

"No," Whatley said. "After that we kind of lost track of him. It seems he disappeared for a while; kind of fell off the radar screen completely—until now. So, you tell me, what's this guy up to?"

"Another time, Jack. I've got an anxious editor in New York waiting to hear from me. Thanks for the information," Williams said.

"You're a sweetheart." He hung up the phone.

Williams thought for a moment, and then glanced at his watch. He picked up the phone again. "I want to call New York," he said and gave the operator the number and then hung up. It would take a minute or two for the call to go through. Williams walked onto the small balcony overlooking the street. It was nearly dusk and the crowds were thinning. The daily ritual had begun—the muezzin were again beckoning the faithful to prayer.

None of it made sense, Williams thought. He couldn't get the pieces to fit. As a journalist, nothing irritated him more. What Abu had said to the men out in the field was like nothing he'd heard before—that made sense. What Abu had said to him on their way into town also made sense, even if he didn't like it. In fact, it had definitely hit a nerve. But now this. The phone rang. He raced over and grabbed it. "Hersch?" he said through the ever-present static.

"Ben?" Strunk's voice was barely audible.

"Yeah," Williams shouted. "What've you got for me?"

"I'm fine, Ben. How are you?" Strunk said.

"C'mon Hersch, tell me."

"Interesting character, this holy man you've hooked up with," Strunk yelled. "You may want to rethink the Mother Theresa angle."

"You may be right," Williams shouted back.

"You already know about the murder conviction?" Strunk asked.

"Yeah," Williams replied. "I've got a source in the Company. Langley has a file on him already."

"Interesting," Strunk said. "You may have just hit on something here, Ben."

Williams didn't mention Dartmoor. He doubted if his editor knew about it. "Can you have someone there contact his lawyer in London?"

"I don't think so, Ben. He's dead. He died of a stroke about a year or so after the trial. We do know that Abu's case became something of an obsession with him."

"Maybe you can get his files," Williams suggested. "His estate may have kept his personal papers. Also, get a copy of the transcript from the trial."

"I'll try, Ben. But it may take some time," Strunk said. "I gather you want to stay on this for a while."

"Yeah," Williams replied. "This is getting too interesting; way too interesting."

Strunk hesitated. There was a moment of silence. "Okay, where do I send the stuff?"

"I'll let you know," Williams said. "Thanks, Hersch."

"Ben, I'm going out on a limb on this one. This isn't news, yet. All you've got so far is a holy man with a prison record."

"With Libyan connections?"

"Just remember, I've got people I have to answer to. This better be good."

"Right." Williams hung up the phone. He sat on the edge of the bed and stared out into nowhere. "Jesus," he muttered aloud. He stood up and paced around the room. He felt agitated. He grabbed his notepad and reviewed what he had written. "It doesn't make sense," he said, slamming the notebook shut.

Williams fell back onto the bed and stared up at the slow-moving fan. Its rhythmic turning was almost hypnotic. In the few short days since he had arrived in Bhopal, his life had been turned inside out. He recalled how he hadn't wanted to come. Now he couldn't escape the overwhelming feeling that there was a purpose to his being there; one that had everything to do with Abu.

But to find out that Abu was nothing more than a convicted killer, maybe a terrorist guilty of unknown crimes, confused and disturbed Williams. There was a knock on the door. Williams shot up. "Yes?" he called out.

"It is Bhaiji Singh."

Williams opened the door. "Come in," he said. "Checking up on me again?"

"No," Bhaiji said. "Abu and I are leaving tomorrow."

Williams was surprised. "Where are you going?"

"We are returning to Kartarpur,"

"Why?"

"I do not know," Bhaiji said. "Abu wanted me to inform you, and invite you to join us, if you desire."

Williams lit a cigarette and eyed Bhaiji Singh with suspicion. Did Bhaiji know about London? He considered asking, but decided Bhaiji might tip Abu off. "Where's Abu now?"

"At prayers in one of the mosques, of course," Bhaiji answered.

Williams hesitated. "Tell him I'll go," he said.

Bhaiji smiled. "Good. We leave at dawn. I must make certain our camel is well-fed," Bhaiji said with a wink as he left the room.

At dawn the next morning, the three men began the roughly one-thousand-mile drive to Kartarpur. For Williams it provided striking reminders of an ancient past and long-lost glory; the vivid contrasts between godly virtue and human deprivation, and the haphazard introduction of modern technology into a medieval culture.

After traveling all day, they reached the city of Agra.

"We will stop here for the night," Abu instructed, pointing to a dhaba, which was a rest stop for truck drivers and tired travelers—remnants from an earlier time when the Mughals had built rest houses along the road. Now they consisted mostly of worn charpoys or cots, set beneath shady trees where one could grab some sleep, enjoy a meal and wash up. Not far away stood the Taj Mahal on the banks of the Yamuna river.

Williams welcomed the chance to stretch his legs and clean off the dust from the day's ride which clung to him like an extra layer of skin. Mosquitoes, flies, gnats and other insects hummed around him as he washed. It was almost dusk as several Muslims knelt in the direction of Mecca and pressed their foreheads to the ground. Abu joined them in prayer. Williams could hear Abu's deep voice softly uttering Arabic recitations from the Koran while, a short distance away, Bhaiji Singh performed his conscientious maintenance on the Mercedes-Benz.

When the prayers were over, Williams saw Abu approach Bhaiji. "Shall we now meditate together, my friend?" Abu asked. Williams watched as the two men sat across from one another in the lotus position and closed their eyes while they performed the Nam Simram—the Sikh meditation. It was through the Nam Simram that Sikhs focused on what they believed was the inner light—the God within.

Afterwards, Bhaiji built a fire and prepared a simple meal over it consisting mostly of well-seasoned rice and beans. It was dark and quiet, and the fire's soft glow danced upon their clothing.

"Where'd you learn to cook?" Williams asked.

"In the army," Bhaiji answered.

"You were a soldier?" Williams asked with surprise.

"I was a corporal," Bhaiji said proudly. "Many Sikhs join the army. We are a warrior people; it is part of our military tradition."

"How about you?" Williams asked Abu. "Ever serve in the military?"

"No," Abu answered. "But I once considered it. I find war and military strategy extremely interesting—it requires humanity's best and worst qualities."

Williams felt that every word uttered by Abu was deliberate; every statement intended to convey a particular meaning. It was as if he was purposely dropping clues for Williams to piece together.

"Why didn't you join?" Williams persisted.

"It was not meant to be," Abu replied.

"You were meant to study law instead?" Williams asked; it was more educated guess than fact.

Abu looked at him. "Yes," he answered with a smile. "I see you've done your research, Mr. Williams."

"Was that in London?" Williams asked.

Abu didn't respond. Instead, he looked off in the direction of the Taj Mahal. "It is very beautiful, is it not?"

Illuminated by a full moon, the white marble edifice seemed to glow in the dark. "Yes," Williams answered. "It's beautiful."

"As it is a tribute to love," Abu explained, "so it should be."

There was a long silence. Williams finally broke it. "Have you ever been in love, Abu?"

Abu glared at Williams. "Yes," he replied. "I was once very much in love."

Bhaiji, who had said nothing for a while, was taken aback by Abu's admission of love. "I have never heard you speak of such a thing," he said.

"Nor will you hear any more," Abu said with finality.

Williams lit a cigarette, inhaled deeply and studied Abu through the smoky haze. "What happened in London?" he asked.

Abu looked Williams directly in the eye. "It is apparent you already know, Mr. Williams. For me to say anything else would merely satisfy your curiosity. It is unimportant."

"Wouldn't you like to give me your version?" Williams asked.

"No," Abu answered.

"Who was Nanaki Kaur?" Williams pressed. "Was she the one you were in love with?"

Abu shot Williams a look that made the journalist realize he had hit a nerve—a very raw one. For a fleeting moment intense anger flared in Abu's black eyes, so much so that Williams felt his own adrenaline surge. Just as quickly the anger was gone. In its place was the same calm demeanor that seemed to characterize Abu. "Would you not prefer to hear about the glorious Mughals?" Abu asked. "It might help you understand this country and its people better."

Abu's quick recovery surprised Williams. He took another drag from his cigarette. "Sure," Williams played along. "I'd love to hear about the Mughals."

"The first Muslims to come to India were Arab adventurers and traders," Abu began. Williams noticed that other travelers in the camp began to move in closer. "In 1398 A.D.," Abu said, raising his voice so that his growing audience could hear, "a Turkish conqueror named Timur invaded India."

Williams wondered if Abu had such ambition. He stubbed out his cigarette on the ground.

"Wasn't Timur an evil man?" Bhaiji asked.

"He was ruthless," Abu responded. "And relentless in his pursuit of new lands to conquer. Timur conquered for the same reason people climb mountains."

"Because they're there?" Williams asked.

"Precisely," Abu answered.

"And you condone that?"

"Timur's conquests shaped the history of the world," Abu said. "He is testimony to the power of one man to change the course of human events."

"How so?" Bhaiji asked.

"Much later, another man would remember Timur's accomplishment—a man named Babur, the fourteenth descendant of the legendary Ghengis Khan. He was 'The Mughal.' " Abu looked at Williams. "Babur studied war and he created a powerful army. But he lacked a kingdom. It was then that he remembered Timur and looked south, to India. But like Timur, Babur could not create a lasting system of government which would survive him. He died at the age of forty-seven."

"Then what happened?" a small boy traveling with his father asked.

Abu smiled at the boy and lifted him onto his lap. "There was civil war for a very long time. Until a boy king took the throne when he was not much older than you. His name was Akbar and he was one of the wisest men who ever lived."

"I have heard of Akbar the Great!" the boy exclaimed.

Abu smiled. "Akbar was the grandson of Babur and he inherited his grandfather's genius. His rule was vast, extending from Afghanistan in the west to Burma in the east. It was one of the largest and richest empires in the world. But Akbar wasn't content. He was fascinated by the spiritual essence of Man and sought the ultimate Truth common to all religions. He created the Din-e Ilahi, the 'Religion of God.' Unfortunately, the Din-e Ilahi met with opposition, and Akbar was compelled to abandon his goal."

"An idea ahead of its time?" Williams suggested.

"Perhaps merely a seed," Abu replied. "One which would take a long time to grow. Is that not what an idea is? Simply a seed?" Abu raised the boy off his lap. The boy hurried over to his father.

"Is such a thing really possible?" Williams asked.

"There is nothing which is not possible," Abu answered.

"Some might consider such a dream to be nothing more than delusions of grandeur," Williams challenged.

"Only by those who are afraid to realize their dreams, who seek refuge in their cynicism."

Williams smiled wryly. "And who do you identify with—Timur or Akbar?"

"Akbar gave the world a vision," Abu answered. "He also created a united India. His reign began a renaissance of art and music in this country. He encouraged advancement in mathematics, science and literature. But, without Timur would Babur have succeeded? Without Babur, India could well have remained a collection of petty feudal kingdoms forever at war with one another. Akbar would not have been given an empire to rule."

Williams offered no response. He studied Abu and the way light from the fire accentuated the sharp features of his face, and shimmered upon the glossy surface of his dark, foreboding eyes.

Abu looked around him at the faces of his listeners. "Perhaps now it is time to sleep," he said softly.

His audience disbanded and moved to their charpoys. Williams stayed by the fire. He watched Abu stretch out on one of the worn cots. His mind raced as he tried to fit all the pieces together. But with each new exchange between him and Abu, with each new revelation, the task became more and more daunting.

CHAPTER 8

Bhaiji Singh maneuvered the Mercedes onto the infamous Grand Trunk Road—India's version of Route 66. Sullen camels, obstinate buffalo and working elephants meandered along the road, and all traffic stopped for sacred cows. Countless bicycles, over-burdened trucks, buses, cars and motor scooters jammed the highway. Oxen-drawn carts, farm laborers, saffron-robed monks and devoted pilgrims moved in an endless stream along the narrow black artery shrouded in noxious clouds of bluish smoke that belched from the exhaust pipes of poorly-tuned diesel engines. The often tedious pace of the trip was occasionally enlivened by the seventy-mile-an-hour game of "chicken" practiced by India's drivers on the road's more open stretches; a game nonchalantly but deftly played by Bhaiji Singh.

"How are you holding up, Mr. Williams?" Abu asked, turning to look back at the journalist from his front seat.

"Just fine," Williams answered. "I've been through worse."

"Not like your American interstates, is it?" Bhaiji said, smiling at Williams in his rear-view mirror.

"Not quite," Williams replied, watching the slow-moving procession. " 'Such a river of life as nowhere else exists in the world,' " he muttered.

"You have read Kipling," Abu observed.

"Yeah. When I was very young. Kipling's *Kim* and Hemingway's *A Farewell to Arms* were two of my favorites."

Abu nodded. "I rather enjoyed *Kim* myself."

"What is it about," Bhaiji asked.

"It is about Kimball O'Hara and a Tibetan Lama who travel the Grand Trunk in search of excitement and adventure," Williams answered.

"And the true meaning of life," Abu added as he stared out of the open window at the passing parade of human and animal life.

For a few moments Williams studied the back of Abu's turban-covered head, as though hoping to penetrate it and discover Abu's hidden thoughts. Then he too turned his attention to the road. He noticed a sign that read "Welcome to Krishna's Birthplace." Orange-robed men with shaved heads, from India, Europe and America moved along the road, shaking their tambourines and chanting. It reminded Williams of the Hare Krishna devotees that sprang up years ago in the United States.

As the Mercedes-Benz slowed, a young Western woman reached into the car and handed Williams a flower. Before he could stop her, she placed a dab of red pigment between his eyebrows. "She has given you a tilak," Bhaiji explained, looking at Williams in the rear-view mirror. "You are now Hindu," he added, laughing.

Williams smiled and pointed to the red mark on his forehead. "And this is my baptism?"

"Not quite," Abu said. "Being Hindu is a state of mind; it's about searching for the ultimate truth—God—an eternal, transcendent, unifying force."

Williams continued watching the procession. "And how is this 'ultimate truth' obtained?" he asked skeptically.

"By losing all attachment to the physical world."

"Not easy for a Westerner."

"Quite so," Abu said. "That is because from the time you are born you are taught to look outside yourself for everything."

Williams felt defensive. "Yeah, well, America is the most successful country in the world."

"But you a pay a great price for that success."

"What price?" Williams asked.

"You live with an emptiness inside that the material world can never fill." Williams didn't respond. In fact, he agreed. "You are afraid of looking inward because of what you might find. And that fear separates you from God."

"And so," Williams said, wanting to turn the conversation back to Abu, "What are you? Muslim, Sikh, Hindu, Buddhist? Surely not Christian or Jew."

"I am none of them." Abu paused. "I am all of them."

"Pardon—?"

"Disregard the illusion of difference and you will see a commonality among all religions."

"I thought you said we need to look for God within."

"The search for God is not as important as the search for yourself," Abu answered. "Find yourself and you will find God."

Williams stared outside. "I don't know," he finally said. "Take a look at the world. It's hard to accept there is a God. I mean, what's he doing up there?"

Abu turned and looked at Williams. "Letting humanity find itself."

"Then what's the point of there being a God?" Williams said with annoyance.

"God doesn't need a point for being." Abu stared at Williams for a moment. "Humanity does not understand what God is because human beings do not understand love. God is pure love and cannot act inconsistent with itself. Would it be loving for God to constantly solve our problems? God has given humanity all the tools it needs to create a better world."

"Abuji?" Bhaiji interrupted, "I am troubled. You have said our souls are part of God, that our souls are helping God to create—" Abu nodded. "Isn't then the world we create—with all the evil in it—God's creation?"

"Yes," Abu answered. Williams listened to the two men, riveted by their exchange.

"Does God create evil, as well as good?" Bhaiji asked.

"God creates, period." Abu answered. Bhaiji seemed distressed. "Bhaiji, define good."

Bhaiji thought for a moment. "That which promotes peace and harmony."

"Now define evil."

"That which causes pain and suffering," Bhaiji said.

"Is it not possible to create peace and harmony through many different ways, some of which might be painful?" Abu asked.

"Yes," Bhaiji answered hesitantly.

"Who defines what is painful?" Abu asked.

"I do," Bhaiji responded quickly.

"Exactly," Abu said. "And that is how you define good and evil."

"Are you saying there is no universal standard of good and evil?" Williams asked.

Abu nodded. "God makes no judgments. Judgment is a barrier to love."

"But if God is within me," Bhaiji proffered, "does not God also feel my pain?"

"No," Abu answered. "You experience pain. What if one inflicting pain on another feels pleasure in it? Is that good or evil? As far as God is concerned, both are creations."

"But," Bhaiji said, as though trying desperately to defeat Abu's reasoning, "have you not said that God desires that we feel joy so that we can create more quickly?"

"Absolutely," Abu answered. "And so it is that there is an alignment of desire between you and God. You wish to feel happiness and joy in all things, and God wishes to create quickly and efficiently. There is alignment of purpose. Is that not good?" Abu asked.

"You argue like a lawyer," Williams observed from the back seat.

Abu laughed. "I do not think you mean that as a compliment."

"So God doesn't care what kind of world we create?" Williams asked. "It's up to us?"

"Yes," Abu replied. "But God does desire for humanity to be without fear."

Everyone in the car was silent again. Williams turned his attention to the Grand Trunk Road. Bhaiji was racing along it at ninety-five miles an hour. Warm, soothing wind shot through the open windows. Williams closed his eyes. He felt a growing anxiety. There was a crack in the wall and something was starting to seep through. Thoughts he never had before invaded his consciousness. When he was younger, it was easy to remain aloof, untouched by his own life. But now, Abu had tapped on the door of Williams' memories and they echoed back at him with a decidedly melancholy and hollow sound.

Abu was right: He was sovereign of his own private world—a world unfrequented by the joy and pain others could give—no one could catch even a fleeting glimpse of the real Bennett Williams.

He began to fall asleep and to dream. He was completely alone in a vast desert—an endless expanse of desolation. "I'm all alone," he muttered. The pain of his loneliness welled up within him. He cried out. His eyes flew open to see Abu staring straight at him. He looked past Abu and saw an ancient truck barreling toward them. At the last second, Bhaiji swerved and the two vehicles passed one another without incident.

"I'm sorry if I scared you," Bhaiji called back to Williams.

"You didn't," Williams answered, looking at Abu. He felt as though Abu had crawled inside his head. Was it a dream? The image was too real and frightening. For a moment Williams wondered if he was losing his mind.

CHAPTER 9

Bhaiji stopped in New Delhi to refuel the car. "We should not delay very long," he said to Abu.

"What's your hurry?" Williams asked.

"Nightfall is dangerous in Punjab," Bhaiji explained.

"We will stop here," Abu said. "Perhaps Mr. Williams has friends in New Delhi he wishes to contact."

"No," Williams answered. "But, thank you."

"As you choose," Abu said. "Then I shall join up with you later."

"Where're you going?" Williams asked.

"To pray." Abu turned and disappeared into the crowded street.

"He sure prays a lot," Williams muttered under his breath but Bhaiji heard.

"Prayer is special to Abu," Bhaiji said. "He does not just talk to God; he listens." Williams nodded half-heartedly.

Bhaiji smiled. "Come, I know a wonderful place to eat."

"Lead on, McDuff," Williams said.

After lunch, Williams picked up a copy of *The Daily Telegraph,* New Delhi's English-language paper, as well as his own *New York Times,* and returned to the Mercedes. Abu was already waiting inside.

They continued driving. Sunset was casting a comforting shawl over the surrounding countryside. "This place was settled by the Aryans over three-thousand years ago," Abu said. Williams looked up from his newspaper. "They were a magnificent people," Abu added, "tall, dark-skinned and extremely handsome. Their name meant 'Noble.' They were the ancestors of all the races of Asia."

"Including the Jats," Bhaiji Singh added with pride.

"Jats?" Williams asked.

"I am Jat," Bhaiji said. "As is Abu's mother. Most Jats are Sikhs. It is the warrior tradition of the Jats that has made the Sikhs feared and admired."

"The Jats are also among the world's best farmers," Abu added.

"Ranjit Singh was a Jat," Bhaiji argued. "And he was no farmer."

"Who was Ranjit Singh?" Williams asked.

"He was the greatest Jat Sikh who ever lived," Bhaiji said almost reverently. "He was a brilliant soldier and king. Abu's mother is a direct descendant of his."

"You don't say," Williams said. "Royal blood, eh?" When Abu didn't respond, Williams looked back at his newspaper. "According to this article, some Sikhs busted into a wedding yesterday and shot a twenty-two year old bridegroom, in front of his new wife, relatives and guests. They burst in with AK-47's, made the young man and five other relatives line up against a courtyard wall and shot them dead. Apparently, just because the bridegroom happened to be the cousin of a government minister," Williams said with disgust.

"They are fighting a war," Bhaiji explained.

Williams was incredulous. "Against whom? A young bride and groom?"

"Innocent people die in war," Abu said simply.

"And what, pray, is this war about?" Williams said with growing contempt.

"Freedom and independence," Abu answered. "As an American, surely you can understand."

"We Sikhs have fought for a homeland since the time of the Mughals," Bhaiji said.

"You count yourself among these terrorists?" Williams asked Bhaiji.

"I am a Khalsa Sikh," Bhaiji answered.

"The Sikhs are passionate about equality and justice," Abu explained. "Their mission is to oppose tyranny and make this world a reflection of God—without famine, homelessness, vice and corruption. And they do this with a warrior's resolve."

"Which means killing innocent people?" Williams said. "That's pretty barbaric, if you ask me."

"Who said humanity was civilized?" Abu asked. "We are still extremely primitive. Over eighty percent of the world's population is poor, homeless, uneducated, and live like slaves. In this world, power is pursued with treachery and deceit by ruthless men obsessed with having dominion over others."

"Christ," Williams said, "I thought I was cynical."

"I am not a cynic, Mr. Williams," Abu responded. "I accept things as they are but dream of something far better."

"Abuji—" Bhaiji interrupted nervously. He was peering through the windshield at an Army checkpoint up ahead.

"Do not worry," Abu said.

"But I am on the government's list," Bhaiji said.

"Why?" Williams asked.

"I was active in the political wing of our struggle," Bhaiji replied.

The headlights were like twin spears penetrating the darkness. Two military jeeps sat nose to nose across the road ahead. Alongside, a handful of government soldiers carried automatic rifles. The Mercedes-Benz slowed down.

"There must have been trouble again," Bhaiji said, bringing the car to a stop. The soldiers held their weapons tightly while they eyed the car's occupants suspiciously. Bhaiji turned off the engine. An officer approached with a flashlight, his heavy boots crushing the gravel beneath his feet. He stopped in front and shined his flashlight through the windshield.

The officer walked to the driver's side. Bhaiji lowered the window. The officer leaned down. He kept his flashlight pointed at Bhaiji's face. Williams felt his heart pounding.

"Identification," the officer demanded.

Abu and Williams watched as Bhaiji handed it over. The officer looked at the photo and then at Bhaiji. "What is your business in Punjab?" he asked.

"He is taking me and my American friend to my farm in Kartarpur," Abu volunteered.

The officer quickly moved the light to Abu's face. "Identification," he ordered.

Williams reached for his bag. Abu's eyes remained on Williams while the officer studied the passports.

"Wait here," the officer instructed. He turned and walked briskly to his jeep.

A moment later, Abu opened his door.

"Abuji!" Bhaiji exclaimed in a fierce whisper, wanting desperately to avoid trouble.

Abu stepped out. The officer immediately pointed his flashlight at the Mercedes and yanked his sidearm from its holster. The soldiers aimed their rifles. Williams heard cartridges snap into place and waited for the staccato crack of blazing AK-47s. A surge of adrenaline coursed through him. He could taste bile.

"Stop!" the officer shouted at Abu, raising his weapon.

Abu kept moving—calmly and deliberately, with his hands in sight and held away from his sides. He stepped in front of the headlights so that the soldiers could see him. The officer aimed his pistol at Abu's head with one hand and the flashlight into Abu's face with the other. Abu stopped and stared into the officer's eyes. The officer seemed unable to break Abu's stare. In the sharp light, Abu's face took on a ghostly tinge. Time stopped.

The officer lowered his weapon and nodded hypnotically. Abu stood for a moment longer, and then returned to the Mercedes. The soldiers looked at one another with confusion. The officer barked another order and the soldiers lowered their rifles. The two jeeps blocking the road backed off to the sides, just far enough to allow the Mercedes to pass between. Williams and Bhaiji looked at each other, and then at Abu as he closed the door behind him.

"I think we should move on," Abu said.

As Bhaiji reached for the ignition, the key turned on its own and the engine kicked in. Startled, Bhaiji drew his hand back and shot a glance at Abu. Abu looked at him but said nothing. Bhaiji put the car in gear and eased out the clutch.

Williams leaned back against the rear seat. He let out a deep exhale. His head throbbed badly; his stomach felt sour. "Well?" Williams finally asked. "Are you going to tell us?"

"How do you feel, Mr. Williams?" Abu asked.

"Fine."

"And your head?"

"Still attached."

Abu smiled. "Perhaps your fear no longer has the hold on you it once had."

Williams wasn't in the mood. "Cut the crap, Abu! What the hell was that all about? You almost got us fucking killed back there!"

"I explained to the officer that it was late, that we were very tired, and I assured him that we were not the ones he was looking for," Abu said.

"Bullshit!" Williams said. "You never spoke a goddamn word! What

56

was it, some kind of mind-control?!" Williams was surprised at his anger. He didn't like witnessing Abu's control over someone else's mind. Could he do that to him?

Abu laughed. "I am beginning to like you, Ben Williams." It was the first time he used Williams' first name. "We shall have a most interesting journey together." Abu's casual dismissal of Williams' irritation annoyed him further.

"But Abuji," Bhaiji began, "how—?"

Abu cut him off. "It is of no importance, Bhaiji."

There was silence in the automobile as they drove on. Williams was tired, but not relaxed. His anger subsided and his head gradually stopped throbbing.

Two hours later they passed through the city of Jullundur. "Kartarpur is not far away," Abu said.

"This must be near the village where you made the bread appear," Williams said, deliberately prodding. There was no response. "How'd you do it, Abu?" Still no response. "Can you really perform miracles?"

"What is a miracle?" Abu asked.

"Making bread appear where there wasn't any," Williams said.

"I suppose you would think so. But a miracle is just something you do not understand. It was not so long ago when it would have been a miracle for a man to walk upon the moon."

"That was a technological achievement," Williams said. "The means existed. They just had to figure out how."

"It was nothing more than a physical manifestation of a thought," Abu said.

"Whatever," Williams said, not wanting Abu to lead him astray. "You were saying about miracles?"

"What happened in the village was God working through me, and every villager. The idea of bread began as a thought, and then the thought became manifest in the three-dimensional world."

"Wait a minute," Williams said. "Divinely inspired or not, we know how a rocket took men to the moon. Someone didn't just think it. How did the bread come to be in the bag?"

"I defined the possibility with thought, my soul combined the energies to make it happen. It wasn't necessary for the wheat to be grown, harvested, milled, and baked. You could have performed the same feat, Ben Williams, if you would learn to master your thoughts and channel your chakric energies to consciously direct your creations."

"Uh-huh," Williams said cynically.

"May I suggest, Ben Williams, that you take the words of Albert Einstein to heart."

"And what words are you referring to?"

"He said 'There are only two ways to live your life. One is as though nothing is a miracle. The other as if everything is. I believe in the latter.' "

Bhaiji veered off the Grand Trunk near the village of Kartarpur. They arrived at a cluster of buildings surrounded by acres of farm land. With sporadic moonlight peering from behind passing clouds, Williams could make out a sprawling house, surrounded by smaller buildings connected by vine-covered walkways, sitting at the foot of a large hill that looked like a hulking protector. A spacious barn loomed behind the smaller buildings. Judging from the size and look of the place, Williams figured Abu's grandparents must have been wealthy.

Bhaiji stopped the Mercedes in front of the main house. They each got out and stood as though waiting for something to happen. In the still of the night, there was only the sound of croaking bullfrogs, and the occasional hoot of a questioning owl.

A few moments later the door opened. A tall, slender woman stepped out cautiously. She wore a scarf over her head and carried an old rifle in her hands. "Who is it?" she demanded. There was no fear in her voice.

"Hello mother," Abu said warmly.

"Abu?!" Satki Kaur exclaimed, searching the darkness.

Abu stepped toward her and she threw her arms around him. "My son! Oh, my son!" she cried, holding him tightly. She pushed herself away, as though remembering something. "Bhaiji Singh?" she asked. "Is he with you?"

"Yes," Bhaiji said, stepping out of the darkness. "I am here."

Satki Kaur embraced Bhaiji. "Have you eaten?" she asked. "You must be hungry?"

Abu laughed. "Yes, mother. We are—all three of us," he said.

"Three?" Satki said peering around. Williams stepped forward.

"Mother, let me introduce H. Bennett Williams, a celebrated correspondent with the *New York Times*. Ben Williams, this is my mother, Satki Kaur."

"A pleasure to meet you," Williams said, extending his hand. "I've heard so much about you."

"Thank you, Mr. Williams," Satki said, accepting his hand. "You are welcome here. Come," she said, taking Abu's arm. "I will cook you a meal you will never forget. And then, I want to hear all about Bhopal." Bhaiji and Williams trailed behind.

Satki prepared what amounted to a small feast, complete with fresh Indian bread called chapati, tandoori chicken, curried rice and vegetables, homemade chutney sauce and a delicious sweet desert made from kumquats and plums. Williams hadn't eaten a meal like this in years.

It was midnight when Abu escorted Williams to a cozy room with simple furnishings and a small bed. Against the opposite wall stood a table with a wash basin, a vase and flowers. Above it hung a portrait of a stern-looking, elderly man with a heavy beard and blue turban like Abu's. "Your grandfather?" Williams asked.

"No. That is the Guru Gobind Singh."

Williams nodded. "Inheriting this large farm must make you a pretty important guy around here," Williams observed. Abu smiled enigmatically as he closed the door behind him. Williams lay back on the bed and within seconds was sound asleep. It was the most peaceful night he'd had since arriving in India.

The sun was already up when he awoke the next morning. He looked at his watch; it was ten o'clock. He glanced at the picture of Gobind Singh on the wall. The guru stared back at him with demanding eyes.

Williams got up, washed, dressed and then began walking through the large, empty house. He found Satki in the courtyard clipping flowers. He watched how she carefully examined each bloom. Her choices were unhurried and deliberate. She was startled when Williams came up behind her. "I'm sorry," he said. "I didn't mean to frighten you."

"Not at all, Mr. Williams. It is just so quiet here with everyone gone."

"Where's Abu and Bhaiji?"

"They have gone to Amritsar."

"Are they coming back?"

"Oh yes," Satki quickly answered. "Abu said he had some things to attend to. I suspect he will be meeting with Sikh leaders."

"For what purpose?" Williams asked, following Satki into the house.

"My son, as you have probably noticed, is interested in politics."

"Passionately, I'd say."

Satki smiled. "Yes, just like his father, I am afraid."

"You don't sound happy about that."

"Politics is a nasty business. People get killed. Abu also inherits my father's role in Sikh affairs." She paused and looked at Williams. "Would you like some breakfast?"

"Yes," Williams answered as he followed her into the kitchen. "But only if you let me help."

"No. You are a guest in my son's house," Satki said firmly and began preparing breakfast. "Did you know, Mr. Williams, that feeding the hungry is the foundation of our faith; it is considered a godly act."

"Why'd you come back here?" Williams asked as he bit into a piece of hot kulchua.

"My husband was dead. Abu returned from England and the civil war was destroying Sri Lanka. The authorities also made it clear they did not want Abu to remain there. I was getting older, and I wanted Abu to know his grandparents. We closed up the house in Jaffna, and returned."

"And your parents accepted Abu?"

"They adored him," Satki answered with a smile. "Especially my father. Abu and my father spent a great deal of time together, riding and talking. My father was passionate about his Sikh faith and thought Abu could become an important spiritual leader among the Sikhs. He told me of his last ride with Abu and how he tried one last time to get Abu to become a Khalsa Sikh. But Abu again refused."

"Did he say why?"

"Abu told him that he could not be aligned with any one religion, nor any one nation. He also told me something about that last ride."

"What's that?"

"They were hunting with my father's champion falcon; he often boasted that it never missed its quarry. But, on that day, it circled while he and Abu talked about Abu's future. My father watched it spot its prey—a dove flying out from the brush near a forest. The falcon began its dive, but before it could seize the dove a handful of sparrows darted out from the forest and surrounded the falcon. They swirled around it and distracted it. The falcon became confused. The dove escaped as the falcon retreated to the sky. The sparrows disappeared. My father tried to recall the falcon but the falcon refused. It just kept circling. My father tried again, but the falcon ignored him. My father persisted and finally the falcon began a slow descent. But rather than return to my father's glove, the falcon flew past him and perched upon Abu's outstretched arm. He had never done that before. My father was stunned and as Abu stroked the falcon's head, it dug its talons into Abu's skin, so deeply that Abu began to bleed. Abu did not even wince. He just extended his arm to my father, and the falcon hopped back to my father's gloved hand. Neither spoke of it."

"Did your father say what he thought it meant?"

"No. But he regarded Abu differently after that, almost with reverence. All he would tell me was that he was certain that the purpose for Abu's life could not be fulfilled on this farm."

"What do you think it meant?"

Satki reflected a moment. "During the time of Gobind Singh," she began, "the Sikhs were in danger of being destroyed by the Mughals. He knew that the Sikhs would have to expand their mission. It would not be enough for them to search for God's truth, and be spiritual examples for humanity to follow. They would have to be warriors. So, Gobind Singh spent twenty-five years living among the Hindus in the Siwalik hills at the base of the Himalayas, patiently building an army. The Hindus there worshiped the goddess Durga."

"Durga?" Williams interjected.

"The divine mother of all creation—God's wife. Her name means 'power' and she is the source of the kundalini that lies dormant in all human beings. Kundalini is represented by a coiled serpent sitting at the base of the spine. When awakened, it rises up through the chakras until it reaches the top of the head. Then it expands outward to connect with God. Once the kundalini is awakened, one's spirit becomes emancipated and wonderful visions and powers come to those who possess it."

"Do you believe in this kundalini?" Williams asked.

"Of course," Satki answered. "You do not?"

Williams smiled. "You were saying about Gobind Singh?"

"At the festival of Baisaka, Gobind Singh summoned all Sikhs to his castle in the hills. Over twenty-thousand responded and the celebration went on for days while the Sikhs whipped themselves into a religious frenzy. All that time, Gobind Singh remained secluded in his tent. When the moment was right, the great kettle drum sounded and

61

Gobind Singh emerged, dressed like a warrior. On his head he wore a steel-blue turban; a sword at his side. To Gobind Singh, God was personified by the sword; his name for God was 'Sarob-loh,' which meant 'All-Steel.' "

"What happened?"

"The great assemblage grew quiet. He announced that Durga had bestowed her blessings upon the Sikhs and had sanctioned his leadership. But, he said, a sacrifice was needed to ensure her continued blessing. He drew his sword, raised it into the air and asked if there was a Sikh brave enough to sacrifice his life. No one came forward. Their timidity angered Gobind Singh. He asked three times until one man stepped forward. And then another came forward, and another, until five in all stepped forward to give their heads—all from different castes. This pleased Gobind Singh. He praised their courage and then took the first man into his tent. The Sikhs heard Gobind Singh cry out *Ya Durga,* followed by the swoosh of his sword slicing through flesh and bone." Williams had just taken a sip of tea and now almost spit it out. "Gobind Singh emerged with blood dripping from his sword. It was the same for each of the five men. After the fifth, he stood before the horrified Sikhs and proclaimed it was the duty of every Sikh to die for the cause. Then, in one swift gesture, he pulled back the side of the tent. The crowd gasped, startled to see all five men standing beside five slaughtered goats. The crowd roared."

"What was the point?" Williams wanted to know.

"They were the first Khalsa Sikhs. Through them, Gobind Singh established an ideal of devotion and courage. He had them drink amrit stirred by his bloody sword, and said any who drank of it would possess the strength to fight without fear. Each man pledged to oppose evil and tyranny. Gobind Singh reminded all Sikhs that their mission was to protect the weak, defy oppression, feed the hungry and care for the poor. But the Sikhs also had to be warriors, and be ready to die for that cause. All male Sikhs would thenceforth have the name Singh, meaning lion, and all women shall be called Kaur. There would be no surnames, no class distinctions. All Sikhs would be of one family." Satki paused, as though arriving at the true importance of her story. "And then Gobind Singh said he would 'teach the sparrow how to hunt the falcon, and one man the courage to fight a legion.' "

"Interesting," Williams said.

"I think God meant for Abu to be the next Gobind Singh—to unite humanity as one family. It was why my father gave Abu the blue turban he now wears, and the dagger he keeps at his side." Williams sat back in his chair. Satki lifted the teapot. "Would you like more tea, Ben?"

"Yes, thank you," he said absently, engrossed in what Satki had said. She had just defined Abu's mission, Williams thought. Or had she?

CHAPTER 10

Just before Abu and Bhaiji returned, Williams invited Satki for a walk. They strolled down through a meadow near the house. "What kind of child was Abu?" Williams asked.

"Most unusual," Satki answered with a broad smile. "He was born on the twenty-seventh of Ramadan—the Night of Power—the night 'worth a thousand months,' according to Muslims. It was the night God began delivering his divine message through the Prophet Muhammad."

"Quite a coincidence," Williams said.

"Perhaps," Satki said, glancing at Williams. "There was a great thunderstorm that night. My contractions came quickly. The midwife told me she'd never witnessed such an easy delivery. The moment Abu was born, he did not even cry—just opened his eyes and looked around, as though instantly aware of everything. He even smiled. My husband Abdullah proudly carried his son out to all the Muslim men who had gathered in our home. And then the storm cleared. Abdullah said it was a sign that Allah was pleased, and so he took Abu out into the night. And then a star suddenly expanded so that it was as bright and as large as the moon. The men all fell to their knees and praised Allah."

"Did Abu have friends as a child?"

"No," Satki answered. "It was as though he did not have time for childhood. He spent most of his time with his father."

"Who I understand had a passion for politics."

Satki nodded. "Merchants would gather at my husband's jewelry shop to engage in the two main topics of conversation in Sri Lanka—religion and politics. In time, Abu began participating in the discussions and he could out-debate even the most educated men. Abu also went to the mosque with his father. Eventually, he spent more time at the mosque than with his father. The mullahs took him under their wings, calling him 'the ancient soul.' " Satki smiled again. "By the time Abu was two years old, he had memorized the entire Koran—word for word." Williams was stunned. Satki smiled. "It's true."

"Did Abu spend time with you?"

"Oh yes," Satki answered emphatically. "He often went with me to visit neighbors to help with food or just talk about their problems. Abu listened and afterwards was always full of questions. It was as though he needed to learn as much as he could as fast as he could. Once you told him something, he remembered it forever."

"Did he attend school?"

"When he was two, my husband enrolled him in a Muslim school. But in one term he learned everything they could teach him."

"What did you do?"

"We hired private tutors—one after another—at first, from the university in Colombo, but then from as far away as Baghdad and Cairo, even Oxford University. Before Abu was twelve, he had a full university education. History was his favorite subject and he understood events as though he experienced them. But then we realized he was simply learning what he needed to know about the world before moving on."

"To what?"

"God and politics. With Abu, they are the same. And it was about that time that my husband was mediating disputes between the Tamil Hindus and Sinhalese Buddhists. Abu went with his father on many of those occasions. And Abu would often visit Buddhist monasteries and Hindu holy men along the way."

"Who taught Abu how to meditate?"

"I taught him the Nam Simram—the Sikh meditation, and about the chakras—the energy portals of our spiritual bodies that connect us to God. After that, there was no stopping him." Satki was momentarily lost in thought. "One day, I looked for him everywhere and finally found him beneath a cluster of palm trees on the beach. He was standing alone, his eyes closed, his hands moving around him in smooth, graceful ways. He had learned to manipulate his own energies and had gained complete unity with his soul. I became very saddened."

"Why?"

"Because I had lost him."

"To what?"

"Something far greater than anything of this world." They walked in silence for a few moments. "He began to spend more time alone. His soul was his new teacher. And then one day, while we were in the house together, there was a woman's blood-chilling scream. We ran outside."

"What was it?"

"A child was sitting near the well. Within easy striking distance from her was an albino cobra with translucent skin and bright red eyes, coiled and swaying back and forth, its hood open and its tongue darting wickedly in and out. The mother pleaded for someone to do something, but everyone was afraid if they did, the cobra would strike. It hissed as it swayed, poised to lunge at any moment. Then Abu moved slowly into the circle toward the snake, until he was in easy striking distance. I was terrified as the cobra turned and faced Abu."

"Then what?"

"Abu stood staring at the snake. It stopped swaying and became like a statue." Satki spoke with the same awe and amazement that she had felt at the time when this event occurred. "And then, Abu took another step towards the cobra. He moved his hands about, in that way I witnessed on the beach. And then, the snake slithered over to Abu and coiled itself cozily between his feet."

Williams' eyes widened. He felt like a kid listening to a horror story. "And then?"

"Abu picked up the great snake and it wrapped itself around Abu's arm like a loving pet. He then stepped through the crowd, walked down the road for a distance and then disappeared. I did not see him again until late that night. We never spoke of it."

"Why not?"

"There was nothing to say."

They continued walking in silence. "How did that change everything?" Williams finally asked.

"Word spread quickly throughout the island." Satki's tone lightened. "In Sri Lanka we have the Jungle Telegraph—anything newsworthy makes its way around very quickly."

"What made it so newsworthy?"

"The cobra is a divine symbol to both Buddhists and Hindus. Legend says that a cobra once came upon Buddha meditating in the rain. He coiled himself around Buddha and sheltered him with his hood.

Hindus believe the gods often take the form of a cobra. And the albino cobra represents the power of kundalini."

"And people began to think that—what? That God curled up under Abu's feet?"

"Yes," Satki said with delight in her voice. "People came from all over to see the man to whom God had revealed itself. Every day there were more people outside our house. It started to become a problem so Abu began traveling around Sri Lanka. In each place, he was accepted as a prophet. But someone highly placed told us that Buddhists in the government were afraid of Abu's popularity among the Hindus, and some Hindus feared his popularity with the Buddhists. We worried that Abu would be arrested or extremists on either side would kill him."

"And so you sent Abu to London?"

"Yes. My husband contacted a man he knew there, an Arab Muslim named Muhammad Jamal Amani."

"Who was he?"

"A barrister, very well connected in London, who served as an unofficial ambassador."

"Why London?"

"My husband wanted Abu to learn about the West, and to learn law. In Sri Lanka, law is an important stepping stone to politics. And I think it was my husband's idea that Abu would one day return and become a very important man in Sri Lankan politics, maybe even president."

"What happened in London?"

Satki's face clouded. "I don't know," she said quietly. "Abu has never spoken of it. There was trouble. People were killed. Abu didn't want me to know about any of it until after the trial was over. It was around that time that my husband was murdered, and my son was in prison for murder in a foreign country. If it were not for Muhammad Amani's urgent pleas for help, I think I too would have died."

"What kind of help?"

"Amani wanted my husband to pressure the government here to have Abu returned. And with my husband dead, it was up to me."

"Who was Nanaki Kaur?" Williams asked.

Satki looked surprised. There was a pause. "Abu's wife," she said sadly.

Williams was startled—he hadn't thought of the possibility of Abu being married. "And she was killed?"

Tears came to Satki's eyes. "Yes. Brutally."

"And Abu was blamed for her death?"

Satki nodded. "And also the death of a young Briton."

Williams started to ask another question but Satki shook her head. "If you want to know more about this, you should speak with Abu. There is much I don't know about this part of his life."

"What happened after he returned?"

"He did not stay in Sri Lanka for long. He was different. He had changed."

"How?"

"When he left to go to London he was only nineteen years old—still a young man." Satki smiled in remembrance. "He was so serious, but still so full of life, so charming." Her face became somber again. "But when he returned, he was withdrawn and angry. And one day he told me he was leaving. I think he needed time alone. He traveled for almost ten years."

Williams remembered what Whatley had said about Abu having disappeared for nearly a decade. "Where did he go?"

"Many places. First, Tibet, where he lived among Buddhist monks who taught him incredible things about control of the mind and body, overcoming gravity and other natural forces. And then he was in China for a while, where he studied ancient techniques of healing. Then he went to Iran and lived with an enlightened Sufi mystic. After that he visited the holy shrines of Israel, the pyramids of Giza, Mecca, and even meditated in the very cave where the Prophet Muhammad received his revelations from God. And from there, he traveled to Peru and lived in Machu Picchu. After that, he stayed in a tiny village in northern Mexico with a man said to have extraordinary powers relating to the manipulation of space and time. Finally, he went to America, living among Cheyenne Indians in South Dakota, where I understand he learned magic from a powerful shaman, and how to connect with the energy of the earth."

Williams nodded absently. "I see . . ." he said, his voice trailing off. But he didn't see—he didn't see at all.

After a few moments of silence, Satki turned to Williams. Her eyes brightened. "And what of you, Ben?" she asked as she studied his face. "Tell me about you. Are you married?"

Williams chuckled. "No," he replied, as though the question was silly.

"Have you ever been married?"

"No."

"What of your mother and father? Are they still alive?"

"Yes," Williams said uncomfortably. "But we're not close."

"I am sorry."

"Don't be. I'm not."

Satki remained thoughtful as she stared at the ground. "And so your work is the most important thing to you?"

"Yes," Williams said.

"Are you happy?"

Williams pondered the question. "I don't know," he confessed. "What is happiness?"

Satki looked at him with surprise tinged with sadness. "I think you must answer that for yourself."

"What if you can't?"

"Then, that is something to look upon."

"Do you think it's important?" Williams asked. He'd never thought so, but maybe he'd missed something along the way.

"Happiness is what life is about," Satki said and then looked him in the eye. "You are a nice man, Ben. You deserve to be happy." No one had ever expressed such a sentiment to him, or about him. He suddenly felt very lonely. "I have to get back to the house," Satki said. "Abu will return soon." Williams watched the tall, handsome woman as she walked back to the farmhouse. Her leaving intensified the sudden loneliness that had come over him.

It was easier to think about Abu. Many of the pieces of the puzzle were being learned, albeit only from people around Abu, but it seemed that the more Williams learned about Abu, the less he knew. What was he hiding? London was the key. He would double his efforts.

He spotted the black Mercedes winding its way up the road toward the farm, a cloud of dust swirling in its wake.

"It is a shame you did not come with us, Ben," Bhaiji said as he retrieved their bags.

"How so?" Williams asked.

"We met a friend of yours in Amritsar," Bhaiji replied.

69

Abu looked at Williams, as though anticipating a reaction.

Williams was suspicious. "Who?"

"A Mr. Whatley," Abu said. "Jack Whatley."

Williams hoped his surprise and concern weren't obvious. "Jack Whatley isn't exactly a friend," Williams said.

Abu was staring at Williams.

"But you do know him," Bhaiji said.

"Yes," Williams answered. "How'd you meet?"

"He was present at a speech Abu gave outside the Golden Temple," Bhaiji explained. It was obvious Bhaiji didn't think there was anything unusual about the meeting. "He was in the crowd and approached Abu afterwards and asked if he could speak with him."

"Yes," Abu said, still looking directly at Williams. "We shared a meal with him at a restaurant. A pleasant man."

Williams grunted. "What was Jack doing in Amritsar?"

"He said he had come to India as a pilgrim," Abu said. "He claims to be interested in religion and philosophy, and said he was in search of a holy man he had heard about."

"Right," Williams said. "You?"

"I do not think so," Abu said. "But he asked many questions."

"He seemed more interested in politics than religion," Bhaiji added.

"Decidedly," Abu agreed.

"How did I come into it?" Williams wondered.

"I mentioned you," Abu said. "He was amazed at what a small world it was."

"Did he say anything else?"

"No," Abu answered. He stared into Williams' eyes.

"Abu's speech at the Golden Temple was one of the best I have heard him deliver," Bhaiji said. "There were many important people there." Bhaiji hurried off into the house.

"Tell my mother we'll be right in," Abu called to him. He turned to Williams. "A penny for your thoughts, Ben Williams," Abu said good-naturedly.

Williams knew it was a pretense for another examination of Williams' emotional state. He wasn't in the mood. "Why's my psyche so goddamn important to you?" he asked. "Doesn't elevating all mankind give you enough to do?"

"Because if you are to have a role in all of this, then you must start to see yourself differently," Abu said gently.

Williams was irritated, on the verge of anger. "Just what the hell is 'all this?' And what is this crap about 'my role'? I don't have a role—I'm a reporter."

Abu smiled. "You are so humble, Ben Williams."

"Fuck you," Williams said. He looked directly at Abu. "Suppose you tell me what happened in London!" He went for it. "And tell me about Nanaki Kaur."

Abu's smile disappeared. Williams studied his face. Did he detect sorrow in Abu's eyes? Had he hit the man's rawest nerve?

Abu looked at him. "We will be leaving in a few days," he said. "By then you will have your package and the answers to your questions." Williams was stunned. How could he have known? Abu headed toward the house just as Satki was coming out to greet him.

Williams watched mother and son lovingly embrace. He thought of his own mother and the fact that they never did, or could, hug each other this way. They never even looked at each other with the love and respect that flowed so easily between Abu and Satki. Williams was envious of this mother-son relationship—it represented yet another loving bond that he believed he would never experience in this lifetime.

CHAPTER 11

"My mother will be joining us when we leave tomorrow," Abu said to Williams and Bhaiji. Both men were pleased. Bhaiji was delighted.

The package had arrived that afternoon but Williams hadn't opened it. He waited until he could be alone.

Retiring early that night, he closed the door to his room and set the box on the bed. He glanced up at the portrait of Gobind Singh. "Get a load of this," he said as he opened the box. It was filled with manila files stuffed with newspaper articles. There was a photograph taken in London of Abu with an older man. Williams guessed it was Muhammad Jamal Amani.

Another file bearing Abu's name contained legal documents and correspondence bearing the barrister's letterhead. There were also some hand-written notes. Beneath that file lay a partial transcript of court testimony. Near the bottom, Williams found a journal. Like an archaeologist who'd just unearthed an important artifact, Williams opened it excitedly. The pages were filled with longhand script. Williams scanned the early entries until he came to Abu. He sat back and began to read.

21 June 1982

My new charge arrived at Heathrow this morning. So young, yet so serious, even intense; yet he has remarkable poise, and obvious intelligence.

The next entry was dated several weeks later.

Abu spent the last two days with my wife and I at our country home in Wiltshire. I am humbled by his genuine piety. He neither drinks alcohol, nor smokes tobacco. He prays five times daily and meditates for long periods. His statements on every subject are thoughtful and reasoned, and never clouded with emotion. He will make an excellent barrister.

Another entry about Abu read:

Abu possesses an innate understanding of law. I have also taken to instructing him in Islamic law. If I have any criticism, it is that he works too hard, and spends too many hours in the library. He is inno-cent in the ways of the world. It is time I introduce him to London society.

Williams searched the journal for the next entry. It was in the early fall.

I introduced Abu to Her Majesty at the official opening of Parliament today. Abu exhibited grace and poise. Seldom have I seen the Queen so taken with anyone. Abu impressed the Prince of Wales in particu-lar. I suspect that the Prince's proclivity for philosophy was the basis for the interest. I also managed an introduction to the Prime Minis-ter. A debate ensued on political matters. Suffice it to say that their respective viewpoints did not coincide. But Abu argued well, without giving the slightest offense.

Williams skipped ahead. There were frequent references to embassy receptions, private dinners, and social gatherings that Amani had taken Abu to. Then Williams came upon something new.

14 April 1983
Abu has discovered love! Her name is Nanaki Kaur, the daughter of Sikh immigrants from Punjab. I have had the honor of meeting her. She is intelligent, virtuous, and quite beautiful. What a change in Abu! I do not see him as often. I understand they are to marry.

Williams turned the page. There was another, more ominous entry.

27 May 1983
Last evening Abu was approached by a Libyan I know only by his nefarious reputation—a close aide to Moammar Khadafi. He invited Abu to the Libyan Embassy. Against my counsel, Abu will go.

There was another entry two days later.

Abu has been arrested for murder! Nanaki is dead. I must begin at once to prepare his defense.

There were other entries, but days apart and they shed little light on what had happened. *Abu is sullen and withdrawn. I fear Abu has retreated into a fiery anger which he keeps suppressed deep within him. The Abu I knew died that night as well.* Muhammad Amani made no further entries. Williams closed the journal.

Williams looked through the newspaper clippings. They bore headlines in large bold type. "BRUTAL MURDER IN EAST END—London Youth Nearly Beheaded!" one article proclaimed. Another: "VAUXHALL SLAUGHTER!" Williams began reading:

> 30 May 1983
>
> LONDON—A savage killing took place last night just after midnight on the working-class streets of Vauxhall. Dense fog rolled silently through narrow streets and alleyways, muffling the blood-curdling scream of Clarence Fox, age 19.
>
> Horrified witnesses watched from inside the Dragon's Head pub as a tall, well-built Arab male choked young Clarence Fox with one powerful hand, while slitting his throat with the other using a curved and bejeweled dagger so as to nearly sever the boy's head from his body. Also found dead at the scene was a young Indian Sikh woman, identified by authorities as Nanaki Kaur, age 18.
>
> Metropolitan police have arrested an Arab male identified as Abu 'Ali Asghar. Nothing is known about Mr. Asghar and the authorities are unwilling to speculate on the motive for the incident. However, according to unidentified sources, Abu 'Ali Asghar is a suspected terrorist. On the same day preceding the incident in Vauxhall, Abu 'Ali Asghar was observed coming and going from the Libyan Embassy. He is being held at the Old Bailey.

Another newspaper in the box had its headline circled with a bright red marker. It was dated the day after the murder. "STAR EXPLODES! Astronomers Observe Rare Phenomena." Williams wondered why Amani had circled it.

He located some witness statements from the police file. Patrons of the Dragon's Head pub on Dante Street all told gruesome tales about how Abu choked the young man with one hand, and slit his throat with the other, and did so with a rage that made him appear like Satan himself. Each saw Nanaki laying dead on the street, but no one had seen how she was killed. A statement from Nanaki's brother said he was a member of the All India Sikh Students Federation, a militant cadre of young revolutionaries, and that Abu had spoken to a gathering of Sikh students earlier that night.

The pub's proprietor said two very drunk young men came in earlier. "They were skinheads," he said, "who wore those gloves with the fingers cut out, swastikas—like Nazis—heavy jackboots, and lots of chains hanging all about them. They were quite abusive. They acted like a wild animals." They were tossed from the pub just minutes before the incident. There was no mention of the other young man, except that one witness saw him flee the scene. What about the one that got away? Did he kill Nanaki? Williams wondered if the police had ever located him.

Forensic reports described a gold, jewel encrusted dagger found at the scene with Abu's fingerprints and the victim's blood. It sounded to Williams like the same one Abu now carried. There were several black and white photographs depicting Abu entering the Libyan Embassy. They were dated the day of the murder.

Williams read with fascination the coroner's report detailing how the young man's larynx had been crushed, and the neck severed down to the cervical vertebrae. The coroner also found that he had an extremely high blood alcohol level and substantial amounts of a drug commonly referred to as PCP. He went on to report that Nanaki's death was due to a severe skull fracture and massive cerebral hemorrhaging. She had also suffered a devastating blow to the face which had broken her nose, displaced several teeth, and caused a severe dislocation of her jaw. She carried a male fetus, not viable at the time of death.

My God, Williams thought, Abu was going to have a son! He put the box on the floor and turned out the light. He stared into the darkness until sleep overcame him. He began to dream. A blood-spattered Abu stood before him. His bejeweled dagger dripped with blood; there was a demonic smile on Abu's face. Williams was seized with fear as Abu came toward him, laughing maniacally. Williams wanted to run but was paralyzed with fright and couldn't move. "I am only here to serve, Ben Williams," Abu said with mock assurance.

Then Abu's head suddenly turned into that of the albino king cobra, with ruby eyes and white, translucent skin. The snake's forked-tongue lashed fiendishly in and out. Then it opened its mouth wide and instead of fangs, Williams saw two curved daggers glistening in the light, dripping with venom. The cobra lunged at Williams. His own scream awakened him. He was drenched in sweat.

He sat up, startled to find Abu standing at the foot of his bed, staring down at him. "We must leave soon," Abu said.

Williams couldn't speak. For a moment he thought he might still be dreaming. He stared wide-eyed as Abu left the room. Williams suddenly questioned his hold on reality. He felt he was losing control and didn't know what to do about it.

The sun was beginning to rise above the horizon when Williams finally appeared from the front door of the house. They were all waiting for him. His bag was slung over his shoulder and the box firmly in his arms. Bhaiji placed them in the trunk. Williams and Satki climbed into the back seat of the Mercedes.

It was nearly evening when they reached New Delhi. Bhaiji maneuvered through the maze of narrow, winding streets in the old part of the city and eventually stopped the car in front of a decaying tenement. "I know the proprietor," Bhaiji said, turning off the engine. "He will give us a good price."

Williams surveyed the front of the decrepit building and told himself he'd slept in worse.

"I will join you later," Abu said, climbing out of the car.

"Where are you going?" Williams asked.

"To the Jami' Masjid," Abu said as he started off. "The city's main mosque."

"I'll go with you," Williams called out, hurrying to catch up. Abu had never been to New Delhi and Williams wondered how he knew where the mosque was. Maybe it was like migrating birds guided by instinct.

Williams spotted the bulbous domes and lofty minarets of the Jami' Masjid. He heard the wail of the muezzin, and saw streams of people moving in a steady procession toward the source.

Inside, over a thousand Muslim men were assembled in neat rows facing Mecca. Abu went further in and disappeared. Williams preferred to stay at the rear, and be inconspicuous.

After prayers, the Imam extended a hand and invited Abu to speak. Abu walked across the platform and bowed to the Imam. He turned to address the gathering. "In the name of Allah, the Merciful, the Compassionate," Abu intoned. "I wish to speak to you about the chains that keep you in bondage." There was murmuring in the crowd. Williams half-listened as he scanned the rapt faces of the congregation, occasionally jotting notes. It was a speech similar to the one Abu gave in Bhopal, but tailored to this particular audience. Williams listened for a while and then badly wanted a cigarette. He stepped out into the cool night air, pulled out his pack of Marlboros and lit one. The smoke calmed him. He could still hear Abu's voice coming from inside. It sounded like the muffled roar of an angry lion.

The stay in Delhi lasted a couple of days. Other mosques invited Abu to speak, and the Muslim newspaper asked for an interview. Abu didn't ignore the Hindus either. When he spoke one night to a gathering of young Hindus at a prominent temple, the response was the same as at the Muslim mosques. People seemed hungry for his words; for his leadership.

The night before they left New Delhi, Williams decided to try and get some information out of Abu about the events in London. Williams knocked on the door to Abu's room and waited. He was about to leave when he heard Abu's voice. "Yes?"

He opened the door. There was a soft glow in the room as evening light seeped through the slats of the closed shutters. A ceiling fan hummed softly. Abu was kneeling on the floor. "I wondered if we could talk—" Williams started to say.

"I've been waiting for you," Abu interrupted.

"You have?" Williams asked.

"Yes," Abu said. "It is time you learned to meditate."

Williams smiled. "That's not exactly what I had in mind—"

"I know. But this is more important than an interview right now." Williams wanted to leave. "Kneel beside me," Abu instructed.

Williams felt silly but maybe this was the trade-off. He'd meditate first and get answers afterward. He rested his hands, palms facing up on his thighs, the way Abu did. "Now what?"

"Close your eyes," Abu said softly. "Allow your mind to drift. Listen to your body; focus upon the sounds and smells around you—feel the air upon your skin." They both sat quietly for a few minutes. "Now breathe deeply." Williams inhaled and then let it out. "Again," Abu said. "Do not force it; let it flow." Williams felt himself starting to relax. The self-conscious feeling was slipping away. There was silence for several moments and Williams grew uncomfortable. He began to fidget; his mind filled with chatter. Abu smiled. "Your conscious mind cannot accept inactivity, so it inundates you with thoughts. Ignore them."

Williams tried. "I can't," he said.

"Breathe," Abu's voice was hypnotic. "With each new breath, imagine a light entering at the base of your spine. As you breathe out, see it—feel it—travel up your spine and out the top of your head."

Williams obeyed and soon he felt his body tingle. He was calm and relaxed, yet more alert, and very alive. Then suddenly, splashes of color appeared—purple, red, orange, yellow, green. They exploded like paint on a blank canvas in rapid sequence. They brought a strangely comforting sensation to Williams.

"Continue breathing," Abu said, making Williams notice that he'd stopped. He breathed in and out, seeing and feeling the white light flowing through his body. "Now," Abu said, "you may ask."

"Ask what?"

"Whatever you wish to know," Abu answered. "And then listen. Say nothing out loud."

Williams didn't know what to ask. The colors stopped. He felt slightly ridiculous all of a sudden. Why? The word came from a voice inside Williams' head; not his own. Then he heard it again—yes, it was his voice after all. You are not crazy, it said.

"Perhaps that is enough for now," Williams heard Abu say. "When you are ready, open your eyes." Abu stood up and began moving about. Williams opened his eyes. It was now dark in the room and Abu was putting on a light. The light blinded Williams. The room looked strange to him, as though he'd been away without really leaving. "Any questions?" Abu asked.

"Is that it?"

"What did you expect?"

"Something magical."

"Tell me what you experienced," Abu said.

Williams stood up and stretched his legs. "Well, I relaxed and then I saw some colors, bright splashes of colors."

"And what else?"

"That's it. Then they went away and I was just talking to myself and reassuring myself that I wasn't nuts."

"Those colors you saw were synaptic firings in your brain. It was your soul trying to communicate with you. So too, the voice in your head was your soul."

Williams eyed Abu skeptically and shook his head. "I'm afraid it sounded like me, like I was just talking to myself."

"You expected God's voice?"

"Yeah, I suppose so," Williams said.

"And What does God sound like?"

"I don't know," Williams said. "Something like John Houston, maybe Charlton Heston."

Abu grinned. "It was God speaking to you—it was your soul." Abu studied Williams, gauging his comprehension. "Define self-confidence."

Williams thought about it. "It's knowing who you are."

Abu shook his head. "Self-confidence is the act of confiding in yourself. It is being your own advisor."

Williams nodded. "I guess that's a plausible definition, too."

"You must understand the many layers of our consciousness, Ben Williams."

"Layers?"

"Your soul is at the core of your being. Shrouding it is your unconscious mind. Around that is your ego—who you think you are, and at the very forefront is your conscious mind."

"What does that have to do with self-confidence?"

"Your conscious mind speaks through your ego. Your soul speaks through your unconscious mind. This meditation enables you to penetrate the layers and hear the whispers of your soul. It will show you who you really are."

"How?" Williams asked.

"By revealing you to you." Abu paused, and looked Williams in the eye. "It will take courage, Ben Williams—it is the path of the warrior." Williams was intimidated by the notion. "I have opened the door. How far you venture inward is up to you."

Williams stood up. "Now can I ask you a few questions?"

"It is not important," Abu said.

"What isn't?"

"What happened in London," Abu said.

"People need to know," Williams countered.

"You need to know."

"Well then, humor me," Williams said. "Why didn't you speak up at your trial?"

"Because it would not have made a difference."

"Just tell me what happened that night outside the Dragon's Head."

Abu stared blankly. Williams tried another tack. "My guess is these drunken skin-heads were aching for a fight that night and you and Nanaki just happened to come along—two dark-skinned foreigners in the wrong place at the wrong time—and they attacked you, am I right?" Abu didn't answer. Williams kept his frustration in check. "One came after you while the other attacked Nanaki. Am I close?" Williams thought he could detect a look of sorrow on Abu's otherwise chiseled face. He was on the right track—he could feel it. "The other guy knocked her down and smashed her head into the pavement, and then the police arrived before you could go after him, right?"

His question was met with silence. Abu turned to look at Williams for the first time in the conversation. Williams knew that he was right but he needed confirmation. His voice became sympathetic, almost pleading. "It was self-defense, pure and simple. Abu, I know you're not a murderer!" Williams needed to hear Abu say it was so, while at the same time, realizing he might never know the truth of what really happened that night. He turned to leave. He stopped at the door. "I'm sorry about Nanaki," Williams said, "and your son." He closed the door behind him, leaving Abu sitting alone, staring at some distant unseen image.

CHAPTER 12

Williams awoke the next morning before sunrise. He stared at the ceiling for a few moments and then decided to try Abu's meditation. After taking several deep breaths as Abu had instructed, the colors returned. Williams smiled. He wanted them to stay but they soon disappeared. He tried to recapture them. *What are you afraid of?* He told himself he wasn't afraid. *Bullshit. You're trying to knock Abu down because you're afraid he's right about you.* The words resounded in his head.

He didn't want to meditate anymore. 'It is the path of the warrior,' Abu had said, and Williams understood why. He took a few more breaths, and then opened his eyes. Again, he felt like he'd been in an alternate reality.

The others were waiting for him outside. As soon as Williams climbed into the back seat next to Satki, Bhaiji gunned the car's engine and they were off.

"Where're we headed?" Williams asked as Bhaiji maneuvered the Mercedes on to the Grand Trunk road once again. He figured they'd be going to Calcutta.

"Bangladesh," Abu answered.

The tiny nation was in pitiful condition. Recent monsoons had caused the Ganges and Jamuna rivers to overflow their banks—three-quarters of the low-lying country was underwater; thirty million people were homeless. A devastating cyclone had followed, killing three hundred thousand more. With all that Williams had seen and experienced over the years, these numbers still seemed incomprehensible. For Abu, Bangladesh was a logical next stop. Despite the tragedy, it was a devoutly Muslim country.

As they drove, Abu noticed Williams as he caught sight of the countless homes made of mud, discarded cardboard and corrugated tin. "We are still a barbaric race to allow such poverty to exist," Abu spoke angrily.

"Les Miserables," Williams said.

"To Muslims," Abu added, "they are *al mustazafin*—the forgotten ones—those for whom governments are created, but whom governments ignore." Abu paused. "What do Americans know about these people?"

Williams looked out the window. "Only what they see on TV, read in the papers."

"Only as victims of disaster—people who must be helped."

"Your point?"

"These people feel, and they have needs, just like you. They are part of God, but are regarded as a burden, an insoluble problem, a monolithic mass that drains the world's resources."

"And so, what is to be done?" Williams asked.

"They must be brought to the forefront of the world's consciousness, but not as victims to be pitied. They must learn to speak out and be heard. Until humanity takes its own constituents seriously, it will always be regarded as a small and petty race, fighting amongst themselves—a primitive people that must be contained."

"Contained? By whom?"

"By the other species that occupy our galaxy," Abu said. There was a sudden silence inside the Mercedes-Benz. Bhaiji shot a glance at Abu. Satki looked surprised.

"Are you serious?" Williams asked. There it was, yet another reason to doubt the teacher, to distrust the message. "Are you saying 'we're not alone'?"

"Are you saying we are?"

"Let's say I'm skeptical," Williams answered, lighting a cigarette and blowing a puff of smoke out the window.

"Why?" Abu asked.

"Where's the proof?"

"Why must you have proof?"

"What else is there?"

"Common sense," Abu suggested. "Do you suppose that human beings are the only form of sentient consciousness in the galaxy? That is very arrogant. There are more life forms out there than you can imagine—some less advanced, some far more advanced. The form of life is far less important to God than it is to human beings."

"So," Williams interjected facetiously, "human beings were not created in the image of God?"

"Very much so," Abu replied. "In the spiritual sense. For God to limit itself to only one form would be extremely inefficient, and God is nothing if not efficient."

"But, you used the word contain," Williams said. "And that sounds like a quarantine—"

"Perhaps it's simply a loving act of self-preservation."

"What do you mean?" Williams asked.

"Before humanity can be allowed to venture out beyond this solar system, it has to learn to live in peace with itself—to be responsible to its own and to respect all forms of life. Humanity is still in the grip of fear and that makes us irrational and dangerous."

"But people are changing," Satki said.

"Yes, mother" Abu said. "It is the evolutionary transition. That is why I am here."

"You keep saying that," Williams said with irritation. "If it's evolutionary, how are you going to influence this change?"

"I will make the transition possible." Abu paused. "When fear is vanquished," he continued, "there will be no barrier to a consciousness beyond what we can imagine, and higher forms of communication—empathic and even telepathic communion."

"And this is what is in store for all humanity?" Bhaiji asked with childlike enthusiasm.

"In the future, yes," Abu answered. "For the present, only some."

"Who?" Bhaiji asked.

"Those who have the courage to be warriors," Abu said, looking at Williams.

"How will it happen?" Williams asked.

"By confronting the devil," Abu responded.

"And what is your definition of the devil?" Williams asked with genuine curiosity.

"The devil is your fear—it is the Antichrist. It is the barrier between God and man, from human beings and their divine souls."

Williams was perturbed. "You're not talking about some gradual change, are you?"

"No," Abu answered, his voice firm.

His tone bothered Williams even more. "Dramatic?" Williams asked. Abu didn't answer. "Cataclysmic?" There was still no reply. Instead, Abu pointed to a dhaba by the roadside.

"We will stop there for the night," he said.

"And I shall cook us a fine dinner," Satki said with her usual cheerful maternalism. Williams was so glad she was with them. Later after they had eaten, Williams felt an uncomfortable silence as he and Abu sat around the nearly-exhausted fire. Williams looked into Abu's dark eyes. He was afraid, and sensed, but did not know, that the path he had chosen was leading him directly to the devil.

Williams couldn't sleep that night. Dawn found him still sitting on the edge of his charpoy. Bhaiji slept soundly not far away, snoring peacefully. Williams thought he saw some movement near the edge of the camp. He strained to see what it was. It was Abu, kneeling and facing West. "Christ," Williams grumbled to himself, "doesn't he ever give it a rest?"

The ramifications of what Abu had said were overwhelming—if they were true. And if they were, then this wasn't about revolution, it wasn't about political demagoguery, and Abu wasn't just another despot seeking power for his own personal glory. It was about one of the most significant events in the history of the world since humanity stopped dragging its knuckles on the ground.

"This is fucking nuts," Williams said aloud, combing his hair back with his hands. But he couldn't just walk away. He couldn't imagine being somewhere else wondering what Abu was up to. He was firmly snagged on Abu's hook, and all the while he thrashed about Abu was patiently reeling him in.

Besides, proof was still needed. Maybe Abu was crazy; maybe he was psychotic, with paranoid delusions of grandeur. And if that was the case, Williams felt he had a duty to tell people, to warn them. That, too, was his job.

Bloated carcasses of dead animals floated in the Bangladesh rice paddies beneath the tropical sun. Most of the human corpses had been taken away, but every so often Williams could see an arm or leg protruding from the shallow water. There was no food, no drinkable water.

Williams had bought an English-language newspaper in the last town they'd stopped at. "It says several hundred thousand people have died, mostly from snake bites. I would've thought it was from starvation or disease."

"That comes later," Abu said. "Human beings aren't the only ones to crowd onto hilltops in search of dry land." Williams had seen people die from snake bites. It was an awful way to go. "How many have died from cholera?" Abu asked.

Williams scanned the article. "They estimate around forty-thousand."

"There will be more," Abu said in a somber voice.

"The administrator for CARE in Dhaka sent a cable to his boss in New York," Williams read. "He wrote: 'Drinking the water is like signing your own death warrant, especially for the children.'" Satki winced at the mention of the children. Williams looked up from the paper. "Did we bring water?"

"Some," Bhaiji answered. "But not enough."

"What'll we drink?" Williams asked anxiously.

"What these people drink," Abu answered.

Williams went back to his paper. "Jesus—they're reporting forty thousand new cases of dysentery and the measles every day!"

"Most of them will die," Abu said.

"Why?" Bhaiji asked plaintively. "Isn't it treatable?"

"Yes, when the body is strong, and medicine is available," Abu replied. "These people live on the brink of starvation even in the best of times. For them, simple diarrhea becomes fatal."

Satki looked at Williams. "Surely there will be some international relief."

Williams read on. "The President of Bangladesh has issued an urgent plea for help. The West, lead by the United States, has pledged millions in aid."

"That is only a drop in the bucket towards what is really needed," Abu said.

Williams folded the newspaper indignantly. "How long is Bangladesh going to remain the world's charity case? Why doesn't its own government do something?"

"There are many reasons," Abu responded.

"Such as?" Williams asked.

"People come here because this land is one of the most fertile areas on earth. But there are more people than land."

"Why don't they build dikes?"

"Look around!" Abu shot back. "Where is the money to come from? Most of these people cannot even read. And in a poor country there is always widespread corruption and incompetency. Some dikes have been constructed, but they are poorly engineered and badly built."

"Maybe their government just needs to clean up its act," Williams noted. He meant what he said, but not for it to sound so cavalier.

Abu turned in his seat and looked directly at Williams. "The world needs to clean up its act. Do you want to know what really caused this flooding?" Williams nodded. "Lumber companies have slashed and burned entire mountainsides in northern India and Nepal. Some of that wood is sent to America and Europe, but most goes to Japan where it is made into chopsticks."

"Chopsticks!?" Williams repeated in astonishment.

"And without trees there is nothing to slow the run-off. When the snows melt and the rains come, the rivers flood and the waters rush unimpeded to Bangladesh. And hundreds of thousands die. No one cares because it is, after all, just Bangladesh—just a few million ignorant peasant farmers."

"Then why doesn't somebody do something?" Williams asked.

"The lumber companies have enormous influence. Bangladesh wants India to build dams and dikes, but is afraid that India will restrict the flow of water to Bangladesh during dry seasons. And India refuses to build dams unless Bangladesh buys the electricity they will generate. But Bangladesh does not have the money."

"What about the World Bank, or the U.N.?" Williams challenged.

"The World Bank has agreed to fund dike projects. But years pass while the projects remain bogged down in negotiations and quarreling. The world must begin to take responsibility for a global problem. If cancer affects one limb of your body, do you wait until it spreads before seeking a cure? Would you sever a limb from your body as casually as you do these people?" Abu paused and stared at Williams a moment. "Why don't you do something?"

"What could I do that would make any difference?"

"I see," Abu said with obvious disappointment. "You are just one person, is that it?"

"You seem to forget, I'm just a reporter. I'm not a politician. All I can do is tell people about what's happening."

"I do not forget, Ben Williams," Abu said. "I just have a different appreciation of your role."

"Then what's your point?" Williams asked.

"Why don't you do something?"

Williams knew the answer. The truth was he didn't give a damn. The people he saw in food lines, huddled together on hilltops, the sick and dying, had nothing to do with his life. He knew it was a tragedy but still he didn't feel anything. He gazed outside and felt nothing inside. But that was the way he felt about everything.

"If you witnessed an injured man dying in the street, what would you do?" Abu asked.

"I'd help him, if I could," Williams replied without hesitation.

"Why? He is nothing to you. What difference would it make if he died?"

He thought about his answer before speaking. "Because I couldn't just walk by without trying to do something. Maybe there was something I could do."

"But yet, you can in this instance."

"You're saying I lack compassion?"

"I'm saying you lack a sense of connection. You would help the dying man in the street because there is an unspoken agreement in your society that someone else—that man—will do the same for you; people need to feel that security. That isn't compassion; it's self-interest—but at least it's a sense of connection. As for these people? You don't see them as part of society—they're not part of the agreement."

"Then there's no such thing as compassion—just enlightened self-interest?" Williams asked. The idea appealed to him; it absolved him.

"Compassion is a higher ideal—something that must be developed. It begins with a sense of connection, but involves actual sympathy for another's suffering and a genuine desire to end it."

Satki sighed. "Why is there so little compassion in the world?"

"Because, mother, there is no real sense of connection."

They arrived at the capital city of Dhaka, a typical third-world-urban-nightmare-of-a-place where a scant few ruled over a desperately poor population. Dhaka was already overcrowded, but the flood had now turned it into a massive refugee camp filled with hopelessness and despair. Bhaiji drove along the narrow streets, past endless lines of men and women with drawn, sunken faces, and scrawny bodies weak from hunger. They held empty, rusted tins, begging for the slightest bit of food—a few ounces of rice—just enough to ensure a tomorrow.

Abu motioned for Bhaiji to stop the car. He got out and headed toward one of the long lines. "What is the matter?" Abu asked an elderly man standing at the front, staring down into an empty rice bag.

"There is no more," he told Abu. "I am sorry," the old man said to the people in line, as though somehow it was his fault. "Come back tomorrow."

"Tomorrow?!" the man in front asked. "My son will be dead tomorrow!"

Abu stepped forward. "Perhaps there has been a mistake."

The old man looked at Abu, as though having been accused. "There is no mistake," he said with dismay. "Look for yourself." He pointed to an old truck. "There is never enough."

The old man followed Abu to the truck. Abu threw back a rumpled canvas. *"Allahu Akhbar!"* the old man exclaimed. "I swear, there was no more."

Abu lifted one of the large sacks of rice and carried it to the waiting line of people. Satki followed with obvious delight. Bhaiji and Williams looked at one another, shrugged and grabbed a sack.

"Establish separate lines," Abu instructed, "so that more can be fed in less time." Bhaiji quickly obeyed, and soon he too was filling tins. A line quickly formed in front of Williams and he found himself looking into the pleading eyes of people who couldn't understand his hesitation. It was a simple thing really, yet he felt like a young surgeon who'd been handed a scalpel for the first time and told to operate. He stared at the expectant faces. Then a man pushed his tin into Williams' face, startling him. He tore the sack open and began to scoop.

Satki walked along the lines of people and saw the relieved, weary mothers of hungry children. She cradled the children in her arms, comforted them, gave them clean water and chased the ever-present flies from their eyes. Williams worked feverishly as though driven. His arms grew tired and his back started to ache. Sweat poured from him, yet he barely noticed.

As each sack was emptied, Abu dropped another at Williams' feet. Finally, the last of the tins were filled. Williams looked into his sack and the rice was gone. He looked back at the truck. It was empty. For once there had been enough to go around.

Williams felt good. It was like the unsullied contentment of a child on a warm spring day. He looked up at the sky and took a deep breath. It smelled fresh, clean. The sky was bluer, the clouds whiter and the breeze more soothing. Then he heard Abu's voice behind him. His stomach knotted.

"This is not a game," Abu said bluntly. "There is an important place for you in what is yet to come, but you must prepare yourself."

Williams was childishly annoyed that Abu hadn't even thanked him for his help. "And how do you suggest I do that?"

"You must end your isolation. The more people you connect with, the more involved you will become." Abu paused a moment. "But it is your choice, Ben Williams."

"I don't know how."

"Begin with a prayer," Abu offered. "Ask for help. That is enough."

Williams bristled at the idea but said nothing. He began walking toward the Mercedes, then running. He jumped into the back seat. Abu watched him like a father watching a recalcitrant child, but one that he knew would someday change.

CHAPTER 13

The next day, Abu had Bhaiji stop the car near a farming village. There, people were rebuilding their homes, huts really, out of mud, pieces of plywood, cardboard and, if they were lucky, corrugated tin. Men, women and children were busy plowing and tilling the rice paddy. Abu, Satki and Bhaiji got out of the car and offered their help to the grateful villagers.

Williams walked to the edge of a ruined rice paddy where he watched an old man trying to remove a large tree branch buried deep within the mud. Williams took off his shoes and socks, rolled up his pants and waded into the ooze. He placed a shoulder to the branch and pushed while the old farmer guided his water buffalo. Nothing moved. Williams pushed again and again. Streams of sweat poured off his forehead. Another push. This time there was a small movement. Williams dropped down and dug at the base. The mud was heavy and warm. He stood up and pushed. There was more movement. He pushed harder. Suddenly the branch pulled free. The water buffalo moved on, dragging the branch away. Williams lost his balance and flopped face down into the mud.

The villagers laughed as he flailed about, attempting clumsily to stand up. "I was just trying to help," he shouted angrily once he was upright. The villagers stopped laughing and looked away. Williams wiped the mud from his eyes and surveyed his muddy body. He realized how ludicrous he looked. He couldn't help smiling. His white teeth beamed out from his mud-covered face and made the villagers laugh again. Williams laughed with them and spied Abu standing with his hands on his waist at the far edge of the paddy.

Just then, a young girl appeared in front of Williams with a cup of water in her hands. The innocence in her large, dark, almond-shaped eyes touched Williams. She held out the cup to him. He smiled and took it. "Thank you," he said, after swallowing the water. He looked at Abu again. Abu scowled and then abruptly turned and walked away.

"Oh my God!" Williams muttered under his breath. He suddenly remembered the CARE administrator's warning: 'Drinking the water is like signing your own death warrant.' Panic swept over him. He tried to leave the paddy, but mud gripped each foot and kept pulling him back. He fell again. He pushed himself up only to become more mired. He sank deeper. He pulled himself to the edge of the paddy and collapsed.

Williams' fear shouted at him; his heart raced. He struggled for composure as he searched for Bhaiji or Satki. He felt a pain in his stomach. There was another surge of fear. "Is there cholera in this village?" he asked Bhaiji, who had just come up to him.

"Yes," Bhaiji answered. "Typhoid and dysentery, too. Why?"

"I'll see you later." Williams started walking. His hands trembled. He could hear his heart pounding. He felt himself sweating beneath the hardening mud. He headed for the river.

The river was swollen and moving with slow, relentless determination. Williams waded in. The water was cool and soothing. The mud dissolved. He dove beneath the surface. As he came up, he exhaled and took a deep breath. His anxiety washed away with the mud. He felt the warmth of the sun. He stepped onto the dry bank, peeled off his shirt and draped it across the low branch of a tree.

He watched the steady current, churning and folding into itself. He didn't want to just survive any longer—he wanted to live. But he didn't really know how. And Abu's suggestion to pray seemed almost silly— a poor substitute for what he felt he probably needed: Ten years of psychoanalysis. Something he had no interest in.

Williams was thinking of his parents, imagining the family portrait. He recognized his mother, father, even his sister. But he couldn't see himself in the picture—as if he wasn't even there. He realized how estranged he was from them. Then, without warning, a wave of loneliness and guilt surged through him. He quit fighting. He began to cry. Tears flowed like the river he'd just emerged from. He started sobbing—deep, wrenching sounds came up from the very well of his being. He wondered if he would be able to stop, and then didn't want to.

The sun was starting to set. Williams, exhausted, got up and put on his shirt, then headed off to find the others. Bhaiji had set up camp near the Mercedes. "Ah, Ben," Bhaiji called out when he saw Williams approaching.

Satki and Abu appeared. "Good," Satki said with motherly satisfaction. "Are you hungry, Ben?"

He had a splitting headache. "Uh, no. Not really. I'm going to lie down awhile." He felt chilled. He unrolled a blanket and covered himself. He fell asleep and awoke several hours later. It was dark and the light from the cooking fire created a soft glow around the camp. He was freezing and his head was pounding. He began to shake uncontrollably.

Satki called over to him. "Are you all right, Ben?"

"I don't know," Williams admitted anxiously. "I'm really cold."

Satki placed her hand on his forehead. "Abu," she said, "he's burning up with fever!" Abu stood towering above him, looking down. "We should take him to a hospital," Satki said.

"NO!" Williams shouted. "No hospital."

"He should not travel," Abu said.

"I will go and find a doctor in Dhaka," Bhaiji said. He jumped into the car and drove off.

"A doctor will not matter," Williams heard Abu say.

"Abu," Satki said, "he could die." She looked at her son with alarm. "What should we do?"

"Keep him warm and make him drink plenty of clean water."

Satki placed another blanket over Williams and tucked it around his neck. "You will be all right," Satki assured him. She propped his head up so he could drink some water. Williams shook too much to drink.

Over the next few hours, intense, sudden diarrhea set in. Watery excrement poured out of him. He tried to get up but his head felt like it would explode and he instantly collapsed. "Oh God," he cried aloud as he lay covered in his own feces. The smell was horrendous.

"It is all right, Ben," Satki said, remaining at his side. She removed his clothes and wiped him down with a cloth and warm water. No sooner had she finished than another bout hit. He felt like his blood was boiling. Every muscle and joint ached so painfully he could hardly move. And he felt unbearable shame.

The diarrhea didn't let up. Gallons of liquid streamed out of him. Each time, Satki cleaned and comforted him. "It is all right," she kept saying.

"Water, please," he managed to gasp at one point. "I'm so thirsty." Satki's strong hand held his head up while she poured water from a tin cup down his throat. She knew that severe dehydration made cholera deadly and usually led to shock, coma and finally death.

The diarrhea was coupled with vomiting of such extreme violence that Williams felt like the veins and arteries in his head and neck were going to rupture, even when there was nothing left but bile. Intense muscle cramps in his arms, back and legs left him writhing and screaming in agony. "Please God, just let me die," he moaned over and over again. His eyes bulged with pain and misery. Abu stood nearby looking down at him, his arms crossed and one hand stroking his beard, like an expectant grim reaper.

Over the next several days, Williams became delirious. He shouted incomprehensibly, tormented by horrible visions. Sores appeared on his icy skin, his face was ashen and drawn, his lips blistered. The cramping continued, racking him with excruciating pain. He simply vomited back up the sugar water with rice that Satki fed him. He fell into a coma, and closer to death. "He may not survive," Abu said, crouching down beside him.

"Can't you do something!?" Satki pleaded.

"I must not interfere."

"But he will die!"

"This is between Ben Williams and his soul, mother." Abu stood up and walked away. She watched him helplessly. It was at such times that she did not understand her son.

Villagers stopped by, including the old man from the paddy. They wanted to help the man who had helped them. They all prayed to Allah for Williams' recovery. Bhaiji returned. "The doctors are too busy to come," he said. The fever, vomiting and diarrhea continued for another two days. Bhaiji joined Satki in her vigil at Williams' side. He too placed cool cloths on Williams' forehead and helped Satki clean him each time he messed.

There was no sign of change for several days—Williams remained in a deep coma. But on the seventh day his fever broke. Miraculously, his torture was ending. He would live.

Williams slept for two more days. Finally, he opened his eyes. He saw Satki and Bhaiji kneeling beside him while Abu stood at his feet. A number of villagers smiled down at him. Williams could scarcely move. He mustered what little strength he could. "I guess I'll be hanging around awhile." Several of the villagers applauded his remark though they didn't understand English.

He slept some more. When he awoke, he realized he was wearing a diaper-like loin cloth. He wrapped himself in a blanket and attempted to get up. "Ben," Satki said as she ran to his side to keep him from falling. "You should not be up so soon." She helped him to a place to sit. "Eat," she instructed, handing him a bowl of broth. Williams took it gratefully. "Thank you so much."

"You are welcome, Ben."

"No," Williams said. "I mean, for everything. I don't know how I'll ever repay you." He swallowed a few spoonfuls of the soup.

Satki stopped and looked at Williams. "I love you like a son, Ben."

Williams felt a surge of emotion. Tears filled his eyes. He put down the bowl. "I guess I'm still pretty tired. If you don't mind, I think I'll sleep some more." Satki nodded and helped him to lie down. He didn't sleep right away, but looked out at the nearby countryside. He remembered the recent moments when he thought he wanted to die, and was glad he didn't. He recalled the loving care Satki had given him, and Bhaiji, and how happy the villagers were that he pulled through. He realized he wasn't alone.

Over the next three days, Williams sat for hours in the shade of a tree at the river's edge, feeling his strength slowly return. Gone was the churning turmoil that had been like a constant dull pain, now made conspicuous by its absence.

He felt close to Satki, closer than he had before. He felt a profound sense of brotherhood with Bhaiji. He even felt closer to Abu. And he had a deep sympathy for the suffering he witnessed among the villagers. Was he developing compassion?

"How are you feeling, Ben Williams?" Abu asked as he joined Williams at the river, just before they were to leave again.

"Much better."

"Good. Then tomorrow we will move on."

Williams didn't respond. He didn't even feel a need to ask where they were going. "You know," he finally said. "As deathly ill as I was, I think that drinking that contaminated water was the best thing that could've happened to me. Does that make any sense?"

"You did not drink contaminated water."

Williams was shocked. "What are you talking about!?"

Abu smiled slightly. "I gave the water to that young girl. I told her to give it to you."

Williams didn't know what to say. "But—"

"You did not have cholera," Abu insisted. "Nor any other disease."

"I was so sick. I nearly died." Williams stared at the river. It seemed to be moving faster than before. He scrambled to make sense of it.

"That was the decisive battle of the war, Ben Williams—your war."

"I don't get it."

"The battle was between your soul and your fear. Your body was the battlefield." Williams just stared at Abu, and then at the river. "It was needed for you to think you had contracted a disease that threatened your life so you could realize your humanity; so that you could experience another's compassion—so you would know 'for whom the bell tolls.' "

"It was all in my head?"

"More, it was all in your fear. It did not want you to be engaged, involved. It wanted you isolated and alone. It would have killed you, Ben Williams, if you had let it."

"Jesus Christ," Williams muttered. He studied Abu's face.

"If it helps you to think you had cholera, please do so. It really doesn't matter. The important thing is that your fear will no longer control you. It may shout at you, but now you are open to hear God's whispers." He left Williams alone to ponder what he said.

Amidst all the chatter in his head, Williams could hear a small, still voice, quietly whispering to him. He couldn't make out the message, but just hearing it, and knowing it was there, soothed him. And then it struck him: He didn't know what to think anymore but he knew how he felt. And that was what all that mattered.

CHAPTER 14

"Why Myanmar?" Williams asked after they had crossed the border into the country. The last time Williams was there it was called Burma.

Abu glanced at Williams. "Why not?"

"Well, most of these people are Buddhists."

"I was raised among Buddhists. But it's not important."

"Why's that?" Williams asked.

"Because truth is transcendental."

"Oh, right," Williams said cynically. "From what I can tell, there's so much bullshit in the world that it seems truth has become extinct, that is, if it ever existed at all."

Abu turned in his seat and looked back at Williams. "God is the only truth. Otherwise, truth is relative, especially among human beings. Yet, even among people there is a fundamental truth."

"What's that?" Williams asked.

"Freedom. It emanates from the human spirit and is undeniable in its desire for realization."

"Very poetic," Williams responded. "But, from what I've seen, truth doesn't do very well when confronted with tyranny."

"Ah, but you're wrong. That is when it shines with the greatest brilliance—and becomes most visible."

Maybe Abu was right. There were times when tyrants tried to destroy freedom, to perjure the truth, but truth prevailed. It made humanity take stock of itself. Was that what Abu was intending—to rally truth through a confrontation with brutality?

Myanmar's lush green hillsides with its cascading tiers of rice paddies came into view. They were surrounded by dense jungle and tropical rainforests which gave the whole place an elusive, mystical quality. It was the gateway to the East, a portal to another world.

"Are things as bad here as in Bangladesh?" Bhaiji asked.

"Perhaps worse," Abu responded.

"How can it possibly be worse than what we have just seen?" Satki asked, shaking her head.

"Because, in addition to poverty, these people endure political enslavement. The two create a misery without hope."

"I've heard that the army runs things here, and they're a bunch of thugs," Williams said.

"They are like most men obsessed with power," Abu said.

As they arrived in Yangon, the capital city, military vehicles and soldiers could be seen on almost every street corner. Bhaiji followed the rectangular intersecting streets to the Cantonment, the oldest part of the city.

"Wasn't there a mass uprising here not too long ago?" Williams asked.

"Yes," Abu replied. "They wanted freedom and the government answered with bullets and tanks. The streets ran with blood. The people looked to the West for help but it never came." Abu's voice trailed off for a moment as he stared out the window, as though silently honoring those who had perished. "These people shall have freedom."

"You're going to get it for them?" Williams wondered. Satki looked at Abu with concern.

"These people want to be free and I can light the way."

"How are you going to appeal to people who think life is merely an illusion in the first place?" Williams asked.

"Nearly one-half of the entire country is less than fifteen years old, and two-thirds are under thirty. They have no work, no money, and precious little food. They are desperate. I will merely—"

"Incite?" Williams interjected.

Abu smiled, as though enjoying the exchange. "They may regard life as an illusion, but that is not to say they do not value it. They may struggle to detach from the world, but not from their freedom."

Bhaiji stopped in front of a dilapidated hotel, and the four went to their separate rooms to rest for a few hours. Williams lay down on the ancient, creaky bed with a lumpy mattress. He couldn't relax let alone sleep. He sat on the edge of the bed and muttered to himself, "What the hell—"

He slid to the floor, positioned himself and closed his eyes. He began to breathe slowly, deliberately, just as Abu had shown him. He felt himself starting to relax. He imagined colored light swirling around him, moving in and out with each new breath. When he reached the crown chakra, or topmost source of spiritual energy, he saw himself in a cocoon of white light.

A sense of peace and serenity came over him. He smiled. Bursts of color appeared. He listened to the birds outside the open window, and the flutter of leaves as a cool breeze swept through his room, caressing his face. Joy welled up in his chest. His eyes teared. *You should call Herschel, you know.* What was that? The happiness was gone, as though suddenly siphoned away. *He's expecting to hear from you.* Where was that coming from? Surely not his soul. *You do have responsibilities, you know. You're supposed to be working, not sitting around being happy.*

He felt dead inside and became angry. Fuck! he thought to himself. *See how easy it is?* The voice was ridiculing and malevolent. It scared him. Anxiety reverberated through his body. *You thought you were rid of me. You will never be rid of me!* Williams shouted out loud, "No!" but his voice belied fear.

He slowly opened his eyes. He felt in control of himself.

There was a knock on the door. Williams jumped up and opened it. It was Abu. "I am going to the Shwe Dagon Pagoda," he said. "Would you like to join me?"

"The what?"

"One of the largest and most important Buddhist temples in the world."

A half hour later, after walking through crowds of vendors and customers in the outdoor marketplaces, and past the red brick British colonial structures of the Cantonment, Abu pointed to a Buddhist reliquary that looked like an enormous golden castle sitting atop a hill.

The reliquary was covered in gold-leaf, painstakingly applied by Buddhist laymen over time. A massive cone crowned the structure, jutting hundreds of feet into the sky with a diamond-encrusted spire pointing upwards, reflecting the sunlight.

Worshipers gathered on an immaculate tiled terrace, surrounded by dozens of smaller pagodas, similarly adorned in gold and guarded by oriental dragons. Shy, saffron-robed monks with shaved heads, walked barefoot over the tiled surface, silently accepting alms from the visitors. It was near dusk and colored lanterns were lit. Williams found the atmosphere to be one of sublime serenity as a soft breeze carried the fragrance of fresh-cut flowers mixed with incense. Then Williams noticed uniformed soldiers standing around with weapons, casually smoking cigarettes and talking to one another. What an ironic contrast, he thought, and wondered if Abu was going to make trouble. Then he reminded himself: Abu was about making trouble.

"Wait here," Abu instructed.

Williams watched as Abu placed fruit and flowers at the base of the towering Buddha and bowed before the statue, then approached an aged monk resting on pillows nearby. Abu handed the monk a leather pouch containing money. Williams continued to watch as Abu and the monk sat and talked for a few minutes.

When Abu returned, the soft sound of a gong, followed by several more, drew their attention. The large crowd fell silent. Williams asked Abu what was going on.

"They have gathered to mourn the deaths of several Buddhist monks recently murdered by the government after being arrested during a protest," Abu whispered to Williams. "They want to free the dead monks' preta."

"Preta?" Williams whispered back.

"Spirits," Abu explained. "The bodies were never recovered, and their spirits must be set free from the earthly plane, so they can find peace."

Williams watched the ancient ceremony that began with chanting, followed by a lengthy recitation by one of the monks on the precepts of Buddhism. There was a sermon by one of the other monks. At the conclusion, the monk looked at Abu and nodded. Abu walked to the front of the gathering.

Abu stood before the assemblage a moment before beginning. When he spoke, his voice echoed off the walls of the Shwe Dagon Pagoda, shattering the tranquil setting. The armed soldiers suddenly paid attention.

"You have gathered today to unleash the spirits of those who died trying to gain freedom for you," Abu began. The soldiers glanced nervously at one another. Williams pulled his notepad from his shirt pocket and began scribbling. "Dharma is the Supreme law," Abu continued in a stern voice. "It is the Divine Truth in a world that is like a great lotus pond. Some lotuses choose to live beneath the surface, others rise just to the surface and remain there, while others extend ever upwards, towering above the rest and radiating divine beauty." Abu paused.

"Buddha taught that carpenters fashion wood and wise people fashion themselves. A man may conquer in battle a thousand times a thousand men, but the man that conquers himself is the greatest of conquerors."

Abu paced some more. He then stood silent and scanned the faces of his audience. "You need not die to achieve Nirvana. It is available to you here and now." There was stirring among the audience. "But denial of desire will not lead you to Nirvana—it will lead you away from Nirvana," Abu said. "Denial of passion will not lead you to Nirvana. It will keep you from Nirvana. And I will tell you that denial of self is not the path to Nirvana."

The gathered Buddhists appeared confused. Where was he going with this? Williams wondered. Was he telling them Buddha was wrong? He stopped writing and listened.

"Nirvana comes only through mastery over the self," Abu continued. "It is the middle way—the path between selfish craving and selfless denial." Abu turned away from the audience and stood before the looming statue of the Buddha. He turned suddenly and faced the crowd so that he spoke as the Buddha.

"How can you find Nirvana while your body remains hungry?" Abu's tone suddenly became angry. He raised a fist. "And there is a hunger of the soul—a hunger for freedom!" His sudden indignation stunned the audience. Williams scribbled more notes, glancing momentarily at the attentive soldiers. "You have gathered here to free the spirits of monks who rose high above the surface of the pond. Will you free their spirits and not your own?"

The audience grew restless. The soldiers fidgeted with their weapons and glanced at the officer in charge for direction.

Abu continued. "The rich, the powerful, the greedy, have insatiable appetites for the fruits of this earth. They feed off your oppression and your misery, and grow fat from your misfortune." Williams kept his eye on the soldiers. The officer seemed distressed and indecisive. Williams wondered how far Abu would go. "The Buddha commanded," Abu shouted, again raising a fist in the air, "to look at evil as evil, and be disgusted by it, cleansed of it, freed of it!" Abu paused for just a moment. Angry rumbling began brewing in the audience. "Who among you will oppose evil?" The crowd was becoming agitated. "Who among you will give their allegiance to the Supreme Law?" The agitation increased. Tension filled the air. Williams own body felt like a coiled spring. "Who will be like the monks—lotuses that radiate strength and beauty to the world!?"

The crowd rose to its feet in unison. The soldiers moved toward Abu, using their weapons to push people aside. "Abu!" Williams called out, trying to shout above the now deafening noise. The Buddhists hurled insults at the soldiers. The soldiers surrounded Abu and grabbed him firmly by each arm. Abu offered no resistance. They led him away from the Shwe Dagon Pagoda as an angry crowd trailed after them. Williams tried to push through the churning mass of people. The soldiers bound Abu's wrists and pushed him into the back of a jeep. The crowd surrounded the jeep while the vastly outnumbered soldiers pushed with their rifles to keep them at bay. The jeep lunged forward, pushing bodies away like debris.

The crowd pressed in and surrounded the remaining soldiers. They shook their fists and shouted; repressed fury oozed like lava from a volcanic eruption. The officer barked orders and the soldiers formed a circle. Sirens wailed in the distance. A helicopter suddenly appeared overhead, its rotors creating swirling wind and thunderous noise. Williams watched, nervous and uncertain. The crowd pressed in. A stone flew out and hit one of the soldiers in the face, knocking him to the ground.

The officer barked another order. The soldiers began shooting point blank into the crowd. Faces splattered; heads exploded and limbs were torn away. The crowd began running in all directions. More bricks hit the soldiers. More bullets were fired. Williams dove behind a wall. The bullets found their marks, exploding flesh and raining blood. More bodies fell to the ground. The soldiers kept firing. Soon the ground was covered in a carpet of blood. Some tried to drag away the wounded, only to become targets for the next round of bullets.

Blood flowed across the tiled surface like rain water after a heavy downpour. Williams watched a defiant youth reach back to hurl a large rock. "Get down!" Williams shouted, just before the youth's chest exploded, spraying Williams with his blood. More soldiers arrived in trucks. Canisters of tear gas flew in every direction. Williams' heart pounded, his eyes started to sting and he couldn't breathe. Nausea was overcoming him. He crawled on his belly along the ground. Finally, he was able to stand up and start running.

And he kept running. Down the hill, away from the Shwe Dagon Pagoda, away from the horrified screams and relentless gunfire. Another helicopter soared overhead, its pounding rhythm shaking the ground. Sirens blared. Army jeeps with heavy machine guns in the rear raced through the streets.

Williams staggered, ran, and when he was on the verge of collapse, miraculously found himself back at his hotel. Bhaiji and Satki were outside. Satki screamed at the sight of his blood-soaked clothing.

"Ben!" Bhaiji said with alarm. "Are you all right?" he asked, searching for wounds.

He couldn't catch his breath enough to talk. "Yeah," he finally said, gasping for air, "I think so."

"Where's Abu?" Satki demanded.

Williams tried to speak. "Soldiers," he managed to say. "Soldiers took him."

Satki's eyes widened with fear. "Where!?"

"I—" Williams gasped, "I—don't know."

An army truck with a loudspeaker rode down the street. Soldiers followed behind on foot. "You are ordered to leave the streets," a voice bellowed. "An immediate curfew has been put in effect by the Chairman of the State Law and Order Restoration Council. Anyone remaining outside will be shot."

"We must get inside," Bhaiji said urgently and put one of Williams arm's around his shoulder to help him into the hotel. Satki followed them. They went quickly to Williams' room. From the street they could hear angry shouting and the sputtering of automatic rifle fire.

"We must find Abu!" Satki pleaded.

"There is nothing we can do for now!" Bhaiji said emphatically. "It is too dangerous!"

"He's right," Williams said, ripping off his blood-spattered shirt. His head was throbbing. "All hell has broken loose out there. They're shooting everyone."

Bhaiji turned off the light. Moonlight streamed in through the gauze-draped windows.

Satki pushed the thin curtain aside and looked out the window at the sight of tanks lumbering down the streets. Armored personnel carriers patrolled. Occasional rifle bursts shattered the silence. Bhaiji went to her and put his arm around her shoulder. "He's all right," he said, more to convince himself than Satki. Williams wondered if this might not be the end of his journey with Abu.

CHAPTER 15

Just a mile from the hotel, Abu sat on the dank floor of a detention cell. The cell was below ground and moisture seeped through the block walls. Beads of water dripped down and dampened the stone floor. The musty smell mixed with the stench of urine and human feces.

There were many cells, cages actually, one after another, each jammed with prisoners. New prisoners were arriving in a steady flow. A row of light bulbs in the corridor partially illuminated the cells, but kept the walls in the shadows. There were no beds, no toilets, just a bucket in the middle of the cell. Rats scurried along the walls and over the tops of the prisoners' feet. Occasionally they'd bite, checking for signs of life. Mostly, they fed upon the contents of the bucket. If a man died, the other prisoners pushed him away from the walls and into the light like refuse to be picked up. The guards didn't always take the body right away. Sometimes the rats got to feast.

The prisoners huddled against the walls. No one spoke. Any one of them could be an informer. No one could be trusted.

At the end of the long corridor was a room. Every so often a man would be taken from a cell and led into the room. The agonized screams that echoed down the corridor betrayed what went on in there. Some went quietly, others struggled violently. But when the door closed, it was always the same. Terrifying, anguished pleas for mercy reminded each man of what awaited him. Sometimes the men came out, sometimes they didn't.

It wasn't long before three soldiers appeared at Abu's cell. One of them pointed a heavy baton at Abu. "You—!" he barked. The other prisoners looked at Abu, grateful it wasn't them. Abu stood up. One of the guards opened the door and grabbed Abu, his wrists still bound behind him.

Abu was escorted into the interrogation room where a blinding light pointed to the spot where the prisoner was made to stand. Clouds of cigarette smoke hung in the air. Within the room were four uniformed soldiers and two civilians. One of the soldiers was bare chested and sweating. He grinned at Abu, grateful for another victim. A gold incisor tooth beamed from his weasel-like mouth.

Abu was pushed inside. He stood silent, staring straight ahead. A video camera sat perched on a tripod. Seated off to one side, lurking in a shadowy corner, was a man who looked American. He lit a cigarette and studied Abu through a veil of smoke.

"Are you still on your spiritual quest, Mr. Whatley?" Abu asked without looking at the American.

"Well," Jack Whatley replied with a smirk, "I'm sort of like Diogenes looking for an honest man. Except I'm looking for that holy man. And you keep popping up."

The officer in charge glanced at Whatley, surprised that he and Abu knew one another. He took a pack of cigarettes from his pocket and offered one to Abu. Abu didn't move. The officer lit a cigarette and blew the smoke in Abu's face. He walked in a slow, steady circle around Abu, studying him carefully.

"From what I am told," the officer began, "you gave quite a speech at the Shwe Dagon Pagoda." Abu didn't answer.

"Tell us what we want to know," the officer said, "and you can go back to your cell. We might even let you go. Otherwise—" He turned and glanced at the weasel-like soldier, then back to Abu. "Do you understand?" Abu didn't respond. The officer sat on the edge of a table. "Who are you?" he asked in a stern voice.

"I am Abu 'Ali Asghar."

"Good." The officer smiled. "You see, it is easy to cooperate. Are you Arab?" Abu said nothing. "Indian?" No response. "Where are you from?" the officer asked.

"I claim no country as my own," Abu answered.

"Really!?" The officer looked around at the others. "So, then, why are you here?".

"I am merely a visitor passing through."

"A tourist!" The officer laughed derisively. The others in the room joined in, except Jack Whatley; he kept smoking and staring at Abu.

"No," Abu responded patiently. "A visitor."

The officer stopped smiling. He became angry. "Do you think we are stupid!?"

"No," Abu said calmly. "I do not."

The officer stood just inches from Abu's face. "Then, tell us why you are here!" he shouted.

Abu remained composed. His voice was steady. "Because I care about these people," he replied "And because you do not."

The officer's face reddened. A vein bulged on his forehead. He nodded to one of the soldiers behind Abu. The soldier's heavy baton struck Abu behind his knees. The officer stepped back, expecting Abu to fall. He grew angrier when Abu didn't. "Admit you are a Communist!" the officer shouted.

"I am not a Communist," Abu answered in the same steady voice. "I profess no ideology other than my own."

"And what ideology is that?"

For the first time Abu looked at the officer. "By what right do you torture and oppress your own people?" he said contemptuously.

The officer was stunned. "What!?"

"By what right do you imprison these men?" Abu asked, as though expecting an answer. The officer remained dumbfounded. "By what right do you deny anyone their freedom?" Abu demanded. "And who are you to demean these manifestations of God?"

The officer's vein bulged again, his face turned beet red. The soldier didn't wait for instructions. He brought his thick baton down across Abu's neck and shoulders. This time Abu fell. The officer kicked Abu in the stomach, then again, and a third time. Using his swagger stick, he pointed to a pulley attached to a beam along the ceiling. "Lift him!" he shouted.

They pulled Abu to his feet and made him stand on a chair. A rope dangled from the pulley. They fastened his bound wrists to the rope. The other end of the rope descended down to a block and tackle on the floor and then up into the hands of the weasel-faced soldier. Abu looked at him. He smiled at Abu. A bit of saliva dripped from his mouth.

Abu fixed his eyes on the officer. The officer nodded and the soldier kicked the chair out from beneath him. Abu fell instantly. The rope cut into his wrists and broke his fall, yanking his arms backward and nearly out of their sockets. His feet dangled off the floor. Abu made no sound nor showed any sign of pain. He simply stared at the officer.

"You are impudent as well as subversive," the officer spat the words up at Abu and then nodded to the soldier. He lowered Abu slightly, and then suddenly jerked the rope, pulling Abu's arms backward again while his body was still moving downward. Abu bounced up and down, yanking his arms backward each time. Jack Whatley took another drag on his cigarette as he watched.

"Admit that you are a Communist!" the commanding officer shouted. Abu still didn't respond. One of the soldiers clubbed him at the back of the knees. Abu began to swing back and forth. Another batted him across the shins like a piñata, while another repeatedly thrust a large pole into his mid-section so that he began to twist around and around. "Tell us who sent you!" No response. "What government do you work for?" Abu continued his blank stare.

"Use the wires!" the officer ordered. A soldier put down his bat and picked up two thick wires from the table. At the opposite end, the wires connected to a crude box with a switch and a small amber light on it. He tied the wires around Abu's ankles, and then stood back a safe distance. The soldier seated behind the box flipped the switch. The amber light glowed as electrical current raced through the wires and into Abu. Abu's body convulsed. The officer nodded again and the soldier flipped the switch off. Abu's body went limp. He lost consciousness.

"Drop him," the officer told the soldier. He let the rope slide from his hands and Abu crashed to the floor. The impact brought him back to consciousness. He sat up on his knees, opened his eyes and stared up at the officer. There was no hint of emotion or pain. Just icy coldness.

The officer looked disbelieving and frightened. He slapped Abu hard across the face with the back of his hand. Abu's head turned slightly from the blow, but he remained upright. The officer hit him again from the other side, then leaned down in Abu's face. "Who are you?" he whispered.

"I am Abu 'Ali Asghar."

The officer stepped backwards. "Why are you here?"

"Because it is time," Abu replied in a calm, deliberate tone that sent a chill through everyone in the room.

"Time? For what?" the officer demanded, nervously eying Abu.

"The end of the petty tyrants," Abu said. "The triumph of freedom and justice."

The officer stared at him. "Take him back to his cell," he ordered his soldiers. They pulled Abu to his feet and led him out of the interrogation room. The officer looked at Jack Whatley.

"The guy's got some steel balls," Whatley said.

"He must die," the officer said.

"I wouldn't recommend that right now. It might be a mistake," Whatley said coolly. "He's been traveling with a reporter from the *New York Times*—Bennett Williams. You'd better find him."

Men came out from the shadows to see Abu walking without assistance back to his cell. They slammed the door shut behind him. He knelt down in the center of the cell and rested his weight upon the back of his legs. He closed his eyes and breathed slowly and deeply. Occasionally, a rat would come to within no more than a foot or so, sniff curiously, and then dart away, terrified. Another prisoner cautiously approached Abu and waited. Abu suddenly turned his head and opened his eyes. "Yes?" he said. "What do you want?"

"I am Chin," the man said in a frightened whisper. "I heard you speak at the Shwe Dagon Pagoda."

"Yes?"

"I was moved. No, more than that. Something happened to me when I heard you speak. I do not know why, but I knew I must speak with you."

"About what?"

"I do not know!" Chin said, nervously looking around to see if anyone overheard. "I want to know how I can be free. There are many like me out there. We all want to be free! But we lack the means. We lack the power."

Abu turned to the other prisoners. "Who else among you would like to be free?" he asked loudly, to Chin's horror.

"*Shhhhh—!*" Chin hissed. "You must be careful! There are informers."

Abu looked at him, and then back at his cellmates. "If you wish to be free you must come out of the shadows." There was silence, followed by a shuffling along the walls. One man moved into the light, then another, and another. Soon, all the prisoners had gathered around Abu. "Each of you alone is like a stone thrown into a pond," he began. "You make ripples that spread outward, changing things, destroying the serenity of the glassy surface. One by one you plunge into the pond until the pond is no more." Abu looked at the attentive faces of his fellow prisoners. "But each of the stones merged together form a great boulder that can fill the pond in an instant. All that is required is unity."

"How?" one of the men whispered.

"By joining together. God hears one voice alone in the wilderness, but those who speak with one voice shout more loudly. The power of the universe will be at your command."

"But the government is very powerful," another man whispered.

"You are the government!" Abu said, in a loud voice that stunned the prisoners, causing some to make sure the guards had not heard. "If you are happy as a slave then scurry back to the shadows and live with the rats. But if you are not willing to live free, what is the point of living? Would you rather be like the ox that pulls the cart—eating what others give you, sleeping when they tell you, going where they tell you, only to be slaughtered when they decide."

"What can we do?" Chin cried.

"Say to others what I have said to you. And continue to say it. Forge a unity but be willing to be the one individual stone hurled into the pond. Rest assured that others will follow. They will be inspired by your courage and your conviction."

"Will you stand with us?" one of the prisoners asked.

"Yes," Abu replied. "That is why I have come."

Just then the guards reappeared at the door of the cell. "You!" the one with the baton said as he pointed it at Abu. The prisoners looked at Abu, while another guard opened the cell door. Abu stood up, but rather than cringe in the shadows, the other prisoners stood as well. They formed a barrier in front of Abu. Because of his height, Abu towered behind the men, like a king protected by pawns on a chessboard.

The guards didn't know what to do. They looked at one another, and then closed the cell door. All three of them quickly hurried down the corridor.

The prisoners in Abu's cell celebrated their victory but within moments the guards returned with six more guards, each wielding a heavy baton.

One of the guards opened the door again. "You, Asghar!" another shouted. Abu didn't move, nor did the men standing in front of him.

"This time," Abu said. "I am afraid you will have to take me."

"Very well," the soldier answered. His voice conveyed some satisfaction in the task. "But you will regret it."

The soldiers moved into the cell. The prisoners closed ranks. One of the soldiers brought his baton down upon the first prisoner's head, knocking him to the floor. The second prisoner struck the soldier, knocking him down. Another soldier quickly stepped forward. The prisoners broke ranks and attacked the soldiers. The soldiers struck back with their batons, crushing one prisoner's skull. He dropped to the floor as blood gushed from his head.

Abu stepped forward. A soldier raised his baton to strike Abu across the head. Abu's hands were suddenly unbound. He reached up, grasped the soldier's arm with one hand and grabbed him by the throat with the other, flinging him backwards. Abu turned quickly and struck another across the face with his forearm, sending him reeling.

The prisoners watched Abu in awe as he proceeded to disable a third and then a fourth guard like a master of martial arts. The prisoners in the other cells were all clamoring to see what was happening. The long corridor erupted in turmoil.

The remaining guards withdrew, slamming the cell door behind them. Seconds later, helmeted soldiers armed with automatic rifles and led by the officer from the interrogation room came running down the dimly lit corridor. They stopped in front of the cell and aimed their rifles. Everyone froze, waiting for the bullets to fly. A tense silence descended upon the entire cellblock.

"Now," the officer said, "you will obey, or you will die. It is your choice." Abu stepped forward to the front of the cell and looked the officer in the eye.

"You will not fire on me or any of these prisoners," Abu said to him in a soft yet commanding voice. The officer did not respond. He seemed unable to break from Abu's eyes. The soldiers glanced at their commander. No one moved.

At the hotel, Williams peered out the window at the street below. The sun was just coming up, and the street was quiet.

"Is it time to go," Satki said anxiously.

"I'd better go alone," Williams said. "I'll find out where Abu is and come back for you two."

"No," Satki said with finality. "I am going with you."

Williams looked at Satki and then at Bhaiji. "I agree, Ben," Bhaiji said. "I am going too."

"Yeah," Williams conceded. "I guess I knew that."

The three left the hotel and cautiously entered the street. It was eerily quiet. Their footsteps echoed off the buildings. Here and there, curtains or shades moved, betraying the presence of someone behind.

"Where are we going?" Bhaiji asked Williams.

"We've got a couple of options," Williams said without much conviction. "If we get that far, we might try the American, Indian and Sri Lankan embassies. But I'm not optimistic that's going to get us anywhere."

"What do you mean, 'if we get that far'?" Bhaiji asked.

"Well, you don't see many folks out for a stroll this morning, do you? My guess is that the police will be here soon, and maybe they'll take us to Abu. If they don't shoot us on sight."

Bhaiji shot a nervous glance at Williams. A moment later, two army jeeps veered around the corner and stopped in front of them. Two soldiers hopped out.

"Are you Bennett Williams?" the soldier in charge shouted.

"Yes," Williams answered, surprised they knew.

"Your passports," the soldier demanded as he extended his hand. Williams, Bhaiji and Satki handed over their passports. "Get in," the soldier ordered, motioning to the jeep.

They arrived at the detention center where Abu was being held and were taken to an interrogation room. An aging ceiling fan rotated lazily overhead. "Wait here," the soldier snapped and then left.

"How did they know you?" Bhaiji asked in amazement.

"Good question," Williams replied.

Satki gave Williams a worried look. "Now what do we do?"

"Wait," Williams answered. "And pray."

Minutes passed before the door opened. Then Jack Whatley walked in. "Well, I'll be damned—" Williams muttered.

"Hello, Ben," a bemused Whatley said. Satki looked quizzically at Williams. "Ben and I are old friends."

"I wouldn't say friends," Williams countered.

"I'm hurt, Ben," Whatley responded. "But I suppose journalists have to maintain appearances."

111

"What in the hell are you doing here?" Williams asked.

"You're not in the best position to be asking questions, old buddy. But, let's just say a 'temporary reassignment'."

"I thought the U.S. suspended diplomatic ties with Myanmar after the military coup," Williams said, "which makes your presence here somewhat surprising."

"Does it really, Ben? You, maybe more than most, should know that things aren't always as they seem."

"Is my son here?" Satki demanded.

Whatley turned to Abu's mother. "Yes, he's here. And I have to tell you that he has upset a great many people in the government."

"Is he all right?" Satki asked.

"I suppose you could say that."

"I want to see him!" Satki insisted.

"Perhaps," Whatley answered and then looked back at Williams. "Let's you and I take a walk." Williams motioned to Satki and Bhaiji to sit tight. "Coffee?" Whatley asked, as they pushed their way through the frantic activity of the detention center.

"Yeah," Williams said as they entered a small room with a desk and two chairs. It was Whatley's makeshift office. "Busy business, oppressing a general population. Always something to do."

Whatley poured each of them a cup of coffee from an ancient Mr. Coffee machine. "You don't fully understand, Ben," Whatley said, handing the cup to Williams. "Like I said, things aren't always the way they appear, especially in politics."

"Politics?" Williams said indignantly. "You call what happened out there last night politics? Christ, Jack, I was there. I had a kid's brains splattered in my face! What the fuck is the U.S. doing here?"

"I'll level with you, Ben, but on condition that it's off the record. Agreed?"

"Yeah," Williams said. "Fine."

"Understand that I'm just an operative, and I don't know what in the hell they're thinking at the White House or Langley, but my orders are to try and maintain informal contact with the regime here. Apparently, Washington has to make a show of suspending diplomatic relations, but is afraid of alienating these bastards. We've got people here. No one wants this regime to pull another Iranian hostage deal, nor does Washington want to give the Chinese-supported

Communists an edge. Got it? Washington is pressing for a return to a democratic government and that ain't gonna happen by totally alienating the junta. And my job is to make sure that doesn't happen."

"Jack," Williams said emphatically, "that's bullshit. What's really behind this, the fucking opium trade? They're fucking butchers! They're torturing and murdering their own people!"

Whatley became visibly agitated. "Jesus, Williams, grow up! You think anything is gonna change if the U.S. maintains some moral bullshit stance? We've got commitments throughout Southeast Asia. Christ, you're as fucking naïve as the people back home!"

Williams sat back in the rickety chair and sipped his coffee. Whatley leaned toward him across his desk. "Ben, now I need you to level with me. Who is this Asghar guy?"

"I'm afraid he's just what he appears to be," Williams answered. "But the interesting thing is that what he appears to be depends on where you stand."

"I don't follow you."

"He claims to be a servant," Williams said.

"Yeah, right!" Whatley exclaimed.

"See what I mean?"

"Okay, he's a servant. What the fuck does that mean?"

"He says he's here because humanity is on the brink of a huge evolutionary leap forward and he's going to help us make that transition. For what its worth, I think he's fascinating, brilliant, and can inspire people like no leader or politician—"

"Sounds like he's brainwashed you," Whatley said. The remark bothered Williams. "So, what's he after?" Whatley asked.

Williams shook his head. "I honestly don't know,"

"Is he dangerous?"

"To whom?"

"Is he crazy?"

Williams thought for a moment. "At first, I wondered. But I don't think so."

Whatley stared at Williams. "We've met before, you know, he and I. In Amritsar." Williams said nothing. "This guy bothers me, Ben. I felt it right away in Amritsar. I can't put my finger on it, but there's something about him." Whatley thought for a moment. "I think he's dangerous." Williams looked puzzled. "They want to kill him, Ben. And that might just save us a helluva lot of trouble later, but my job is to make sure this situation doesn't erupt into another bloodbath and cause further problems for the West. Besides, the way I figure it, if they kill him, they're gonna have to kill you, too." Whatley spoke coldly—it was business to him, not personal. But it got Williams' attention. He wished he had told Herschel where he was. "And I don't think the *New York Times* and the rest of your colleagues would take too kindly to having one of their own murdered," Whatley said, and sat back in his chair. "We don't need that kind of press right now." He paused. "So, you see my dilemma."

"Yeah, rough. Sorry to be so much trouble, Jack."

"I want you and your friends out of here," Whatley said, leaning forward again. "I want you gone by tonight, got it?"

Williams nodded. "Of course, Sheriff. We'll take the next stage out of Dodge."

"I'm serious, Ben. Fuck with me on this and you'll all end up dead." Williams knew Whatley was right.

Whatley took Williams back to the interrogation room. "Come on," Williams said to Bhaiji and Satki, "we're getting out of here."

"What about Abu?" Satki asked.

"He's coming, too," Williams answered.

Jack Whatley led them out a side door. The Mercedes-Benz was waiting with its engine running. Their things were inside and the vehicle had been thoroughly searched. Williams noticed that the box of papers from Abu's trial was missing. He chose not to say anything.

A moment later, Abu appeared, his wrists bound behind his back. One eye was nearly swollen shut, and a large cut on his cheek had barely stopped bleeding. Satki gasped when she saw him. Two soldiers untied Abu's wrists and pushed him into the back seat of the Mercedes. Satki climbed in next to him and immediately began to examine her son's wounds.

"These boys are going to escort you to the Thai border," Whatley said to Williams. "They've got orders to shoot you if you stop to so much as piss. After that, you're on your own. Good to see you again, Ben. Take care of yourself now, ya hear?"

Williams didn't answer. When the jeep in front moved out, Bhaiji quickly followed.

CHAPTER 16

As soon as they entered the predominantly Muslim country of Malaysia, Abu instructed Bhaiji to drive directly to Kuala Lumpur, the capital city. There Abu had been invited to speak in several mosques, and Williams, Bhaiji and Satki were grateful there were no incidents. It was a brief, two-day stop, and they were off again. They journeyed to the Phillippines via freighter.

"Have you been to Manila before?" Abu asked Williams as they disembarked.

"No," Williams answered.

"Come with me," Abu instructed.

They walked the crowded streets in silence. Teenage prostitutes, male and female, were everywhere. Some of them, Williams was certain, were no more than thirteen or fourteen years old. Nightclubs, X-rated movie houses, and brothels—once havens for bored and horny American servicemen—still flashed their neon signs like titillating magnets. But business was down in Manila. The closure of the U.S. naval base at Subic Bay, and Clark Air Force Base had hurt. Downtown Manila wasn't the same.

"The Filipinos have always been a traditional people," Abu explained. "But their values have been replaced by Western standards," he said as they passed yet another nightclub advertising nude dancers. "They have seen their culture decimated. Many of these people are Roman Catholics, but they share the same hopelessness and despair of their counterparts elsewhere in the world. Religion is the most important aspect of their lives, but it affords them little hope in this world. The Church has come too far away from Christ's original teachings."

"How do you mean?" Williams asked, intensely curious.

Abu looked at him. "Jesus purposely involved himself in the politics of his day. He was here to help humanity evolve—spiritually and politically. He knew that it was impossible to separate politics from spiritualism—religion, yes; spirituality, no. He knew his teachings would bring him into conflict with the religious and secular leaders of his time. And he knew that it was the only way he could fulfill his destiny. He began the transition."

Williams wanted to stop Abu right there in the street and ask: 'Do you honestly believe you are the new Christ?' If Abu said yes, it would certainly prove that he was mad—a possibility that frightened Williams. Then he realized he wouldn't get a straight answer anyway. "This transition—you've talked about it before—"

"Yes. It began two thousand years ago with Jesus. It is nearly complete."

"Jesus didn't finish it?"

"No," Abu replied.

Williams proceeded carefully. He remained skeptical. "So, then the prophecy that Christ will return is true?"

Abu continued to look at the people on the streets—he was more interested in them than his discussion with Williams. "Yes," he said. "To complete the transition; to confront the Antichrist."

"The Antichrist," Williams repeated. He wasn't buying it.

"Yes," Abu answered.

"The devil?" he asked sarcastically.

"Yes," Abu replied matter-of-factly.

"Uh-huh," Williams said. He thought for a moment before continuing. "So, we're just about there. The end of the transition, I mean."

"Yes," Abu said. He looked at Williams. "Can you not feel it?"

"Feel what?"

"A sense of impending change. An acceleration of events. A strange combination of anxiety and wonderment. A stirring in the soul of humanity, like an infant stirring in its mother's womb."

Williams didn't respond. He refused to be distracted by what he was thinking. "This reappearance of Christ," he began, ignoring Abu's question, "and confrontation with the Antichrist—is this—?"

"Yes, it is the Armageddon—the war between good and evil—predicted by all the world's religions."

"And how do you fit into all of this?" Williams asked, finally arriving at the question.

"As I've said before, that is for humanity to decide."

"Where the hell are you?" Herschel Strunk asked with irritation when Williams phoned him a few days later.

"Manila," Williams said.

"Jesus Christ! Last time we spoke you were in India. Where've you been since?" Williams rattled off the list. "Myanmar!" Strunk exclaimed. "Were you there during the riots?"

"Yes," Williams answered.

"Well, goddamn it, where's your piece? You must've been the only Western journalist to cover it. Why are you sitting on it?" Strunk was characteristically gruff.

"It's bigger than that," Williams said. "Much bigger."

There was a pause. "Well then, when am I going to get another installment?"

"Soon," Williams said, "I'm working on it."

"Lemme just tell you, Ben, it'd better be good or I might be forced to pull the plug on this assignment."

"Yeah," Williams responded. He wasn't intimidated.

"What's this Abu up to?"

"I don't know. He's been speaking at mosques and churches all over the city—I don't think anyone but the Pope could attract so many people."

"Has it occurred to you that maybe this guy isn't who or what you thought?" Strunk sounded worried.

"No," Williams said. "There's something here. I just can't put my finger on it yet. I'll call you from Indonesia—that's where we're headed next," Williams said. He hung up before Strunk could respond.

When they left Manila by freighter, Williams stood on the deck as it plowed through the South China Sea toward the island of Java, and studied the endless horizon, wondering if he was too close to Abu. Maybe he was losing his objectivity. In the distance loomed the large island of Sumatra. A stream of smoke wound its way into the sky from a small, active volcano. Abu came up to him on the deck. As The ship neared the island, the volcano looked more ominous, and mysterious.

"Four of the world's most devastating eruptions occurred in Indo-

117

nesia," Abu said. "The worst one was in 1815. Ten thousand people were incinerated by the explosion, and over eighty thousand died from the famine and disease that followed."

"My God—" Williams said.

"It altered global climate for many years." Abu continued. "Months later, temperatures dropped around the world. The skies over London turned crimson, and six inches of snow fell in July in Rhode Island. There was severe summer crop damage reported worldwide. Throughout the entire summer, temperatures fell below freezing. People panicked; they thought the world was coming to an end. There were epidemics of typhus and cholera all over Europe and Asia. Sixty-five thousand more people died." Abu stared at Williams for a moment, then abruptly left the deck.

Williams thought it uncharacteristic of Abu to talk about this sort of catastrophe. Was there some hidden clue in this information that he was supposed to pick up on? What the hell was Abu really trying to tell him?

Nearly all Indonesians, about a hundred million of them, were Muslims and most lived on Java: A primeval island of astonishing beauty. The capital, Jakarta, was on Java, and it was home to one of the world's largest and most impressive mosques—the Istiqlal.

Abu and Williams walked along the narrow back streets that catacombed Jakarta. The air was oppressively humid; the constant brushing of bodies against one another caused unavoidable familiarity. Vendors with pushcarts sold black-market goods from the West. At every corner prostitutes, perfumed transvestites and rickshaw drivers with sinewy legs and scrawny bodies, offered their services. Arabic melodies set to rock rhythms blared from car radios. Beggars lined the avenues, thrusting their empty hands into the faces of everyone who passed. A cacophony of car horns and angry, shouting cab drivers echoed off the dilapidated, moss-covered buildings.

Abu went from mosque to mosque. Williams waited while Abu visited with the mullahs, often for long periods of time.

"What'd you talk about in there?" Williams asked after the first visit.

"The physical and spiritual deprivation of these people."

It was the same old stuff. Williams thought of Herschel's impatience. He had to send him something, soon. "What can you do for them?"

"Give them hope, give them a voice."

Williams jotted down the last part. "Abu," he said, trying to keep up with him as they walked quickly through the sweltering streets. "This Mother Theresa stuff you do—going to hospitals, schools, orphanages—it's all well and good, but it's kind of a drop in the bucket." Abu looked quizzically at Williams. "What I mean is, with your intelligence and charisma, not to mention your public speaking talents—" Abu smiled—"Why not just go for it? Quit screwing around in the back streets of the world's ghettos. Pick a country, hell you could become President or Prime Minister just about anywhere you chose."

"Why don't you just ask what you really want to know?"

"And what's that?"

"Is it my ambition to be a world leader?"

"Well?"

Abu heaved an exasperated sigh. Williams almost felt embarrassed. "Your mistake, Ben Williams, is in thinking change must occur from the top down."

"At least put yourself in a position where people can be made to act," Williams shot back defiantly. "If your ambitions are truly noble, then we need men with your ideals in government."

"There are men with my ideals in government!" Abu's tone was angry. "But they have no more voice than these people."

"Because they've been corrupted by the system?"

"No. Because they are part of a system that does not work."

"I see," Williams said, but in fact, he didn't—and Abu knew it.

"We must have a new system," Abu said with intense conviction. "We must invert the pyramid!" Williams wondered why Abu's words made him feel anxious. Did it have to do with where he was in the pyramid? "Power should never be aggregated in the hands of a few, nor the one. It should remain where it belongs—with the people. One who governs is a servant but would you allow a servant in your house to command obedience from you, or inflict punishment upon you because you insist upon respect, or because you demand freedom and justice?"

"No," Williams was obliged to say. "Of course not. But what makes you think your ego isn't at work here, or that you're any different from any other politician?"

Abu looked at him as though Williams hadn't heard a word. "My motives." His eyes were fiery. "Do you want to know my ambition? I want nothing more than to elevate these people to the status they deserve. And I will do whatever is required. I humble myself to no one but I respect and admire all, for each is God."

"And if you succeed? What then?"

"The purpose for my life will have been served. But the success will not be mine, it will belong to humanity."

"And once the pyramid is inverted, who will rule? You?"

"No one will rule," Abu answered. "Everyone will govern."

"Sounds like anarchy to me," Williams said sarcastically.

"Check your dictionary, Ben Williams. Anarchism is defined as a political theory that advocates cooperation and voluntary association of individuals and groups as a means of satisfying needs." Abu became stern again, as though admonishing a foolish student. "Stand aside from your limited perceptions, Ben Williams, and you will discover a new world."

Although early evening was approaching, the heat and humidity of Jakarta clung to Williams like a damp rag. Insects swarmed around his head and buzzed in his ears as he walked alongside Abu. A warm breeze carried a fetid stench from a nearby canal.

He wondered if Abu could awaken the masses to reclaim their power, would they act responsibly? Would they exercise their power wisely? Or, would they just give it over to someone else—to someone who said all the right things? And who better than a messiah?

They had arrived finally at a large square called Medan Merdeka— Freedom Field—situated in the heart of Jakarta. At the edge of the square was the Istiqlal mosque. A steady stream of the faithful were making their way through the streets to come and pay homage to Allah.

At the crest of the Istiqlal's spired center dome stood the Arabic character for Allah: A golden metallic symbol stylized in the shape of a trident. It reminded Williams of a pitchfork. Abu stared up at the trident. The orange and red rays of the setting sun struck the shiny trident and reflected on the ground.

Abu pointed to the ornament. "That shall be the symbol of the new order, and it shall be borne upon the flag of a new nation." He walked toward the two giant entrance doors of the Istiqlal. Williams followed. They removed their shoes and entered. Williams remained at the rear while Abu went ahead. He surveyed the great hall: Its ceiling loomed like an immense sky, resting upon a forest of magnificent columns that extended upward hundreds of feet. The immaculate floor was covered with Arabic rugs except for two aisles on each side. It was impossible not to feel a sense of reverence in the great room, even humility. Over five thousand Muslims were kneeling in neat rows, each had just enough room to touch his forehead to the floor during prayer. It was an act of submission to Allah that, repeated since childhood, left the visible mark of a true believer indelibly stamped upon the forehead.

After prayers, the Imam delivered a sermon. At the conclusion, he looked at Abu and then back at the congregation. "There is a visitor among us who wishes to speak to you," the Imam told his followers. "He is an Arab Moor from Sri Lanka." With that the Imam stepped back and sat down at the rear of the platform.

Abu stepped onto the platform. He pressed his palms together and bowed to the audience. "Salam," he said. Strategically placed microphones picked up his voice and carried it through the hall. There was silence, broken only by an occasional cough. Abu turned and bowed to the Imam, who responded with a brief and subtle nod.

"In the name of Allah, the Merciful, the Compassionate One," Abu began, "I am Abu 'Ali Asghar. I am here to speak to you of the tide of change that will soon sweep across the world with all its might like a great tsunami unleashed by a volcanic eruption of incandescent fire from the Earth's core."

That got their attention, Williams thought.

"I am here to speak to you of your enslavement, of your servitude to the rich and powerful of the world. And I have come to liberate you." As Abu spoke, a tidal wave of emotion swept through the vast room. Near the end, Abu stared at the people before him. "I am not here to tell you what to do, only what you can do. The choice is yours. But you are not alone, and I will join you. I will stand alone if necessary, I will even die for this cause. But know that there are many like you, many more than those who are rich and powerful. They can kill you, and they can kill me, but they cannot kill all of us. There will come a time, and it will be soon, when the masses of the world, the billions on the planet like you, will rise up and reclaim their power, and demand justice. Tyranny will be abolished, and freedom will reign!"

Abu bowed. The audience rose, one by one, until they were all on their feet. "Abu 'Ali Asghar," they chanted, softly at first, but growing louder with each repetition. The chanting reached a thunderous crescendo. Abu raised his hands in the air, and strutted from one side of the platform to the other. Williams thought he saw a nervous look cross the Imam's face.

CHAPTER 17

Williams was glad when they left Jakarta the next day. He didn't want to experience another incident like Yangon, he confided to Satki when they were seated in the back of the Mercedes.

"Nor do I," she agreed, just as Abu opened the front door and climbed into the car.

Then a more cynical thought crossed Williams' mind: What if the CIA had decided it would be better if Abu wasn't around to stir up trouble? Maybe that's what they'd intended to do all along, but they just wanted Abu and Williams out of Yangon. After all, Williams had known more obscure figures who had died mysteriously and he knew the CIA was responsible. He'd just never been able to corroborate it. And, of course, to cover their tracks they'd probably kill him, too. Just like Jack Whatley had theorized.

At the western tip of Sumatra, they entered the territory of Aceh where the government had constructed its crown jewel: The immense P.T. Arun gas liquefaction plant. It was a symbol of Indonesia's great leap into the industrial age.

Aceh was also home to over three million Muslims engaged in a bloody 'jihad,' or holy war, against the government. The Koran was the only law recognized by the Acehnese, who were zealously dedicated to establishing an independent nation.

Right now they were being punished for their rebellion, deliberately ignored and deprived by the government. The plant's employees were imported from elsewhere, and lived in hilltop enclaves of expensive homes and clean streets. The Acehnese lived in filthy, rotting slums.

Bhaiji drove directly to the port city of Banda Aceh, the provincial capital. The rivers that flowed through the city were polluted with human waste and debris, yet were the only source of drinking water. Giant disease-carrying flies and cat-sized rats fed off mounds of festering garbage. The pothole-ridden streets rendered navigation by car painstakingly slow, and often impossible. But looming over a sparkling blue reflecting pool was the black-domed Masjid Raya Baiturrah–man mosque. It stood, ageless and beautiful, surrounded by the poverty of its devoted people.

When the Acehnese learned that an American journalist was in their midst, they clamored to talk to him. Abu explained to Williams that they possessed an almost universal belief that once the American people were told the truth, they would come to their rescue. "You tell them!" Williams was instructed on more than one occasion. "They will help us!"

"Tell them what?" Williams asked.

"They butcher our people," a man said.

"Who?" Williams asked, surrounded by shouting Acehnese when he and Bhaiji had gone to a restaurant one afternoon while Abu and Satki were at a local hospital.

"The government!" several people called out from nearby tables. "They are murderers! All of them!"

One young man grabbed Williams by the arm, nearly tearing his shirt. "They slaughtered over a hundred of our people yesterday! Women and children. It happened at the funeral of one of our leaders, martyred in the fight for our freedom!" Hatred spewed from his mouth. "They will suffer, as they have made us suffer! Allah is with us! We will destroy those followers of Satan."

Williams looked nervously at Bhaiji. He said, sotto voce, "Let's get out of here." Bhaiji nodded and the two got up from their table, quickly paid the bill and left.

"What's wrong, Ben?" Bhaiji asked as he hurried to keep up with Williams who was racing toward the car.

"You ever heard of Krakatoa?"

"You mean the volcanic eruption—"

"Yeah. Well, if they blow the P.T. Arun plant, the explosion is going to make Krakatoa look like a hiccup."

"I see your point," Bhaiji said as he slammed the car door shut.

They drove quickly to the hospital only to be told that Abu and Satki had left and were at the Great Mosque. Bhaiji and Williams raced there, Bhaiji driving almost recklessly through the narrow streets.

Abu was already on the mosque's stage, delivering an impassioned plea for the people of Banda Aceh to fulfill their destinies, reclaim the power of their divinity and carry out the will of Allah.

The zealous Muslims were on their feet, chanting *"Allahu Akbar,"* followed by the name of their new savior. Abu climbed down from his lofty perch and entered the throng of devotees who cleared a path before him. They poured into the street, sweeping Williams along. "Allah has sent us a Prophet!" one man exclaimed to Williams, "a messenger to show us the way!"

Williams watched in awe as the frenzied crowd turned into a great artery that wound its way through the streets of Banda Aceh. Demonstrations, chanting and protesting continued through the night and spread to surrounding cities and villages. Abu was declared the Amir al Muimin—Commander of the Faithful. It wasn't Abu admonishing them to act—it was Allah—a call to arms they dared not disobey.

The next day, the Acehnese captured the P.T. Arun plant and held its employees hostage. Government troops soon arrived. The Acehnese said if their demands weren't met, they'd blow up the plant, and all Sumatra with it.

Hersch is gonna love this, Williams thought as he banged away on his laptop. Within hours he wired the piece to Strunk, and in less than twenty-four hours the *New York Times* ran the story. It wasn't until the next day that the rest of the world's media even knew what was happening. Williams had scooped them. Herschel Strunk was happy. He'd let Williams stay on the assignment as long as he wanted. He, too, was beginning to see the Pulitzer potential in the stories being sent to him.

The capture of the plant brought correspondents and TV crews from around the world—they descended on Jakarta like a colony of ants on honey. Moscow and Washington voiced grave concern and stern messages were sent through ambassadors of every nation advising Jakarta to take all necessary steps to avoid a catastrophe. The United Nations Security Council passed a resolution demanding that the Indonesian government sit down and negotiate an immediate end to the war with the Acehnese.

The government responded by dispatching heavily armed troops. But the Acehnese knew jungle warfare. They attacked and destroyed many of the troops while en route. Finally, the government sent one of its top officials to Banda Aceh. He immediately asked for a meeting with Sheik Abu 'Ali Asghar. He and his aides were taken to the Masjid Raya mosque, where they found Abu seated serenely in a chair, surrounded by armed Acehnese. Williams, Satki and Bhaiji sat nearby, silent and nervous.

"End the rebellion," the minister instructed Abu.

"Give them what they want. Give them justice!" Abu said.

"You must order them to leave the plant!" the minister countered angrily.

"I do not control these people!" Abu said, leaning forward and looking at the minister with menacing eyes. "Only you can stop this by recognizing their dignity and giving them respect."

"You do not understand!" the minister exclaimed, obviously under enormous pressure. "Millions could be killed if the plant is destroyed. The entire nation would suffer. Is that what you want?"

"It does not matter what I want!" Abu said. "These people suffer every minute of their lives! They watch their children grow sick and die! They watch the survivors grow up and live the same wretched lives as they have been made to endure! What is death to these people but a release from their anguish! I will not stand in their way," he said. "The choice is yours." His voice became calm, yet sounded more menacing than when he was angry. "I suggest you choose wisely." The minister was stunned. He looked at the young Acehnese and their automatic weapons. He mopped the beads of sweat on his forehead with a handkerchief. Abu stared at him. "Go now," Abu said. He motioned for the armed guards to take them away and looked at Williams.

"My God," Williams muttered under his breath. Satki and Bhaiji both looked at him anxiously. "This is it," he said, returning their gazes. "This is what it's about."

Within hours, the minister had returned. "What have you decided?" Abu asked from his unproclaimed throne.

The minister looked exhausted and defeated. "My government will agree to the demands of the Acehnese people." He paused. "On condition—" he said tentatively.

Abu raised an eyebrow. "Yes?"

"You must leave Indonesia at once."

Abu sat back in his chair and smiled. "I will be happy to do so." The minister sighed with relief, and mopped his sweaty brow with a damp handkerchief. With a deep laugh, Abu stood up and left the room.

Tens of thousands appeared at the dockside in Banda Aceh to see Abu off. He stood at the ship's railing, arms raised, waving. Bhaiji, Satki and Williams stood nearby. *"Allahu Akbar!"* Abu shouted. *"Allahu Akbar!"* the multitude answered, "Abu 'Ali Asghar!" The vibration made the aging dock tremble.

As the ship sailed west, the chanting sounded like distant thunder, a storm gathering on the eastern horizon. Abu disappeared below deck. Williams stayed at the railing with Satki and Bhaiji. None of them spoke.

Williams pulled a cigar from his shirt pocket. Satki looked at him. "I thought I'd give up cigarettes," he said. He unwrapped the cigar and lodged it securely on one side of his mouth. He remained quiet, listening to the distant thunder. Every so often, the cigar would dip and twitch as his teeth clenched. "My God, it's really happening," Williams mused aloud, removing the cigar from his mouth.

"Did you doubt it?" Satki asked.

"I guess so," Williams confessed. "I mean, it's one thing to attract a small following in Bhopal, but to rally hundreds of thousands, probably millions—" Williams shook his head in amazement.

Satki frowned. "More and more, I think back to simpler and less dangerous times, when Abu was a boy." Her voice trailed off.

Williams looked out at the sea and recited a poem he'd been made to memorize long ago:

> *Turning and turning in the widening gyre*
> *The falcon cannot hear the falconer;*
> *Things fall apart; the center cannot hold;*
> *Mere anarchy is loosed upon the world,*
> *The blood-dimmed tide is loosed, and everywhere*
> *The ceremony of innocence is drowned;*
> *The best lack all conviction, while the worst*
> *Are full of passionate intensity.*

Satki looked at him. "William Butler Yeats," he explained, "a poem called *The Second Coming.*" Williams turned back to stare out at the sea.

Bhaiji smiled at him. "Since you are also a great fan of Mr. Hemingway, you must be excited that we are heading to Africa."

"Of course," Williams said. In fact, he had been thrilled when they packed up the day before and Abu had announced their next destination. But then he realized that to let Abu loose in Africa was like placing a lion in the middle of a flock of sheep.

As the ship sailed toward Africa, Williams spent most of his time alone, thinking. He reviewed his notes over and over again, and walked the deck staring out at the open sea. Banda Aceh showed what Abu could do. But Banda Aceh was merely a foreshadowing. And therein lay the story. But what was it? He just couldn't connect with it. It mocked him, laughed at him from atop a mountain he couldn't scale. The harder he tried, the more elusive it became.

Was Abu simply another obscure political demagogue seeking notoriety and power on the backs of the masses? Or, could it be that humanity was actually on the verge of some profound leap forward into a higher consciousness? Was it about an ultimate conflict between good and evil? Armageddon? Why had he, Bennett Williams, been sent to Bhopal? Was it a story he was destined to tell? Was his job—his duty—to put the pieces together?

He also knew the story was too big, too important, to simply be a series of newspaper articles, something that would end up in a trash bin, or lining the bottom of a bird cage. He wanted to write something meaningful and lasting. But the desire was immediately followed by the self-doubts he had as a writer. They danced before him like demonically possessed creatures.

Then Abu appeared at his side as he stood on the deck on a chilly, foggy morning. "How are you, my friend?" he asked.

Williams glared at him. "I'd prefer to be alone right now," he said, turning his gaze to the line of white foam trailing behind the ship.

"To wallow in self-pity?" Williams hated Abu second-guessing his thoughts.

"I don't think you'd understand," Williams said facetiously. "Fallibility isn't one of your characteristics, is it?"

"Then, perhaps I can apply the whip," he said. "It must be awkward for you having to reach behind like that."

"Go to hell."

Abu ignored Williams' hostility. "Maybe you sabotage yourself."

"How so?"

"You construct Mount Everest in your mind, and then tell yourself you are not capable of climbing it. Besides, it is much safer at the bottom. But then again, you never get to see the magnificent view." Williams looked at Abu. "Do you know what you will see from up there?"

"What?"

"Other mountains to climb."

Williams sighed. "Thanks. That's discouraging."

"Why?"

"Because there is no end."

"That, Ben Williams, is the greatest gift you will ever know." Abu paused a moment. "Those who achieve greatness never realize it; those who perceive greatness never achieve it. Do not presume to change the way people think, Ben Williams. All you know is your truth. Simply speak that truth." Abu turned and walked away. Williams stared down at the moving water, no longer conscious of the swirling chaos below.

The next day Williams heard the ship's whistle blow, followed immediately by a knock on his cabin door. "Good Morning, Ben," Bhaiji said cheerily as Williams opened the door.

"What's up?" Williams asked. "Where are we?" He knew it couldn't be Africa, they hadn't been at sea long enough.

"Colombo, Sri Lanka," Bhaiji explained with delight. "We only have a few hours. We are going ashore. Abu asks that you join us."

It was a short walk from the docks to the heart of Colombo. "Oh, Abu, do you remember?" Satki said nostalgically as they neared the old Dutch fort.

"Yes, mother, I do." Abu said. Williams noticed something strange about Abu's look and voice. He seemed distracted, as though anticipating something.

"I must visit the Somali embassy here to make sure we all have visas for our arrival at Mogadishu," Bhaiji said as hurried off. "I will see you back onboard," he called to them.

Abu nodded. "We will meet you at the ship in three hours," he said to Bhaiji, as he motioned for Satki and Williams to follow him.

As the three travelers walked through the streets, Satki said to her son, "I can remember so clearly the day your father and I first set foot on these shores. It's still the same."

"It has changed," Abu said ominously.

But to Satki, it appeared nothing had changed. Rain trees still lined the streets, mischievously lying in wait for unwitting victims upon which to pour their cradled water. Rickshaw drivers scurried along, competing with the ever-growing number of vehicles for the right of way. There was the Queen's House built by the British, surrounded by the beautiful Gordon Gardens, and there were the bright colors and rich aromas of the Pettah District.

But Williams could feel something lurking just beneath the seemingly peaceful surface. It permeated the city like the acrid smell of vinegar. And then Williams knew what it was: Fear, a strong and powerful fear. It belted him in the stomach; it assaulted the emotions like a wave of noxious vapor. And then, suddenly, Satki felt it too. As they moved deeper into Colombo, it became worse.

The place Muslims believed was the original Garden of Eden had become contaminated by hatred and prejudice in a way that surpassed most other places. The never-ending war between the Tamils and the Sinhalese had developed into rampant barbarism and cruelty. Government terrorism had become national policy. The slightest hint of dissent was punishable by death.

Williams knew it was only a matter of time. "Do you wish to return to the ship, mother?" Abu asked.

"No," Satki answered. She refused to shield herself from the horrors that had befallen her adopted country.

And then, the three of them stopped in their tracks as they spotted a charred and maggot-ridden corpse lying just ahead in the middle of the street. Satki covered her face with her hands and buried herself in Abu's arms. Williams had to look away, but he noticed how everyone else on the street seemed oblivious.

"Such barbarity," Abu muttered.

"What happened?" Williams asked.

"He was probably killed by soldiers who placed a gasoline-soaked tire around his waist, and then set it aflame for all to watch. It is a horrid way to die but it is intended more for those witnessing it than the victim. When the screaming stops, the stench of burning rubber and human flesh touches even those who try to block out the horror. The bodies are left as warnings."

"Why doesn't somebody remove it, or at least cover it up?"

"Anyone caught doing so receives the same punishment." Abu's voice rose angrily. "But this is no secret to the world, Ben Williams. What you should ask is how is this allowed to continue?"

"What a nation does to its own people is like a man brutalizing his own family—no one wants to interfere," Williams said.

"But this was my home!" Abu shouted with rage. "These people were my family!" Abu stepped toward the body. He stopped and looked at the people in the marketplace. "Why do you allow yourselves to live like this!?" he demanded of them. People stopped and stared. His face became red; the vein in his temple throbbed. Williams had never seen him so angry. It frightened him.

Abu stepped abruptly to a merchant's stand and grabbed a large rug on display. He gently covered the body and then knelt and prayed.

At that moment, three government soldiers rounded the corner. Williams saw them as they spotted Abu. "Oh shit," Williams said under his breath. The soldiers raised their rifles and began running toward Abu. Williams and Satki stood frozen while everyone around them fled in a screaming panic. "Abu!" Satki and Williams called out in unison.

Abu stood up, turned and faced the oncoming soldiers. They stopped a short distance away, and pointed their automatic rifles at him. One of them shouted furiously in Sinhalese. Abu glared at them, his laser-like eyes spewing rage. The vein in his right temple looked like a tree root about to burst through.

The soldier continued shouting and cursing as Abu met his gaze with a challenging glare, as though daring him to do something. He stepped toward them. The soldiers were startled by Abu's boldness. The one who had shouted suddenly dropped his rifle and grabbed at his throat with both hands—he was choking and struggling to breathe. His face reddened and his eyes bulged. He fell to the ground, gasping and clawing at his throat, trying to free himself from some imaginary

131

grip. The others stepped back, frightened. Abu stood over the writhing soldier, staring down at him with a rage Williams had never seen in Abu before.

The other soldiers looked at one another and aimed their rifles at Abu. "Abu!" Williams yelled.

Abu spun around and fixed his eyes on the soldiers as though locking in on a target. They pulled the triggers of their rifles. Williams braced himself but nothing happened. They pulled the triggers once more, but again nothing. One drew his sidearm and tried to fire at Abu, but it remained silent in his hand. Another soldier extended the butt of his rifle and ran toward Abu. Just before he reached him, Abu waved his arms in front of him, in what looked to Williams like something only a black belt in karate could do, then pushed outward suddenly and explosively. The soldier lurched backward. Abu stood completely still. The remaining soldier dropped his rifle and fled.

Abu walked to the choking soldier and stood at his feet. The soldier began to breathe again. Abu pulled him up. "Go," Abu ordered, "while you still have your life." The soldier stumbled as he ran away. Abu scanned the faces of the stunned Sri Lankans just beginning to emerge from hiding, and then at Williams and Satki. They heard the ship's whistle blow. Without a word, Abu began walking toward the docks with Williams and Satki hurrying behind.

CHAPTER 18

To Bennett Williams, Africa was Mecca. It summoned his spirit. It epitomized adventure and daring—a place intolerant of weakness, where nature reigned supreme and courage was as essential to life as water and air. It was a place where a man just might find himself.

But Africa had changed. It was now the most exploited place on earth. Torn by bloody civil wars, disease and unimaginable famine and poverty, Africa had become the industrialized world's ghetto and Black Africans were humanity's impoverished relatives, a blight on the family of man.

Their first stop was Somalia where, in Mogadishu, Williams witnessed yet another of Abu's remarkable powers. Somalian warlords had just about destroyed the country over the past several years. After only two days in the capital city, Abu began gathering the warring clans and, after several more days of impassioned argument and mediation, a truce was finally announced. Abu had succeeded in abating the bloody clashes—he had succeeded in doing what no other country's emissaries had been able to do. Williams' piece about the truce once again scooped the international press. In New York, Herschel Strunk was delighted.

"You seem to have accomplished the impossible," Williams said to Abu when they were back on the road again. "Bringing those enemy tribes together was, well, almost miraculous." Satki beamed with motherly pride as Williams spoke.

Abu turned around in his front seat to face Williams. "Have you ever heard of the 'Mad Mullah?' "

"No," Williams said, "but you're going to tell me."

Abu smiled. "He was Sheik Mohammed Hassan, and he united the Somali warlords and their clans, and inspired them to fight a jihad against the British. They gave him the name 'Mad Mullah,' but the Sheik's people proclaimed him 'the Mahdi.' "

"The who?" Williams asked.

"The Awaited One," Abu explained. "The one who would hold back the forces of evil until the arrival of Judgment Day."

"Armageddon?" Williams asked. Abu didn't respond. "I gather the British finally won."

Abu nodded. "After twenty years of fighting, and only because Sheik Hassan died of influenza. The mighty British army could never defeat him. But without his leadership, solidarity among the clans was destroyed."

"So he wasn't the Mahdi after all?" Williams asked.

"It would seem not," Abu answered.

"So this Awaited One is . . . still being awaited?"

"It would seem so."

Williams looked out the car's window at the hordes of refugees who trudged along the highway, paying no attention to the passing Mercedes.

"Can't the Red Cross or other relief agencies help these people?" Williams asked.

"They try to," Satki offered. "But it is never enough."

Abu nodded. "A grain of sand in the Sahara. Something more radical is needed."

"Like what?" Williams asked.

Abu fell silent for what seemed a long time. When he spoke it was not directly to Williams, his gaze was somewhere out the window, past the people on the road, to a distant horizon. "Sometimes it is necessary to demolish the existing structure in order to rebuild the new one," he said.

Bhaiji glanced over at Abu for a moment. Satki stared at her son. Williams, too, thoughtfully studied the man in front of him. No one spoke.

It was dusk by the time they arrived in Ethiopia. Abu instructed Bhaiji to stop at one of the makeshift refugee camps that were throughout the Horn of Africa. A dry, stiff breeze whipped dust and sand into the air. There were small fires scattered about the camp from which streams of smoke meshed with the haze—it looked like the hellish vision of some tormented artist. Odorous sulphur mixed with the smoke; there were mournful wails from mothers whose lifeless babies lay limply in their arms, and from men who had only stumps where hands, arms or legs once were. Naked children with distended stomachs roamed about, their eyes begging for food. Starvation and misery were the great equalizers in this camp of almost forty thousand; fighting was left to the politicians and their armies—the only ones who always managed to remain fed.

Then, from the far end of the camp, a man's frail voice began to chant. "God is most great," the Ethiopian Muslim sang out in Arabic. "There is no God but Allah . . ."

The Muslims in the camp who could, began moving toward the self-appointed muezzin, while on the camp's other side, a priest of the Ethiopian Church was conducting Christian services.

"It is truly amazing, *non?*" Williams heard a voice say with an unmistakable French accent. He turned to see a man in his late fifties, with tanned and weathered skin, his grey hair unkempt, his face unshaven. He was dressed in denims and a red kerchief was tied loosely around his neck. He extended a strong hand toward Williams. *"Je suis* Doctor Phillipe Bertone. I'm with *Medicins Sans Frontières,* part of the U.N. relief effort."

Williams shook the doctor's hand. Abu bowed to him and introduced the group.

"Why did you say 'amazing'?" Williams asked Bertone.

"Because despite their condition, they still find the strength to pray. Perhaps they believe God will answer their prayers, deliver them from this hell." The Frenchman paused, placed both hands on his waist and sighed deeply. *"Pour moi,* I look around this abominable place and wonder if God even listens, or where God could be looking, for *certainment* it is not here."

"We have come to help," Abu said simply. Bhaiji and Satki nodded.

Bertone smiled. "Excellent. There is much to do." He craned his neck toward the entrance of the camp. "You have brought food?"

"No," Abu said.

"Are you with the U.N. or Red Cross?"

Abu shook his head. "But there will be food in the morning. And medicines."

The doctor's face clouded. *"Pardonez-moi, monsieur,* but I've heard that promise many times. Always tomorrow. But nothing ever comes. Only death."

"Tomorrow," Abu said firmly. "When the sun rises."

Phillip Bertone looked skeptically at the tall man in the blue turban and flowing robes but said nothing.

Abu bowed slightly. "Excuse me," he said politely, "I would like to pray with those people." Without waiting for a response, Abu turned and walked away.

"Show us the rest of the camp," Satki said, taking the doctor's arm. With Bhaiji and Williams following, Bertone escorted them through the tents where those most in need, and closest to death, were kept.

"So many children," Satki said with tears in her eyes.

"Oui, the young men are either dead or in the army."

"Which army?" Bhaiji asked.

Bertone shrugged. "Any army. They simply come in and replenish their ranks from the villages. Young men either fight or they are killed so they cannot fight on the other side."

"And where are the women?" Satki asked.

"Most are raped and killed, usually by the same soldiers who steal their husbands and sons."

Williams fought not to become sick at the sight of so much disease and death, of people whose skin clung to their bones like taut canvas wrapped around protruding skeletons. This is what they looked like at Auschwitz and Dachau and Bergen-Belsen, he thought.

Satki stopped at the bed of a badly wounded boy. He actually looked as though he wanted to die—as though death would be a welcome relief. Satki stroked his forehead as he stared blankly at her. "He was the only member of his family to escape from his village," Bertone said. "His father was taken by soldiers, his mother and sisters raped. He was shot and left to die."

"Will he?" Williams asked.

The doctor nodded. "If not from his infected wound, it will surely be from the cholera and dysentery and typhus that is everywhere."

In another tent, the group saw several dozen children just sitting and staring into space. They were unlike the other sick and malnourished youngsters, and even appeared slightly better off than most, although they too were scrawny and weak. But their illness seemed to go beyond physical pain and deprivation.

"What is wrong with these children?" Bhaiji asked.

"Their minds are gone," the doctor said flatly. "Most of them have seen their mothers and fathers brutalized and killed. Quite honestly, it's a miracle these children find their way here at all. They often arrive by having followed a trail of corpses, those who died on the road leading to the camp. These *pauvre enfants*—they go insane, their little minds simply cannot comprehend the horror of what has happened, they are so terrified and confused, so lost. We try to nurse their bodies back to health, but we are not equipped to treat their minds."

"God have mercy," Satki said softly.

It was dark when they got back to the middle of the camp. There, a large fire burned brightly, illuminating a wide area around it. As Bertone led the group to his tent near the main infirmary, he stopped and looked at Abu standing near the fire, surrounded by hundreds of refugees, apparently mesmerized by his words of hope and comfort.

"A most unusual man, your son," Bertone said to Satki.

"Most," she agreed.

"Where on earth could he have gotten so much wood? I've never seen a fire as big at that."

Satki merely looked at it and smiled.

Dr. Bertone didn't know what made him wake up so abruptly the following morning. It was not quite dawn, that interval between night and day when darkness is beginning to evaporate as quickly as dew upon the desert sand.

Still dressed in the clothes he had worn the day before, Bertone sat up quickly on his cot, ran his hands through his thick, unruly hair and rubbed the back of his stiff neck. He grabbed his boots and inspected the insides of them for any unwelcome visitors.

There was a strange quiet about the camp as the doctor looked out through the mesh walls of his tent. Not far from his own cot, Satki, Williams and Bhaiji were still sound asleep. But he noticed that Abu's bed was empty and the olive green blanket was still neatly folded.

Bertone splashed water on his face and quickly stepped outside the tent. Nothing seemed out of the ordinary. The ground was covered with uneven mounds of blanketed refugees, and a small trail of smoke rose from the still smoldering fire where Abu had spoken the night before. The faint glow of the orange sun was just showing on the eastern horizon. Everything was very still.

Then Bertone saw it. The silhouette of a huge, black, rectangular shaped 'monolith' that had inexplicably risen from the Ethiopian dust during the night. It eclipsed the ascending sun, producing around it a corona of blinding light. For a moment, the doctor thought he might be hallucinating.

The sun rose further, allowing the mountainous shape to come into focus. Just outside the camp's entrance, Bertone saw row upon row of neatly stacked burlap sacks, reaching thirty-five feet high and a hundred and fifty feet across.

Just beyond the sacks were more rows of crates and boxes, stacked in equal proportion to the burlap sacks. Bertone looked around for signs of trucks or airplanes, any kind of vehicle that could have brought this mountain to him.

Then Abu suddenly appeared, walking toward the doctor, carrying a large sack beneath each arm. The sun rose fully as Abu walked, as though trumpeting his arrival. Bertone raised one hand to shade his eyes, squinting through the harsh glare, half expecting this 'mirage' to disappear. But when Abu stood directly in front of him and dropped the sacks at his feet, the doctor knew it wasn't an illusion.

"As the sun rises," Abu said, looking at Bertone, then turned and walked into the tent to wake Williams and Bhaiji.

Commotion filled the camp as Bertone's jubilant staff quickly began ferrying the crates and sacks toward the tents. Bertone himself hastily inspected the boxes and stacks, looking for whatever markings might betray their origins. He couldn't stand not knowing where this astonishing windfall had come from. It was more food and medicine than he had ever seen delivered to any refugee camp anywhere. It must have taken enormous effort and manpower. How on earth did it get here? Who was the anonymous benefactor? Bertone hated mysteries.

He stood off to one side of the diminishing bounty of supplies and spotted Abu lifting a sack.

"Who sent all this? Where is it from?" Bertone asked.

Abu dropped his sack and walked up to the doctor, stopping just inches away from him. "Why is it so important, good doctor, that you know the origin of these supplies? It is not enough that they are here, and so desperately needed?"

"Who are you, *monsieur?*" Bertone demanded indignantly.

"I have told you who I am," Abu said calmly.

"Do not play games with me, *monsieur.* I must know where this came from."

Abu paused. "You are gravely mistaken when you said last night that God does not hear or see what is happening here, that God does not care about the suffering of these people. God does see, and God cares. You are a most powerful man, doctor, much more than you realize. These supplies have come because you have demanded that it be so. You are much more visible than you think. Your desire to help was like a beacon of energy that could not be ignored. I felt it, and so has God."

"I am a scientist, *Monsieur* Asghar. I do not believe in miracles."

Abu smiled. "Neither do I, doctor. But you are also a human being who sees and feels with his heart, and his soul. Your desire to help is as powerful as the need to survive is among these people. You have responded to that need, and through you, so has God."

"And what is your role in this, *monsieur?*" Bertone asked.

"Think of me merely as a broker, a middleman."

The doctor's attention was riveted on Abu, as if waiting for further explanation. "Your skepticism is healthy, Dr. Bertone. But do not let it make you cynical. For then, you will lose your ability to truly see." Abu bowed to the doctor and went back to the ever-decreasing mountain of crates and burlap sacks.

With small tins in hand, those who could stand beneath the hot sun waited patiently in line for their ration; those who could not had food brought to them. Bertone watched Abu, a short distance away, walking with a small group of children who were, for the first time that Bertone could remember, smiling and playfully tugging on Abu's robes.

As he stood watching, Williams came up to his side.

"How does he do it?" the doctor asked, not looking at Williams.

"I don't know, doc," Williams said, "I've been trying to figure that one out myself."

"Haven't you come to any conclusions?" Bertone's voice was almost pleading.

"I think," Williams offered, "that to Abu, reality is only a state of mind. To him, anything is possible. He has no doubts, he believes there are no limitations. Maybe that's what makes the impossible happen." Williams paused. Bertone looked at him curiously. "Perhaps Hamlet was right," Williams continued, "when he said, 'There are more things in heaven and earth, Horatio, than are dreamt of in your philosophy.' "

Bertone started walking toward the children's tent. "I shall try to remember that, *Monsieur* Williams," he called back.

CHAPTER 19

They were on the road once again, driving through Zaire, after having visited refugee camps in the Sudan which were interchangeable with the ones they'd been to in Ethiopia and Somalia. The tragic portrait was always, numbingly, the same. Only the canvas was different. Disease, starvation, atrocities, and premature death were the common lot of these vast African populations. And the children seemed to be its largest number of victims.

"You know, Abu," Williams said, venturing into unchartered waters in hopes of provoking him, "most of the industrialized world wonder why these people keep having so many children. I mean, overpopulation is a major threat to the entire world, but it's destroying this continent."

"What would you have me say?" Abu replied. "That black Africa is where the idea of family is as ancient as the land? That is true, but it is too easy. It's the same as in the West—children represent their dreams for a better tomorrow, children enable them to feel a connection to something greater than themselves."

Williams hesitated to say what he was thinking. "But it's selfish to bring a child into this world. In the West, at least a kid has a pretty good chance for a decent life. Here the chances are they're gonna watch 'em die."

"And that is the truth of it, Ben Williams. Harsh reality compels a man and woman to bear as many children as possible in order to ensure there will be enough who survive. It is not birth control that black Africa desperately needs, Ben Williams, it is assurance that the children who are born will live. In the West you take that assurance for granted."

Williams didn't respond. Abu continued. "Do you know what the leading cause of death is in most of Africa?"

"No," Williams answered.

"Measles. And there is only one doctor here for every fifteen thousand people," Abu added. "Coca-Cola is unaffordable for most, yet much easier to obtain than drinkable water. These people deserve their place at the table. It is time we recognize that the problems of the world are global. If we are going to solve them, we must sit down together and do what is necessary."

Williams stared at him. "Sounds like you're advocating some kind of world government." Abu said nothing. "Is that it? With you at the top, running it?" Williams asked.

There was a strange look in Abu's eyes, one Williams couldn't read. "When this comes to pass," Abu finally said, "when the pyramid is truly inverted, I will no longer be needed."

"Oh? And who will stop the despots from taking over?"

"The ones hungry for power and desperate to dominate others will always be a threat to guard against. But is that a reason not to move forward? A world government is not an end in itself, Ben Williams; merely one step in an ongoing process."

"What are you saying? That all this is part of some cosmic plan?"

"Yes, if you like."

"And that plan is what?"

"From the time humanity walked upright it has embarked upon the path of change—of evolution and growth. It has wavered on that path, and often stumbled. But it has always moved forward." Abu's voice was growing impassioned. "Humanity must continue on that path or it will cease to exist. That is its covenant with God."

They did not stop in Zaire, but crossed over into neighboring Uganda. The beauty and tranquility of the countryside belied the political turmoil that plagued the nation. What had once been known as the "Pearl of Africa" was now being called the "Land Beyond Sorrow."

Bhaiji found a place for them to camp for the night. It was along a river that fed into the mighty Nile. Here, for the first time, Williams experienced the Africa he had read and dreamed about for so many years. Hemingway's Africa. There were prides of lions and leopards, elephant herds, rhinoceros, giraffe and zebra, hippopotamus and gazelle, all roaming the plain, and easily spotted from their campsite. As they sat around a fire, eating a spicy dish of rice and beans that Satki has prepared, the sounds of the distant animals could be heard in the still twilight.

"Do you miss America at all?" Bhaiji asked.

Williams smiled. He hadn't thought about being homesick, until Bhaiji's question.

"Yeah, sometimes," he said.

"What do you miss most?" Satki asked.

Williams reflected for a moment. "Lazy summer afternoons, listening to baseball games on the radio, the smell of fresh-cut grass, backyard barbeques with ice cold beer and hamburgers, and Fourth of July fireworks, and Thanksgiving dinners and autumn weather when the leaves turn orange and red and yellow—it's very beautiful."

"Where is your favorite place in America?" Bhaiji asked.

"Well, New York is my home, and it's a great city, but when it closes in on me—when I have to get away—I go out West, to the Rocky Mountains." Williams stared off into the starry night sky as though looking at a distant projection. "To appreciate it, all you have to do is stand on a mountain ridge, surrounded by snow-capped peaks and watch a bald eagle silently descend from the blue sky and snatch a fish right out from the smooth surface of a lake with a simple, graceful flick of its talons." He shook his head. "The Indians who lived there used to say, 'Only the rocks live forever.' "

"What I know of America," Bhaiji said, "I have learned from your movies and television. Actors like John Wayne and Gary Cooper— they portrayed America at its best, no? The good guys against the bad guys. And eventually the good guys won, right? The choices were much clearer then, but now, I have seen on American television how much everything has changed."

"And what's your view on my country these days?" Williams asked.

"America is a place where ethics and morality are in a constant struggle against power and the pursuit of wealth. Everything is measured in money. America is a very rich country in material things, but I think very poor spiritually."

"Why, Bhaiji," Williams said with affection, "you're a philosopher." Bhaiji smiled shyly as Williams turned to Abu. "And how do you see America?"

Abu gazed out across the river. His tone was measured and there was an almost mystical look in his eyes. "Yours is a country that has abandoned its vision, a people who have forgotten their heritage.

Americans have squandered their precious gift, but it is still there, ready and waiting."

"What gift?"

"You once had a grand purpose—you worked together and sacrificed to build a great and powerful nation."

"So that was the gift, the pioneer spirit?" Williams asked.

"Oh, much more, Ben Williams. Americans had the courage to rebel against tyranny, to fight for liberty, freedom and justice. To create a political system that guaranteed fundamental human rights. But then, an obsession with materialism, competition and greed replaced the old values. Americans like to think of themselves as a generous people, but you rank at the bottom in foreign aid. What you spend on one Stealth bomber could feed all the starving of Ethiopia, Somalia and the Sudan. For the price of one MX missile, America could eradicate measles in all of Africa—"

"I know my country's not perfect," Williams interrupted, "but it's the best around." He heard the hollowness of his own words, yet felt the need to defend his country, not out of a sense of patriotism, but rather the hard fact that what he was saying was simply true.

"Do you remember your early public schooling, Ben Williams? When you said the Pledge of Allegiance every morning before class began?"

"Yes. Why?"

"Can you speak it for us?"

Williams looked up at the sky, as if searching for the words. "I pledge allegiance to the flag," he began tentatively, "of the United States of America, and to the republic for which it stands: One nation, under God, indivisible and with liberty and justice for all."

"And now, Ben Williams, to what do you give your allegiance? Now when you look at your country and what it has become, do you think it acts in accordance with those principles?"

Williams hesitated. "No," he finally said, "not very often."

"To be a nation under God is a lofty ideal," Abu said. "Such a nation must adhere to a self-imposed standard that is higher than for other countries. It must be more self-critical and be able to admit mistakes, learn from them, see that they are not repeated. It need not be perfect, but it must be willing to seek the truth of itself." Abu paused for a moment, then continued. "You Americans have a saying: 'If you are not part of the solution, you are part of the problem.' "

"But we do try to be part of the solution. We do call for an end to human injustice and misery—"

"Yes," Abu interrupted, his eyes flashing, "while all the time you are playing a chess game of geopolitics, supporting repressive dictators, turning a blind eye to the suffering on the planet, to the ethnic cleansing and the intolerable violence. America hides behind a great war machine and allows its rich and powerful citizens to own the country's politicians." Williams couldn't deny the truth of Abu's words.

"And where do you think all this will lead?" Williams asked.

"The changes that are sweeping the planet and causing great upheaval and pain will also one day produce a fruit that will taste sweeter than anything humanity has ever known. America can lead the world into the next century and create a free and just society for all people. How America responds now is most important."

"And if it resists?" Williams asked.

"Then it will inflict great pain and suffering upon the rest of humanity before the new epoch dawns. That is what I need you to understand; it is vitally important that you do."

There was silence around the campfire, broken only by the deep, proud roar of a distant lion.

Before Williams fell asleep, he lay on his blanket and studied the night sky. In the constellation of Taurus was a star that seemed to shine with greater luminosity than any other around it. Then, as Williams watched it with fascination, it suddenly expanded for a few seconds, and shone even brighter. Just as quickly it shrank back to its normal size, but as it did, Williams felt a wave of exhilaration and joy flow through him, as if he'd been zapped by a sudden burst of energy that emanated from the star itself. For those brief moments, it made him feel better than he had ever felt in his entire life.

He immediately sat up, still looking at the star, hoping it might do it again. After a moment or two, he lowered himself back down on his blanket and began to doubt it had really happened. As he turned to make himself more comfortable, he saw Abu looking at him from the other side of the fading campfire, leaning on one elbow. There was an odd smile on Abu's face. Without a word, Abu turned his back away from the fire and went to sleep.

The next morning they arrived in an area of Uganda that held the most fertile farmland in all of Africa. Williams couldn't help remarking on the beauty of the gently rolling hills and luxuriant foliage that he saw from the car window.

"I am afraid," Abu explained, "this is where nearly half a million Ugandans were beaten and tortured and murdered." Williams sat back in his seat, like a child who'd been properly chastised.

A few minutes later they reached the small town of Nakaseke. Standing alone in a field of tall elephant grass was a frail-looking man with a hoe resting against his shoulder, staring down at the ground.

Abu instructed Bhaiji to stop the Mercedes along the dirt shoulder of the road. "Come," Abu said to Williams. The two men got out of the car, Abu in the lead, striding quickly over to the Ugandan. When the man started to back away fearfully, Abu held up one hand and spoke to him in a Bantu dialect.

Standing next to the Ugandan, Abu pointed to the ground.

Williams recoiled as he looked down and saw a human skull and beside it a small pile of bones. Next to the bones were two old and rusted shock absorbers. The man spoke to Abu.

"What's he saying?" Williams asked.

"This is all that is left of his wife. Soldiers raped and killed her." Abu pointed to the rusty pair of shock absorbers. "With these, and then hacked her to pieces with machetes."

"Why?" Williams was incredulous.

"She was Baganda," Abu explained.

The man motioned for Abu and Williams to follow him. Then, using his hoe, he cleared away the grass to reveal another human skeleton. The man said something to Abu.

"This is his daughter," Abu said to Williams. "They shot her as she tried to escape. They raped her as well."

"Where was he?" Williams asked.

Abu asked the Baganda farmer who cried as he explained. Abu turned to Williams. "They held him and made him watch. Then they released him so he could run. They fired at him. One bullet hit him and the

146

soldiers left him for dead. But some neighboring farmers found him and saved his life."

"Why doesn't he bury his family?" Williams asked.

"Bagandans do not believe in burying a body that is not whole. The soldiers knew that."

Williams could no longer look at the horror at his feet. He felt his stomach turn, he thought he would cry as he watched the tears streaming down the man's weathered face. He looked at Abu. "Tell him . . . tell him I'm sorry," Williams said, and for a moment, as he hurried back to the car, a wave of guilt washed over him.

In town after town they encountered dead bodies in various states of decay, empty half-destroyed buildings with gruesome scenes of torture illustrated on their walls—the graffiti left behind by drunken soldiers who proudly painted lasting reminders of the atrocities they committed. In another village, in the middle of a dusty street, stood a fifty-foot long wooden table that was once used to display the vast array of fruits and vegetables grown in the area. Now, hundreds of human skulls were neatly stacked upon it, with stacks of larger bones carefully placed behind them. They had been collected from the nearby killing fields, and dozens more were being retrieved every day.

"Dear God," Williams said under his breath, as he and Abu walked along the side of the table.

A local farmer suddenly appeared from nowhere. "You are American?" he said, tugging at Williams' sleeve.

"Yes," Williams replied.

"Tell the world what has happened here!" he insisted. "This is all that is left of the people who once lived here—my family, my neighbors. Tell the world! Please tell them. Make it stop—please!"

Dumbfounded, Williams nodded. "I'll try," he said helplessly.

Back in the car, driving once more, Williams looked out the window and noticed people on foot and on bicycles, carrying bark-shrouded corpses on their way to burial.

"They are not victims of the soldiers," Abu said. "Most died of the disease they call "slim'." Satki gave a confused look. "AIDS," Abu said. "Others die of tuberculosis or some parasitic infection."

"Why are you doing this? Why are you showing me all this?" Williams demanded. He'd had enough.

"If Muhammad will not go to the mountain," Abu answered, "the mountain must come to Muhammad. Do you want to know what to tell your readers? Tell them what a barbarous, primitive world exists outside their shining city on the hill. And that it's coming closer and closer to them."

Williams looked Abu straight in the eye, trying to stare him down, but that, of course, was impossible. The corners of Abu's lips turned up in an ironic half-smile.

"And so, Ben Williams, again I ask: To what will you give your allegiance?"

CHAPTER 20

The Great Rift Valley of Kenya, with its massive, steep cliffs and bizarre rock formations, its fluorescent-colored mineral springs, active volcanoes and vast open savannahs, was home to herds of wildebeest, lions, cheetahs, jackals and hyenas. There were crocodiles and hippopotamuses, giraffes and baboons. And tens of thousands of flamingos that formed an enormous pink canopy as they flew over the region's lakes and rivers. The Valley was also home to the Masai, a warrior tribe that had, in the past, always commanded fear and respect from their enemies. The Masai were nomadic herdsmen—they roamed freely over the open plains, having no wish to own it, divide it or measure it.

"The British changed all that," Abu explained to Williams, as they drove through the bustling, skyscraper city of Nairobi, Kenya's capital. "They taught farming to the other local tribes, and the fine art of politics as well. The Masai resisted change and the encroachments of the modern world. They called the British railroad the 'black snake' and the 'iron rhinoceros.' They had no interest in government or cities or boundaries. They merely wanted freedom."

"And these other, more 'Westernized' tribes, have taken over the region?" Williams asked.

"Yes. The modern farmers have usurped what was once the domain of the Masai. They can no longer migrate over the vast distances between the rainy seasons, so they are forced to over graze the land. It is now dying, and they along with it. The predictions have all come to pass."

"What predictions?"

"The Masai were once united under a great spiritual leader, a laibon, who foretold of the terrible events that would occur. First a massive drought which decimated the Masai cattle herds, then a plague of smallpox killed thousands of their people, and finally, the hairy pink men arrived riding a black snake. They now pray for a new laibon who will deliver them from their suffering and restore their greatness."

Williams stared at Abu. "A new laibon . . . sort of a messiah?"

Abu looked at Williams but said nothing.

When they crossed over into neighboring Tanzania, Abu said to Williams, "I will show you another former Masai grazing land that is now forbidden to them. It is near something you want very much to see."

Williams was about to ask what that "something" was, when suddenly he spotted it. "There it is!" he cried out with child-like exuberance, and pointed to Mount Kilimanjaro. "'Wide as all the world, great, high, and unbelievably white in the sun'."

"How poetic, Ben," Satki said.

"Hemingway's description. Not mine."

Williams asked Bhaiji to stop the car so he could get out and look at the mountain for a few moments. Abu nodded to Bhaiji. Williams jumped out and stood on the shoulder of the road, staring in wonder at the mountain's snow-capped peak. It reminded him of a great collar of ermine on the shoulders of a king as he stood looking out over his realm. Kilimanjaro reflected the afternoon sun in shades of pink and purple.

Abu came up to him. "Look over there," he said, pointing toward the distance. "That is an extremely active volcano. It is where Enkai lives."

"Enkai?" Bhaiji asked as he walked up to Williams and Abu.

"The Masai name for God," Abu replied.

"They believe God lives in a volcano?" Williams asked.

"Yes. But she—"

"She?" Williams exclaimed. "Their god is a woman?"

Abu nodded. "And she exists in the trees, the air, the rain and the grasses of the plain. It is through the volcano, however, that she makes her will known." He tapped Williams on the shoulder. "Come, we must arrive at the manyatta before dark." Williams gave Abu a puzzled look. "It's the village where the Masai warriors live," Abu said.

Williams flashed a look of concern at Bhaiji, then at Satki.

When the Mercedes arrived at the manyatta, it was immediately surrounded by stern-faced warriors—or moran—as the Masai called them. They had shoulder-length dreadlocks and wore ochre-colored togas that accentuated their lean, muscular torsos. They carried cowhide shields and tall spears with elongated, double-edge blades that took up nearly half of the spear's shaft.

"Be careful what you say and do," Abu cautioned. "The Masai are suspicious of strangers."

Williams looked at the unsmiling faces surrounding them and at the pointed spears. "No problem," he said.

A great convocation had been called and hundreds of Masai were now gathering at this village to discuss important business. Abu, as tall as any of the warriors, but broader than most, placed his palms together and bowed to a handsome young man who had chiseled features, deep-set eyes and a strong jaw. There was an aristocratic and intelligent look about him. He was Tipilet Ole Simel, the son of the spiritual leader of the Masai.

"I seek your father, Menye Tipilet," Abu said, speaking the Masai language.

The young man eyed him warily. "And why do you seek Menye Tipilet?"

"Your father knows who I am, and why I have come. He is waiting."

Tipilet looked over at the Mercedes and its occupants. "And the *mzungu?*" he asked, gesturing toward Williams.

"He is an American journalist. He wants to tell the world about the plight of your people."

Tipilet studied Abu for a moment, then said, "I will take you to my father."

Abu motioned for the others to get out of the car. As Tipilet led the group into the manyatta, several warriors followed behind, spears pointing menacing at their backs. A group of women and children walked alongside, pointing at Williams and shouting, *"Mzungu, Mzungu!"*

"What's *Mzungu?*" Williams whispered to Abu.

Tipilet turned to Williams and spoke in perfect English. "It means white person. It is not a compliment."

Bhaiji turned to look back, alarmed as a number of moran and children were descending on his treasured possession.

"There is no need to worry," Tipilet said reassuringly. "They just wish to touch your vehicle."

"Is this the first time they've seen a car?" Williams asked.

Tipilet shot Williams a patronizing look. "We are aware of modern society's machinery, and we know about automobiles, but we find their fumes and noise greatly displeasing."

Williams pursued. "Then why the special interest in this one?"

"If there is anything the Masai respect," Tipilet replied, "it is power. And the emblem of a Mercedes-Benz is a symbol of power—it appears on army vehicles. In fact, Mr. Williams, the word 'Mercedes' is the only white man's word that many Masai ever bother to learn."

Tipilet led them past igloo-shaped huts made of cow dung and mud, surrounding a kraal, where scrawny cattle idly roamed within the thorny fences. Several warriors stood guard to protect their herd from lions and leopards. Abu leaned toward Williams. "The Masai believe that all the cattle on the face of the earth were given to them by Enkai, to watch over and care for."

Tipilet nodded in agreement. "Even when we take cattle from other tribes, we are merely reclaiming what is ours."

"How do you distinguish that from stealing?" Williams asked.

"We cannot steal what we already own, Mr. Williams."

Tipilet motioned for Abu and Williams to follow him into one of the large huts while Satki and Bhaiji remained outside. Masai women were clustered nearby, whispering among themselves and occasionally letting out shy little giggles. Satki smiled at them and went over to the children who, fascinated by her clothing, tugged at her and asked her to join in their play.

Inside the hut, the three men walked through a short corridor designed to keep out the wind, dust, and rain. They arrived at a cool, central chamber. It was dark; the only light came from an opening in the roof to allow smoke from the fire to exit. As Williams' eyes adjusted to the darkness, he could make out a group of old men seated in a half-circle on the floor. In the center, seated on a chair covered with animal skin, was a burly and uncompromising-looking man who peered through narrow, scrutinizing eyes. His closely-cropped hair and moustache were steel grey, his coal black skin was leathery. His earlobes, stretched in youth, now hung like loose bands anchored by heavy, beaded earrings. An azure-blue cloth cloaked his body over which he wore a leopard skin. A metallic, cylindrical baton rested in his hands. Intricately-beaded leather secured a chain at each end that looped around his neck. He held it proudly, like a king's scepter. Williams felt the scene before him was almost surreal.

"I am Menye Tipilet," the old man said in English.

"I am Abu 'Ali Asghar," Abu said, bowing to the great warrior. There was a long pause, then Menye Tipilet said, "You are the one Enkai told us would come?"

Williams eyes widened.

"Yes," Abu said matter-of-factly.

"You are not Masai," Menye Tipilet said with obvious disappointment.

"But I am a warrior, and it is the soul of the warrior that makes us one."

"And the *Mzungu?*" Menye Tipilet said with disdain, looking at Williams.

Williams adjusted his weight, trying not to look nervous or offended. Abu glanced at him, then back to the old man. "He is here to learn," Abu said. "And to write about what he sees."

The younger Tipilet snorted. "The lion and the white man are alike," he said. "They are to be respected, even feared because of their power. But they are never to be trusted. They also go crazy in the head and that makes them dangerous."

"This one has my respect," Abu said, "and my trust."

Menye Tipilet look at Williams. "We shall see," he said skeptically.

"Tell me of your message from Enkai," Abu prodded the chieftain. "You saw a light in the night sky, then a star grew very bright, is that not so?"

Williams instantly remembered the star he'd seen a few nights ago in Uganda. A shiver went down his spine. Was that why Abu smiled at him across the campfire?

Menye Tipilet nodded. "We felt it in our hearts, and from its power we knew we must gather now. It is a time of great sorrow for my people. The government has modern weapons and they will surely destroy us." Tipilet raised his head high, his chin jutting forward, his eyes blazing. "But we will die as Masai, as warriors. We will return to the Earth from which we were born. I am old, for me it does not matter." He looked over at his young son. "But our children will pay the greatest price."

"It is for them that I have come," Abu said. He turned to the younger Tipilet. "I will help you become a great laibon; I can show you another way of being the warrior, and the way by which the Masai can regain their power." Tipilet Ole Simel said nothing, suspicious of Abu's words. "Your name, Tipilet—it means 'New Dawn,' does it not?" Neither younger nor elder Tipilet responded. "I will help you lead your people into a new dawn," Abu continued. "You will possess much shade," he said, making reference to the ultimate proof of a great spiritual leader.

"Can you cause the skies to bring forth rain?" Tipilet challenged. "Can you make the plains green and the rivers flow so that our cattle can feed and produce fresh milk, so that our children are not sick and weak?"

Williams could feel the young man's smoldering rage just beneath the surface. The elders looked at Abu, eagerly awaiting his response. He turned back to Tipilet. "My brother," Abu said firmly, "I will do what you ask, if that is what you need. But know that there is little time for distrust between us." With that, Abu turned and walked quickly out of the hut.

Bhaiji looked at Williams. "Where is he going?"

"To do a rain dance," Williams said.

They both bowed to the old men in the hut and then left, followed out by the younger Tipilet. Williams turned to him. "You speak English very well," he said.

"I also speak French, German and Swahili," Tipilet said with a self-assurance that somehow avoided conceit. "We are not stupid people, Mr. Williams. Nor are we uneducated, although the education offered by the white man is of no particular value to us. When I was a boy, all I wanted to be was a herder and grow up to be a warrior, but my father sent me away to the white man's school. He foresaw the changes that would threaten our survival—he knew it was necessary for me to the know the white man's world. I attended Nairobi University and London University. It cost my father many cattle."

"You chose to come back?"

"Of course. This is my home," Tipilet said emphatically. "These are my people. You may think of us as ignorant and primitive, but I think it is the white man's world that is ignorant and primitive. You see the land as something to own and exploit, which you then destroy in the process. It wasn't until I lived in your world that I truly came to appreciate my own. You call your cities—with their crime and pollution and corruption—civilized. But to me, here is where it is truly civilized."

"But what about education and modern medicine?"

"Whose education? Whose medicines? Our laibon have medicine made from herbs and roots that can cure anything, except those diseases brought by the white man." Tipilet had become haughty.

"I suppose you're right about that," Williams conceded. "But your country's been ruled by a black government for over thirty years."

"They are white men in black skins," Tipilet said with disgust. "You cannot live by the white man's rules and be Masai. Your friend understands that; do you?"

"Not yet. But perhaps with your help—"

Tipilet nodded. "Yes. Another time. I have to go now. Tomorrow is an important day—new warriors are to be initiated. And there will be a lion hunt."

Williams looked surprised. "Isn't it illegal to hunt lions?"

"Yes," Tipilet said with a smile. "But is there a better way to die?" He turned and hurried away.

Williams walked past a group of Masai women who were constructing the ceremonial huts for the next day. Surrounded so completely by these people and their world, Williams suddenly felt transported back to another time and place—to the fascinating continent described in the books he'd read as a young boy.

Then, a sudden stillness fell upon the village. Tension filled the air. The women stopped working, the children ceased their play. Only the wind could be heard, as it whistled through the acacia trees and dried grasses. The cattle stirred in their pens. The Masai warriors looked at one another in anxious anticipation.

From the direction of the volcano, Williams could see Abu walking toward the manyatta. Above the volcano, ominous dark clouds were forming against the clear blue sky. The wind blew harder, leaves and branches whirled in a chaotic frenzy. Rolling thunder came from the direction of Enkai's home, following Abu as he drew nearer. Jesus, Williams thought, he's bringing the goddamn storm with him! The huge, black clouds blotted out the sun, turning day into night. Menye Tipilet and the elders emerged from their hut. Abu appeared to grow taller as he walked. His robe, blowing wide in the wind, seemed to merge with the clouds overhead. As he entered the village, thunder shook the ground and a large drop of water splattered at the feet of the younger Tipilet, followed by another, and another, until the heavens opened up and unleashed the rains that cascaded out of the clouds like a gigantic waterfall, cooling, cleansing and nurturing the parched earth.

The Masai celebrated nature's gift with loud excitement and joy. There would be green grass again, and milk would flow. The Masai would survive.

The rain pelted Williams' face as he grinned from ear to ear. Abu went up to the young Tipilet and his father.

"Perhaps now we can speak," he said. He went back into the hut. The elders followed.

CHAPTER 21

"My youngest brother was killed by the government police," Tipilet said to Williams. The two men were sitting in the Masai warrior's hut, beside a warm fire. Outside the rains continued to bring healing relief to the manyatta.

"Why did they kill him?" Williams asked.

"For taking his cattle into Olduvai Gorge. They were starving and he needed to find a place for them to graze. We are not farmers; our animals sustain us. If they die, so do we."

Williams nodded sympathetically, then smiled at Tipilet. "Tell me about becoming a warrior," he said. "How old were you?"

"I was fourteen. Since then, I have become the leader of the moran—the first among equals. Even the poorest family becomes wealthy when their son becomes moran: He will defend them and provide them with cattle. Moran have special privileges, immense freedom and are afforded great respect. We are forbidden to marry but we have many lovers—all Masai women lust after the moran." Tipilet noticed Williams' grin and he smiled back. "We live in warrior villages like this one, only in the company of other moran. A Masai warrior is very strong and has tremendous endurance—he can run forty or fifty miles a day without stopping. Above all, he is brave; he alone must face dangers that no other Masai has to concern himself with."

Williams tried to think of some American equivalent. The boy scouts? Hardly. The Marines? Not quite. "How did you qualify to be the leader of the moran?" Williams asked.

"I have killed more lions than any warrior in my age group. My first lion was a *simba marara*—they are the most powerful and dangerous of lions."

"Tell me what the initiation ceremony is like."

"A great deal of celebration and dancing. And, of course, I was circumcised." Williams looked at Tipilet in shock. Tipilet smiled.

"Do you know that the word 'moran' means 'one who is circumcised'?"

Williams shook his head. "And I suppose you . . . you had to . . . bear the pain."

"Of course. It is a young man's first demonstration of courage; he must not even wince or he will bring shame upon himself and his family."

Williams let out a low whistle. He shuddered trying to imagine the physical agony. "For days before the event," Tipilet continued, "the boy is ridiculed by his elders, told that he is weak and frightened. He is made to sharpen the knives that will be used to cut him. And to guard them from those who would steal them and dull them."

"Why in God's name would they do that?" Williams asked.

"To shame the boy and his family." Tipilet replied.

"The whole ritual sounds incredibly cruel."

"It is only through danger and cruelty that one's courage is tested."

"And now it's time to stop being a warrior?"

"Yes. It is time to assume responsibility as laibon."

At that moment, Abu entered the hut. He sat down beside Tipilet. "Is he learning?" he asked, gesturing toward Williams.

Tipilet smiled. "He is a good student, for a *mzungu.*"

Abu nodded, smiling. He sat down beside Tipilet. "I will tell you a story," Abu said in a voice as soft as the light that danced upon the hut's walls. "There was once a lion whose mother abandoned him at birth. He wandered alone, doing his best to survive. He had never seen another lion before and did not even know what they looked like. Desperate and starving, he came upon a flock of sheep and they took him in. They fed him milk and taught him how to graze. He learned to act and sound like a sheep, but in time, the lion grew large and powerful.

"Then, one day, along came another lion who eyed this one with despair, for he knew not the truth of himself. At first, the young lion was afraid of this stranger for the sheep had taught him to be wary of lions. But the other lion showed him that he only wanted to help the young lion discover himself. He tried to teach the young lion to roar, but all that came out was the bleat of a sheep. So the stranger took him to a pool of water and showed the young lion his reflection. At first he did not recognize himself and was frightened. Then he realized it was him and he marveled at his impressive head and body. Then the stranger gave the young lion a piece of meat. The lion did not like the taste and choked on it, but eventually swallowed it. The stranger gave him another piece of meat and this time it tasted better. Soon he realized that he liked the meat and it made him feel strong. Then, suddenly, he let forth a mighty roar, sending the other animals of the plain running in all directions. Then, the young lion and the stranger headed off together into the bush, leaving the sheep behind forever." Abu paused. "That is why I have come, my friend." Before Tipilet could say anything, Abu rose and left the hut.

The next morning, the entire manyatta was busily preparing for the ritual and celebration of the young boys who would become warriors that day. An army truck pulled up to just outside the village and a group of *askari,* well-armed soldiers, appeared.

Menye Tipilet came up to his son. "There can be no lion hunt," he said, pointing toward the soldiers. "They have permission to shoot any Masai warrior found hunting wild game, you know that."

The younger Tipilet looked at his father and shouted, "Without a lion hunt we are not warriors!" Other moran cheered him, jumping up and down and jabbing their spears into the air. Williams, Satki and Bhaiji watched apprehensively from a short distance away. They certainly did not want to witness a confrontation between the Masai and the military police.

"Spears are no match for bullets," Menye Tipilet said angrily. "Even if we killed all of them, more would come. It would give the government their best excuse for eliminating our people forever."

Abu suddenly appeared and went up to the father and son. "My friends, the Masai are the bravest warriors on earth, but what is needed is a new kind of warrior." He turned to Menye Tipilet. "Allow the hunt and I will show you what I mean."

The old man was pensive for a few moments, then nodded. The other moran began shouting and cheering. The hunting party was formed, with Abu in the lead and Williams and Bhaiji following behind the group of warriors. They headed out, walking the distance of a few miles to Olduvai Gorge. Williams' mouth and lips were parched, but he refused to drink because none of the Masai—nor Abu—seemed even slightly bothered by the heat.

And then the warrior at the very front of the line raised his spear into the air and stopped. He crouched down, followed by all the other moran. Williams looked up to see stiff-winged vultures circling patiently overhead. He watched the lead warrior gesture to Tipilet, and then Tipilet turn and silently signal for the other moran to fan out. Williams felt his stomach tense, his heart was racing.

Stooped over, Williams followed the warrior in front of him. He was suddenly aware of the noise he made in contrast to the quiet stealth of the Masai as he moved silently through the tall grass. When the moran had formed a huge circle, they all stood up.

There was an eerie calm that made Williams' skin crawl. He leaned toward Bhaiji. "Maybe it's a false alarm," Williams whispered.

"Oh, I doubt it," Bhaiji said.

Williams pictured a massive lion charging out from the tall grass right at him. His chest heaved, every muscle in his body was taut. As terrified as he was, Williams never felt more alive in his whole life.

And then a thunderous roar ripped through the still grass. Another roar followed, then another, in quick succession—too close together to have been made by just one animal.

The moran began whooping and dancing in place, some making guttural noises that mimicked the roar of the lion which was intended to confuse and scare the beast. Tipilet signaled and the circle began closing in. Caught up in the frenzy, Williams found himself jumping and whooping along with the warriors.

As the circle grew smaller, the lions could be heard more clearly and Williams soon smelled the sickeningly sweet odor of blood.

The lions could now be seen amidst the blond grass that camouflaged them so well. There were about ten of them—several males, a number of females and a few young cubs. The pride, although acutely aware of the moran, was feasting on a large zebra whose blood oozed from its slashed hide, its innards being torn by lion claw and teeth.

Williams suddenly remembered the *askari* and looked over in their direction. They weren't moving, just watching, but ready to intercede. Williams was glad because the Masai were as worked up as the hungry lions at that moment and would probably just as soon kill the *askari*.

Then, the dominant male of the pride, with a huge black mane and saber-like teeth, roared and lunged toward the moran.

"Simba marara! Simba marara!" Tipilet shouted excitedly. The other

moran echoed his shouts and Williams realized they were deliberately trying to provoke the lions into attacking. Killing a lion on the attack would bring the greatest honor to the warrior. The lions, their faces smeared with the blood of their kill, laid their ears back and roared, exposing pointed fangs and cavernous jaws. They angrily thrashed the air with their claws in defense of the spoils of their hunt. Williams' breath grew more rapid; sweat poured off him, he thought at any moment he might begin hyperventilating. He saw Abu glance over at the *askari* who were now moving in, just as the moran were closing their circle around the lions. Abu, unarmed except for the sheathed dagger buried in his robe, his bare hands hanging loosely at his sides, began walking, slowly, deliberately, calmly. He might as well have been taking a stroll through a meadow on a pleasant summer day, Williams thought.

Then, with lightning speed, the *simba marara* sprang toward Abu, its fangs bared, its huge paws swiping the air. Steadily and unyielding, Abu continued moving toward the lions, most of whom were now pacing in agitation, roaring and hissing with consummate feline ferocity. Abu's gaze stayed fixed on the dominant male. When he was a few feet away from the awesome beast, Abu stopped. It was suddenly dead quiet except for the wind through the grass. The *askari* watched. Bhaiji's eyes were wide with excitement and admiration. Williams stood more still than he would have thought possible; he knew he was witnessing a moment that transcended any perception he'd ever had of fearlessness. And of connectedness to all living things.

The great lion stopped roaring and stepped softly toward Abu. The two were like bronze statues, facing one another, their eyes speaking a silent language that both understood.

The hair on the *simba marara*'s back smoothed, his enormous muscles relaxed beneath his coat, his ears were no longer pinned back in anger. The rest of the pride were confused and continued to pace and eye the surrounding moran with intense suspicion.

It was then that Williams thought he must be dreaming—he watched as the *simba marara* rested on his hindquarters, gently raised a paw and preened his foreleg. Abu smiled and placed a hand on the lion's head in the way that a Masai warrior greets a child. The lion looked up at Abu and quickly rose on his hind legs and placed his front paws upon Abu's broad shoulders. He tenderly swabbed the side of Abu's face with his large coarse tongue, as if grooming him, one lion to another. Abu threw his head back and laughed, and slapped the lion's muscular shoulders with burly affection. The two stood together for a few moments like comrades in battle—victorious and united.

Abu stood back from the *simba marara* and walked among the other lions, rubbing each of them on their heads and patting their sides. The lions responded with gentle submission, rolling on their backs, while the cubs yapped and frolicked at Abu's feet.

The *askari*, still a safe distance away, watched in amazement. Abu walked around the circle of moran, challenging each warrior with his eyes. Then he went back to the *simba marara* and standing beside him, called to a stunned Tipilet, "Come meet your former enemy. He is now your new ally."

The Masai warriors watched their leader as he handed one of them his weapons. Tipilet slowly stepped into the circle and walked toward Abu and the lion. The animal eyed Tipilet ferociously and bolted toward the Masai with a bone-chilling roar. Tipilet stopped in his tracks. He remained motionless, swallowed hard and glanced at Abu. He desperately wanted to turn and run for his spear but to do so, and even kill the lion after a valiant fight, would now be seen as nothing more than cowardice.

"He smells your fear," Abu said to Tipilet. "That is why he sees you as a threat. But which do you fear more: Death or disgrace?"

Tipilet could feel the eyes of every warrior upon him, searing into his flesh. He stared only at the lion, afraid to look away for fear the animal would surely pounce and rip him to shreds. Out of the corner of his eye, as he moved toward the lion, Tipilet saw Abu smile at him. A sudden and unexpected surge of strength and confidence swept over him. He felt an exhilarating sense of freedom. And then, in a moment that would be retold by all Masai forever, Tipilet Ole Simel smiled. His fear had melted away, vanished, and it was replaced by a roaring laugh that sent the lion scampering back to Abu.

Williams stood transfixed. A few seconds ago, Tipilet had been prepared to be savagely mauled, even killed by the lion, and was now placing a hand on the formidable beast's head. The *simba marara* stood silent and calm, satisfied that his pride was no longer in jeopardy. The *askari* looked on, scratching their heads and exchanging animated reactions to the remarkable scene before them.

The moran began to sing in praise of their new laibon whose feat of courage was nothing short of miraculous. It would make the young Tipilet a legend among the Masai. The story of this day would be told over and over, spreading throughout Masailand and beyond. Whenever they spoke of their great warrior leader, the Masai would always add, *"Eta Oloip,"*—he had shade—and nod in unquestioned agreement.

When they returned to the manyatta, dozens of young girls ran out to greet them and guide them home. There was tremendous excitement and celebration as everyone learned of the day's events. In front of an immense fire, the singing and dancing continued into the night. Abu danced the dance of the Masai as if he were a native of the tribe. Satki beamed with delight and clapped her hands. Williams and Bhaiji hesitatingly accepted the moran invitation to join the dance. Williams did his best as several warriors laughed good-naturedly at the clumsy *mzungu* who possessed a clean heart.

Tipilet raised his hands and the drumming and singing and dancing stopped. He went over to Abu and embraced him. The moran whooped and hollered. Then Tipilet grabbed a beaded gourd and filled his mouth with cow's milk. He spat the white liquid directly into Abu's face in the ancient Masai custom which signaled respect. Abu took the gourd and repeated the ritual, spitting a mouthful of milk into Tipilet's face. The two men laughed and the celebrating continued with even more jubilation.

A short while later Abu raised his hands and the revelers grew silent. Only the crackling of the fire could be heard, and the sounds of the animals on the Serengeti plain. Abu's voice filled the night air. "My friends, when the sun rises, we must leave you, but we shall remain with you forever in spirit. Watch the night sky. There is a light growing brighter—it is the light of Enkai. It will lead us from darkness into a new dawn. It will illuminate the fears that live deep in the heart of humanity. Those who have not learned to master their fear will feel its terrible wrath; those who are warriors will bask in its warmth. Those who have lived as slaves will find freedom, those who have enslaved others shall feel the sharp blade of justice." Williams was trying to scribble down every word Abu said in the dim light of the fire. The Masai were whooping and nodding at Abu's prophecies. "The light will tell you when it is time, and you will feel the earth beneath you change. It is then we shall be united again."

The celebrating began again, and continued until daybreak. As the sun crept over the horizon, Abu, Williams, Satki and Bhaiji said their goodbyes to the Masai. Tipilet accompanied the group to the entrance of the village and the waiting Mercedes, now being guarded by several moran.

"I want to thank you," Williams said to Tipilet.

"Did you learn?" Tipilet asked.

"Yes," Williams answered.

"So did I," Tipilet said, nodding toward Abu. He turned back to Williams. "What will you tell your readers about the Masai?"

Williams thought for a moment. "What would you like me to tell them?"

Tipilet smiled. "Tell them . . . tell them that we are coming."

As the Mercedes pulled out of the manyatta and Williams could see Tipilet raise one hand in a final farewell, he pictured a hundred thousand Masai warriors, armed with modern weapons, marching in a precise phalanx. The image sent a terrifying chill down his spine.

CHAPTER 22

All across the African continent, bloody civil wars were ongoing. In the nation of South Africa, where the African National Congress went from revolution to ruling the country, rival parties were waiting in the wings, ready to grab power. Meanwhile, tribal feuds and constant conflict with the government and the military (in most instances, they were one and the same) had led to a wave of genocide, atrocities, disease and starvation unparalleled in the history of these countries. The millions who had been driven into refugee camps—crossing borders into temporarily safe havens in a neighboring country—were then rounded up by the militia and forced to return to their decimated countries. Tens of thousands had fled the soldiers by running off into the nearby hills and forests, without food or water. There seemed to be no solution to a catastrophe on so monumental a scale, no way to control the chaos that was taking over.

It was into these devastated countries that Abu and the others would stop for a brief day or two so that he could visit the local churches, mosques, hospitals and schools. Williams took the time to send off another article to Strunk. The editor no longer questioned Williams' lengthy stay in Africa; what he was writing about now was too important and too dramatic—the best damn stories Strunk had ever read. He found himself both horrified and fascinated by Williams' accounts of the overwhelming events that he was privy to. The Masai story— especially Williams' powerful and poetic description of Abu's confrontation with the *simba marara*—was absolutely spellbinding. Strunk now only worried that his journalist was a little too close to the action, to the danger. He genuinely feared for Williams' life.

As Bhaiji guided the Mercedes through a particularly war-torn region of Botswana, Satki and Williams viewed with horror the sights before them—the burned villages, demolished trucks, smoldering tanks and shattered artillery along the roadsides. Here and there the bloated bodies of dead soldiers and civilians littered the landscape, while endless columns of weary, frightened refugees trudged north. In the distance, the muffled explosions of gunfire were heard, and plumes of smoke drifted across the African sky. Abu remained silent and stoic during the slow journey when they often had to stop and let the advancing caravans of army trucks pass them on the road.

Satki was clearly disturbed by what she saw. "Abu," she said, breaking the solemn silence, "why do we go so far south?"

"There is one I must see," he answered.

"Are you protected, Abu?" Williams asked, half-facetiously.

"Yes."

"Then I hope you've got a big umbrella," Williams said. Bombs began exploding as they drew nearer to the fighting. "Tell me, Abu, do you ever envision a time when there will be no more wars?" Williams asked.

Abu nodded slowly. "One day there will be no need for war; it will become obsolete. It will serve no purpose because humanity will finally understand its own purpose in the universe's grand design. But we are a long way from that."

"So, you see us as pretty far down on the evolutionary ladder?" Williams asked rhetorically.

"I'm afraid so. First, humanity must learn to see itself as a reflection of the fear that exists within its collective consciousness. Right now, that awareness is at the level of the man who continually beats himself upon the head with a hammer simply because he doesn't know any other way to live, and because it feels so good when he stops. Human beings are still self-destructive, still their own worst enemy. Until that changes, war will remain the method of choice for conflict resolution, and as a curative for many of society's ills."

"Such as?" Williams asked.

"It decreases the population, puts people to work, produces technological advances, provides new economic markets for the victor, creates heroes to be emulated and admired. But above all, it furnishes an outlet for the fear that drives the lives of almost every human being on the planet."

"And is there no such thing as a just war, like our World War Two or the American War of Independence?" Williams asked.

"Wars are fought for many reasons, and from a historical perspective you could argue that if the cause is worth dying for, if it ends persecution and oppression, then it is just. But that is only because humanity hasn't quite figured out how else to right its wrongs. All war is absurd, and destructive. And unenlightened." Abu looked out the window at the refugees.

"And too many innocent suffer and die," Williams said.

"Indeed, too many innocent suffer and die," Abu echoed. "It is because of them that the foundation must be laid for a new order."

"And so, Abu, I'm not quite clear on this yet: Are you here to end war or make war?" It was a question Williams had been burning to ask for months, ever since he first heard Abu exhorting the Muslim masses in the mosques.

Abu paused, staring out at the throngs of people on the road. "I shall be the hammer."

As dusk approached, Bhaiji suddenly noticed something up ahead and began slowing down. He glanced over at Abu. A few hundred yards away Williams could make out a sentry point manned by a dozen soldiers. Two of them were standing in the middle of the road, their rifles raised.

"What shall I do?" Bhaiji asked nervously.

"I would suggest we stop," Abu answered.

The soldiers surrounded the car the moment it came to a halt. "Abuji?" Bhaiji asked, clearly seeking guidance.

"Just do as I say," Abu replied calmly.

One of the soldiers yelled something in Tswana and the others raised their weapons and pointed them at the group in the car. For one wild moment, Williams thought maybe they only wanted the vehicle—it was, after all, a Mercedes. But then he heard Abu say, "He would like us to get out of the car, and I recommend we do so, slowly." The others moved exactly as Abu did. The officer shouted and gestured with his gun. Abu translated. "He wants us to stand at the side of the road, in this field, and requests that we put our hands behind our heads." Williams doubted the officer had been quite that polite. Abu clasped his hands behind his turban, the others on the back of their heads.

Two soldiers kept their weapons pointed at the group. Bhaiji said a silent prayer as he saw several other soldiers open the car and begin searching under the seats, opening the trunk, rifling through its contents.

When the soldiers were finished, an officer barked more orders. Abu responded in Tswana. The officer shouted at Abu and waved his pistol in Abu's face. Williams wondered if Abu had pushed his luck too far. Then, without warning, the officer brought the butt of his pistol down across Abu's forehead, knocking him to his knees.

"Abu—!" Satki cried out and went toward her son. But before she could do anything, another soldier stuck the barrel of his rifle in her face.

"Do not worry, mother," Abu said. Blood was running down his cheeks, into his beard. "They are merely afraid."

"Good," Williams muttered under his breath. "We've really got 'em where we want 'em." At that moment the officer shouted something at Williams and waved his pistol toward him. "Look," Williams said, "I'm an American—"

The officer brought the butt of his pistol down on Williams' head. Everything went dark. Williams staggered and fell to the ground. He could hear voices and felt warm blood spreading down the side of his face. He heard the sputtering of automatic rifles. "God no," he gasped. The sounds faded as total darkness enveloped him.

When Williams awoke, he was lying in a room, face down on a dirt floor. He was blindfolded and his hands were tied behind his back. The barren earth was cool and damp and smelled of urine.

Suddenly, a door opened and sunlight streamed in. He heard Abu's familiar voice, as someone else removed his blindfold and untied his hands.

"Are you all right, my friend?"

"Thank God," Williams said. "I thought they killed you."

"It is not yet time for me to die, Ben Williams."

"Excuse me, *sahib,* I forgot who I was talking to. Guess I'll live to fight another day, too," Williams said as Abu helped him up. Williams squinted in the harsh light and saw an imposing black man wearing a red beret, standing alongside Abu.

"Meet an old friend of mine," Abu said to Williams. "He is General Mubambo."

The name instantly registered; he hoped his face didn't betray his surprise. Williams remembered his conversation with Jack Whatley about the Botswanan who had been in Dartmoor Prison with Abu and how he'd become Abu's chief lieutenant in those terrible days.

"Luxurious accommodations you have here, General. And the welcoming committee couldn't have been more hospitable." Williams tried in vain to brush off the dirt and dust that covered his pants and shirt.

"I apologize for your treatment, Mr. Williams, but these are wartime conditions. My men are suspicious of strangers, particularly white ones. You could have been a CIA spy for all they knew."

"Oh that's rich," Williams snickered. He felt the bruise on his forehead and winced. "A CIA spy wouldn't be smart enough to pass as a journalist."

"Well, certainly not one from the *New York Times*," Mubambo said and let out a booming laugh. "Come, let's get you out of here and to more 'luxurious accommodations.' "

When they walked outside, Williams realized they were at a large army base. Uniformed soldiers were everywhere; tanks, jeeps, plane hangars, artillery, rows of wooden buildings. Along the barbed wire perimeter of the compound, soldiers were hunkered down in sandbag machine-gun nests.

"General Mubambo is the Supreme Commander of the Botswanan Army," Abu explained to Williams.

"Very impressive, General," Williams said. "You've come a long way from Dartmoor Prison."

Abu and Mubambo exchanged surprised looks. Then Mubambo laughed. "Are you sure you're not a CIA spy, Mr. Williams?"

"Just a reporter who does his homework."

"Yes, Mr. Williams, I am a long way from my notorious past. And all because of this man," Mubambo said, placing a hand on Abu's shoulder as they walked.

"Another student of yours?" Williams asked Abu.

"Oh indeed," Mubambo said before Abu could reply.

"And what did you learn, General?"

169

"I learned that it is not so important to know who you will become than who you will not be."

"And who is that, General?"

"Another man's slave. That is why I do what I do."

"With all due respect, General, what you seem to be doing here is a great deal of brutality and senseless killing," Williams said in a voice rising with passion. "What in your mind justifies so much carnage?"

"In great part it is the legacy of apartheid—division and distrust. Political alliances have now collapsed. The old tribal conflicts resurfaced. The revolution that brought down the white government became a victim of unfulfilled expectations."

"But aren't you just perpetuating that victimization?" Williams asked.

The group was now seated in Mubambo's barracks headquarters, around a large table where a meal consisting mainly of army rations was being served to them by other soldiers. Mubambo turned to Satki, "For you, dear lady, I deeply regret we have nothing better to offer."

"Please don't apologize, General. With all the starvation we've seen, I'm just grateful to have something to put in my stomach."

Mubambo turned back to Williams. "When I first returned to Botswana, Mr. Williams, I took up arms against the injustices of the white ruling minority. It was not a preferred solution but until there is another way, it is how it must be done. Today, conflict and chaos threaten to undo everything we fought for. The system of hatred must be vanquished. That is the enemy I oppose. I do not enjoy war, Mr. Williams, but I cannot and will not allow the legacy of evil to continue."

"So you kill to stop the killing? That's insane."

"Is it, Mr. Williams?" Mubambo asked. He studied the journalist for a long moment. "Let us suppose you are walking down a street and you see a man brutally beating a child. What would you do?"

"I'd try to stop him."

"Why?"

"Because he has no right to beat the child."

"And how would you stop him?"

"I'd try to reason with him."

Mubambo laughed cynically. "Reason with a man who is brutally beating a child? That is very civilized of you, Mr. Williams. Suppose he refuses to listen?"

170

"I'd call the police."

"While he continues to beat the child. *Tsk, tsk,* Mr. Williams. And if the police refuse to come, then what would you do?"

Williams could see where this was leading, but he knew he couldn't back down. "I'd try to stop him any way I could."

"With violence?"

"I suppose . . . if necessary."

"Would you kill him?"

Williams pondered the question. "That depends."

"And so, with each choice, you escalate your involvement until you and he are locked in mortal combat. And then you kill him. Does that make you a murderer?"

"Not necessarily. Society's laws provide for such exigencies."

"Whose laws? American? South African?"

Williams was uncomfortable; he felt like a trapped animal. "Natural law then, the law of human decency."

Mubambo leaned forward; his irritation no longer concealed. "Show me such a law, Mr. Williams. Where is it written?"

"It's an unwritten law. It stems from accepted standards of human conduct."

"Then I submit, Mr. Williams, that if human conduct defines the laws under which we are governed, the man who beats the child is acting legally, and you are the criminal because you interfered. If human conduct defines the law, war is the law."

"That is sick, twisted logic. You are no different from those you fight, no different from the white South Africans."

"Mr. Williams," Mubambo said, his voice growing tired. "I employ the only means humanity has left me. And you, too, Mr. Williams, given a certain set of circumstances, you would choose to stop violence with violence. An eye for an eye, as your Bible defines justice."

"The way things are now, in this part of the world, might makes right, isn't that true, General?"

"No," Mubambo shot back. "But might determines what will be."

"But who gets to decide? You?"

"Yes. I do not believe that Allah alone determines our fate. Allah merely provides us with opportunities to test our beliefs. We create our own destinies."

Williams glanced at Abu, realizing that the African general had indeed learned from his mentor and fellow prison inmate. Abu looked at both men with a slightly bemused expression. "Perhaps Ben Williams will expand on all of this in his book."

Bhaiji looked surprised. "What book?"

"The one Ben Williams is going to write," Abu replied.

"Well, it's just an idea at this point," Williams confessed, "that's all."

"But the seeds have been planted," Abu said. "Be glad; it will make you famous." Before Williams could respond, Abu had turned to Mubambo. "General," Abu said, his voice solemn and resolute, "we can only stay here a few more days. I want you to invite the leaders of the various black factions to come and meet with you."

"All of them?" asked a surprised Mubambo. Abu nodded. Mubambo studied Abu for a moment. "What reason shall I give?"

"I will leave that to you. It need not be important. They will know it is necessary to come because your invitation will coincide with thoughts they have been having on their own."

"I see. Yes, of course, I'll do it right away."

"Good. Then I will bid you each goodnight," Abu said, his voice softening.

Mubambo rose too, and offered to escort Bhaiji, Satki and Williams to their rooms, apologizing again to Satki for the minimal amenities. "General, I am so tired I could probably sleep in that cell that Ben was put into," she said with a weary laugh.

Williams remained seated. "Ben, aren't you coming?" Bhaiji asked.

"Soon. I want to sit here for a while. Sleep well."

When the others had left the room, Williams got up and walked outside. He leaned against the shingle exterior of the one-story building, lit a cigarette and looked up at the night sky, searching for the star that had shown so brightly in Uganda. He thought he found it. There was one that shone brighter than the others, but he wasn't sure.

"Can't be sure of anything these days," he said aloud to no one in particular. "Not anything, anymore."

CHAPTER 23

Within a few days, convoys of cars and trucks began appearing at the military base carrying the leaders of the warring factions, along with the official aide to the South African president. The meeting Abu had requested took place beneath the large tent that was normally used as the camp's main mess hall. Tables had been arranged in a "U" shape. A row of lights dangled along the center of the tent, beneath which a swarm of small insects gathered in the humid night air. Abu and Mubambo sat at the closed end of the tables, and on either side of them sat Mubambo's aides. Williams, Bhaiji and Satki sat behind them, in the shadows.

Like the discordant sounds of a symphony orchestra tuning up, the voices in the tent reverberated throughout the compound. When Mubambo rose from his chair, an expectant hush fell upon the assembly.

"I bid you all welcome and wish to thank you for coming," the general's voice boomed out. "This is not an official meeting; I'm not acting on behalf of my government—"

"Then why have you brought us here?" one of the leaders called out.

"So that we can sit together, as brothers, and bring an end to the wars in this region." Mubambo scanned the faces around the tables. "And to introduce you to Abu 'Ali Asghar," Mubambo said, nodding toward Abu, "a man who has my deepest respect and admiration. I ask that you to listen to what he has to say."

As Mubambo took his seat, Abu stood up. Williams noted that he seemed even taller than usual. "My friends," Abu began, "it is time for you to unite and bring peace and justice to this stricken land."

"Who are you to tell us what we have to do!?" shouted one of the Pan Africanists. "Are you South African? If not, this is none of your affair!"

"I hold allegiance to no one nation," Abu said calmly. There were murmurs in the room, then a cacophony of voices began jarring the air. Abu held his hands up for silence. "My allegiance is to humanity. My only purpose is to unite humanity as one race, one people. I seek to establish a new world order and I am here in search of warriors who will join me in that crusade."

The gathering was quiet again. Outside, soldiers stood in rapt silence, listening. In the tent, Abu's eyes searched those of the leaders. "Do you not see the profound changes underway upon this planet?" he said, his tone impatient, demanding.

He pushed his chair out of his way and began to walk the length of the tables, his gaze riveted on the leaders as he walked past them, slowly, deliberately, like a well-seasoned trial lawyer making an impassioned plea to the jury. "Or are you so mired in your earthly ambitions that you are blinded to everything else occurring in the world?" He paced around the tent, stopping only to lock his eyes on one representative or another for a fleeting moment so that his point was made all the more personal. His tone turned conciliatory. "You are leaders of your people; your revolution would not have been possible if not for the fundamental changes happening." Some of the men in the audience turned to one another with puzzled looks, other stared at Abu, mesmerized by his words.

"There is a light in the sky that is growing brighter with each passing day. It is an enigma to astronomers and scientists; it is a beacon of visible energy being directed at this planet from deep within our galaxy. A celestial spotlight has been placed on humanity, forcing us to see ourselves in a way we have never seen before; it is illuminating all the misery and suffering, all the horrifying and barbaric human behavior, all the fear and despair—all that is borne of hatred and greed is being brought from the dark shadows and into the bright pure light. It is meant to show us how we have been, and to make us realize that it is now time to end this madness and move on to the next step in the profound process we call evolution. Have you not noticed the acceleration of changing world events? It is because the universe itself wants us to move faster, wants us to reach that which we desire, sooner."

Williams was fascinated by Abu's words. They made sense. Look at what had happened on the world stage in just the last decade—the demise of old world orders, the shifts in the balance of power, more technological advances than ever before and yet more environmental disaster, more disease, mass starvation, violent crime and global wars. Historic and cataclysmic events had been occurring with the dizzying speed of a runaway train, faster than our ability to comprehend them.

"And now," Abu said, his voice sounding operatic in its resonance, "due in large measure to instantaneous communication, it is no longer possible to deny what is happening, or to hide from it. All of humanity—the very planet itself—has a great yearning to finally be done with the pain and fear and violence, to go beyond it. The world you live in today is merely a reflection of each and every one of you. It is based on the choices you have made for many millennia. Are you going to let them continue? Evolution knows there is no turning back, that there is no movement but forward. We must go forward in peace."

Every man in the tent was now either gazing at Abu in awe or nodding in agreement. "There are many in the world who predicted that without the white man's control, the black man would turn on his brother, that you yourselves would become tyrants and punish those who oppose you." Abu's listeners shifted uncomfortably in their seats. Abu raised his large hands in the air. "And were they not right? You have been given a light to illuminate the brutality and slavery that still exists in your countries and to courageously say, 'NO MORE!' To take that light and show the world that you can live in peace and harmony." Abu's voice turned angry, demanding. "You must put aside your anger—it comes only from your ancient belief of being inferior to the white man. You have nurtured that fear into a hatred so strong that it blinds you, makes you see enemies everywhere. You burn each other's homes, kill each other's families, bring ruin to the people in whose name you fight. Do you not see that you are still serving apartheid? You must cease focusing on the differences between you and seek what is common between you. The greatest of the coming changes is the end of tyranny. If you seek power because you believe that you alone hold the truth, then you are a tyrant. The consciousness of humanity must now see its connection to the universe, and the universal family to which we all belong."

Abu scanned the faces of the African leaders one more time. "You have much to do; the choice of how to do it is yours." Then placing his hands together, he bowed to the gathering.

Later that evening, Abu stood alone near the camp's perimeter, staring up at the stars. He didn't turn to see who was approaching when he heard the sound of crackling twigs and brush behind him. The man came up to Abu, stopped and gazed with him at the starry sky.

"Quite fantastic," Muthezi Kansala, the South African leader said softly. "The potential of the human mind is so vast, like the universe itself. Yet we can barely appreciate either one."

Abu turned to Kansala, almost pleading. "That is what makes everything we do here so important. There will never be another moment like this one—it is like a raw gem taken from one of your country's diamond mines; it must be cut and shaped into something precious and lasting, or be of no value at all."

Muthezi Kansala took a deep breath, continuing to look up at the sky. "These are extreme times for my country, Sheik Asghar. The fires of my own hatred have long softened to a simmering anger, and a deep sadness. But then I am an old man. Half my country's population is under twenty years of age; they lack patience. They want vengeance more than justice, soldiers in a great cause of liberation."

"Your leaders need unity of purpose, and discipline among themselves."

"How is that possible?" Kansala asked with an ironic laugh.

"Emphasize the commonness between you."

"But all of us want something different."

"Only in appearance."

"I have tried before, many times—"

"Allow me to suggest," Abu interrupted, "that you use what you do not want as a starting point. You will discover that each of you do not want the same thing. Build upon that—it will lead to a common ground. Then solidarity will be possible."

Kansala stared at Abu for a moment. "I shall consider what you have said, Sheik Asghar. And now I bid you goodnight."

Abu nodded. "Goodnight, Mr. Kansala. May you dream of a better tomorrow."

The next day, Muthezi Kansala asked General Mubambo to convene another meeting of the African leaders. It lasted for several days. Bitterness, anger, and mistrust spewed out in venomous words, hurled like spears at perceived enemies. Williams sat on the sidelines, watching and taking copious notes, and finding it almost impossible to keep up with all the sound and fury.

At one point, Williams went up to Abu who was mediating the assembly and asked, "Doesn't South Africa have one of the best equipped armies in all of Africa, maybe in the world?"

"I believe they do, Ben Williams."

"And nuclear weapons."

Abu nodded. "They also have the precious minerals needed by the West to survive militarily and industrially, and over half of all the gold exported to the world each year. And when paper currency soon becomes obsolete, gold will be one of the few commodities of agreed value. That and oil."

"Sonofabitch!" Williams hissed. "That's part of your plan, isn't it?" He recalled a dream he'd had a few weeks ago where he saw Abu being carried on the shoulders of frenzied worshipers, and the beast with ten heads, and a mushroom cloud looming in the background. "That's why you're here. You don't give a rat's ass about these people!"

Abu looked at Williams unperturbed. "I am just one man, just as you. I am simply fulfilling my part, just as you."

"And what part is that?" Williams asked defensively.

"I told you, I will be the hammer. But remember, Ben Williams, a hammer is used to build, as well as destroy. And sometimes you have to do one in order to do the other."

"You are mad," Williams said.

Abu looked Williams directly in the eye. "From the beginning you perceived that in me there was a story to tell. You sought me out. What drove you was your need to win a Pulitzer prize, to be recognized as a great journalist. You can leave right now if you choose. But there are many others waiting to sell their souls for this exclusive. What will you do?"

Abu's words ricocheted in Williams' mind, making him realize his own thinly-veiled hypocrisy. He was willing to risk everything to be part of Abu's story. He hadn't followed him this long because of his love for humanity.

As if reading his thoughts, Abu smiled. "I thought so." Abu turned his attention back to the assembled representatives and their contentious wrangling.

After several more days of meetings, the fierce and dogmatic leaders were drained of energy, and even of desire to continue their verbal warring. A calm rationalism began to emerge and soon prevail over the gathering. Abu spent time with each leader in his respective tent, walking and eating with him, quietly listening and compassionately responding, and always making practical suggestions. Little by little, the Africans began to see their common purpose. A last meeting was held and reconciliation took place. A new pact was forged; the combatants agreed to lay down their arms. For the first time in history, these men embraced in a spirit of unity.

Abu congratulated them, and told them, "There are almost thirty million people in your nation that await you. You have created a new government here. Now it is time to go before your people and demonstrate your unity."

"Come with us, Sheik Asghar," Kansala shouted. "Stand with us." The others joined in his plea.

Abu placed his palms together and bowed. "As you wish," he said humbly. "I am your servant."

The gathering, led by Abu, left the tent. Mubambo was still there. Williams came up behind him. *"Déjà vu,* eh, General?"

Mubambo turned. "Ah, Mr. Williams. I didn't know you were here."

"Looks like you're being promoted, from Abu's chief lieutenant to his Supreme Commander. What's next? The world?"

"The future is what it will be, Mr. Williams."

"But you and Abu have no doubt worked out a plan. Right?"

"Perhaps. But to find out, you will have to wait and see. There are no more exclusives for you, Mr. Williams." Mubambo placed his beret on his head and tucked his baton under his arm. He marched out of the tent, leaving a perplexed Bennett Williams behind.

In Johannesburg, South Africa's largest city and unofficial capital—the new government proclaimed it to be the site of a mass celebration. What had happened in Botswana would now be the cry heard 'round the world. But before the international media converged on Johannesburg, Williams had already sent his exclusive story to Strunk. It would, however, be his last scoop.

Newspaper headlines around the globe heralded the great event. "PEACE IN SOUTH AFRICA—CIVIL WAR ENDS" proclaimed the media, and in the telling of the story, Abu 'Ali Asghar emerged as the man who had done what no one else could do.

Abu's efforts had been remarkable, the results were nothing short of a miracle; he appeared to be the greatest humanitarian anyone had ever seen. But appearances can be deceiving, Williams thought, and behind all the miraculous events Abu was fostering there was something sinister in the making. Something evil will hatch out, Williams kept thinking.

The celebrations began throughout Johannesburg. At one park, where two hundred thousand people had converged on an enormous grassy expanse, loudspeakers blared out Muthezi Kansala's introduction to Abu. When Abu stood up and raised his arms, the audience cheered him with a deafening roar that lasted twenty minutes.

"People of South Africa," Abu shouted into the microphone, "I stand in awe and with deep admiration for you and the men with whom I share this platform." Abu paused and waited for the audience to quiet down. "What you have taught the world, my friends, is that tyranny is an evil demon and will be exorcized from this world. You have overcome your differences and shown the overwhelming strength of unity. You are symbols of the power of the human spirit." Shouting and singing broke the stillness of the early evening air. Abu called for silence.

"But, my friends, do not rest on your victory. Look outward to the world, extend your wisdom and strength to those who are oppressed by evil masters, to those who yearn for freedom and justice. I humbly ask you to join me in continuing this quest. Together we will change the world!" He raised his fist into the air. *"Amandla!"* (Power!) he shouted, using the African National Congress's rallying cry.

"Awethu!" The crowd roared back the Bantu word for "to the people."

"AMANDLA!" Abu cried out.

"AWETHU!" the people responded.

As the chanting continued, Abu stepped back from the microphone and bowed deeply to the immense crowd. Then they began chanting his name. He turned to the other leaders on the platform and acknowledged their adoration. The international news media filmed and photographed and wrote of the momentous event and, in particular, of the legendary man who possessed extraordinary power and magic.

But during the days and weeks that followed, the new government fell into disarray; public utilities were inoperative, its manufacturing facilities, mining operations, refineries and transportation system were idle. Money from the West, desperately needed to jump start the nation's industries, was not forthcoming. Frustration and fear of failure were felt by both the leadership and the general population. Angry demonstrations filled the streets, while in the government buildings, rival factions began jockeying for position, and plotting a second revolution.

Williams felt he was witnessing the birth of a new nation and wondered if this was what it had been like for America's founding fathers.

Abu stepped in to mediate, to help bring about compromise and resolve the disputes that ranged from the petty to the profoundly serious. At last, when the arguments began turning into agreements, and the nation was finally on the road to recovery, financial suitors from around the world arrived with offers of aid and investment. America, Japan, and the European community came courting. Even Cuba and Libya sent envoys. And each of the suitors had a friend in the government. Many of South Africa's leaders became concerned.

"These money lenders," one minister charged, "they are scavengers, here to mortgage our country and make us their slaves once again."

Abu responded in a tone both blunt and decisive. "You are part of a complex interdependent system of countries—isolation is no longer an option. Your people must not only become involved in the rebuilding of their country, but it is now time for them to become involved in the whole world."

Another member of the group stood up. "Sheik Asghar, what you are proposing will lead to disaster for us. We will simply be replacing one master with another."

"Do you know the difference between the slave and the master?" Abu countered.

"The master is free, the slave is not," the council member replied.

"Not quite," Abu pointed out. "The master thinks he is the master, the slave knows he is not. As in all things, it is a matter of perception. Your fear of enslavement is rooted in the past; I am not asking you to forget that past, but to not remain a prisoner of it. Know in your hearts that you are not slaves, that you will never be slaves, and you can never be slaves."

There was nodding agreement and even a few of the officials present applauded Abu's words. "What is it you would have us do?" one of the men asked.

Abu wasted no time. "Some hard facts, gentlemen. You have an enormous supply of cheap, unskilled labor, but because under apartheid so many were denied a decent education, there are very few who can manage the banks, run the manufacturing industry, the mines and nuclear power plants. Where are your engineers to supervise the rebuilding of bridges, dams, roads, and transportation systems? You need hospitals, schools, universities—who will design them? You need doctors, nurses, teachers—where will they come from?" Abu looked from member to member, his eyes riveted on their faces. "If you close the door to outside help, you will hold your country back. Besides, the West needs you—needs South Africa's strategic minerals. When world currencies collapse in the global depression that is on the horizon, your gold will become even more valuable. Seize the opportunity, gentlemen, and you can make South Africa one of the major powers in the world. Or you can let it slip into anarchy and ruin."

There was a palpable silence in the room. Abu scanned the faces around him and smiled. "To govern is a difficult task. First you must learn to govern yourselves. Then you will be warriors, and able to face what will come." Abu put his hands together and bowed to the group. *"Amandla,"* he said, his voice soft as velvet, strong as steel.

Williams watched silently as Abu left the room, then looked at the gathering, all the members now animatedly talking to one another. Did they completely trust Abu? Would they follow his dictates? And where was he leading them—into a great new dawning or into a fiery abyss?

CHAPTER 24

They left Johannesburg that same day, returning to Mubambo's camp in Botswana. Abu and the general immediately sequestered themselves in Mubambo's tent for several hours. Williams desperately wanted to be privy to their conversation; after all, things were starting to gel—hell, they were starting to really cook. He loitered near Mubambo's tent like a beggar waiting for a handout.

When Abu finally emerged, Williams fell in step with him as Abu strode across the compound. "What's happening, Abu?" Williams asked almost defensively. Ever since they first came to Botswana, he felt he was being pushed aside, excluded.

"We are going to Gaberone," Abu said flatly.

"To the capital? Why?"

"There is something I must do there," Abu answered coolly.

"Care to clue me in?"

"No," Abu replied and headed into his tent.

Williams heard loud sounds and turned around to see Mubambo barking orders to several of his aides. There was an instant flurry of activity within the camp.

An hour later, a small caravan of military vehicles and the Mercedes-Benz were heading toward Gaberone. Mubambo rode in a jeep equipped with a large machine gun mounted on its rear. A heavily camouflaged truck carried Mubambo's elite Praetorian guard. The capital city had been well-defended by Botswana's small army, but even so, it showed the ravages of recent missile attacks and artillery barrages. The convoy threaded its way through Gaberone's streets and stopped at a large, well-guarded, and surprisingly unscathed government building. The soldiers in front snapped to attention when Mubambo stepped from his jeep. Abu and the others got out of the Mercedes without much notice.

Abu and the general walked together, striding purposefully into the building—the two men exuded a rare measure of power and confidence. Williams, Satki and Bhaiji hurried to keep up with them. Army guards snapped to attention as the group passed.

They waited briefly in a large well-appointed anteroom. Abu and Mubambo stood, as though knowing they would not be kept waiting long, while Williams and the others sat in the ornate overstuffed chairs.

A tall black man in his early forties, dressed in a dark, Western-style suit and tie, with a sober and officious air, came into the room and nodded to Mubambo. "General," he said with a clipped British university accent, "the President will see you now."

Williams started to get up, thinking for a moment that he might just have one more exclusive to send to Strunk. But Abu glanced at him, indicating that he, Bhaiji and Satki were to remain in the waiting room. Williams was being snubbed again. His resentment was barely contained as he watched Abu and the general being ushered into the Botswanan leader's office.

President Serowe was an aging, bespectacled man who sat unsmiling at a large mahogany desk. On the walls behind him were photographs of himself with a former British prime minister, other African leaders, and one with the President of the United States, taken in the Oval Office.

Mubambo removed his beret and saluted the President. "Your Excellency," Mubambo said.

"It is good to see you again," President Serowe said. "Allow me to congratulate you, General. You have protected your country well."

"Thank you, Excellency," Mubambo responded. "I merely did my duty."

"You are far too modest, General." The president turned to Abu. "And you, Sheik Asghar, have become quite a celebrity in the region. Apparently all of southern Africa owes you a debt of gratitude." Serowe studied Abu for a long moment and shifted uneasily in his high-back leather chair. "So, what interest do you have in our small country?"

"I am only here to help, your Excellency," Abu said with genuine sincerity.

Serowe looked at Abu like a teacher about to admonish a troublesome student. "I am well aware that you speak of solidarity to the black man, Sheik Asghar, but you seem to have a disconcerting talent for creating instability." He paused. "Nevertheless, you have my attention."

"Your Excellency, Botswana has one very important commodity that has not been fully utilized."

"And what is that?" the president asked.

"Geography, combined with a unique history."

"I do not quite understand—"

"Botswana is a landlocked country; most of your exports go to Europe, but most of your imports come primarily from South Africa. Botswana has unquestioned credibility among its neighbors. And right now South Africa needs your help."

"I see what you're getting at, Sheik Asghar, but allow me to play devil's advocate. Why should Botswana help South Africa now? The value of my country's minerals and diamonds has increased as a direct result of the slowdown of production in South Africa. But once awakened, South Africa could become like a powerful python, and swallow up a small country like mine. We here remember the vast Zulu empire that once dominated all of southern Africa."

"That is precisely why you must act now, President Serowe," Abu said, his tone both passionate and persuasive. "South Africa will recover. Wouldn't you rather it be an ally than an adversary? Nations do not have friends, they only have interests that must be promoted and protected."

"So, what is your proposal?" Serowe asked, his curiosity genuinely piqued.

"A federation—both economic and political. Botswana is in the best position to forge greater ties between the nations of South Africa, Namibia, Zimbabwe, Zambia, Angola, Zaire, Tanzania—the entire southern half of Africa." Abu leaned forward. "Consider how the wealth of all the members could be enhanced by forming cartels to export certain products to the industrialized countries. Imagine the power that would flow from such cooperation, rather than the instability and chaos of competition." Abu paused. President Serowe nodded for him to continue.

"Imagine a political federation that is also committed to the human values of justice, equality and freedom. Consider the possibility of a combined military organization dedicated to the security of its member nations. Consider the leadership role that such a federation could provide."

"You are an ambitious man, Sheik Asghar."

"So were those who created the Arab League, and NATO, and OPEC, even, if you will allow, the United States of America. It merely requires leaders who possess the vision to make it happen."

Serowe smiled almost imperceptibly. "And generals, of course."

"I think you begin to see," Abu said.

The President stood up from his desk, and walked to a large window behind him which looked out onto the city. He gazed thoughtfully into the distance. Then he turned back to Abu. "What you have proposed will require careful consideration. But, assuming I followed your recommendation, how would you suggest we begin?"

Abu's excitement mounted. "Call for an immediate convention of the Southern African Development Conference to take place here. Make the first item on the agenda the prompt admission of South Africa as a member. Make the next item of business the measure that can be taken to get South Africa back on its feet, economically and politically. Take small steps and always be clear about your intentions. Move the Conference toward integration with the Organization of African Unity and a strengthening of that body." Abu paused and weighed his words before speaking again. "And remember, Excellency, the mistrust you felt when I entered this room, it will be prevalent among others. It is merely an inevitable part of the change that is coming."

"I understand," Serowe said solemnly.

"Good," Abu said as he and Mubambo rose to leave.

In the weeks that followed, Williams saw Abu's popularity grow like a political candidate whose campaign had suddenly taken off, leaving his opposition far behind in the dust. The international media was everywhere, making Williams begin to feel increasingly irrelevant—just one of Abu's entourage, like some celebrity groupie. Yet he would not, and could not, leave. There were still important pieces of the puzzle that obsessed him; he had to know where this steamroller, with Abu as its self-appointed engineer, was headed.

Williams sat in a bar in Gaberone, drinking scotch and pondering the puzzle and its random pieces that fit nowhere. The whiskey allowed him to wallow, and feel lonely, disconnected from everyone and everywhere. The bar had a jukebox that played old rock and roll songs. The soulful harmony of the British group Queen filled the small, dark barroom.

Caught in a landslide;
No escape from reality.
Open your eyes;
Look up to the skies and see—

What does Abu want? Power. He knew that much of the puzzle. But what would Abu do with power? Make war? With what—he had no army, not even a country. What he did have was an extraordinary ability to win the hearts and minds of the Third World's population. And he was raising the stakes all the time, awakening a sleeping serpent that, once aroused, could become a fire-breathing dragon. Williams couldn't think of any leader who could do that and not have it devour him. Some had tried—Napoleon, Caesar, Hitler—but each was consumed by the tempest they'd awakened. Suddenly, a piece of the puzzle fell into place. Maybe that was what Abu was trying do. Maybe he had no intention of keeping it under control. Maybe Abu wanted to create a tempest no one could control.

Too late
my time has come.
Sent shivers down
my spine;
body's aching all
the time.
Goodbye everybody;
I've got to go.
Gotta leave you
all behind and
face the truth.

Williams felt an ineffable sadness come over him. He downed another whiskey just as Bhaiji entered the bar, looking for him. Williams smiled tipsily at Bhaiji and waved him over. "I'm glad you're here, pal. I hate to drink alone."

"What is the matter, Ben?"

"Nothing. Not a goddamned fucking thing—"

186

Bhaiji looked at Williams sympathetically. "Abu asked me to find you. He is going to address the Southern African Development Conference. He thought you might want to be there."

Williams got up shakily from the table. "Wouldn't miss it for the world. Lead on, McDuff," he said and put an arm on Bhaiji's shoulder for support.

At the meeting, Abu was already speaking when Williams and Bhaiji took their seats. "Black Africa must take sole responsibility for where it is today," Abu said sternly to the group. "You are squandering Africa's potential through corruption and tribal warfare. And blaming or lamenting the injustices of the past is a misguided waste of precious time." The delegates did not like what they heard. Williams sensed a collective anger building toward Abu. "Alone, none of you can overcome the enormous obstacles you face. Together, you can become a power to be reckoned with. But you must rise above your petty differences and see the limitless advantages of cooperation."

At that moment, President Serowe's aide entered the room, whispered something to the president and handed him an official-looking piece of paper. The president nodded, and the aide quickly left the room. Almost immediately, he returned, this time followed by Satki and a horde of reporters and photographers. Abu continued to speak to the conference leaders.

"Do not look to the white man to save you in retribution for past offenses," Abu said passionately. "Stand up and command respect. Then the white world will listen; then the entire world will listen, for they will have no choice."

As the assembly began applauding, President Serowe rose quickly from his chair and took the microphone.

"It would seem we have reason to celebrate," the Botswanan president said, his voice a bit shaky with excitement, "for I have here a telegram that allows me the distinct honor and privilege of informing you that Sheik Abu 'Ali Asghar has been chosen to be this year's recipient of the Nobel Peace Prize—" The room was suddenly abuzz, and Serowe called for silence. "—For his—" Serowe looked down at the piece of paper in his hand and read aloud, "for his efforts in bringing peace and stability to the nation of South Africa, and for his continuing efforts to bring justice and comfort to the oppressed and afflicted of the world."

Visibly moved, Serowe put down the telegram, removed his glasses and extended his hands to Abu. "I think I speak on behalf of all of us, Sheik Asghar, when I offer you our heartfelt congratulations."

Instant clamor filled the room. Williams jaw fell open. He looked at Abu whose expression hadn't changed. He looked over at Satki who face had an almost incandescent glow about it. Tears of joy and pride streamed down her cheeks. Bhaiji, too, was crying silent tears of admiration.

All the African leaders rose to give Abu a standing ovation. Abu acknowledged it by bowing several times—to the right, to the left, to the center. You're good, Williams thought to himself, a master.

Camera strobes flashed all over the room, journalists took notes furiously, reporters with microphones tried to get near Abu. He held up his hands to quiet the din.

"My friends," Abu said, "you fill me with humility. I am deeply honored to have been chosen for this distinguished award. But its true recipients are the leaders and people of South Africa, and all the oppressed people I have encountered on my journey. I shall accept it in their name. And with that responsibility in mind, I shall use it appropriately." Abu bowed again. Applause and congratulatory shouting broke out, reporters and photographers went into a feeding frenzy. Abu found Satki and embraced her, then turned to Bhaiji and embraced him. Abu's eyes searched the room and when he spotted Williams, he nodded once. "Yeah, you're welcome," Williams muttered under his breath as he watched Abu leave the room surrounded by an adoring, exultant crowd.

Williams saw Mubambo standing off to one side of the room. He threaded his way through the throng and stood facing the general. "A legend in his own time, eh, General?"

Mubambo smiled at Williams. "I cannot think of anyone who deserves it more. Can you?"

Williams made a wry chuckling noise. "Hell no," Williams said. "He deserves all the awards." Then, almost inaudibly, he added, "Let's give him an Oscar too while we're at it—"

"A what?" Mubambo asked.

"Never mind. You know, General, I still haven't had a chance to find out exactly what happened back in Dartmoor, and it is something I want to write about in the book—"

"Not now," Mubambo said.

"Oh, I didn't mean now, I meant I'd like to sit down with you some-time soon, for a few minutes—"

Just then, Abu re-entered the room and headed toward Mubambo and Williams. The General smiled politely at Williams. "If you will excuse me, I must see to my guests." He nodded to Abu as he walked past him and left the room.

Williams was utterly confused as Abu came over to him. "What's up? You look like you've got something to say."

Abu looked at Williams. There was a hint of compassion in his eyes. "It is time for you to leave."

Williams felt like he'd been punched in the solar plexus. For a long moment he couldn't breathe. When he found his voice, he didn't know what to say. All he could manage was "Why?"

"Perhaps you should call your editor at the *New York Times,*" Abu suggested.

"What for?" Williams asked, his heart racing.

"Call him." Abu turned and walked out of the room.

Williams looked at his watch. It was still early in New York. He went off to find a telephone and placed a call to Strunk's direct line. The editor answered.

"Hersch, it's Ben."

"Williams! Where you been, for Chrissakes?! I've been trying to track you down all week." He paused. "It's time to come home, Ben," Strunk said. His voice was firm but unusually gentle.

"Oh? What's up?"

"It's your father, Ben. He's quite sick. Your sister called. They don't think he's got much time left."

"Sonofabitch," Williams muttered, running a hand through his hair.

"I'm sorry, Ben."

"Yeah, me too." Williams wanted to smash the receiver into the wall.

There was static on the phone line. "Listen, Ben—can you hear me? I feel like we're gonna lose this connection any minute." Strunk's voice faded in and out.

"I hear you," Williams shouted.

"Ben, there's some good news. In fact, great news. I've been con-tacted by Brandon House. They want you to write a book. And to get started on it the minute you get back."

"But I'm not finished here yet. I still need to—"

"Ben, you haven't got the exclusive anymore. This story is bigger than anyone ever dreamed. *Time* and *Newsweek* are putting Asghar on their next covers! He's a world-class celebrity, and let me tell you, it'll be for a lot longer than fifteen minutes."

"I bet it will."

"And this is going to do it for you, too, Ben. This is going to be your goddamn Pulitzer Prize! And you know what that means—your mug on the cover of *Time* and *Newsweek!*"

"Jeee-sus . . ." Williams said softly.

"Speak up, Ben—I can't hear you," Strunk yelled.

"Thanks for everything, Hersch. Okay. I'm coming home. I'll see you soon."

"Good. I'll call the publisher and let them know. And I'm really sorry about your father, Ben."

"Yeah," Williams said and hung up the phone. A reception for Abu was taking place in the adjoining room and the noisy din penetrated Williams thoughts. The scotch he'd been drinking hours earlier had long since worn off, but he still felt lightheaded and confused. He didn't know what to think, or even what to feel. He walked into the adjacent room where the celebrating was in full swing. Abu saw Williams, and from across the room made eye contact, but Williams couldn't read his expression. Bhaiji and Satki came up to him.

"Is anything wrong?" Satki asked. "You look so worried."

"What—?" Williams looked down at her distractedly. "Oh. I have to go back to the States. It's my father. He's taken ill."

Bhaiji frowned. "It's not serious, I hope."

"Apparently it is," Williams said. Satki and Bhaiji exchanged surprised glances at Williams' obvious lack of concern about his father.

"Then you must go," Satki said.

"I don't really have a choice. Your son is kicking me out, now that he's gotten what he wants from me."

"What do you mean?" Satki asked gently.

"He used me, Satki. I served his ambitions well. Nobody did a better public relations job for him than I did," Williams said bitterly.

Satki scowled at Williams. "Used you? How? For what gain? The success you always wanted?"

190

Williams looked at her, unable to answer. There was no denying it. Abu was right; they'd both used each other. Williams felt suddenly spent, a wave of exhaustion swept over him. He wanted desperately to lie down and sleep for two days.

"My son cares about you, Ben. You and Bhaiji are like brothers to him. Except for the short time he had with his wife, he has never been close to anyone other than his father and me, and now you and Bhaiji. We are his only family. He loves you, Ben. I know it hurts him to see you go. He has given up everything for what he believes he must do, even his own happiness. Please do not be bitter, Ben."

Williams put his arms around Satki and hugged her. "I'm going to miss you," he said, his voice shaking. He turned to Bhaiji and they embraced. "Well, you'll have a little more room in the Mercedes now."

"Ben, I am glad I have been with you all this time," Bhaiji said, his eyes brimming. "I wish you good luck when you get back to America."

Williams nodded. "Thanks. You both mean a great deal to me."

"And you to us," Satki said. "Now go over and say goodbye to Abu," she urged him, like a mother wanting her two sons to make up after having had a fight.

"No," Williams said. He leaned over and kissed Satki, then shook Bhaiji's hand and began walking toward the door. Abu's gaze followed him, but Williams never returned the look; he did not want Abu to see the tears that were welling up.

CHAPTER 25

Satki sat quietly, sipping tea in the small garden of the Gaberone Hotel where, the day before, her son had been awarded the Nobel Prize. Their lives would never be the same from that moment on, of that she was certain. The air was dry and dusty, but all around Satki, the sweet-smelling flowers made her wish she could stay in the courtyard garden for another week or two. But when she saw Abu walking toward her, she knew this would be their last day in Gaberone.

"Mother," Abu said, sitting on the bench next to her. "It is time for me to leave."

Satki nodded. "I shall get ready." She started to get up.

"No, mother," Abu said, "you are not coming with me."

Satki looked puzzled. "Are you sending me away like Ben Williams?"

Abu smiled and gave Satki a kiss on the cheek. "Of course not. I need you to do something for me which I do not have the time to do."

"What is it?"

"I want you to go to Oslo, Norway and accept the Peace Prize on my behalf. I must finish my work here in Africa. Greater fame than I already have would be a distraction, perhaps even a detriment. The time will come. But for now, it is better that you go in my place."

Satki nodded. "I will do what you ask."

Abu hugged her. "There is much more that I need you to do."

"And what is that?"

"As part of the Nobel award, I shall be given a sum of money—it's approximately one million dollars." Satki's eyes widened. "I want you to take that money and establish a langar, in the Sikh tradition—a kitchen to feed the hungry."

Satki jumped up. "Abu, that is wonderful!" Then she thought for a moment. "But even a million dollars won't go very far. Perhaps we should donate it to the Red Cross instead—"

"No," Abu said firmly. "The langar cannot be associated with any

192

existing nation or organization. As for the money, this million dollars will only be the beginning. There will be much more." Satki smiled as Abu continued. "When you accept the prize money, I want you to pledge it for the betterment of humanity. Announce that I have authorized you to form a world organization dedicated to the elimination of poverty and hunger. Then begin soliciting donations. You will need to travel throughout Europe, Asia and America, raising money in my name. Consider it a sacred mission; ask for help and support wherever you go. The langar shall become a worldwide organization; we will distribute food and medicine to the sick and homeless and dying. We will stop mass starvation and disease. Eventually, we will fund agricultural projects to create new food sources. The world will never be hungry again."

"And where will this noble enterprise be headquartered?" Satki asked.

"In Geneva. You will obtain office space, hire a staff—however many people you need—and soon we will create offices in every major city to administer langars around the globe. Mother, do you see? We will be fulfilling Muhammad's message of mercy and compassion on a grander scale than ever imagined."

Satki hugged her son. "Your father would be so proud of you. How I wish he were here."

"He is, mother." Satki nodded with tears in her eyes.

As mother and son walked back into the hotel, Satki took Abu's arm. She looked up at him, taking a deep breath before she began. "Abu, I must talk to you about Ben. You know that he was so angry and hurt when he left—"

"Yes, I know," Abu replied without looking at her. His voice turned sad. "I'm afraid he needed to feel that way in order to leave. And he knew it."

"Do you think the two of you will ever reconcile?"

Abu didn't want to answer but Satki's eyes demanded a reply.

"It is not over between us," he said.

"Good," Satki said, reaching up to embrace him. Abu wrapped his arms around her.

"Have a safe journey to Europe." Abu smiled. "What is it the Irish say? 'May the road rise up to meet you.' "

"For you too, my son."

Abu looked lovingly at his mother. "Bhaiji will be in touch with you regularly. If there is anything you need, let us know. Oh, and mother—"

"Yes?" Satki opened the door to her room.

"I cannot think of anyone better suited to undertake this mission than you. It is your nature, it is your heritage."

Satki nodded modestly. "It will be an honor to do this work." She gently touched her son's cheek, then walked inside her room and closed the door. Abu stood there for a moment, turned and started down the corridor, his stride picking up momentum as he walked—the embodiment of passion served by purpose.

The Mercedes-Benz seemed empty to Bhaiji without Williams and Satki in the back seat. Abu was quieter too, as they drove west, across the great Kalahari Desert. Bhaiji could sense that things were changing; and it made him anxious. He tried not show his fear; he had to be strong for Abu, for whatever he might be needed to do. Abu counted on him, trusted him, and none of the journey could have been accomplished if not for Bhaiji's expert driving. He felt a sense of pride and gratefulness that he was a part of the life of someone so important as Abu. But lately, more and more, a sense of foreboding had been creeping into Bhaiji's consciousness. And now, the fact that he missed Williams and Satki only added to his anxiety.

The drive across the desert brought them to Namibia where Abu was granted an audience with Samuel Majamu, the country's president, and feted at a mass rally in Windhoek, the capital city. Tens of thousands of people turned out to see the man who had brought peace to southern Africa.

"I must confess, Sheik Asghar," President Majamu said, when Abu was about to depart, "I am glad you are leaving." Abu's dark eyes shot a questioning look at Majamu. The president attempted a smile. "If you decided to stay, you could become Namibia's next president, and I would be out of a job." The president laughed. Abu nodded but said nothing. He climbed into the Mercedes and closed the door. Bhaiji was forced to carefully and slowly maneuver the car through the cheering, waving crowd clamoring to say goodbye. President Majamu stared coldly at the departing Mercedes. An aide stood obediently at his side. "There is no office high enough to satisfy that man's ambition," Majamu grumbled. His aide nodded in sycophantic, silent agreement.

In Angola's capital city of Luanda, Abu received another red carpet treatment, complete with a military reception, twenty-one gun salute and, most importantly, a private audience with the Angolan president. There were interviews with the local press, a mass rally and a meeting with Angola's opposition leaders. When Abu left the country, there were again hordes of people waiting to bid him farewell, to get one last look at him, to perhaps hear a few more words of hope and glory.

Abu grew excited as they crossed into Zaire. He knew the country's president and was looking forward to meeting with him. Zaire itself was one of the largest nations in Africa and played a dominant role in African politics. President Zubala was considered one of the most skilled, cunning and ruthless leaders in Africa, and Zaire had one of the most successful economies on the continent. Also greatly in its favor was the fact that both the U.N. Commission on Human Rights and Amnesty International had removed Zaire from their list of countries accused of human rights abuses.

President Zubala found his allies and sources of aid wherever he chose. Most recently he had formed alliances with Libya and Iran, reinforcing the fact that his foreign policy was becoming increasingly anti-Western. He had even gone so far as to allow the Islamic terrorist group, Hezbollah, to use Zaire as a military base and for the training of its growing army.

Abu was met with a tumultuous reception when he arrived in the capital, Kinhasa. Tens of thousands of people lined the city streets to greet him. A media event was staged, and there was a parade that allowed the president to show off his well-trained and well-equipped army. Abu's speech went over the airwaves—he was on television, radio, written about in every newspaper and magazine; he had become omnipotent. Bhaiji watched all the fanfare and ceremony with awe and admiration. He never respected nor loved his great mentor more than he did when seeing the effect that Abu had on the people who heard his words. Abu was one of them, understood them, lived and suffered with them, and yet he alone possessed what none of them had: A transcendent presence. It allowed him to inspire, enlighten, and above all, create a public groundswell of support, of unbridled devotion.

"We are kindred spirits," President Zubala said to Abu when they were comfortably seated in the living room of his palatial home. In the adjacent elegant dining room, a dinner party was being readied in honor of Abu. The guests were a select, powerful and influential group of Zaire's elite—high-ranking government officials and wealthy friends of the president. It was now evening and the dinner was the culmination of a long day of festivities honoring Abu. That afternoon, Zubala had taken Abu's hand as the two men stood on a platform at the soccer stadium where a hundred thousand people had come to see the peacemaker, and had raised them high in the air in a gesture of solidarity. He formed a clenched fist with the other and held it equally high. The crowd had sent up a deafening cheer. President Zubala had never heard anything like it. Now, seated on a sofa opposite the one Abu sat on, he had his first opportunity to speak candidly.

"It is essential for black Africa to stand on its own, to leave our colonial past behind," Zubala said and Abu nodded in agreement. "I have been struggling to instill pride in my people, for who they are and their ancestral heritage."

"You have done admirably, your Excellency," Abu said.

"But I put this to you: The history of black Africa is one of tribal cultures, based upon a pastoral economy. To draw upon that past in order to give back to Africa its true identity, while at the same time trying to build an industrial infrastructure and compete in the international market, is a daunting task. And fraught with many dangers."

Abu's laser-like eyes bore into the president's with riveting intensity. "That is precisely why the nations of Africa must set aside their differences and begin working as a cooperative, economic unit." Abu leaned forward on the sofa, speaking as if to a longtime, trusted confidant. "Zaire is the heart of Africa. Because of its size, population and central location, you already have considerable influence on the other countries. With a unified system, Zaire's influence would only expand." The president nodded in understanding. "But it is not only up to Africa's leaders to change; ultimately it will depend on the people. They must feel a sense of purpose, and be involved as an essential part of the new order."

The president leaned over the coffee table that separated the two sofas, and reached for one of the cigarettes that filled a small antique silver cup. The lighter that he held up to his cigarette was made of exquisitely cut crystal that gave off prisms of color as it caught the light from the chandelier above them. The president inhaled deeply and slowly let out a long stream of smoke. "I find one thing most curious in the plan you propose," he said, concern registering in his voice. "You advocate consolidation, but isn't that inconsistent with the trend of current history?"

"Not at all," Abu responded quickly. "I advocate a confederation, not an empire. By combining parts to strengthen the whole, and with unity allowing for cooperation, the whole then becomes greater than the sum of its parts."

Zubala looked admiringly at Abu. "There is no question, as I saw earlier today, that you have won the hearts and minds of the people. Obviously, politicians and generals are a little harder to win over."

"I shall succeed, President Zubala. My cause is just; the people of Africa know that."

"The whole world now knows it, Sheik Asghar."

Zubala took another drag on his cigarette, blew out the smoke and crushed the cigarette in the large round crystal ashtray on the coffee table. "I shall give your proposal my most serious and careful consideration. I want only what is best for my people."

"As do I," Abu said solemnly.

From the dining room, the voices of Zubala's guests could now be heard and the delicate aroma of food began wafting into the living room. "Come, my friend," the president said, "we must not keep the dinner party waiting any longer." He opened the tall carved teakwood double doors and he and Abu entered the dining room amidst bursts of applause, excited chatter, and champagne glasses raised in toasts to him. Abu bowed gracefully to the guests, acknowledging their accolades. Zubala could not help but feel that he was in the presence of a spiritual warrior whose messianic message had begun to change the lives of millions of people. The world will never be the same again, Zubala thought.

THE MAHDI

PART TWO

"The world and time are the dance of the Lord in emptiness. The silence of the spheres is the music of a wedding feast. The more we persist in misunderstanding the phenomena of life, the more we analyze them out into strange finalities and complex purposes of our own, the more we involve ourselves in sadness, absurdity and despair. But it does not matter much, because no despair of ours can alter the reality of things, or stain the joy of the cosmic dance which is always there."

— Thomas Merton

CHAPTER 26

When Bennett Williams walked off the plane at Kennedy Airport he was already feeling the effects of jet lag; the last thing he wanted to do was make a connecting flight to Milwaukee. And to face the family he'd been estranged from for twenty years. *My God, twenty years.* He shook his head in amazement as he sat in the Northwest Airlines boarding area. Twenty years of only occasional contact with his mother, just enough to let her know he was alive and well. No visits home for Thanksgiving or Christmas or a wedding, a birthday milestone—nothing. There hadn't even been a funeral to attend. The years had pressed on and all familial ties had remained severed—no attempt to mend fences was ever undertaken. Not by Williams, his mother, and least of all, his father. He had no idea how it would feel to see his parents again, but his apprehension made him queasy. He wanted to turn and run, never to have to deal with his past and his demons, let alone the present pain and sadness of his father's imminent death.

"Flight 73 for Milwaukee is now boarding—" a voice came over the loudspeaker. Bennett Williams lifted his exhausted body and, too tired to think anymore, trudged through the passageway and onto the plane.

Herschel had told him which hospital. He grabbed a taxi and settled into the back seat, too drained and disinterested to look at the passing scene of city streets that were all too familiar. He stood outside the hospital entrance for a moment, not wanting to go in. It reminded him of his first encounter with Abu in Bhopal. He took a deep breath, trying to steel himself for God knows what. The automatic sliding doors opened and he went into the hospital. As he walked down the corridor that the receptionist at the front desk had directed him to, he was assaulted by that smell he hated—it resurrected the memory of the many times when he'd been in the hospital as a young boy. All those tests, lying endlessly in bed, only to learn that his physical problems were largely undiagnosable and were finally determined to be psychosomatic. It was all coming back—the pain, discomfort, the humiliation; a wave of depression engulfed him.

"I'm here to see my father, Bennett Williams, Sr." he said to a black nurse at the nurse's station. She flipped through her register. "That's intensive care, sir. Down this corridor and then make a right and follow the signs."

Williams obeyed, walking faster now despite his fatigue. Anxiety was propelling him; and the desperate wish that all this would soon be over. This too shall pass, he told himself.

He entered the I.C. unit and scanned the room. The light was dim. He saw the bed off to one corner but his eyes avoided looking at it. He saw his sister Margaret standing against a far wall, staring at her feet. Then he spotted his mother, sitting in a chair next to his father's bed. He made himself look at the bed. His father lay motionless, eyes closed, tubes running from his arms and nose. His sister looked up. Her face was drawn and pale. Williams thought the dark circles under her eyes made her look like a hunted animal.

"Hello, Ben," Margaret said. Her voice was flat, emotionless. "We didn't think you'd come."

His mother looked up at him, and in her eyes, for a fleeting moment, he detected her sadness and vulnerability. But in a second it was gone, replaced by the stoic coldness that was typical of her. It was his mother's defense mechanism for everything unpleasant in life.

"I got here as soon as I could," he said apologetically.

"Of course you did," his mother said with a tinge of sarcasm. She looked him up and down quickly. "You look fit, Ben, except you really ought to change your clothes—"

"Mother, I've been on planes for the last twenty-four hours," he said defensively.

He wanted to scream at her. A few feet away, her husband of almost fifty years lay dying and she was annoyed with her son's appearance. Old angers began churning in his stomach. His sister came over and embraced him. It surprised Williams; it was the first time she'd ever done anything like that. "It's good to see you," Margaret said. Then, turning to her mother, she took her arm and helped her up from the chair. "Let's give Ben some time alone with Dad."

"Thanks, Maggie," Williams said as his mother reluctantly left the room with his sister.

Williams looked at his father and then at the monitors on both sides of the bed—electronic sentries posted to keep watch.

He pulled up a chair and sat down. He barely recognized the man who lay before him. The chemotherapy had made all his hair fall out, his skin looked parched and decaying, barely clinging to its skeletal frame. The face was ashen, the cheeks hollow, the nose more prominent. He was not the man Williams remembered, a man once larger than life, a towering figure of a father, to be feared if not respected—the closest thing to an image of God as Williams could imagine. The family had always referred to him as 'Big Ben' so as not to confuse the two. He was always 'Little Ben.'

Williams knew he should feel something. But he just felt empty inside, completely numb. Maybe it was the long trip, and being sent away by Abu. Or perhaps he had simply chosen *not* to feel. To be numb to the pain of the past. When it came to his father, all he had ever felt was anger and bitterness. He'd always sought his father's approval, but it never came. He seemed to have been constantly disappointing the man he was named after. And when he had decided to enroll in Northwestern University and study journalism, his father scoffed and criticized his choice—irate that his only son was not going into a more lucrative and worthwhile profession, such as "doctoring" or "lawyering," as his father had advised. "You won't make it as a writer, you'll be out of work half the time—" Bennett Williams, Sr. had said vehemently.

"It's my life; I'll do what I want with it!" Williams had yelled back.

"Well, I'm not going to watch you waste *your* time and *my* money. Pay your own way and see how you like it!"

"Fuck you, you sonofabitch!" Williams had shot back. The memory made him wince.

"Hello, Ben," he heard his father say so faintly he thought he'd imagined it. He slowly raised his head up to see his father looking at him through glassy eyes, deadened by pain.

"Hi, Dad," Williams answered. "How are you feeling?" It was a stupid question, but he didn't know what else to say.

"I'm dying, thank you." His father coughed. "I feel rotten."

"Shall I get the doctor?"

"Hell, no." Bennett Williams, Sr. stared at his son. It made Williams uncomfortable. He thought he should say something, do something.

"Things have kinda turned around, huh, Ben?"

Williams didn't know what his father was referring to. Then it struck him. All those times he'd been in the hospital as a boy with his father looking on. The reversal was profound. "I guess your old man's not so tough after all," his father said and coughed again.

"No, I guess not." Williams wasn't bitter or accusatory, just applying the same standard by which he'd been judged so many years ago.

His father tried to lean toward the box of tissues on the table next to his bed but the tube in his arm made it awkward. Williams quickly pulled a couple of tissues from the box and handed them to his father. "Thanks," his father said and coughed again, spitting into the tissue. Williams took the used tissue from his father's hand and dropped it into the plastic wastebasket, plucked another one from the box and gently wiped around the old man's mouth where some saliva still remained.

"I read a few of your articles in the *New York Times*," his father said.

Williams was dumbstruck. "Yeah? Well, what didya think?"

"They were good, damn good."

"Thanks." Williams brightened. Maybe there was a common ground beginning to emerge. Maybe even a truce. "I've been asked to write a book, based on the articles. For a major publishing company."

His father smiled slightly. "Excellent," he said. Williams felt as if he'd just been given a high mark on an exam. There was an awkward silence for a few moments. Then Williams, Sr. looked up at his son. "I'm sorry, Ben."

His father's apology took him completely by surprise. "For what?"

"I was hard on you, son. Maybe too hard. It was just that—" He coughed again. Williams reached for a glass of water and held it to his father's lips. It was like being in Bhopal again. No, this was worse. His father took a sip and then let his head fall back onto the pillow, his breathing was labored. "It was just that I wanted you to be strong."

"Like you?" Williams didn't mean to let the bitterness seep through.

The old man looked surprised, then sad. "No. I wasn't strong at all. As a matter of fact, I didn't want you to be like me—afraid; I wanted you to be able to stand on your own. I knew I'd succeeded when you cussed at me and walked out. But when I didn't hear from you all these years, I knew I'd gone about it the wrong way."

Williams looked down; he couldn't bear to hear the painful reminders. He felt ashamed. Were father and son finally resolving the terrible issues that had haunted them for twenty years? Were they going to heal the wounds after all this time?

"I guess it's too little, too late," his father said, reaching for his hand. Williams took it, stroking the wrinkled, dry skin. It felt so frail. "But I want you to know that I love you, son." It was the first time in his life his father had ever said the words.

Williams awkwardly reached out and put his hand on his father's forehead. "I . . . I . . . love you too, Dad." His voice was barely audible.

"Forgive me," Bennett Williams, Sr. said, squeezing his son's hand as hard as he could manage. Then his grip loosened and his eyes closed.

Williams sat, staring at his father, stroking the man's nearly bald head. He remained that way for a long time, oblivious to any other sound or movement in the room. The constant beep of the heart monitor attached to his father suddenly fibrillated and became a steady whine. Williams looked at it, then at his father, lying there, so still and quiet. So fragile. So far away.

Williams leaned over. "Godspeed, Dad," he whispered.

A nurse came over and looked sympathetically at Williams as she gently removed the tubes and turned off the machinery that had pumped a few more days of tortured life into the dying man. Williams walked out of the room and down the hall to find his mother and sister, and tell them the news.

Williams flew back to New York the day after the funeral. Herschel Strunk had found him an apartment—a sublet from a friend of a friend. The co-op was owned by a successful entrepreneur who would be traveling on business for the next year. It was on the upper West Side, a few doors off Central Park, in an elegant high-rise building. The apartment was spacious, airy, quiet, tastefully and expensively furnished. It was larger than Williams needed and far more lavish than he was accustomed to. But it felt empty; and a gnawing angst took over every time he walked into the place. He had been living there for a month and still couldn't shake the feeling of terrible aloneness. He tossed his keys, and a small stack of mail that he hadn't even looked at, onto the entryway table and listened to the silence. He felt lost, bereft, in a state of animated suspension. He went into the burgundy-and-grey-tiled bathroom with its art deco-patterned wallpaper and matching accessories. Not something Bennett Williams would ever have thought to do—decorating—but he rather liked the superficial comfort it provided. He climbed into the large, smoked-glass shower stall and let the steamy hot water wash away some of his anxiety. It helped. So did the scotch he fixed for himself a few minutes later. He popped a CD onto the player and settled into the oversized tan leather Eames chair. The scotch slid smoothly down his throat; he could feel its heat inside his body. He laid his head back and closed his eyes.

Williams wanted to cry but he couldn't. Tears began to build behind his eyes. If only he could let it out, he'd feel better. He tried to make himself cry, but realized how silly that was.

He thought of his father's deathbed confession of guilt and remorse. How ironic. After all the years of wanting his father's approval, when he finally got it, when the old man actually paid him a compliment about his work—his career—it seemed to hardly matter. The appreciation he had dreamed of, hoped and prayed for, when it came, was somehow anticlimactic. Had he really needed that paternal approval after all? Or was it just some childhood craving that he had long since outgrown? His own guilt began to creep over him. Should he have reached out sooner, years ago? Had pride and stubbornness been greater than understanding and forgiveness? Should he have tried harder to reconcile with the man he had been afraid of for so long? Or could it only have happened when it finally did?—in the last moments of his father's life, in a hospital room, as death hovered like an impatient vulture.

The CD ended just as a bolt of lightning lit up the living room, followed immediately by a powerful clap of thunder. Williams remembered how, as a boy, he loved the dazzling display that lightning often created, but thunder had always terrified him. His mother used to refer to it as "God's anger," and the louder the thunder, the angrier God was. Bennett's mother rarely thought of a benevolent or merciful God—she chose only a wrathful one.

Williams got up to pour himself another drink and then walked to the front door and picked up the mail he'd left on the small antique table with its dark green marble top. He rifled quickly through the bills from Visa and MasterCard, the electric and gas companies and wondered how much longer he'd be able to afford this apartment. It was more than he was used to paying, and he hated the possibility of going into debt. Maybe the book advance would take care of his financial worries. Strunk, who was acting as Williams' agent, had promised a meeting with the publishers in the next few days. He was getting anxious about that too.

Then he noticed the envelope marked with a return address he didn't recognize. He looked at it curiously before opening it up. The announcement inside was from the President of Columbia University. It read:

> This letter shall serve as official notice that H. Bennett Williams has been awarded the Pulitzer Prize for outstanding journalistic achievement in the category of International Reporting for his series of articles written during Mr. Williams' travels in India and Africa with Sheik Abu 'Ali Asghar, and published in the *New York Times* between February and September, 1998.
>
> You are cordially invited to attend a dinner announcing this award, to be held on November 15, 1998 at the Waldorf Astoria, 7:00 PM, Black Tie.
>
> *We congratulate you on winning the Pulitzer Prize and we look forward to meeting you in person on November 15th.*

The letter was signed by the President of Columbia University. Williams read it again and then once more. He telephoned Strunk and told him the news in a voice shaky with excitement.

"Goddamn it, I knew you'd do it!" Strunk was ecstatic. "Congratulations, Ben. Come to the office tomorrow. I've got a bottle of champagne I'm gonna pour over your head." He laughed heartily and shouted, "Way to go, Ben!"

"Thanks," Williams said. "I couldn't have done it without your help, Hersch. You made it all possible." Williams had never felt the kind of love he reserved for Strunk. A combination of respect and trust and a warmth that bordered on vulnerability.

When he hung up the phone, he sank down into the leather chair again, the scotch in one hand and the letter in the other. He looked around the room, then his eyes drifted upward.

"Hey, Dad," Williams said out loud, a grin starting to spread across his face. "Guess what? I won. I won the Prize. I won the fucking Pulitzer

Prize! How about that?" Williams paused and leaned back in the leather chair.

This time the tears came. They rolled down Williams' cheeks and into his lap. He couldn't stop them; he didn't want to. They poured out of him—a watery catharsis that was washing away years of hurt and anger.

Williams walked over to the window, still crying. Outside, a hard rain had begun to fall. Williams watched through his tears as the rain washed away Manhattan's daily accumulation of dirt and pollution. The city's lights twinkled and danced through the downpour, sparkling like tiny diamonds. Slowly, Bennett Williams' tears abated and he started to smile at his reflection in the window.

CHAPTER 27

The Pulitzer award banquet was, for Bennett Williams, one of the high points of his life. Nothing remotely like it had ever happened to him. He wondered if Abu knew about the prize. And if he did, what he thought. Would Abu care? Would it simply be another of his predictions come true—something that wouldn't surprise him at all? Or was it something that Abu would use to his advantage? How could he resist the added publicity of this prestigious award having been given for a series of stories written about him? Surely he'd get some mileage from Williams' new-found celebrity. Williams felt a surge of resentment welling up inside him as he rode in the taxi to the Waldorf-Astoria in midtown Manhattan.

But once the evening's ceremonies had begun and Williams was seated next to Herschel Strunk at the elegant dinner table, where the food was excellent and the champagne flowed, and he was surrounded by the country's finest journalists, publishers, university professors, and newspaper editors, his anger toward Abu dissipated. Tonight Williams' star was on the ascent, he was center stage, and the accolades were for him. It was a wonderful feeling and Williams allowed himself the luxury of reveling in it.

He heard his name announced by the Chairman of the Pulitzer Prize board, he heard his work being lauded, a small portion of which was read aloud, and then the applause, the standing ovation as he was called up to the podium to accept the award.

"Thank you," he began, his voice faltering slightly as he spoke into the microphone. "This is a most humbling experience." He paused. "I want to thank my editor at the *New York Times,* Herschel Strunk. If it hadn't been for his support and patience, and the wisdom to let me have my way," Williams said with a chuckle, "I wouldn't be standing here right now."

Williams became more relaxed as he saw the faces in the room, smiling up at him. His voice became stronger, steadier. "There's one other person I must also acknowledge. Without him there would be no story. And so, wherever you are tonight, Sheik Abu 'Ali Asghar, my deepest thanks."

As Williams stepped down from the podium another round of applause broke out; it continued as he headed back to the table. Suddenly he realized that this was a mere fraction of the appreciation and admiration that Abu experienced *all the time*, everywhere he went. Williams reasoned that only someone as evolved as Abu, as completely detached from his ego as he was, could possibly handle such a heady brew.

In the weeks that followed, Williams was invited to luncheons and receptions and cocktail parties. He was written about in *Time* and *Newsweek*, he appeared on the major morning TV shows, on CNN and *Larry King Live*. Now he was the one being interviewed; it felt strange, but he basked in it. Those editors and fellow journalists who privately thought he had gone over the edge by traipsing after some obscure holy man in India and Africa, now publicly praised him for his unerring intuition. Several newspapers came courting, but the *New York Times* and Strunk wouldn't let him go. The book contract was also looming, and there was even serious talk of a major motion picture based on Williams' travels with Abu. One movie studio executive likened Williams to the reporter who had journeyed with Lawrence of Arabia. There was no doubt about it: Bennett Williams had arrived. He looked around the luxury apartment he was subletting and suddenly realized he could afford it. Abu had not only brought him fame, he'd brought him financial security.

Yet, all the newly-acquired prestige and prosperity—and becoming this season's darling on the literary-cocktail party circuit—didn't really add up to much and did little to assuage the emptiness, the loneliness that he felt all the time, deep inside.

He came back to his apartment one evening after attending a small dinner party given by a wealthy New York socialite who loved to surround herself with the literati of the moment. He poured himself an unusually large brandy and gulped it down. He had drunk almost a whole bottle of wine at the party, but he now still needed a nightcap—

something that would help click off the noise in his head, something to fill up the emptiness. He thought of the meditation that Abu had taught him. He hadn't done any since he'd returned. Ironic. It was probably the one thing that would help him—the one thing he needed to get in touch with again.

The evening had unnerved him. When one of the dinner guests had dismissed Abu's spirituality and his 'miracles' as 'the work of a charlatan' and compared him to 'that deluded swami who used to ride around in Rolls Royces,' Williams found himself coming to Abu's defense.

"He's not like anyone else," Williams had said. "You'd have to have met him and traveled with him to understand. You'd have to have seen what I saw."

"Bennett's right," said a thin, bejeweled woman sitting next to Williams. He noticed her diamond bracelets and emerald earrings and the necklace that matched. What were they worth? he wondered. Probably enough to feed one of the starving countries he'd been to in Africa. She took his hand and leaned toward him, whispering loud enough for everyone to hear. "Pay no attention to Geoffrey; he's just an elitist New Yorker who thinks anyone who's the least bit different is either looney tunes or dangerous. Or both." She pointed a silver fork at the man sitting across the table. "Now, Geoff darling, you keep your nasty remarks to yourself," she said good-naturedly, then turned back to Williams. "Go on, Bennett, tell us more about Abu; he's so fascinating. I'll bet women are forever throwing themselves at his feet. You know, a lot of these gurus have numerous wives, whole harems of them. Or is your guru celibate?" Before Williams had a chance to open his mouth, she prattled on, answering her own question. "Oh, but of course he must be. How on earth could he do all that traveling and preaching and healing and peacemaking, and still have the time, let alone the energy, for sex?" Everyone at the table laughed. "I'm sure it's not a priority with him. Isn't that so, Bennett?" Williams stared at the woman and nodded.

He wanted desperately to get out of there, and an hour later, apologized and told his disappointed hostess that he had an important breakfast meeting in the morning. As he was on his way out, several guests mentioned that invitations to cocktail or dinner at their homes were being sent to him. Williams mumbled his thanks as he left. Outside on the street, he wondered why he went at all. Despite the chilly weather, he had decided to walk the twenty blocks back to his apartment. The air would do him good.

Williams poured more brandy into the snifter, swirled it absently and sipped it this time. He automatically reached for the TV remote and clicked on the set, then walked over to the window and opened it a few inches. Fifteen stories below, police and ambulance sirens pierced the air, momentarily overriding the honking cars and taxis and the grinding sounds of the city's busses. No wonder New York had the dubious honor of being the most noise-polluted city in the country. Williams could even make out the muffled clamor of the subway beneath the traffic-clogged streets.

In the background, the eleven o'clock news had just come on. Williams heard a woman's voice that sounded terribly familiar. He turned and stared at the television in excited surprise as he recognized Satki. Wearing a blue and white sari, her thick hair neatly pulled into a large bun at the back of her head, she was addressing a European parliament on behalf of Abu. Satki was pleading for the salvation of the world's hungry and homeless. Williams sank down into the leather couch, his eyes riveted to the screen. He remembered how she'd cared for him in Bangladesh; how she'd been more a mother to him than his own mother. Now she was like a mother to all the suffering people of the world. Tears welled up in his eyes as he watched Satki speak. He raised his glass in a silent toast to her.

The news segment was followed by another one about Abu. It began with a background report on his travels, as chronicled by "H. Bennett Williams of the *New York Times.*" The narrator told how Abu had begun in India, moved through the Far East and Asia, and then East Africa. There wasn't any mention of what had come before—nothing about the murder in London and Dartmoor Prison.

There was videotape of the rallies in Johannesburg, Namibia, Angola, Zaire, and some of the smaller nations. There was a clip of Satki in Oslo accepting the Nobel Peace Prize on behalf of her son.

Then they showed Abu in Lagos, Nigeria, walking among the impoverished people of the massive ghetto. Even more compelling were the scenes of Abu visiting a leper colony, kissing the forehead of a woman horribly disfigured by the disease while he carried her baby in his arms. He moved through the throngs of the sick and suffering, touching them all with his outstretched hand. As he watched, Williams realized how much he wanted to go back to Africa. He regretted the way he left things in Gaberone—his own childish pettiness that had prevented him from saying goodbye. But it was more than that, it went much deeper. It wasn't finished between Abu and him; he knew it and he was certain Abu knew it as well.

A network news correspondent was now talking about the terrible tensions in the Middle East.

Williams stared out the window, searching for the glowing star he'd seen in Africa, but a layer of storm clouds filled the sky. A torrential rain descended upon the city. Sheets of water, driven by heavy winds, pelted against the window panes, creating a liquefied world that blurred all distinctions. He felt a tightness in his chest. He quickly shut the window and returned to the TV set.

The newscaster was now talking about a strange phenomena that was of great concern to the world's leading astronomers. It was centered in the Pleiades star system, in the constellation of Taurus. Originally thought to be a supernova when discovered years earlier—a star that had finally reached the end of its long life was now ready to burst into a trillion pieces—scientists were being forced to rethink their previous conclusions. It wasn't acting like a supernova, at least none that the experts had ever seen before. This one was expanding and contracting, and emitting incredibly high levels of radiation at irregular intervals. They'd never encountered anything like it.

But Williams was only half-listening. An awful sense of loneliness had welled up and consumed him. Maybe it was the shallow, superficiality of the evening's dinner party, and maybe it was seeing Satki and Abu on CNN, but never before had he felt so alone—it was like nothing he'd experienced since coming back to New York; it was more intense than anything he'd ever felt in his entire life. He realized it was the source of tightness in his chest and it was growing into real pain. He couldn't breathe, it was suffocating him. He didn't want to be alone any more. "God, please deliver me from this pain," he muttered, fighting back tears, afraid to let them flow for fear they might not stop. "I am so lonely," he said, as if in desperate prayer.

Then, outside, a sudden crack of lightning split the heavens with a flash of blinding light. Williams almost jumped off the couch. The tremendous rumble of thunder that immediately followed felt as though it rocked the building's foundation. Rain turned to hail. Large, marble-sized stones of ice hurled themselves angrily against the windows. Jagged lightning ripped the sky. A shiver began at the base of Williams' spine and raced upward with a force so great it was as if the lightning bolt itself had been shot straight through him.

The city lights flickered, and then everything went dark.

CHAPTER 28

Abu and Bhaiji drove through the tiny, reed-like African nations of Benin and Togo, stopping only for fuel and food. Abu was anxious to get to Ghana, one of the West's star pupils.

Years earlier, under the leadership of a young flight lieutenant who had seized control of the country in a military coup, the new government instituted harsh economic measures as dictated to it by the International Monetary Fund and the World Bank. Ghana devalued its currency, drastically downsized its civil service, and liberalized import restrictions—making it easier for Western goods to fill the store shelves and for foreign loans to flow into the country.

But the hoped-for investments never materialized. Instead, the economy suffered, food prices soared and unemployment was rampant. The nation's leaders watched helplessly as worldwide recession dashed their dreams of building a new Ghana.

The young flight lieutenant needed to appease the terrible plight and growing dissatisfaction of his people. Abu arrived just in time. When he spoke of economic imperialism and third-world enslavement, it struck a deep chord in the Ghanaian people. And when he met with the lieutenant/president and other government officials, they listened attentively to his words. They saw great opportunity in what he said; their hope for a better tomorrow was suddenly rekindled.

In Liberia, a small nation of less than three million people, and once an American colony founded in the early 19th century as a refuge for freed slaves, Abu was again met with wildly enthusiastic crowds—whether in mosques or public rallies—he had now become a national hero. In a country that had massive unemployment, a civil war and a bitter resentment toward the United States, Abu's message was immediately embraced by all Liberians.

Abu and Bhaiji traveled on, farther north, where the preponderance of Muslim nations increased, moving ever closer to the Arab countries of the great Sahara; nations that had once been the heart of the vast Islamic empire. Abu gained new followings in Sierra Leone and Guinea before traveling to his next destination: Senegal. This country's black Africans had proclaimed Islam as its official state religion. Senegal itself was run not by its government, but by the dominant Islamic brotherhoods, the most powerful of which were the Mourides. They were not the largest nor most ancient brotherhood, but they were the richest. Their wealth controlled the economy of Senegal and, therefore, they controlled the country. They owned and operated Senegal's transportation systems, they owned most of its urban real estate and ruled over the peanut industry—the country's largest export. The Mourides employed millions of Senegalese, providing economic as well as spiritual nourishment.

But in recent years, the Mourides had amassed too much wealth at the expense of the general population, creating hardship and deprivation for the majority of Senegalese. And the political power they wielded had resulted in a surfeit of corrupt politicians, beholden only to the interests of the Mourides.

It was to Touba, the Muslim Mourides' holiest city, that Abu came. Touba was to the Mourides what the Vatican was to Roman Catholics. And like the Vatican, Touba was a state within a state, where government representatives possessed no authority, and even less influence. But it was the most sacred place in Senegal, and contained a great mosque—a gleaming white edifice with the tallest minaret in black Africa; it blinded the naked eye in the noonday sun. The mosque contained the spiritual writings of the founder of the Mourides and, therefore, was the reason that millions of black Muslims made an annual pilgrimage to Touba every year. The only event more sacred was going to Mecca itself.

Abu wanted to speak in Touba's great mosque, but to do that required the permission of the Caliph General, the marabout or leader of the Mourides. Not much happened in Senegal, or in all of Africa for that matter, that escaped the attention of the Caliph General.

Abu was invited to the marabout's official residence just outside of Touba. To see him sitting on the carpeted floor of a plain, bare room in his home, one would never guess that he presided over an extraordinary financial empire.

"Are you Muslim?" the Caliph General asked when Abu made his request to address the Mourides in Touba's mosque.

"My father was Bedouin Arab, and a Muslim. I was raised to believe in the principles of Islam."

"But are you Muslim?"

Abu looked at the Caliph General for a moment. "I believe there is one God and it is Allah. And I believe that Muhammad was the messenger of God."

The Caliph General nodded thoughtfully. "I have heard and read many of your speeches, and I find aspects of your theology which seem to conflict with the basic tenets of Islam."

"Perhaps more in appearance than substance," Abu said.

The Caliph General shook his head. "Sheik Asghar, you believe in reincarnation, of the soul being reborn. But there is no such belief written in the Koran, nor in Islamic thought. Indeed, the Muslim believes there is but one life, and depending upon the manner in which one lives it, there is only heaven or hell."

"But yet the soul is eternal, is it not?" Abu challenged.

"Yes, as is Allah," the Caliph General answered.

"And that is what I teach. And what I also teach is that the soul is part of Allah, it is one with Allah. That is not inconsistent with Muslim beliefs."

"True," the Caliph General acknowledged.

"I do not deny that I have said the soul of each lives more than one life—that the essence of the soul lives on after the body dies. And that is because the soul knows no separation from God, from Allah, and only when it connects to a human body does it gain a sense of separation, of personal identity. I teach that the soul will incarnate countless times, but in the union of soul to the body, it will create only one life that is unique and that is never repeated. It will not carry with it the same identity, nor the memories of its past lives. It is that uniqueness which makes each life special."

"And you perceive each life as a manifestation of Allah—that there is no difference. But, as Muslims, we must surrender to the will of Allah, and serve him."

"Again," Abu responded quickly, "this is not inconsistent with what I teach. Allah, as an indivisible aspect of all that is, must enter into a relationship with the world as creator. That relationship becomes manifest in all of humankind. As one great Sufi master has observed: 'God is the mirror in which thou seest thyself as thou art, His mirror in which He contemplates His names.' "

"And what of heaven and hell? What of Satan?" the Caliph asked, eying Abu skeptically.

"That which we call Satan, the devil, is merely the fear that we hold within and that influences our actions toward other human beings. It is that which causes us to inflict pain upon ourselves in self-loathing and hatred of others. Hell is not punishment reserved for the next life because of evil wrought in the present, but rather the pain experienced by those terrible actions in the here and now. And the 'kingdom of heaven' is here, on earth, as Jesus once preached. And according to the Koran, it is Jesus who shall return again one day after the reign of the Mahdi—'the Awaited One'—and after the chaos of the Antichrist. I mention Jesus as the example of one who had come to so high a level of communication with God through his own soul that he then became the direct instrument of God on earth. He represented all that humankind is capable of becoming—there is not one person upon this planet who does not contain the same potential as that one."

"And how best do you believe we can we serve God?" the Caliph General asked.

"By improving the communication between our souls and our conscious mind. Only then can humanity create a world society based upon equality, justice, compassion and mercy, as set forth by Allah in the Koran. Perhaps that is the divine will to which it is said all men must surrender."

The Mourides marabout smiled obliquely at Abu and adjusted the folds of his embroidered orange scarf. "It is also written in the Koran," his tone was ominous, "that a time shall come when the forces of chaos, violence, and destruction shall break through the wall of divinely imposed order, and darkness shall befall the world. At that time, there shall also be a brief return to spiritual integrity, delivered by a Mahdi."

A young boy, a servant in the Caliph General's house, entered the room carrying a black-lacquered tea tray with a small teapot and two china cups and saucers. He placed the tray on the floor between Abu and the marabout, then bowed slightly and left the room. The Caliph General poured two cups of tea and handed one to Abu. Looking over his teacup at Abu, the Caliph General studied him for a moment. "There is a traditional belief that the Prophet ordained that the Mahdi would be of his own stock, perhaps meaning that he would be Bedouin, and 'broad of forehead and aquiline of nose.' But you, of course, already know this, I am sure."

Abu offered no response, his expression remained cryptic.

He sipped his tea. The Caliph General continued. "And there are those who believe that under the Mahdi, justice will be restored, law will reign in place of lawlessness, order will replace chaos. But the Mahdi will be followed by the coming of the Antichrist, the one the Sufis call 'the great deceiver.' And then there shall be Armageddon." The Caliph General's eyes bore into Abu's. "I wonder, Sheik Asghar, are you the Mahdi? Or are you perhaps the great deceiver?"

Abu placed his teacup back on the tray and adjusted his seated position on the carpeted floor opposite the Caliph General. Abu's arm rested on his knee as his gaze turned slightly away from the Caliph General. "Perhaps it reads too much into the divine revelations to assume that either shall take the form of a man. Perhaps they refer to states of being. Perhaps we shall pass through a time of great fear, a global purging if you will, which shall then usher in a golden age which shall be characterized forevermore by the mastery of our fear as a race of human beings."

"But you agree that Allah works through his human instruments, do you not?"

"Most definitely."

"Thus, whether the revelations speak in metaphors or physical actualities, the vehicles by which such changes shall occur are through God's human instruments. Would you not agree?"

"Indeed I would," Abu replied.

The Caliph General smiled at his guest. Then instantly turned serious again. "And what if I choose not to grant your request to speak at the Touba mosque? After all, from everything you have said here today, I could easily perceive you as a threat to the Mourides authority." He paused. "To its very existence."

"That, of course, is your prerogative." Abu spoke politely, diplomatically, but with the assurance of someone who knows they will ultimately win the debate. "But your people have heard of me and they will wonder why I have been denied access to speak to them. Can you afford further disaffection among your followers?" Abu paused and looked directly into the eyes of the Caliph General. "There are, of course, the other brotherhoods in Senegal who would be less fearful of allowing their people to hear me, who would see an advantage in undermining Mourides dominance in the country."

The Caliph General looked coldly at Abu. "You are indeed a persuasive man, Sheik Asghar."

Abu smiled. "I can also help you."

"How is that?" the Caliph General asked.

"There is widespread and increasing discontent among your people. They are hungry to hear what I have to tell them. They yearn for spiritual guidance and a means to recapture their lost power. If you let me speak to them, they will see that you truly have their interests at heart, and their anger will not be unleashed on you. But if you oppose me, your empire will crumble beneath you."

"Your point is well taken, Sheik Asghar."

"But I could be of help to you as well."

The marabout looked at Abu with genuine interest. "Please go on."

"There is increasing conflict between Senegal and its neighbors, Gambia, Guinea-Bissau, Mali and, most importantly, Mauritania. I can put an end to those conflicts."

"How do you propose—"

Abu put up his hand, interrupting the Mourides leader. "Leave that to me," he answered.

The Caliph General took a deep breath and exhaled. Slowly he nodded. "Very well. You shall be permitted to speak at the Touba Mosque."

Abu got up and bowed slightly. "I am most grateful." He turned and walked out of the room, the marabout watching his every step.

CHAPTER 29

"*Jeee-sus Christ!*" the taxi driver grumbled with a strong Brooklyn accent.

"What's the problem?" Williams asked, leaning forward in the back seat of the yellow cab. He stared out at the traffic jam that surrounded them.

"*Noo Yawk,* that's the problem!" The cabbie was bearing down on the horn, adding angry comment to the already screeching, blaring, shouting cacophony brought on by the city's gridlock. The cabdriver stuck his head out the open window, his left hand pounding on the outside of the car door. "Move yer ass!" he barked at the vehicle in front of him. The only response from the driver was a hand out the window, jabbing its middle finger into the air. "Yeah, fuck you too, asshole," the cabbie shouted back.

"Now I really feel like I'm back home," Williams grunted.

"This city's one big fuckin' sewer," the driver said, and laid on his horn again. "And the drain is startin' to back up, if you get my drift." Despite Williams' obvious lack of interest, the cabbie continued. "And what about that guy who's been shootin' people in Central Park—in broad daylight! Just walks up to 'em and bam! And then disappears! And that big-shot-Wall-Street guy—they found him with his brains splattered all over his desk; how'dya like to walk into that first thing in the a.m.? I'm tellin' ya, the whole city's fucked. Everything's breakin' down. And then you got all the niggers up there in Harlem all pissed off again. I hear they had most of 125th Street in flames last night. Pretty soon they'll be coming down like fuckin' barbarians and burning us out too. Just like they torched L.A. years ago with them riots, remember?"

Williams remembered it all too well. He had gone out there on assignment to cover the disaster that was the result of the first Rodney King verdict. He recalled seeing whole square blocks of the city streets turned into exploding infernos by violent young men who rode in cars

221

and on motorcycles, tossing Molotov cocktails into the storefronts along Los Angeles' major boulevards. He remembered seeing, and from a not very safe distance, people being pulled out of cars and trucks, beaten by raging mobs in South Central Los Angeles—several people killed, scores injured. He could still hear the constant wail of police and fire sirens, and the helicopters that rumbled endlessly overhead. He could still smell and taste the smoke that burned the eyes and throat as it hovered over the city and permeated homes and buildings. He could still see the choking layer of gray ash that fell for days on streets, houses, cars, blanketing everything, even the trees. He remembered the marching gangs as they looted and rioted. He shuddered at the memory.

"Listen, I'm late," Williams said. "And I only have a couple more blocks to go—I'll just get out and walk."

"Suit yourself," the driver said as he took the ten dollar bill that Williams handed him.

"Keep the change," Williams said.

The cabbie nodded, and for the first time his voice softened. "Hey, have a nice day."

The moment Williams was out of the cab, the driver honked again and began shouting at a pedestrian who was weaving in and out of traffic. The well-dressed jaywalker, carrying an attaché case, stopped long enough to say, "You taxi drivers are the worst, you know that?" You ride up on the sidewalk just to run over a pedestrian!"

"Aw, go soak yer head!" the cabbie yelled back. Just then, traffic started moving again and the cabbie immediately gunned his engine, sideswiping a delivery truck and starting another round of angry cursing.

Bennett Williams joined the sea of humanity that moved along Manhattan's streets where people walked much faster than any of the cars or taxis rode. New Yorkers never strolled; they walked quickly, with purpose, like a procession of determined ants being directed by some greater force. Or maybe, Williams thought, it was just to avoid the ubiquitous panhandlers, or the ever-burgeoning homeless population, or keep one step ahead of a potential mugger. Survival—psychological and physical—was what made New Yorkers walk faster than people anywhere else. They ran across streets, dodged cars, jumped into cabs, hurried into buildings, pushed onto subway trains and busses. It was a daily struggle and the city's inhabitants endured it because they were resigned to the way things were—they couldn't imagine it was ever going to get better. They were probably right.

In fact, things were getting worse. Power outages and rolling brownouts were becoming more frequent, even in the dead of winter. And, making matters worse, the city was experiencing a garbage collection crisis—the sanitation department was on strike. Mounds of torn plastic garbage bags spilled their contents onto curbsides. Manhattanites were getting used to gingerly maneuvering their way around the mountainous piles of refuse. The other city inhabitants—the rats and cockroaches—were enjoying an unexpected daily banquet.

Williams finally entered the marble lobby of one of New York's celebrated landmarks—the Chrysler building. Its graceful art deco architecture and interior design bespoke of a more civilized era, one that Williams was convinced was lost forever.

The elevator that took him to the twentieth floor emptied into the dark-oak-paneled, stylishly-furnished reception room of the venerable publishing giant, Brandon House. The moment Williams gave his name to the pretty young woman seated behind a rosewood desk, she said politely, "Oh yes, Mr. Williams, they're waiting for you." She immediately pressed a button and before Williams could sit in one of the upholstered chairs that made the place look like the reading room of an exclusive men's club, another woman came into the reception area, greeted Williams and asked him to follow her.

As she led him down a corridor and past open areas where secretaries and various entry-level trainees sat—young men and women who were smartly dressed—it occurred to Williams that he should have worn something other than his standard attire of blue jeans and khaki shirt. At least he'd shaved, and was sporting a pair of ninety-dollar tan leather shoes. It was the most he'd ever paid for a pair of shoes. Having some frivolous spending money was one of the perks, Strunk had told him. "Go, spend, you've earned it," his boss had said.

Inside a small, elegantly-appointed conference room, several people were waiting for Bennett Williams. When he walked in, they put down their coffee mugs and croissants to greet him. At the head of the conference table sat the publisher, Henry Fairlie, a tall, dignified looking man in his sixties. Fairlie rose from the table.

"Bennett Williams," he said, in a deeply resonant voice. "Good to see you again." He was referring to the first time they had met when Herschel Strunk introduced them at the Pulitzer awards dinner. He extended a firm handshake.

"Good to see you too," Williams said, shaking Fairlie's hand.

"I've asked these folks to join us." Fairlie indicated the others at the table "This is Robert Johnson and Carol Stevens from our legal department, Tom Miller and Barbara Flannigan from Marketing and Sales. And this is Aimee Argent who's to be your editor, and will work closely with you on this project." He gestured to an attractive woman, slender, with long dark hair that fell in gentle waves to her shoulders. As she got up to shake his hand, he could see her beautifully rounded breasts beneath the rose-colored silk blouse. Her well-fitted, charcoal gray wool skirt revealed narrow hips and shapely legs. Sheer black stockings and black patent pumps added the right amount of sexiness to her tailored look. She had high, chiseled cheekbones and dark eyes that exuded intelligence and confidence. She was accustomed to working in a highly competitive, male dominated business, undoubtedly the kind of woman who had to be assertive, even aggressive, if she was going to succeed.

"A pleasure to meet you," she said. Her voice was slightly husky. Williams liked the sound of it. "And congratulations on your Pulitzer."

"Thanks," he said, shaking her hand.

"Please everyone, let's sit down and get started," Henry Fairlie said in a gentle but paternalistic voice. For a split second Williams wondered what it would be like to have had Henry Fairlie for a father. "Bennett, I'm going to let Aimee take the floor, since it was her proposal that sold me on the idea of a book. That, of course, and your rather brilliant writing." Everyone around the table smiled and nodded, politely attentive. "Aimee . . ."

"Thank you, Henry," Aimee said. She brushed back a strand of long hair from her face and gazed directly at Williams; he felt a warm sensation flood through him. "Ben, when I read your articles, I knew the public was ready for this story—it's what they're hungry for. And the timing is perfect."

Williams looked at her, slightly skeptical. He was attracted to her, of that there was no doubt. But was she just another ambitious hypester? He knew the publishing industry had become more show business than literary over the last eight or ten years. It was all about box office. Best sellers now made millions of dollars for authors and publishers; then there were the foreign rights, the feature film, the TV mini-series, the CD rom, the sequel. And all the merchandising in between. Writers were the creators of multi-million dollar 'products' that had to be packaged and marketed like a Hollywood blockbuster film.

"And just what is it they're so hungry for?" Williams asked.

Henry Fairlie sat back, lit his pipe and smiled at Aimee.

"A spiritual message," Aimee said, "a reassurance, an awakening of hope and faith. Historically, people have always had an obsession with change at the end of every century. On one hand, it's a very frightening time—fear of the unknown, of what lies ahead. On the other hand, it's a very exciting time, and people become intrigued by the prospect of a new and better century, a chance to start again—wipe the slate clean so to speak—let go of obsolete ideas. And with this comes not only a renewed interest in global matters—in how to create a better world—but, in spiritualism, in God, in our relationship to the entire universe."

"And to the coming of a messiah who heightens that connection," Williams observed.

"Exactly," Henry Fairlie said enthusiastically, leaning toward Williams. "And what makes it all even more exciting this time, even more profound, is the fact that we are not only at the end of a century, but at the end of a millennium. And the beginning of a new one: A thousand years of history ending and another thousand beginning. In the year 999 A.D. there weren't many people around who could read, much less write! You have an extraordinary opportunity to make a contribution no one ever has, and to do it with your insight and eloquence. Think of it, Ben! The dawn of a whole new age, as told by H. Bennett Williams. It will be a classic, it'll live for a thousand more years! Aimee is right—the world is waiting for it." Fairlie sat back in his plush leather chair, and took a satisfied puff on his pipe.

"Yes, I suppose it is," Williams acquiesced.

"You just might wind up with another Pulitzer; hell, you might even get a Nobel for this one," Tom Miller of Marketing and Sales chimed in.

Williams turned to him, annoyed. "Hold it, hold it," he said. "Let's not get that far ahead. Let me write the book first."

Aimee smiled at Tom. "Ben's right," she said. "At least wait till it's on paper. Then you can market the hell out of it."

Williams shifted uncomfortably in his seat. Fairlie smiled at him. "I'm hoping you'll get started as soon as our legal department works out the final details of your contract. That okay with you, Ben?"

"Yeah, sure, sure."

"And Aimee will put her other projects on hold so she can work exclusively with you. She's not only a terrific editor, she's also a helluva researcher." He turned to Aimee. "Take good care of Ben. I'm counting on you."

"I'll take great care of him." She smiled broadly. That throaty voice again. Williams wanted to hear much more of it.

Fairlie brought the meeting to an abrupt end, and headed back to his office for a conference call that would set up an international distribution deal for Bennett Williams' book.

Out in the corridor, walking toward the reception room, Williams fell in step with Aimee. "It's almost lunch time," Aimee said glancing at Williams. "I hope you don't mind, but I took the liberty of making some arrangements."

"Oh," Williams said, caught off guard. The truth was, from the moment he laid eyes on her, he'd hoped they'd have lunch.

"You don't have plans, do you?" Aimee sounded concerned. "This is a great day, we have to celebrate." She wanted to spend more time with him, if for no other reason than to make sure he was firmly on the hook. And where she planned to take him would ensure they'd be seen by a lot of people in the publishing business. Colleagues and competitors would take notice of her with Brandon House's new author, a Pulitzer Prize winner, the celebrated friend and confidant of Abu 'Ali Asghar—it was almost as good as being seen with Abu himself. What she had trouble admitting was that she too felt the increasingly undeniable attraction.

"By all means, let's celebrate," Williams said.

Aimee again noticed his smile. It aroused feelings she hadn't felt in a very long time, feelings she had forgotten were possible. They made her a little nervous. She picked up a small pile of phone messages from the receptionist and then turned to Williams. "Wait here, I'll just get my coat." He watched her long legs receding down the hall-way toward her office.

"The Monkey Bar," Aimee said to the cab driver as she and Williams got into a waiting taxi in from of the Chrysler building.

The way Aimee took charge was new to Williams. American women had changed. It was the '90s, he reminded himself, and he'd been gone a long time. "A new place?" he asked. "I've never heard of it."

"I think you'll be pleased," Aimee said, smiling. "It's a favorite of mine. It's in the Elysee Hotel," she added. Williams nodded. The hotel was new to him too.

The taxi ride, as if by magic, was quick and uneventful. No traffic jams, no cursing drivers, no delays. Once they entered the crowded, noisy restaurant the outside world suddenly melted away.

"Good afternoon, Ms. Argent," the maître d' said to Aimee and then quietly motioned to a waiter to seat them. Aimee ordered a very ex-pensive bottle of champagne as she placed the cloth napkin on her lap. "It's on the house," she said. "Brandon House," she added, grin-ning. A few moments later the wine steward had filled their glasses.

"To new beginnings," Williams said, touching his glass to hers and holding it there just a bit longer than usual.

"And happy endings," Aimee said.

They ordered fresh lobster salads and then went back to their appe-tizers of Beluga caviar with chopped hard-boiled eggs and onion on the side. Aimee covered a small cracker with caviar and popped the whole thing into her mouth. Williams was impressed.

"This is how the Russians eat it," Aimee said. "If you try to take tiny bites of the cracker, the caviar ends up on your nose."

"I see," Williams said, smiling. He popped a crackerful of caviar into his mouth, chewed and swallowed it. "You know, I'm not even sure I like caviar."

"Oh good, more for me," Aimee said with a laugh.

Williams took another sip of champagne and stared at her. "So you know everything about me—sort of—but, aside from 'helluva re-searcher' and 'great editor,' plus possessing a pair of legs I'd follow anywhere, I don't know who Aimee Argent is. Except that her name is French."

"True."

"Go on, tell me about yourself."

"Am I being interviewed?"

Williams nodded. "It's what I do for a living."

"And I'm your editor. Which means I get to delete what I don't want you to know."

"Ah, a woman of mystery—"

"Sorry to disappoint you, but what you see is what you get—"

Williams stopped her. "I like that too—straightforward, no bullshit, truthful."

"Please don't make me sound like a girl scout."

Their entrees arrived and Aimee attacked her lobster salad with gusto. Williams smiled. "And I really like a woman who enjoys her food." Aimee nodded. Williams studied her for a few seconds. "You don't have a New York accent, so I'd say you're originally from the Midwest."

Aimee nodded. "Iowa. I come from a long line of farmers. They came here from France just after World War One."

Williams smiled. "And so, small town girl with lots of ambition comes to big city and works for—"

"Wait. You forgot college."

"Oh right. Where'd you go to college?"

"Northwestern—" Williams dropped his fork and stared at Aimee. "What's the matter?" she asked.

"I went to Northwestern, too."

"Hope it was a few years before me."

"It was. Okay. What happened when you came here?"

"I struggled along for a few years, then a few more years, then decided that being poor really sucks. Especially in New York. I was on the verge of a major depression when I managed to get invited to a literary luncheon—agents, publishers, and young editors looking for jobs. I pawned my TV set and bought the most expensive outfit I could afford. At the luncheon I was seated next to the editor-in-chief of Brandon House. We talked, I convinced him he needed me, and the rest is history. Excuse me, *her*story."

"And no 'significant other' along the way?"

"I was married for a couple of years. It should never have happened. We had loneliness and lack of money in common."

"And these days?"

"These days I don't have time for relationships. I've become a workaholic. But I love what I do—someday I want to have my own publishing company—"

"You are ambitious."

"So are you."

Williams nodded absently. "Yeah. But something's missing. Something's definitely missing." His gaze drifted away as he thought about the loneliness he'd felt the night before, and that still tugged at him. She watched him as he suddenly snapped back, as if coming out of a daydream. His eyes locked on hers. "So, little ex-farm girl, tell me about growing up in Iowa."

"It was wonderful. There were lots of animals—I had a horse, three dogs, four cats, two ducks, and a macaw."

"A macaw?"

"Yes. You know, the big rainbow-colored parrot." Williams nodded. "I still have him."

"How old is he?"

"Ninety-five. He'll probably outlive me. If they're healthy, they can live to a hundred twenty-five, thirty," Aimee said matter-of-factly.

"Are you saying he's been in your family—?"

"Forever. He keeps getting passed down in the family will, from generation to generation."

"And now he's yours?"

Aimee nodded. "He's a great guy. Real smart."

Williams looked worried. "Does he talk, too?"

Aimee shook her head. "Just a few loud screeches at around five in the afternoon. Like they do in the jungle when the sun goes down."

"I see. And what is his name?"

"Napoleon."

"Figures."

The waiter came over and took their plates, refilled their glasses with the last of the champagne and asked if they'd like to see the dessert cart.

"I'll just have coffee," Williams said and looked at Aimee.

"And I'd love to see the dessert cart," Aimee said.

Williams watched with delight as Aimee ordered the richest dessert on the tray—a thick slice of chocolate mousse with raspberry truffle, topped with a dollop of whipped cream and dripping with fresh raspberries. "Where do you put it all?" Williams asked.

"Must be the farm girl in me."

Williams drained the last of his champagne and looked at Aimee as she swallowed a mouthful of mousse. "How is it?" he asked.

Aimee put her fork into the mousse, carefully including a few raspberries and extended it toward Williams. He opened his mouth slightly, Aimee glided the fork between his teeth, he closed his lips around the fork and with his hand on her wrist, slowly slid the fork out of his mouth. "I think I'd like to let you to feed me all sorts of food—"

Aimee blushed and sipped her coffee. Then she gazed directly into Williams eyes. Her delicate silver earrings with dangling quartz stones bounced as she shook her head from side to side. "Ben, what's going on here?"

"I'm not sure. But whatever it is, I don't want it to stop. I don't want this afternoon to end."

"I know," she said quietly. "But I have to get back to the office."

"Do you?"

"I can't mix work with pleasure."

"Where is that written?"

"Ben, this is crazy. We really don't know each other—"

"Oh yes we do. I feel like I've always known you. I just hadn't met you."

Aimee sighed softly. "When I read your first article in the *New York Times,* I felt as though . . ."

Williams took her hands in his and whispered, "As though what?"

"As though . . ."

"Say it."

"As if we'd met somewhere before, like a *déjà vu,* that I connected to what you wrote about in a way that was like finding—" Aimee stopped.

Williams looked at her with intense longing in his eyes, a feeling of desire and need and yearning coursed through him. "Finding—?"

Aimee met his gaze. Their eyes locked on each other. "Another part of myself."

Williams stared at Aimee, as though contemplating something. He leaned forward. "Aimee, stay with me. Don't go back to the office. Let's take a room upstairs."

Aimee stared back at Williams. There was a hint of fear in her eyes.

"I can't, Ben. I just can't. It wouldn't be a good idea, not very professional, you know."

Williams leaned over and kissed her softly on the cheek. "That I *know* isn't written." He paused. "For what it's worth, I have *never* felt like this in my life. Never."

Aimee reached up with one hand and gently touched his cheek. Williams took her hand and kissed her palm as it grazed over his mouth. "Nor have I," she said in that husky whisper that Williams knew he'd never get enough of.

CHAPTER 30

Williams awoke to the sound of sirens racing through the streets below. He turned to look at Aimee, sound asleep beside him in the satin-sheeted bed in the hotel suite he had rented for the rest of the day. He marveled at how innocent her face looked—so peaceful, he thought. He doubted that he ever slept that way. Taking care not to wake her, he lifted some stray hairs that had fallen across her cheek, leaned over and brushed his lips on her forehead. He glanced at his watch; it was just after midnight. He'd slept only a few hours but was energized and alert.

They had made love several times throughout the remainder of the afternoon and into the evening. Passionate, intense, romantic lovemaking. It surprised them both—the extent to which each was hungry for the other. But the need was much more than physical— that too they both knew. They held one another and talked in soft, hushed tones. Williams was deeply touched when Aimee told him why she loved books. "My father was a great storyteller," she said as she lay in Williams' arms, "and when I was a little girl, he would make up fascinating stories with wonderful characters—make them up as he went along. He'd tell them to me before I went to sleep at night or whenever he'd let me sit on his lap on the tractor. And some-times he'd stop right in the middle of a story and have me add some-thing, just to get my imagination going, and as a challenge to him." Aimee smiled at the memory. "Then he'd take off with my contribu-tion and weave it perfectly into his story. And they always had happy endings, no matter how scary or sad they might have been in the middle."

"How did he die?" Williams had asked.

Aimee sighed. "A heart attack. Right there on the damn tractor. He was lying in the field when we found him."

"Well, at least he didn't suffer. Didn't die in pain, with regret—"

Aimee held Williams tightly against her breast, instinctively realizing the reference. "We had very different fathers," Williams said.

Sirens continued to wail in the city below but something beside the sirens had awakened Williams. An uneasy feeling churned beneath the surface of his consciousness. He got up and went to the window. Fire trucks and police cars were heading toward Harlem. In the distance Williams could make out a fiery glow illuminating the night sky. Riots had erupted again. He wondered where the people of Harlem would go when they'd burned their buildings and businesses to the ground. Where would they turn next? Maybe they didn't care.

Except for a taxi ride through Harlem once or twice in previous years, Williams had never really been to the ghetto that had become like dry rot in an old house—a steady, relentless decay that had been allowed to spread through apathy and constant neglect. Harlem was just a place to pass through quickly on the way to somewhere else, a place smart people avoided. But now, he suddenly realized that the people who lived there were hardly any different from those in Calcutta or Manila or Jakarta. He now saw how much they had in common with the masses he had encountered in Mogadishu, the refugees in Ethiopia and throughout the devastated African nations. He even saw their common bond with the Masai people in the Great Rift Valley.

The images of the day came back—the taxi driver who cursed the world around him and saw no way to change it, the moment he walked into the conference room at Brandon House and met Aimee. He remembered their lunch hours earlier, and how all he could think about was wanting to make love to her; and the moment he entered her—their lovemaking was like nothing he had ever known. As Williams watched her, he felt an indescribable sense of elation and peace. He also realized that the feelings he had for Aimee would never have been possible before Abu. It was Abu who first chipped away at his fortress until the walls began to crumble. Abu had taught him about connecting with himself and the outside world. He understood now that he was not so different from all the rest of humanity. Everyone was afraid of something, and often it was the same thing. To be afraid was to be human. But love was the key that opened the door to a deeper meaning. Fear was the anchoring clay of existence; love was the liberating rain that cleansed and nurtured. The struggle against fear and the need for love was what connected everyone together. Abu had shown

Williams the world around him. More importantly, he showed Williams the way home. Now it was up to him.

Williams saw Aimee reach out in her sleep to touch him. Finding only the empty spot, she awoke, peering around the dark room. "Ben?" she said in an anxious voice.

"I'm here," he said.

Aimee got up from the bed, wrapping the satin sheet around her as she walked over to Williams. She snuggled next to him on the settee. "Are you okay?" she asked softly.

"Yeah," he said, stroking her hair. "What woke you?"

"I felt you gone. I thought you left."

"Not a chance," he said, gently kissing her head.

"Wanna do it again?" Aimee asked playfully

"Are you trying kill me?"

"There are worse ways to die. In fact, I'd say this was about the best way to go," she teased.

Williams laughed and took her in his arms. He kissed Aimee and she began to respond with more intensity. Williams gently stopped her. "I need to ask you something."

"You want to know if I'll respect you in the morning—"

Williams smiled. "No, I'm serious. It's about the book." Aimee looked puzzled. "I want to know what gave you the idea for a book about Abu."

Aimee looked at Williams with disbelief. "You want to discuss this now?"

Williams nodded. "It's important."

"You pick odd times to work, Bennett Williams." She paused and thought for several moments. "Okay. The answer to your question is Nostradamus."

"The man who made those extraordinary predictions that keep coming true?"

"Yes. I'd been to a party one night where people were talking about New Age writings, and they discussed apocalyptic prophecies, and how all the religions of the world have their own but similar versions. Someone suggested I read Nostradamus' book *Centuries*— the quatrains, the four-line stanzas that predicted major events of history. Did you know that the quatrains can be interpreted to have foretold the French and Russian revolutions, World War One and

Two? There is even a prediction about World War Three."

"What's all this got to do with Abu?"

"Nostradamus prophesied that an Antichrist would return,"—Aimee spoke as though she were finishing one of her father's stories—"wearing a blue turban, and he would come to power in the Middle East. He would bring about the final Armageddon, followed by a new age of peace and splendor." Aimee paused to look at Williams. "What better manifestation of this than Abu 'Ali Asghar? You understand I'm not saying that I'm absolutely convinced of any of this. But he has certainly captured my imagination—and those of a lot of people—through your articles. Some think he's the nineties' version of Mother Theresa and the Dalai Lama combined."

"Don't you think you're reading too much into this?" Williams asked, but he felt more the way Aimee did than he was willing to admit.

"Maybe. But think about it, Ben," Aimee said, her enthusiasm growing as she spoke. "It all fits, doesn't it?" Williams looked at her in silent agreement. "And from what little I know about the Sikhs, they're highly venerated warriors. Right? And Abu is half Arab, half Sikh."

A disturbed look crossed Williams' face; he got up from the settee and walked over to the window. Aimee came up to him and put her hand on his back. "What's the matter?"

"I just remembered something Abu once said." Aimee looked at Williams quizzically. "Humanity, with its constant resorting to warfare as a method of resolving conflicts, reminded him of the man who beat himself over the head with a hammer, and when asked 'why,' the man said 'because it feels so good when I stop.' " Williams took a deep breath. Aimee waited quietly. "And so I asked him if he was here to make war or to end it?"

"And what did he say?"

" 'I shall be the hammer.' "

"Ben, where is he now?"

"The last I heard, North Africa. He's heading to the Middle East."

"We need to talk about Abu." Aimee's tone was serious. "Tell me what you know about him, what *you* think he's up to."

"In that case," Williams said, "let's go out and get some breakfast. This is going to take a while."

They dressed quickly, but both were ambivalent about leaving the hotel room, neither wanted the romantic fantasy they had begun at lunch to end. "Maybe we should just order room service," Williams said, embracing Aimee as she was brushing her hair.

"Oh, you're bad," she said as she kissed him. A moment's hesitation and then: "No, we have to leave, or we won't end up talking." Aimee paused. "And we need to discuss Abu; I feel it's important. Besides, you started it."

Williams held her tightly in his arms and kissed her. "To be continued . . ."

They held hands in the elevator and as they walked out of the hotel. Around the corner they found an all-night coffee shop and slipped into a booth with a window facing the street. They ordered juice, coffee and sweet rolls. Williams told Aimee of Abu's coming of age in Sri Lanka, his life in London and his wife, Nanaki.

"And right now, Ben, *today*, what do you think Abu wants?" Aimee asked.

"He's after power, I'm certain of that—but not in the political sense. He wants to be in a position to affect great change all over the planet. That's why he wants to be leader of the Third World."

"Why does he want that?" Aimee asked as she took a large bite of her sweet roll. It reminded Williams of the way she ate the caviar cracker at lunch. He smiled at her.

"I love watching you eat," he said.

Aimee grinned at him and took a sip of coffee. "Go on, why leader of the Third World?"

"Because there isn't one; because there needs to be one." Williams downed his orange juice and cut off a piece of his roll, then put it back down on the plate and looked into Aimee's eyes. "But understand, Abu's message is an intensely spiritual one. I think he's a great spiritual master, maybe even in the same league with Jesus and Muhammad."

Aimee looked at Williams with skepticism. "Now maybe *you're* reading too much into him?"

Williams shook his head. "Abu is not like any other human being on this planet. He's not merely the champion of the poor, the suffering, the homeless, those dying of starvation and war. I think he's been sent here to . . . teach."

"Sent here by whom?"

"God. By the spiritual energy and consciousness that connects all human being to one another, and to the universe. Abu always said he was here to serve humanity and he will do whatever humanity chooses for him to do."

"And so, you believe that he's come now, at this time, for some divine purpose?" Aimee said the words slowly, carefully.

"Yes." Williams' tone was unequivocal. "Aimee, no one was as skeptical as me when I first met Abu. But I've seen too much, too much has happened—it's not an accident. The universe doesn't operate randomly."

"You're saying there's a plan?"

"Yes, and no. According to Abu, about two thousand years ago humanity began another transition—an evolutionary and spiritual change that started with Jesus and was followed by the prophet Muhammad, and the teachings of both came from the early Hebrew faith—Judaism gave rise to Christianity and shaped Islam as well." Aimee nodded as Williams continued. "Now we're on the brink of another major transition—a new period of human evolution."

"A transition to what?"

"A new level of consciousness. One which recognizes that humanity is nothing more than the sum total of its separate parts: A consciousness based on love."

"Oh, like the Age of Aquarius?"

"No, something way beyond that. A consciousness of cooperation and commonality. Of respect and appreciation for differences in order to end intolerance. A state of consciousness devoid of judgment and fear. It's possible, according to Abu."

"How is it possible?"

"He teaches that we're much more than physical beings, that our souls exist in a realm unaffected by the physical reality we live in; the three-dimensional concept of time and space. That we're actually ten-dimensional beings with abilities and potential far beyond anything we currently know or use."

"How does this relate to my idea for a book about Abu?"

"Because he says that our souls are conduits to the universe, to God. And we're all linked together by that common network and, therefore, in direct communication with everything and everyone around us. We're all playing our roles in one great drama: Our evolution as a species. And that evolution is based entirely upon our actions, the choices we make as individuals, societies, nations, all of humanity."

"Okay, I'm with you so far. But why a book?"

"It's part of the connectedness of things; there's no coincidence here. It's the reason I found myself in Bhopal—because I was desperate to find the one story that might win me the Pulitzer. Maybe for the same reason you and I found each other. You see, it's not just about Abu, it's about all of us, the whole damn world—that's what he wants us to see and understand. He wants us to realize our collective consciousness and use that 'higher power,' if you will, to bring about harmony and peace. To see beyond our petty, narrow sphere of vision and embrace something far greater, far more noble and wiser. It would certainly be the beginning of a brave new millennium, don't you think?"

"Yes, of course. But is the world ready? I hardly think so, Ben. Most of us can't get past the petty prejudices we experience on a daily basis."

"Ah, but the world is changing and shifting, and these polarities are part of the pain of transition, moving from everything we've known and accepted as true into the great unfathomable unknown. And to do that, everything is being brought up to the surface to look at in undeniable technicolor."

"You mean this is like some collective, universal labor pain before we give birth to a better world?"

"Yes, and it will be so much better. But Abu says that first there must be an awareness of how barbaric we still are as a species before we can begin to understand and feel and change."

"So when you traveled the Third World with Abu, and he wanted you to see the suffering and horror and write about it, it was to show the world what is going on there *in order* to bring about that change."

"Right. But I'm afraid Abu isn't going to let humanity come to that realization when it's good and ready. If, when all the facts are presented, through my book, and through his worldwide appearances and speeches, if nothing is done about the terrible injustices and suffering, if humanity chooses to hide in its fear, then Abu is going to bring that fear out and expose it. He will force us to confront it. And it won't be a pretty sight. He will do whatever is necessary so that the lesson is finally learned. No matter how terrible or apocalyptic."

"You think he has that power?"

"I *know* he does. But if we find the courage to change, then Abu will simply drift into obscurity; there won't be any need for him. However, my faith in humanity isn't quite up to believing that that is what will happen."

"Then what *do* you think will happen?" Aimee's voice was a mixture of trepidation and intense curiosity.

Williams took a final swig of his coffee, got up and tossed some money on the table. "Come on, I'll show you."

"Where are we going?"

"To see the shape of things to come."

The taxi driver had to be bribed several hundred dollars after Bennett Williams had asked to be driven to 125th Street and Lenox Avenue."

"Harlem?!" the cabbie said incredulously. "You nuts? There's riots going on up there."

Aimee looked frightened. "Ben—"

The driver took the money from Williams, but was now regretting his acquiescence as they reached the famous Harlem intersection. It was called "Africa Square" and was the cultural and economic center of Harlem with its African-American art museum, the National Black Theater and the Apollo where history's black jazz greats, rhythm and blues and soul artists still performed. Nearby was the Audubon Theater where Malcolm X was assassinated several decades earlier.

But tonight, 125th Street was burning. Its shops were being looted and the whole area had been cordoned off by police barricades.

"Can you go around?" Williams asked the driver.

The cabbie took an immediate left on 123rd Street and Adam Clayton Powell, Jr. Blvd. and went right on Eighth Avenue heading back toward 125th. Suddenly, the driver slammed on the brakes throwing Aimee and Williams forward. They both looked up to see a group of young black men standing in front of the taxi's headlights.

They encircled the cab and closed ranks. "Hey, honky mutha–fuckahs," one of them shouted. Another spotted Aimee in the back seat. *"Ooooh, baby,"* he said, "I ain't had no white pussy in a *loooong* time." The others joined in, leering at her, whistling, making obscene gestures and laughing.

"Oh God," Aimee muttered. Williams quickly locked the doors. The driver shifted into reverse and frantically tried to back up. The engine stalled. "Ben!" Aimee cried.

"It's okay, we're gonna be fine," Williams said as he put an arm around Aimee without taking his eyes off the youths who had ambushed the cab.

"Shit, goddamn it—" the driver yelled as he kept turning the ignition key to no avail.

The attempted escape seemed only to anger the boys, who now began pounding on the windows and roof and rocking the car from side to side. Aimee was terrified. "They're going to kill us, Ben," she said, clutching his arm tightly.

"Easy, easy . . ." He was surprised at how calm he was, as though none of it was real. The driver reached under his seat and pulled out a revolver. "Here," he said, handing it to Williams. "Don't be afraid to use it." He continued trying to get the engine to roll over, but it was dead. Then a baseball bat shattered the window on the driver's side. Flailing black hands reached in and pulled the cabbie out of the car. The boys gathered around him, and began kicking and punching him until he fell to the ground. Aimee screamed. Williams checked the revolver and released the safety. As he was getting out of the taxi, the attackers stopped, looked down the street and then ran. The taxi driver writhed on the sidewalk in pain. Just as Williams leaned over, trying to lift him up and back into the cab, he saw a dozen or so tall, young black men walking slowly and steadily toward him, carrying sticks and clubs. Beneath long, black coats, they all wore white shirts buttoned up at the collar, but without ties. They were clean-shaven and had closely-cropped hair. Their somber expressions were identical and ominous. When they reached the taxi, one of them, a particularly tall and intense-looking young man, knelt down to the cab driver. "He will live," he said, then stood up and glanced at Williams. "Are you all right?"

Williams was struck by his polite demeanor and the way he enunciated his words. He bore a stunning resemblance to the Masai warrior, Tipilet Ole Simel. "Yeah, I'm all right," Williams said.

The young man pointed to the revolver in Williams' hand. "Are you going to shoot me?"

"No," Williams replied.

"Good," the young man said with a bemused smile.

"Who are you?" Aimee asked, clutching onto Williams.

He noticed Aimee for the first time. His smile disappeared.

"We are Muslims," he said. "Members of the Islamic Brotherhood. We are not going to hurt you. We seek to rid our streets of the vermin that pollutes them. We work to make life better for our people, not more desperate."

Aimee let out an audible sigh of relief.

"Well, I want to thank you," Williams said gratefully. "I think you saved our lives."

"Oh," the young Muslim leader said, looking off in the direction where the assailants had run, "I am certain we did. And if I were you, I'd leave here right now."

"We need to get him to a hospital," Williams said gesturing to the taxi driver who was now being lifted up by two of the young Muslims.

"We'll take care of him," the leader said. "There's an emergency clinic around the corner."

Before Williams could decide how he and Aimee would get back to midtown Manhattan, the Muslim leader hailed a passing taxi. As soon as the cab stopped, he opened the door and gestured for Williams and Aimee to get in. Once they were in the back seat, Williams opened the window and extended his hand to the black man. He looked at it but did not accept it. "Do not think because we have saved your lives that we are friends. Sir, this is our community, and we are trying to save it. Unless you have come here to help, you are not welcome. Go. You do not belong here. A day will come when you and I may face one another again, but then it will not be my intention to save you."

Aimee looked startled and swallowed hard to control her fright. The Muslim slapped the roof of the cab with his hand and the taxi took off quickly, jolting Aimee and Williams against the back seat. After they had been riding for a few minutes, Aimee started to relax and took a deep breath. "Helluva first date, Bennett Williams," she said.

Williams laughed and held her tightly. "I don't know if I can promise this much excitement indefinitely."

Aimee smiled. "This was enough to last a lifetime, thank you." Aimee's smile faded. "And you made your point—it isn't real to most people, not in this country anyway."

Williams kissed the top of Aimee's head as she nestled into his chest. The churning inside him had stopped. He noticed how serene he felt. A direction was beginning to open up to him, and a clarity he had never experienced before. He had found Aimee, and with her a sense of completeness that had escaped him all his life. He also realized that the book he wanted to write was beginning to take shape in his mind. Williams wrapped his arms more tightly around Aimee as the taxi sped them further and further away from danger.

CHAPTER 31

Abu's father had made certain his son knew what it was to be Bedouin—those ancient people who were born in the Arabian desert and who, down through the centuries, had remained there. Like seafaring adventurers of maritime nations—free and independent—wanderers unfettered by constraints of place and time. The Bedouin knew that no one was greater than the desert; no one was stronger than the group.

When he was a small boy, Abu's father told him the stories of Saladin, the greatest of Arab heroes, the embodiment of the Bedouin ideal, and it did not escape the young Abu that Saladin, like himself, wasn't an Arab.

Saladin was born a Kurd in Iraq, but as a youth became deeply interested in the study of Islam. He was both statesman and military leader by the time he was thirty-one. For twenty years he reigned as Sultan of Egypt and Syria.

He zealously united all Arabs under the Islamic concept of jihad. But Saladin saw the holy war in its purest form—that of bringing light to the world, righting injustice and advancing the message of the Prophet Muhammad.

Abu understood clearly that Saladin's dream lived on, that the Arab people still possessed their glorious memory of a once-great civilization, and that the heart of the Arab people could still be made to beat as one.

As Abu traveled through the Moroccan cities of Marrakech, Casablanca and Tangier, wherever he went, he gained an audience of Arabs. He spoke of their past glories and he spoke of the abyss—the Dark Ages into which the Arab people had descended. "Muslims everywhere will rise to reclaim that glory. We are over one-billion strong and in every country in the world. *Nothing* will stop us from bringing justice to the world!"

Abu and Bhaiji drove to Algeria where, at the Great Mosque of Pasha in the Casbah of Oran, he exhorted his Muslim audience to recapture their former greatness. His acceptance was immediate, passionate and devoted. And then, just as quickly as he'd come, he was gone, but always leaving in his wake thousands more admiring, often adoring, followers.

On a particularly clear and cool day, Abu and Bhaiji moved onward, along the jagged, rocky coastline—known as the Turquoise Coast—toward Algiers. Bhaiji deftly negotiated the winding road that went through forests along the sea and around steep cliffs. It was along this road that Abu told Bhaiji to stop.

Abu got out of the Mercedes and walked to the edge of the cliff where he stood looking down at the waves smashing against the rocks below. A light breeze made his robes flutter. Bhaiji sat back in his seat, turned off the engine and recalled a similar moment with Williams and Satki on the Serengeti Plain.

Bhaiji missed Satki and his American friend. He was disturbed by a growing tension in Abu, and a feeling that Abu was distancing himself. It bothered him that Abu kept more to himself. Abu had become a *celebrity*. People were always clamoring to meet him, or at least be seen with him. Bhaiji was beginning to feel less like Abu's friend and more like one of those political lackeys that buzzed around government officials like flies. He wished things had stayed the way they once were.

Quite unexpectedly, Abu turned and motioned for Bhaiji to get out of the car and join him.

Abu looked back out at the sea, and then down at the white sandy beach. "Walk with me."

The two men followed a steep and narrow path down to the shore. They walked along the water's edge. "This place reminds me of Sri Lanka," Abu said wistfully. "There were beaches like this, but even more beautiful. I used to watch the fisherman cast their nets. I was without a care in the world then, and I was very happy." Bhaiji walked in silence. Abu had never confided in him in quite this way before. "But things changed. My world changed. I changed. My soul desired that I become more, experience more, and as a human being I desired to become more than I was, to fulfill my destiny. I could have remained in Sri Lanka, married and had children, perhaps become a fisherman or a farmer. To try and hold onto what was dear to me. I could have chosen that path." Abu stood for a few minutes, quietly staring out at the sea. "Bhaiji," he finally said.

"Yes, Abuji?"

"The joy of life, Bhaiji—the richness of living—only comes to those who have the courage to keep moving forward. You *must* learn to accept that things are going to change. They may not be as you think they should be. I know it is difficult for you. But there are things you cannot know. Such knowledge could put you at great risk and I do not wish you harmed."

"I would die for you, Abuji."

Abu placed a hand on Bhaiji's shoulder. "But I will never ask that of you."

As they sat in silence, Bhaiji sensed it would be their last time to do so together.

Everyone of importance in Algiers turned out to greet Abu at the Palais du Peuple near the Parc de la Liberté. There was pomp and circumstance befitting a royal visit.

Before moving inside for private discussions, the president led Abu up onto a platform for what he assumed would be a perfunctory statement by their honored guest. But when Abu finished, the crowd was chanting his name.

There were official receptions and dinners, and while Abu was afforded all the respect given a winner of the Nobel Peace Prize, there was something more—as though Abu was being accorded the status of an Ambassador at Large, a diplomat without portfolio, even a head of state.

There were parades and celebrations, and the Algerian legislature proclaimed a national holiday in his honor. He was accepted as an Arab, and seen as a hero; even better, he was seen by Algeria's politicians as having no agenda that could threaten them. He would distract Algerians from their problems, and by his presence show the people that the government was indeed on their side. The country's leaders gladly welcomed Abu.

Abu spoke at the one-thousand year old Djemaa El Kebir mosque, and addressed the National Assembly with the same ease and humility that he showed when he walked the streets of Algiers and visited the men and women who worked and shopped the Fish Market, across from the Place des Martyrs on the Boulevard Che Guevara. He helped the merchants uncrate fish and sweep the floors while admiring throngs of people watched. Even the cynical international press couldn't help but remark on the Sheik's extraordinary lack of guile.

As Abu walked through the city's streets, Bhaiji noticed something remarkable happening. People began falling in step with Abu, walking alongside and in back of him, gathering to him the way a magnet attracts slivers of steel. Soon, there was a parade of men, women and children a mile or more long. They blocked intersections and brought traffic to a halt.

Abu entered Algiers' spectacular amphitheater atop the hill of the Esplanade de l'Afrique and waited at center stage. His followers crammed themselves into the rows of seats and overflowed into the aisles. There was barely room to move, and those who could not waited outside and transmitted what was happening to those yet further away.

A hush fell over the expectant crowd. Only the cool sea wind whispered through the palm trees. Abu scanned the faces of his audience.

When he spoke his voice was like rolling thunder, amplified by the walls of the amphitheater so that it could be heard outside. "My friends, my brothers, my sisters: You have welcomed me into your hearts and your homes and showered me with your love, your generosity and your hospitality. You have embraced me as one of you, and raised my spirit. I have felt a warmth and acceptance in your presence that transcends even our common Bedouin heritage, and I feel a kinship with each and every one of you that has become an everlasting bond between us." His voice became somber. "But, because we are one family, I feel your suffering. My heart calls out for vengeance against those who harm you."

Abu paused while the crowd rose to their feet and cheered, as though wanting to convey that they too felt kinship with him. After a few moments, they settled into their seats and the amphitheater grew quiet again. "And," Abu continued, his voice resolute, "I make a solemn oath to each and every one of you: I shall strive to create a new world order that will ensure that *you* are recognized as the true source of worldly power, and *you* are afforded the respect and dignity that befits all of Allah's children. One world, under God, with liberty and justice for all! I will not fail you!"

Again, the large crowd was on its feet, and the amphitheater was filled with exultation. "Our Bedouin forefathers," Abu continued, speaking over the crowd until they were silent, "believed in one Arab nation without borders wherein all Arabs were equal, wherein all Arabs could live in peace and prosperity: One house, united and strong. The time has come, my brothers and sisters, for us to begin constructing that house!"

The crowd roared. They chanted his name for several minutes before Abu raised his hands to quiet them. "There is an ancient Arab saying: 'Me against my brother, my brother and I against my cousin, my cousin and I against the foreigner.' We have allowed the evil-doers of the world and foreigners to enter our house. They turn us against one another by fueling ancient rivalries and jealousies, and they have caused us to kill our brothers. And just as our Bedouin ancestors gave us an understanding of the strength of the group, so did Allah give us through his messenger Muhammad the understanding that we all deserve to live in a world free of disease, free of famine, free of oppression. And Allah has given us to know that it is the duty of all Muslims to create that world. And the time has come to do so!"

Once again the crowd jumped to their feet while Abu waited. "Of all the people of the planet, Allah chose the Arab people to receive his message through one of them, and he chose the Arab people to spread that message to the world. Why? Because Allah placed the Bedouin in the desert to study and learn. And the Bedouin learned that none of us is as strong as all of us, and that the needs of the many outweigh the wants of the few. Allah asked: 'Have you thought of him that denies the Last Judgment? It is he who turns away the orphan and does not urge others to feed the poor. Woe to those who pray but are heedless in their prayer; who make a show of piety and give no alms to the destitute.' "

As Abu paused he paced before the assembled crowd. "And Allah asked 'Have you thought of the Event which will overwhelm mankind? On that day there shall be downcast faces, of men broken and worn out, burnt by a scorching fire, drinking from a seething fountain. Therefore give warning. Your duty is to warn them: You are not their keeper. As for those who turn their backs and disbelieve, Allah will inflict on them the supreme chastisement.' "

Abu paused and paced, never breaking eye contact with the audience. "And Allah," Abu continued, his tone more ominous, "has warned us of the coming Day of Judgment. 'When the sky is rent asunder, when the stars scatter and the oceans roll together; when the graves are hurled about; each soul shall know what it has done and what it has failed to do.' And, my friends," Abu said, "know that the Day of Judgment is near."

"How can we know?" a man shouted from the audience. "Can you give us a sign?"

"Read your Koran," Abu quickly responded in a stern voice. "What does it say to you on this matter?" There was silence in the audience. "Does it not speak of a time of change? Does it not speak of the time when the hypocrites and evil-doers of the world will be revealed to all? And have you not seen changes occurring in the society of Man? Have you not observed that the hypocrites of the world are being discovered, and the evil-doers revealed for all to see? Can you not *feel* the changes occurring in the world and are you not filled with a sense of anxiety about the future? Are you not witness to great shifts and the death of established empires? Is not the might of imperialist America waning? Is not the vast atheistic empire of the Soviet Union in ruins and consumed by chaos? And most importantly, are you not observing worldly power slipping from the grasp of the few and into the hands of the many?" There were again nods in the audience. "Does the Koran not speak of the planet quaking and trembling; when mountains are blown away? And watch the night sky. See the light in the heavens that grows brighter with each passing day. Does the Koran not speak to you of this 'Nightly Visitant'?" Abu stopped for a moment and looked at his listeners, his eyes intense and foreboding. There was a collective nodding in the audience.

" 'By the heaven,' " Abu said, quoting from the Koran again, and sounding as though he was invoking the power of God, " 'and by the nightly visitant! Would that you knew what the nightly visitant is! It is the star of piercing brightness.' "

"Are you a prophet of God?" a man shouted from the audience.

Abu looked at the man. "I am here to warn humanity. I am here to be part of the great changes to come. Does that make me a prophet of God? You decide."

The audience was murmuring, a sense of agitation could be felt throughout the amphitheater. "But, must I be a prophet of God before you will hear me?" Abu asked. "Did the ancients listen to Noah? Did Pharaoh listen to Moses? And what of Lot? Did the people of his once great city listen to him when he beseeched them to change their ways? Or did they turn their backs, label him a religious fanatic, and thereby seal their own destruction? Did they listen to the Prophet Jesus when he walked the earth with his message of peace and love? Or did the people not allow the Roman eagles to crucify him?"

Abu waited for a moment for effect, and then continued: "And Allah has warned the faithful that: 'When the sun ceases to shine; when the stars fall down and the mountains are blown away; when camels big with young are left untended and the wild beasts are brought together; when the seas are set alight and men's souls are reunited; when the infant girl, buried alive, is asked for what crime she was slain; when the records of men's deeds are laid open and the heaven is stripped bare; when Hell burns fiercely and Paradise is brought near: Then each soul shall know what it has done.' "

"But, Sheik Abu," the same man shouted again from the audience, "we desire to follow only Allah and those who are truly his apostles. How do we know you are one? How do we know that you are not the Great Deceiver of whom the Koran also speaks?"

The vast audience registered its disapproval of the man's insolence. Abu raised his hand to still the crowd. "It is good that you question those who invoke the name of Allah, and decide for yourselves whether they are who they say, and deserve your trust. I offer only my deeds; my actions have been recorded for all to know. Look inside your own hearts, and decide for yourselves."

Abu allowed silence to fill the amphitheater. "Has it not been said that 'If thou canst walk on water thou art no better than a straw. If thou canst fly in the air thou art no better than a fly. Conquer thy heart that thou mayest become somebody.' For those of you who seek a sign, know that Allah desires for you to join him in bringing his light upon the unbelievers of the world to unveil the hypocrites and discover the evil-doers. I am only a man, a servant, at best a humble messenger."

"What would you have us do?" another man called out. "We are poor people, we have nothing."

"You have more than you know," Abu answered forcefully. "YOU ARE ALLAH!" he shouted out.

"Blasphemy!" someone yelled. There was a stirring among the crowd. "Allah is supreme!" someone else asserted. "Allah is great; we are merely his servants."

"You are right," Abu quickly agreed. "Allah is supreme, Allah is greater than anything you can touch, see or feel, Allah is the divine Master of all that is. And we *are* his servants. But Allah is greater than each of us in the way the great Sahara is greater than each grain of sand. But is each grain of sand not the Sahara?"

Many in the audience remained uncertain, but many others nodded in understanding and agreement. Abu paced the stage from one end to the other, his eyes cast downward, deep in thought. "It is said in the Koran that life is but a sport, a pastime. That sport—that illusion—distracts us and so Allah sends down his prophets from time to time to show us the way out of the darkness into the light."

Abu surveyed the faces of his audience for a moment before resuming. "Only within that light can you know the power of which I speak. 'Allah loves those who fight for his cause in ranks as firm as a mighty edifice,'" Abu said, again quoting from the Koran. "'Believers, be Allah's helpers! When Jesus said to his disciples: "Who will come with me to help Allah?" they replied: "*We* are Allah's helpers."'

"You," Abu said—his right arm made a sweeping gesture, "each of you are his blessed creations. There is not one of you who is better or less than another. You are sent forth to be his warriors; to carry his message in your hearts, and demonstrate the godly virtues that are befitting his name. Allah now looks upon the world created by Man and sees those who are denied their dignity, who are treated unjustly. He sees the greed and decadence and inequity. And Allah says 'This is not right; this is not what was intended for my children.' And Allah feels righteous indignation. It is for that reason that He now summons forth the true believers, and commands by all that is just, and good and merciful, that it be put right, that humanity put its house in order.

"Who among you shall heed Allah's call?" Abu asked. One man, in the center of the amphitheater, rose to his feet, followed by another, and another, until everyone in the audience was standing. Abu raised his hands high in the air. *"Allahu Akbar!"* his voice thundered out.

"Allahu Akbar!" came back the response in a united voice that shook the very foundation of the amphitheater; and then added "Abu 'Ali Asghar!"

Abu suddenly stepped down from the stage and waded through the vast throng of his newly devoted followers, his new disciples. As he passed, they chanted *"Allahu Akbar*—Abu 'Ali Asghar!" and reached out to him. Those who were able to touch him claimed they felt his divine power.

Bhaiji watched the frenzied adulation that surrounded his mentor and teacher—his spiritual guide—and realized this was how millions of people felt about him. Abu belonged to them now—he had become their Mahdi.

CHAPTER 32

The next leg of the journey was south, into the Sahara desert. The drive worried Bhaiji and he instantly set about preparing for it. He refitted the Mercedes with "Sahara tires" designed to withstand intense heat, and special air filters to protect the motor against blowing sand. He bought a spade for digging themselves out of any sudden sand storms. He bought scorpion and snake-bite serum, as well as plenty of engine coolant, motor oil, and fuel. He bought food and drinking water, a new compass, a mirror for signaling, and two smoke bombs—one black and one red. And he made certain he had the most current maps, knew what highways to take and marked the location of each oasis along the way. Still, his anxiety about this trip remained constant.

Just before they left Algeria, Abu thanked the thousands of people who had turned out to say good-bye, and kissed the cheeks of the most important officials, including President Alfez Massoud. He then stepped back and stared into Massoud's eyes. "Your Excellency," Abu said, "please issue a most urgent message to the people of this region."

With raised eyebrows, Massoud said, "What message is that?"

"There will be a powerful earthquake in seven days. Its epicenter shall be just off the coast of Tunisia, near Tunis, but it will be felt throughout all of the Maghreb and even in Spain and Italy. But it shall be Tunis that suffers most. For the true believers of Tunis, tell them to seek sanctuary within the Great Mosque Jamaa ez-Zitouna. None who seek refuge in that place will be harmed." President Massoud simply stared at Abu, unsure how to respond. "If you do not do as I ask, many will die needlessly. Do not forget—the Jamaa ez-Zitouna." Abu then kissed the president on both cheeks once again.

"*Allahu Akbar*—Abu 'Ali Asghar!" the populace chanted as the Mercedes sped off behind an army jeep filled with military escorts.

"Did you inform the newspapers?" Abu asked Bhaiji.

"Yes, of course, Abuji, Just as you asked."

"Good," Abu said, staring out the car window. They were heading to Tamenghest, a thousand miles to the south. The endless expanse of sand brought an unavoidable sense of solitude—the only comfort begrudgingly offered by the hostile desert—a scorching inferno with a searing wind. Heat radiated off the blacktop, blurring the horizon. Bhaiji could feel his skin crawl with static electricity as the air leached moisture from his body. He reached into the bag next to him and popped another lozenge into his mouth.

With each passing oasis the journey became more difficult. During the second day of travel, Bhaiji thought he would die of boredom. Every attempt to engage Abu in conversation was met with silence.

They ascended into the Ahaggar mountains. The scenery was eerie, but at least there was something to look at. Steep, jagged mountains rose from a high plateau. Burned by the relentless heat, and with deep claw-like marks etched by time and erosion, they stood like brooding old men gazing down at their domain. Their cold, utterly lifeless visage belied the churning currents of molten earth that swirled just beneath one of the thinnest layers of crust on the planet's surface.

Bhaiji anxiously surveyed the multi-colored metallic rock mountains. The barren terrain was inhospitable and unforgiving—what purpose could possibly justify coming there?

Light and shadows played tricks on Bhaiji's eyes. With the advancing sunset, the shadows grew longer and more ominous. Bhaiji felt as though extra-terrestrial creatures might suddenly appear to investigate the intruders. He pressed harder on the accelerator.

"I am going into the mountains," Abu told Bhaiji when they arrived at Tamenghest. "Alone."

"But, Abuji," Bhaiji said with alarm, "it is not safe. Let me go with you." Before leaving Algiers, Bhaiji had been warned that Tamenghest had the highest known temperatures on earth, duly recorded by astronomers at the nearby Jules Carde Observatory.

"No," Abu said emphatically.

"Then take the soldiers." He was referring to the Algerian Army escort that had traveled with them.

Abu shook his head. "No, I must go alone."

Bhaiji looked at Abu nervously. "For how long, Abuji?"

"Five days."

"Why?" Bhaiji asked as Abu began walking toward the mountains. "Take some food!" He rushed to open the trunk of the Mercedes. "And water! You must take water!" Abu ignored him. Bhaiji watched helplessly as Abu disappeared into the mountains. The soldiers stared at Abu in confusion.

The next day, Bhaiji began to worry when the shade temperature shot above 100 degrees. As sunset approached, his concern shifted to the below-freezing temperatures of night that would surely follow.

Bhaiji waited in the dingy little room of his hotel, staring at the ceiling, consumed with anxiety. By the third day, Bhaiji was convinced Abu could not survive that long without food and water. He pressed the soldiers to contact their superiors in Algiers for help.

The Algerian government dispatched several army helicopters to Tamenghest, and a battalion of troops to conduct a search of the mountainous region. The activity attracted the attention of the media, who descended upon Tamenghest by plane and helicopter, eager to report on the mysterious disappearance of the Nobel Peace Prize winner. "Why did Sheik Asghar go into the mountains?" a reporter asked Bhaiji as a group of journalists gathered around him, pushing and shoving to get closer, sticking microphones in his face.

"I do not know," Bhaiji answered with annoyance. "You will have to ask him."

"Is it true," another asked, "that Sheik Asghar predicted there will be a major earthquake in Tunis?"

"Yes," Bhaiji answered, uncomfortable with all the media attention.

"What's the basis for that prediction?" another reporter asked.

"I do not know," Bhaiji confessed, exasperated. "Again you will have to ask him.

"Do you have any hope of finding him alive?" one shouted.

Bhaiji stared at the man, unwilling to confront the possibility. "Yes," he answered.

By the early morning of the fourth day a search began and helicopters criss-crossed the sky over the difficult terrain. Soldiers set out on foot, but by nightfall the search ended without any sign of Abu. Headlines around the world reported the mysterious circumstances surrounding the disappearance of Sheik Abu 'Ali Asghar.

After five days few people believed Abu would be found alive—if at all. Some speculated he'd fallen into a crevasse and might never be found. The reporters grew bored. At a daily press conference, the army spokesman announced they would search just one more day. Then it would be over.

But then, something strange began to occur above the mountains near Tamenghest. Thick, black clouds started to form and fill the sky. They swirled and churned. Everyone watched the clouds as darkness enveloped them. There was rumbling thunder, and then cool, dry wind. Lightning bolts lashed out from the clouds, illuminating the night with a radiant light. The wind became a squall. Dust and sand whirled up and danced around the spectators, stinging their eyes. More lightning split the sky, one bolt after another in a super-charged tempest, accompanied by a nearly constant roll of thunder that rocked the ground.

And then it started to rain; cool, soothing, torrential rain lasting only a minute or two, followed by large nuggets of hail—icy rocks mercilessly pummeling the onlookers, who covered their heads with their arms as they ran for cover. It too lasted only a minute or two and then stopped. Everyone stood waiting for what would follow.

The wind subsided, and all became still. "Look!" someone shouted. A hole in the clouds appeared in the near distance, like the eye of a hurricane, growing ever larger. Within the opening, the stars twinkled serenely, but around it the clouds swirled as if in a frenzy.

Amidst all the other stars, one star expanded until it glowed like a gleaming moon. And then, as everyone watched, mouths agape and stunned, the star ruptured, sending a narrow beacon of blinding light into the mountains. And as quickly as it had darted out from the heavens to touch the ground, it retracted again. Then the star disappeared among the others.

"What the hell was that?" someone asked.

"It must've been lightning," another suggested.

"That wasn't lightning," yet another responded adamantly.

The clouds dissipated. The amazing celestial show was over. Bhaiji returned to his room, and sat down on the ancient, creaky bed. He stared up at the ceiling. He knew Abu was alive. He felt a knot grow in his stomach and wondered what Abu had done.

The next morning, Bhaiji awoke from a restless sleep. The town was quiet except for the soldiers already stirring in their camp and preparing for the last day of their search. Bhaiji collected his belongings and loaded them into the Mercedes in anticipation of Abu's imminent return.

He waited, slumped behind the steering wheel, near where Abu had disappeared. Finally, he saw the tall, stately figure in flowing robes walking towards Tamenghest with that familiar purposeful stride.

Reporters swarmed around Abu. Soldiers tried to push them away while the officer in charge escorted Abu to a makeshift infirmary. Abu had survived the ordeal remarkably well—no signs of fatigue, dehydration or exposure—confirmed a bewildered army physician.

"I regret any inconvenience I may have caused my hosts," Abu said. The commander authorized his release.

The reporters pounced upon Abu as soon as he reappeared. Abu walked to the Mercedes. "Where are you going, Sheik Asghar?" one of them called out in frustration.

"Tunis," he answered through the open window.

"Haven't you heard?" the same reporter asked. "There was an earthquake there last night. A horrible earthquake."

"I know," Abu answered coldly.

"Then why are you going?" the reporter persisted.

"To help, of course."

"Sheik Asghar," another called out in an accusing voice, "how did you know?"

Abu gestured with his hand to move on. Bhaiji started the engine and pressed on the gas, spinning the rear tires on the gravel surface as they sped off to the Trans-Saharan highway, toward Tunisia.

CHAPTER 33

Bhaiji never asked Abu what happened in the mountains of Tamenghest. He wasn't sure he wanted to know. Had Abu summoned the Tunisian earthquake? The notion was unthinkable—not because he doubted Abu could do it, but because he didn't believe Abu would inflict such suffering on innocent human beings. He was dedicated to helping people, to ease their misery, not create it.

Yet there was something unmistakably different about Abu's mood and temperament. He'd even changed physically. He was older; his face was more lined and tired, even his beard had grayed over the last few months. Somehow, he'd aged in the mountains of Tamenghest.

Bhaiji was exhausted. He'd been driving for nearly fourteen hours straight. Abu just stared out the window the whole time. "Abuji, we must stop for a while," Bhaiji pleaded.

"No," Abu said. "We must get to Tunis."

"But Abuji," Bhaiji protested, "I have to sleep."

"Then I will drive."

Bhaiji looked at Abu in surprise. Abu never drove. But Bhaiji wasn't about to argue. His body cried for rest. He pulled over to the side of the road and crawled into the rear seat. He was asleep in minutes.

Without consulting a map, Abu veered west at Tourggourt onto a highway leading directly to the Tunisian border. Two hours later, Bhaiji awoke when he felt the Mercedes slowing down. He looked up to see an army escort pulling off to the side of the highway. Ahead lay Tunisia.

By now Abu's fame had spread through all of Africa, and even in remote villages the local inhabitants often recognized the black car and the blue-turbaned man who rode inside. It was no different today. They waved and cheered as the Mercedes went by, but this time Abu did not wave back or stop as he usually did.

He raced on, as though spurred by some mighty and invisible force.

Closer to Tunis, the destruction wrought by the massive quake became evident. The city was in ruins. Thousands of Tunisians had been killed, tens of thousands left homeless and injured. Devastation and chaos were everywhere. An enormous *tsunami*, or tidal wave, had arisen from the sea and cascaded upon the city. Water mains were broken, raw sewage ran openly in the flooded streets; there were increasing reports of cholera and dysentery. An army of workers dug through the rubble, frantically trying to rescue those who might have survived. In the center of the city, remarkably unscathed, sat the Jamaa et-Zitouna mosque.

Abu told Bhaiji to find Satki. She was on the scene with the relief organization that Abu had instructed her to create a few months earlier. "Tell my mother I'm here," he said to Bhaiji as he headed toward a crew of workers searching through the large chunks of a collapsed building with dogs sniffing for the bodies that were buried alive.

The World Peoples' Organization, with Satki as its head, had set up its relief operation near the undamaged mosque. Satki, along with a group of doctors and nurses was busily dispensing blankets, food, water purifying tablets and medical supplies to the thousands of newly homeless, traumatized, terrified and wounded Tunisians. The WPO was the first disaster relief agency on the scene—arriving within hours of the quake—a fact widely reported by the international press. The media also noted the mysterious prescience demonstrated by Sheik Abu 'Ali Asghar in connection with this, the worst earthquake in over a century.

"Is Abu with you?" Satki asked as she and Bhaiji embraced.

"Yes, of course," he replied. He noticed how tired she looked but then her face lit up when Bhaiji told her Abu was helping the volunteer crews digging through the debris.

"Take me to him," Satki said.

Almost immediately, a BBC correspondent with his film crew in tow, recognized Satki and Bhaiji. "Say there!" he shouted and began following them as they hurried away from the mosque.

Arriving at the site where Abu and others were moving huge blocks of concrete, the reporter was excited to discover that Satki and Bhaiji had led him straight to the most important man in this part of the world. He tried to coax and cajole Abu into giving him an interview but Abu paid no attention to the anxious correspondent; he just kept working. The reporter pleaded for Abu to just say a few words, but to no avail. The BBC cameras, however, kept rolling and recorded an event that would be seen around the world. Abu had stopped lifting the huge cinder blocks and tossing them aside with ease, when he heard a tiny, human sound coming from a part of the mountain of rubble that was several yards away from him. He went over to it and began removing the mortar and fallen bricks until he found what he was looking for: A small girl, trapped in a coffin-sized opening, uninjured but with a blank look of horror across her dirty, scratched face. She was holding the hand of her dead mother crushed by two large fallen beams.

Abu reached into the rubble and gently lifted the child, speaking softly to her. The girl looked at Abu with vacant eyes and let go of her mother's stiff, lifeless hand. Abu took the frightened child into his arms and held her head to his shoulder, whispering gently to her. The other workers cheered and cried. The BBC crew kept filming.

Satki went over to her son and embraced him. She looked at the little girl in his arms and touched the child's head and face with a comforting hand. "Come," she said to Abu, "I have brought doctors."

The film crew followed once again as Abu carried the child to the WPO relief center. It was a few streets away and Bhaiji fell in step with Satki as everyone walked quickly, carefully skirting the fallen debris that was everywhere. Bhaiji looked at Satki; he had to tell her what he was thinking, to share his burden. He took hold of her arm as they hurried along the street. "Abu caused this," he whispered to Satki.

She stopped suddenly and looked at Bhaiji in disbelief. He nodded silently.

"No," Satki said. "That cannot be."

"It is."

"Why?"

Bhaiji shook his head. "I do not know."

Satki started walking again, faster this time. She and Bhaiji were practically running. Abu turned to look at his mother. His face was cold and dark, his stare was sinister.

Satki studied him as though he was someone she no longer recognized. And then she knew it was true.

Bennett Williams also knew it was true. He was watching a CNN newscast of the earthquake. It showed Abu's rescue of the little girl and talked of the swift, well-coordinated and highly efficient disaster relief operation of his WPO agency; its efforts had saved thousands of lives. Then a special correspondent reported Abu's prediction and the lack of preparation by the Tunisian government. He also told of Abu's disappearance in the Ahaggar mountains and his bizarre, unexplained reappearance. There was even brief mention of the strange storm that had occurred over Tamenghest on the night of the earthquake.

Williams sat back in his leather chair near the TV set. He felt his stomach tighten. "He did it," Williams muttered under his breath.

"Did what?" Aimee said as she came into the living room holding Williams' half-finished manuscript in one hand and a mug of coffee in the other.

"Abu caused that earthquake in Tunisia."

Aimee sat down next to Williams on the couch. "Ben," Aimee said gently, not wanting to upset him, "I think you've been working too hard—"

"I mean it, Aimee. He made it happen."

In the short time that they'd been together, working intensely on the book, and falling more deeply in love with each other—sharing feelings and thoughts and an intimacy that neither had ever experienced before—in all their days and nights barely apart from one another, Aimee had never heard him say anything about Abu with such complete certainty. And fear. Still, she found his words incomprehensible.

"How, Ben, *how* could he cause it?" She tried to sound like the voice of reason.

Williams shook his head as the news segment stopped for a commercial break. "I don't know. But he did."

"Ben, that's crazy. Why would he do such a terrible thing?"

"Maybe to make a point."

"What point?" Aimee was becoming exasperated.

"To get people to take him more seriously. Maybe he's saying 'from now on, when I speak, listen; when I warn you, take heed.' "

She went over to Ben, her eyes imploring him. "Darling, no human being can *cause* an earthquake. Or a tornado or a hurricane."

"Aimee, don't patronize me," Williams said, looking at her with annoyance.

"But listen to what you're saying, Ben! It sounds—it's, it's preposterous."

"Not if you knew Abu. Not if you'd been there." His expression softened. "Aimee, I know it sounds nuts, but Abu is not like other human beings. Maybe he's not even . . . human."

The commercial was over and Williams and Aimee both stared, transfixed, at the TV screen. Abu was seen emerging from the WPO center, instantly surrounded by hundreds of Tunisians who were grabbing his hands and kissing them, fighting to reach and touch him, some falling to their knees in front of him, crying and praying. Others kissed his robes. The reporter's words were irrelevant. The images said it all.

"There's Bhaiji and Satki!" Williams exclaimed as he spotted them in the background. Aimee leaned forward, intensely studying the scene on TV. Bhaiji's eyes found the television camera and he looked directly into it. Williams saw the deep concern in his Indian friend's eyes. Aimee noticed it too.

"Ben, what do you make of the way he's staring into the camera?"

Williams didn't want to tell Aimee what he was thinking, but he wondered if Bhaiji was trying to connect with him, trying to send him a message. Instead of answering Aimee, Williams picked up the remote and clicked off the television. He got up. "Let's get back to work. There's not much time."

"What do you mean?"

"I mean that the world has to know about Abu."

"If you're in such a hurry, why not write what you want to say in an article for the *Times*?"

"No. The book will have more credibility. People need to see the whole picture, they need to know everything."

"Ben, even in the book, if you talk about Abu causing this earthquake, no one's going to believe you."

Williams suddenly grabbed Aimee and held her so tightly that she winced. "Ben, you're hurting me."

"I'm sorry," he said, releasing his grip. He held her head between his hands, looking deeply into her soft dark eyes. "I love you, Aimee. Oh God, I love you."

Aimee kissed Williams; not with lust or desire but with a tenderness and compassion that spoke her most intimate feelings.

"I know," she said. "I love you too."

"Please, Aimee, don't think I'm crazy. I need you to trust me. You're the only one I can ask that of."

Aimee wondered what her lover knew. If he was in danger. If they were all in danger. If there was even the slightest, smallest, microscopic chance that he was right. Aimee was frightened as she embraced Williams, but she tried not to show it. "Come on then," she said emphatically, "let's get back to work."

Colonel Moustafa al Karbarek, the notorious Libyan leader—the man President Ronald Reagan once called "the most dangerous man in the world"—excitedly awaited the visit of Sheik Abu 'Ali Asghar to his oil-rich country. Karbarek had arranged for ceremonies and celebrations to greet the man he had heard and read so much about. If Asghar was making a personal pilgrimage to meet with him, Karbarek thought, it must be of vital importance. He would show his fellow Arabs—those who condemned his terrorist tactics and considered him a pariah in the Arab world—that he, too, was important and powerful enough to warrant a private visit by the man whom many had now begun to call "the Mahdi."

Libya's economy, despite its oil resources, was failing. Secret cadres were forming in Karbarek's own government, elements of his army were becoming increasingly bold in their open disapproval of him. Other countries dismissed or ignored him, some even considered him a joke. America despised him, and once unleashed its military might in a ludicrous attempt to assassinate him. A team of F-111 bombers, dispatched like a herd of elephants being sent off to kill a mouse, missed their target, killing the Colonel's young daughter as she slept. The Libyan strongman vowed he would one day have his revenge. He was brash and bombastic, but he was no fool. Karbarek knew that he and the Sheik had much in common and he intended to use the publicity of this visit to shore up his image on the world stage—it would be just the public relations coup he needed. The Colonel was determined to impress other leaders and regain the respect and power that he coveted.

Attired in full-dress army uniform, complete with medals, and wearing his trademark hat with the elaborately braided visor, and his baton tucked under his left arm, Karbarek effusively greeted Abu on the steps of the People's Palace. He kissed his guest warmly on both cheeks as a huge crowd of onlookers screamed and cheered, and a military band played marching music. In the distance, a twenty-one-gun salute could be heard.

The two handsome men stood side by side, smiling as hundreds of photo-ops were being recorded for posterity. The only thing that annoyed the Colonel, but he did his best not to show it, was the fact that Abu was five inches taller and towered over the military president.

Once inside Karbarek's private office, he motioned for Abu to sit in the oversized upholstered chair across from the Colonel's massive mahogany desk. The moment Karbarek sat in the throne-like chair behind his desk, the broad smile he had displayed from the moment Abu had arrived, instantly disappeared. The Libyan leader's face turned dark and brooding. He leaned confidently toward Abu.

"You and I are much alike," Karabarek said, his black eyes staring directly into Abu's.

"Is that so?" Abu responded. "In what ways?"

"We are both Bedouin. And both Muslims. Above all, we share a commitment to Arab solidarity and Islamic justice. And we both derive our power and our sustenance from the people. Is that not true?"

"But I," Abu said firmly, "do not impose my will upon the people. I do not sit atop a brutal police state and seek to control their thoughts and actions."

The Colonel's eyes momentarily flashed with rage. Then he remembered his Arab hospitality. "Your reputation for frankness is well deserved. But perhaps, like so many, you do not fully understand my motives."

"On the contrary, Brother Leader," Abu said, using the accepted Arab title that Karbarek was fond of. "I understand your motives better than you think. And I know of your background as well."

"Do you indeed?" the Colonel asked, his curiosity piqued.

"As a young man you were a devoted disciple of Egypt's President Nasser, you were inspired by his Pan-Arabism. And you became dedicated to revolution in your own country. You had your military training in England, and in 1969 you led a bloodless coup against your nation's king. You were all of twenty-seven at the time."

Karbarek was flattered and impressed with Abu's knowledge of him. "You've done your homework well, Sheik Asghar. Please continue."

"To your credit, Colonel, after you came to power, you did use your best efforts to rid your country of corruption: You banned alcohol and gambling. And you endeavored to rebuild your country's sadly neglected systems of health and education. But I also know you have likened yourself to Jesus, and the prophet Muhammad—"

Karbarek's face clouded. "And you, Sheik Asghar, have referred to yourself as the Mahdi—the Awaited One—the rightful leader of the Arab world. Perhaps we are in competition for that much coveted position." His tone had turned cocky and challenging.

Abu's amused smile annoyed the Colonel. "I make no such claim," Abu said calmly. "I covet no such position. But there is a vacuum which must be filled. And it is the Arab people—and only they—who will choose."

"But Nasser himself appointed me his heir," the Colonel said petulantly. Karbarek's egotism was evident in every word he said, every gesture he made. Abu would have found his puffed-up self-importance almost cartoonish if he were not quite so wily and dangerous. "Just before he died, he told my Libyan countrymen that I was to be the representative of the Arab revolution and of Arab unity." He sat back in his chair, a smug look on his face, like a chess player who had just trapped his opponent's king.

Abu continued to smile. "That was over a quarter of a century ago, Brother Leader," Abu said, his voice stern. "Today is what matters. And today, your people plot against you. You torture and imprison those who disagree with you. Justice and equality may be what you preach, but brutality and oppression are what you practice. How can you possibly expect the Arab people to follow you?"

Karbarek grew defensive. His face reddened and his voice rose. "I love my people! I have sacrificed everything for them! And they return my love!"

"If you were loved by your people," Abu said, his eyes narrowing as he leaned toward the Colonel, "there would be no need for this ruthless police state."

Karbarek barely contained his anger. "I have built hundreds of schools, dozens of hospitals," he shouted. "Prostitutes no longer walk our streets, beggars have been banished. A national development program costing sixty-two billion dollars has been implemented."

"That money comes from the oil you sell; it belongs to your people. It was theirs. But what of the billions you spend on modern weapons, much of which still sits in the desert in unpacked crates? What of the millions you spend on terrorism? What of your new underground chemical and biological weapons arsenal? Is that for your people? How do they benefit? Or is it not for you, Colonel Karbarek—to show your power, to let them know you are a man to be feared?"

Karbarek rose from his ornate chair, his eyes staring intently at Abu. He put the palms of his hands on his desk as he leaned toward Abu. "Since you have apparently come here to insult me, Sheik Asghar, I see no reason to continue this discussion. Our meeting is—"

"Wait!" Abu said as he stood up. "Colonel Karbarek, I do not wish to become your adversary." His tone softened, became placating. Karbarek eyed him suspiciously. "You said we had much in common. In that regard, perhaps you might consider me as a mirror, a reflection of you, for that is all I truly desire to be." He smiled at the Colonel. "Please hear me out." Karbarek sat down slowly, never taking his eyes off Abu. He leaned back stiffly and nodded for Abu to continue. Abu sat back down. "Brother leader, it is your fear of not being given respect that keeps you from receiving the very respect you seek; it is the fear of not being regarded as powerful that denies you the power you pursue so fervently."

Karbarek adjusted himself in his chair. He was no longer angry, but still uncomfortable with Abu's words. "You have used your army as an instrument of power to suppress your countrymen. But now, you fear a coup from that same army—so you must watch everyone and trust no one. I tell you, Brother Leader, no such threat would exist if you were truly loved by your people. But as long as they withhold their trust and confidence in you, you will always fear the assassin's bullet. You cannot compel the power and love you desire from your people; you can only become worthy of it."

The Colonel gazed off into some vague distance, beyond Abu, beyond the room itself. Then, slowly, he returned to stare at Abu. Karbarek had not expected to hear any of this, he was unprepared for Abu and the truths he uttered with laser-like clarity. But neither was the Colonel ready to fully accept or completely believe the man who sat across from him. "What is it you really want, Sheik Asghar?" he asked, his eyes never more penetrating.

"I am only here to help you realize what *you* want, Brother Leader."

There was an awkward silence. Then Karbarek asked the question that had been bothering him for weeks. "There are some who say you are responsible for the great earthquake in Tunisia. Are you really so powerful?"

Abu smiled modestly. "If I had any part in it at all, it was merely as an instrument of Allah, perhaps only a conduit for Allah's will, but only that."

"Aha!" Karbarek said, like a predator pouncing on his quarry, "then you claim a divine connection to Allah."

Abu shook his head. "It is no more and no less than the connection to Allah that we all possess. That is what I want humanity to understand. That is what I am here to teach."

Karbarek reached for his baton on the desk and tapped it lightly against the palm of his left hand. "I see," he said suspiciously. "Suppose, Sheik Asghar, that I denounce you and expel you from Libya?"

"That would be extremely foolish, Brother Leader. It would only exacerbate your unfortunate reputation with your Arab neighbors. If you oppose me, you will bring about your own destruction. Besides," Abu said, like a magician reading someone's mind, "you already believe that you can use me to get what you have always wanted. In truth, it is only *through* me that you can ever hope to possess what you've sought all your life."

Karbarek could not help but be impressed by Abu's assessment of him. Even if the Sheik were a madman, was he any madder than Karbarek's enemies had accused *him* of being? He looked at Abu. Yes, indeed, they had many things in common. "And if I joined with you, what would you require of me?"

Abu realized Karbarek was his. The Colonel's interest was now genuine. Abu spoke softly but his tone was adamant. "Immediately disengage Libya from its involvement in the civil wars of Africa. Your contribution to the instability of such countries as Liberia, Chad and Niger— to name a few—must end at once. Once you resolve your dispute with Chad, I can assure you, you will be given access to the uranium there."

Karbarek bristled at the idea of having to back away from his long-standing conflict with Chad, but he now knew better than to protest Abu's demands. He was tight-lipped as he said, "What else?" Abu's authoritative tone somehow managed to avoid sounding condescending. "You will place a moratorium on Libya's involvement in state-sponsored terrorism."

"You want me to give up the struggle against Western imperialism?" the Colonel asked incredulously.

Abu nodded. "For the time being, it is important that the West begin to feel a sense of peace and calm, to gain a perception of order." Abu sensed Karbarek's resistance. "Brother leader, I must have not only your allegiance, but your trust and confidence."

The Colonel's dislike at being regarded as a subordinate was apparent, but he was willing to continue listening to Abu. "Go on," he said without enthusiasm.

"You must make peace with other Arab leaders. Libya must be seen as an important ally, cooperating with other Arab nations. How you signal such an intention I will leave up to you." Abu paused. "Lastly, you must initiate political reforms that are truly in the best interests of your people. You must invert the pyramid, become a consensus builder, a servant rather than a ruler."

"Is there anything else?" the Colonel asked with sarcasm.

"Only to wait," Abu answered. "And sense the coming event—perhaps the most significant one in all of recorded history."

Karbarek studied Abu with an amazement that bordered on respect. He smiled wryly. "Sheik Asghar, can your ambition be so great? Can you really achieve such power?"

Abu rose from his chair. "Colonel, I am only your reflection; I am what humanity has asked for."

CHAPTER 34

The lights in Bennett Williams apartment flickered and then went dark. His computer went down with them. "Sonofabitch!" he exclaimed, staring at the darkened P.C. screen.

"Ben—?" Aimee called out from the blackness, "what's happened?"

"It's another goddamn power outage! That's twice this week. I've lost everything!"

"You have it backed up, don't you?" Aimee asked as she groped her way down the hall to the den.

"Yeah, except for what I've been working on for the last hour. Shit! I knew I should've saved it."

Aimee lit a candle and the room took on a warm glow. She walked over and stood behind Williams. "Don't worry. You'll get it back. If worse comes to worst, I'm sure you can reconstruct it." She started to massage his shoulders. He leaned back, his head against her breasts. But he couldn't shake his irritation. He seemed more angry with himself than with the current blackout. "Something's missing," he said. "It's not really me; it's coming from Abu."

"Everything I've read so far has been really good. You're just tired." Aimee bent down and kissed the top of his head and rubbed his temples. "Maybe we need to take the weekend off—have some R and R—"

Williams was distracted and agitated. "No, I've got to keep working."

Aimee began to nibble the lobe of his left ear. "I think I know what might help," she whispered. She moved down his neck. Williams suddenly stood up, pivoted around and kissed her hard. He ripped open her silk robe to reveal soft, bare flesh. He grabbed her so tightly Aimee gasped. They dropped to the floor. Williams moved his lips along the contours of her breast, then over her satiny stomach. She groaned as Williams' passion ignited her own desire. He knelt between her legs and opened his pants. His member was rock hard. He pushed his pants down to his knees and dropped forward. He thrust himself inside of her. Aimee wrapped her legs around his waist and dug her fingers into his back.

"Oh, Ben!" she cried out. "Oh my God! Yes!"

Williams kept thrusting, relentless in his intensity; pouring his frustration out through his loins. His body tensed; he groaned and then let go. With a few more violent thrusts, it was over. He collapsed onto Aimee, his chest heaving to suck in air. He rolled over and lay on the floor beside her.

Aimee caught her breath and then closed her robe. She sat up and ran a hand through her hair. It was over so quickly she didn't know what to make of it. He'd never made love to her like that before—if that's even what it was. Williams lay silent for a moment or two with his eyes closed. Then he stood up abruptly and grabbed a pack of cigarettes from his desk. He lit one and with the cigarette poised between his lips, he pulled his pants up.

Just then the lights suddenly came on and the computer booted itself back into operation. Aimee wanted to laugh but she was too confused and disturbed by what had just happened between them.

"Ben, what's going on?" she asked pointedly.

"I don't know," he answered flatly. He took a deep drag on his cigarette and ran a hand through his tousled hair. He walked over to the window and raised it. The muffled sounds of street traffic floated up and into the room. "I can't work here. I feel . . . trapped, the walls are closing in on me, the *city's* closing in on me—"

"Are you sure it's only the city?" Aimee asked, afraid to find out the answer.

But Williams didn't even respond. It was as though he hadn't heard her. "Listen, Herschel's got a small place upstate, in the Catskills, on a lake. He said I could use it anytime. We can work up there."

Aimee sat down on the sofa. "We?"

"Yeah. Whatd'ya say we go?"

"Ben, I'd love to, but what about my job? My work?"

"Fuck your job," Williams said, then wished he hadn't sounded so demeaning. He knew how much her career meant to her and how hard she had worked to get where she was.

"No, Ben," Aimee shot back angrily, "I'm not going to fuck my job."

"Well, Brandon House isn't going to fall apart if you're not there for a few weeks."

"You selfish sonofabitch! What the hell is wrong with you?"

Williams wished he could tell her he was sorry, that he didn't mean it, but something ugly and dark and deep inside him was glad he said it. He wanted to hurt Aimee, push her away, but didn't know why.

There were several long minutes of silence between them. Aimee got up from the sofa and went into the bedroom. She returned, dressed in her brown wool slacks and a peach-colored cashmere sweater. It set off her hair and dark eyes and delicate pale complexion; she's so beautiful, Williams thought.

He finished his cigarette and tossed it out the window. He watched it fall to the street below, then turned back to Aimee.

"You're leaving?"

Aimee nodded. She paused, then: "Ben, I have to tell you something—and I realize that this is not exactly the best time to be telling you, but I guess neither of us can help that."

He looked at her, puzzled. Was she going to break up with him? For good? Was he going to lose her forever? He wanted to run to her, take her in his arms, apologize and make everything all right again. But he didn't. He just stood there, waiting for her to say whatever she was going to say.

"I'm pregnant, Ben." The words came out almost matter-of-factly.

"What!?" was all Williams could spurt out. He felt like he'd been hit with a blast from a howitzer.

"You heard me. I said I'm pregnant."

Williams sat down on the window sill. He swallowed hard. "How long've you known?"

"About a week."

"Why didn't you tell me?"

"I was afraid, I guess."

Williams got up and began pacing the room. "Jesus Christ," he muttered.

"I'm not sure I'm going to keep it."

Williams spun his head around. "Don't I have anything to say about that?" It wasn't as though he really wanted her to keep it; it was more a matter of principle.

"To be honest, no." Aimee spoke without defiance or anger.

Williams snorted and shook his head. But then he remembered that small baby in the Bhopal hospital, the first day he met Abu. 'Would you accept responsibility for his life?' Abu had asked. 'Would you raise him as your own?' Was he prepared to accept the responsibility for the life of a child—even his own? He barely felt responsible for himself. But yet, he was already responsible for the child. He had never asked Aimee if she used birth control; he just assumed she did. Now, a new life had been created. He looked at Aimee in confusion, even disbelief.

"Listen, Ben, I think you should go up to Herschel's place, alone. I think we need some time apart," Aimee said softly.

He hated to admit that she was right. Aimee went to the foyer closet, took out her trench coat and put it on. She took her tan leather shoulder bag down from a hook on the carved oak umbrella stand with its beautifully beveled mirror centerpiece. Aimee usually gave herself one last check of face and hair in that mirror before going out of the apartment. But not tonight. She walked silently to the door.

Williams didn't want her to go, but he didn't know how to make her stay. "Take the umbrella," he said. "It's starting to rain."

Aimee shook her head. "I don't need it. The doorman'll get me a taxi." She opened the door and then turned back to Williams. "Call me," she said.

He nodded without looking at her. The door closed and she was gone.

Williams sat alone in the apartment. It was suddenly very quiet. His mind was racing; his emotions a jumble of thoughts and feelings that threatened to overwhelm him. All he knew was that he felt utterly alone. He wished Abu was there. He wished he could go to him and ask what all this meant. Abu would show him the truth; he always did. But, at that moment, he had absolutely no idea where Abu was.

Williams went into the bedroom and sat down wearily on the unmade bed. He lay across it, staring up at the ceiling as if searching for answers that wouldn't come. For a moment, he wished he was under a starry night sky, somewhere in Africa, with Abu and Bhaiji and Satki. His head rolled over onto Aimee's pillow and he buried his face in it. The smell of her hair and perfume filled his nostrils and made him long for her again. He wrapped his arms around the pillow, clutching it tightly.

By the time Abu had left Libya, he'd won the hearts of its people. He'd spoken at the mosques in Tripoli and toured the country's factories, schools and hospitals. Wherever he went, the media followed; recording the reverence and devotion that Abu engendered in mass populations. Colonel Karbarek was pleased too; he'd never enjoyed greater credibility and trust from his countrymen. But Libya was merely foreplay for Egypt, where Abu was now headed. Egypt had sixty million people—more than any other Arab country. And it was the poorest. Egypt was a vast desert; arid and lifeless, where people of ancient Bedouin traditions fought a never-ending struggle for daily survival. But Egypt had one saving grace: The mighty Nile River that wound through the country like a giant python; its nutrient-rich, life-giving waters, spreading over an enormous delta, was where most Egyptians lived: Ninety-nine percent of them on four percent of the nation's land.

Abu's first stop was Alexandria, Egypt's primary seaport and once the great center of scholarship and science. Where Cleopatra seduced Julius Caesar and bore him a son; where she and Marc Antony ruled Rome's eastern empire from atop golden thrones. And where she died by her own hand upon a bed of gold, thirty years before the birth of Jesus.

Abu spoke to the poor, homeless and working class Alexandrians. He walked the streets, prayed in the mosques, and visited the hospitals. When he and Bhaiji left, thousands turned out to say farewell.

They moved on, south, to Cairo. It had been described as a place difficult to love but impossible to hate. The Arabian cities of Mecca and Medina possessed the soul of the Arab world but Cairo was the custodian of its heart. A timeless city where past and future were oddly juxtaposed in the present, creating a convoluted reality where yesterday became tomorrow—and linear time was simply an illusion. A modern industrial city, the largest in Africa, and home to over fifteen million people, Cairo was surrounded by the mystical grandeur of Egypt's antiquity: The magnificent remains of its temples and great pyramids, of its once mighty pharaohs, and its enlightened culture.

Now, its spiritual legacy was seen in the centuries-old mosques, its minarets pointing up to Allah, and where five times a day, the chants of the muezzin floated across the city. But in the cafes and nightclubs on the streets below, after prayers were ended and women and children were in bed, men opened whiskey bottles and ogled buxom belly dancers. Rock-and-roll bands belted out faithless versions of the West's latest hit songs in crowded, smoke-filled clubs. The city of Cairo was run by a bloated and inefficient bureaucracy whose principal credo was *"malesh,"* which meant "never mind."

Cairo had earned its reputation as a place of contradictions. It was where the "Gulfies" came to play—the rich oil sheiks of the Persian Gulf—and where Western tourists stayed in luxurious hotels, experiencing exotic Egypt from a safe distance. A place where pleasing and delicately scented tea gardens and quaint outdoor cafes served as front for a continuous maze of dark, narrow back-streets that led to a netherworld of walkways lined with trash and human waste. It was a place where the advantaged arrived in chauffeured limousines to attend sumptuously catered cocktail receptions for visiting dignitaries and world celebrities. But just outside, on the streets of the hot, crowded, noisy and noxiously polluted metropolis, millions of impoverished and homeless begged for their daily ration, only to be met by the callous indifference of the rest of the Cairo population.

To the minority of wealthy Arabs and Westerners of Cairo, Abu was a new celebrity with whom to be seen. To the starving and destitute of the city, he was something quite different. To them he was "the Awaited One." They believed he would rise in the East, cast his light upon the West and bring balance to world—just before the end of time.

Egypt was important to Abu because it was the cultural capital of the Arab world, because it possessed the largest army in the Arab world—equipped with state-of-the-art American weapons—and it controlled the Suez Canal, the vital link between Europe and Asia. Egypt was also a powerful member of the Organization of African Unity and a voice for the Third World. Within the country, Arab radicals and Muslim fundamentalists decried America's dominance over the Middle East. They still spoke about how America had set up Saddam Hussein to crush him, to provide an excuse to send troops into Iraq and place its boot over the jugular vein of oil-dependent Europe and Japan.

The Arab house that Abu entered was bitterly divided. Some were

jealous of Egypt's influence in the Arab world; others still deeply re-
sented Egypt for making peace with Israel. Egypt's leaders walked a
tightrope between competing interests: They badly needed American
aid to keep their economy alive, yet Egypt's relationship with the United
States alienated its government from the Arab world and worse, the
Egyptian people.

And so, Abu's visit to Cairo caused a small crisis between President
Mahtasi Bakar and his cabinet. Bakar had decided not to welcome Abu
with open arms. "We will wait before inviting him to meet with me. I
want to see what his intentions are," he said to his ministers on the
eve of Abu's arrival.

"Mr. President, according to Sheik Asghar's aide, who requested
the meeting with you, Sheik Asghar wishes to propose a plan for a
new Arab federation."

"Hah!" Bakar scoffed. "How different can it be from all the other
federations that have never succeeded?! An Arab alliance isn't meant
to be. Nasser tried and failed. My mentor, the great Sadat, tried and
failed. What has Sheik Asghar got to offer that will build a lasting
federation?"

"His aide said you will understand that after you have heard him
speak at Al-Azhar University," the minister replied.

"I do not entertain any interest in meeting with him," Bakar said
stubbornly.

Another cabinet minister became extremely upset. "But he is a hero
to so many—a savior. We ignore him at our peril."

Bakar's most trusted advisor beseeched, "Mahtasi, other countries
have given him grand welcomes—"

The president looked at the members of his inner circle with annoyance. "This is not Libya. I am not Karbarek," he said in a voice
filled with disdain for the pompous Colonel.

There was no further discussion of the matter.

Bhaiji had made arrangements for Abu to speak at Al-Azhar University. It was actually a one-thousand-year old mosque surrounded by
the venerated University of Cairo. Al-Azhar was the citadel of Islamic

intellectualism and the oldest continuously operating university in the world. When it came to interpreting the Koran, the influential sheiks of Al-Azhar had evolved into the equivalent of Western judges, and the university was the Supreme Court of Islam. Although Al-Azhar's 150,000 students from 75 countries studied medicine, agriculture, philosophy and literature in the hot, crowded classrooms of the university, the single most important area of study was still the Koran. In order to gain admittance to this prestigious institution, a student had to demonstrate that he or she had memorized every one of its nearly 80,000 words.

The concept of separation of church and state was unthinkable in Muslim society. The law of Allah applied to all human endeavors—especially government. And Egypt's government depended on the support of the sheiks of Al-Azhar—they possessed the ability to bring the country's ruling body to its knees. It was why the rector of Al-Azhar held a cabinet post in the government equivalent to the Prime Minister. And why interpretations of the Koran often conveniently endorsed government policies.

When Anwar Sadat made a separate peace with hated Israel, Al-Azhar pointed out that Muhammad had also entered into treaties with the Jews, and at one time allied himself with them. And when Egypt aligned with America against Saddam Hussein, Al-Azhar declared that it was not a desecration of Islamic holy land to allow an army of infidels into Saudi Arabia to defend another Muslim country.

Other Arab leaders saw it differently. Colonel Karbarek had called for a popular invasion to restore the university to its rightful role, and the Saudis offered to buy it and move it to Saudi Arabia. Even Cairo's leading independent newspapers complained that Al-Azhar was more interested in turning out Western-style businessmen, video salesmen and discotheque operators than religious scholars.

Abu disagreed with everyone. In an interview with Egypt's leading newspaper, *Al-Ahram,* he declared, "It is not the sheiks of Al-Azhar who hold the true power. It is the students. They are not insulated from the outside world; they are deeply affected by it. They see the suffering, the poverty, the unemployment, the bureaucratic corruption. At Al-Azhar they are imbued with the purity and idealism of the Koran. And they feel the growing shifts; they are the ones who object to the inequity and injustice in the world." The sheiks of Al-Azhar were offended by Abu's comments, but they were not the ones Abu wanted to reach.

"Twenty thousand years ago," Abu's voice bellowed out across the huge hall at Al-Azhar where tens of thousands had come to hear him speak, "when all of Europe was buried under the ice age, this land was fertile and green, and teeming with life. Where there is now only lifeless desert, there were once flowering meadows, fields of tall grasses, forests and marshes, animals in numbers too vast to count. And mighty rivers that coursed like arteries, pumping life into the region."

Abu paused. His audience was enthralled. Not a sound, not a whisper, could be heard. Abu's face clouded. "But then, Allah willed that the earth undergo a massive change. The polar caps dissolved, the rains moved north. Green mesas were replaced by desert, the lakes and rivers dried up and the land became a hostile environment. In Egypt all that was left was the great Nile. But even though the land was parched, the plants perished, the grasses withered and the animals fled, a new society of people made this place their home. Despite the hardships, they survived and flourished. And were the first to create a glorious and enlightened civilization. They were the Egyptians!"

In the presidential palace, in a private screening room, President Bakar sat with several advisors and cabinet members, gathered around a large TV set, watching the imposing Sheik Asghar arouse and inspire his listeners with the often-forgotten fact of their once splendid culture.

"Do you see, Mr. President, what I meant about mesmerizing his audience?" one of the ministers asked.

"Shh—" Bakar hissed, "I am listening."

The minister turned to an aide sitting beside him. The two men smiled discreetly at one another.

"Thousands of years ago," Abu was saying, "while Europeans were barbarians living in mud huts and could barely speak, Egyptians had already created a complex language, they had invented papyrus so as to record their magnificent history, they constructed the pyramids and built a system of irrigation to fertilize the delta. They invented engineering and studied the stars; they divided the day into twenty-four hours and the calendar into three hundred and sixty-five days. They created government and formal education, the libraries of Alexandria were one of the seven wonders of the world.

"When the Bedouin tribes of neighboring Arabia came here to settle the land, they brought with them something of inestimable value: Islam. And the glorious will of Allah."

President Bakar nodded. "He is quite impressive," he said. "Perhaps we need to be even more careful of him than we think."

"But he makes great sense, does he not?" an aide asked. "He speaks the truth."

"Perhaps with a forked tongue," the president replied.

Abu began chiding his listeners—most of whom were under the age of thirty—in order to show them who and what they have become in today's world. "Arabs are regarded as ignorant! 'Camel jockeys.' 'Lazy sand niggers,' they call you! A pathetic, backward people who practice a medieval religion!"

The audience was on the verge of rioting. The police and university guards stationed along the walls and exits grew nervous. "Is this true?!" Abu shouted, holding up his hands to the crowd.

"NO!" came roaring back.

"Is this how you wish to be regarded?" Abu asked.

"NO!" was the collective retort.

"Then why," Abu asked, his voice indignant and incredulous, "in the name of Allah, do you allow it to be?"

In Bakar's screening room, the assembled group applauded and cheered. They seemed no longer concerned with their president's skepticism and reticence. Mahtasi Bakar continued to stare at the TV screen with cautious interest, then said to no one in particular, "But what does he offer in the way of a solution?"

As if the same thought were in the mind of someone in the audience at the great hall, a voice called out to Abu, "What can we do?"

Abu's words were a command. "Act with the dignity that is rightfully yours! Stop denying your heritage. Examine yourselves and your society, examine the entire Arab world! You, whose culture once gave the world its greatest philosophers, poets, explorers, inventors, have now become intimidated by the technologically advanced Western world and you have allowed them to hold you in contempt; you are pawns in their global game of exploitation and control. But I say to you: No more. No more!"

"NO MORE!" was shouted from thousands in the audience. It reverberated off the walls and ceiling, and shook the very foundation of the building.

President Bakar got up from his chair and began pacing the room as he watched the TV screen. He knew what his ministers and aides were thinking: Sheik Abu 'Ali Asghar is unstoppable.

A senior aide watched his commander-in-chief pacing and said, "You must meet with him, Mr. President."

Bakar said nothing, he didn't even look at the man who was his most respected advisor.

In the hall of Al-Azhar, Abu raised his arms and strode across the platform as he spoke. "Allah knows what evil exists in the world, and Allah understood from the beginning that it would require an army of believers to create the society that is in accordance with the will of Allah. Who better than the Arab people to carry out that will?"

"Allahu Akbar!" was the chant that rang out through the hall. It fairly rocked the ancient building.

"Allah sent forth his prophets—Moses and Abraham and Jesus—to teach us the right way. But the world failed to heed their message, and so Allah sent Muhammad, who delivered the means of achieving Allah's true desire for all mankind."

Abu continued to bring his audience to their feet in a show of both solidarity for his words of anger and near-worship of his spiritual persona. "Every human being has its moment of truth—the moment when you declare allegiance to the role Allah has given you to assume. It is time for the Arab world to reclaim its destiny. There are now over one billion Muslims in the world—believers who have surrendered to the will of Allah. And they look to the Arabs as the leaders of Islam. It is time to overcome the differences that divide the Arab world and unite in the name of Allah. We must establish a new world order based upon his will. My friends, together we can do it!" Abu stopped for a moment. His eyes scanned the thousands of people before him. There was a sudden hush—as if everyone had stopped and held their breath.

"Who among you will join me in that quest?" Abu called out.

The response was a tumultuous, deafening roar, so loud it caused the radio and television sound technicians to tear off their headphones as the gauges on the panels before them shot off the scale.

In President Bakar's screening room, the cabinet members looked at their leader, a man they respected and genuinely liked. No one said anything. The president stopped his pacing and sat down again. He used the remote to click off the TV set and his eyes gazed for a moment at each of the men seated around him. When he spoke, it was in a voice filled with resignation.

"I shall meet with Sheik Asghar. You are right; not to see him would be foolhardy. Even dangerous." He turned to one of his aides. "Arrange it."

"For when?" the aide asked.

"As soon as possible."

The other men smiled, grateful and relieved. Their president had realized that, indeed, discretion was the better part of valor.

CHAPTER 35

The CNN anchorman spoke directly into the camera. Behind him on the wall was a huge blowup of a map of the Middle East. "We're going to switch now to our correspondent, Veronica Basmanti, with a live report from Jerusalem. Veronica?"

"Thank you, David. I'm standing here at the Damascus Gate in the Old City of Jerusalem." Basmanti, speaking into the camera with microphone in hand, gestured toward an enormous crowd of people. "As you can see, there's a huge turnout awaiting the arrival of Sheik Abu 'Ali Asghar. We just received word only yesterday from Bhaiji Singh, the Sheik's aide, that he'd be arriving here today. So far, however, we've not seen the now famous black Mercedes-Benz and its celebrated occupant."

From the CNN newsroom, David Dawson broke in. "There does seem to be a lot of commotion there, Veronica; what's the mood like in Jerusalem?"

Basmanti pressed a finger to her left ear. She nodded while listening. "Well, David, it can only be described as electric. I heard one veteran correspondent say that he hadn't seen anything like it since Anwar Sadat came here over twenty years ago to make peace with Israel. And this is a city not easy to impress."

From the CNN production booth, word came down to Dawson to fill the time until the Sheik arrived. "I can imagine that's quite true, Veronica. Even from this distance, looking at the ancient wall of the Old City, it's easy to sense the weight of history and religion."

"Absolutely true, David. Words just cannot describe the feeling you get as you walk the streets that Jesus, and King Herod and the disciples walked. So little has changed since then. It's as though you are living in the time of the Roman occupation; you can feel the splendor of the Age of Saladin. It's surely the world's most intensely spiritual and religious city—next to Mecca, it is the holiest city in the Islamic world; to the Jews, there is no place more sacred; and to Christians, it is the birthplace of Christianity."

"And at the center of it all is the Temple Mount. How far is it from where you're standing?" Dawson asked.

"It's just inside the walls of the Old City, David."

"And it's the most sacred of places, isn't that right?" Dawson asked as the screen showed Basmanti looking toward the Mount.

"Indeed. Even Orthodox Jews are not allowed to set foot on it. In the center of the Mount is a large rock where, according to the Old Testament, Abraham—the patriarch of the Jews and Arabs—was instructed by God to sacrifice his son, Isaac, as a test of faith. Later, it became the place where the Temple of Solomon was built to house the Ark of the Covenant and the Ten Commandments. And the Koran tells of a night when Muhammed was brought to Jerusalem by the Angel Gabriel; and there, waiting for him were Abraham, Moses and Jesus. They all prayed together upon the Temple Mount. Then, according to the Koran, Muhammed left his physical body and ascended upward through the 'seven heavens' that separated the physical world from Divine Reality. So, to Muslims, the Temple Mount represents the divine connection between man and God. That's why the Arabs built the Dome of the Rock on that very spot. It's interesting to note, David, that around the exterior of the structure are inscriptions from the Koran about Jesus—and warning of a coming apocalypse."

"And the Dome of the Rock is where the Temple of Solomon once stood, isn't that right, Veronica?"

"Yes, David. What remains of it. The second temple was built by Herod the Great, then destroyed by the Romans in retaliation for Jewish rebellion. All that remains of these temples is the famous Western Wall, the one venerated by the Jews as the Wailing Wall."

A sudden, heightened commotion took place within camera range and Basmanti turned around and craned her neck to see better. "As you can probably tell, this increased excitement can only mean one thing—yes, I believe that Sheik Asghar is now arriving!"

The CNN anchorman adjusted his earpiece and nodded. "We're being told back here, Veronica, that the Sheik is indeed approaching the Damascus Gate."

"Yes, David. I can see his Mercedes moving very slowly. There's a mob of reporters and photographers surrounding the car—"

"Can you get close enough to ask Sheik Asghar a few questions?"

"I'm certainly going to try, David." Veronica Basmanti began moving toward the Mercedes, her crew following closely behind her. Then she stopped and faced the camera. "I can tell you, David, that anyone who has seen the Sheik knows what an incredibly imposing man he is. His physical stature and his blue turban make him easily distinguishable from the crowd." Basmanti looked back toward the car, then to the camera again. "He's out of the car and is heading this way now; I can see him grasping the outstretched hands of his followers. Quite a few people are laying palms at his feet, everyone is waving to him. It's an incredible sight, David; the emotion from this crowd is overwhelming. Men, women, children, all are ecstatic to see Sheik Asghar. Many people are crying, some have fainted—everyone in a state of worshipful adoration of him."

"We can see him now, Veronica. He seems to be headed your way."

"Yes, David, here he comes. I'll try to get his attention. Sheik Asghar! Could we ask you a few questions?" Abu stopped a few feet away from Basmanti, then stepped toward her. The other reporters shoved microphones and tape recorders in front of Abu's face. The CNN correspondent wasted no time. "Sheik Asghar, why have you come to Jerusalem?"

"To seek communion with God."

"Then this is a religious journey as opposed to your travels in Africa which had decidedly political overtones—"

"My message throughout Africa and all of the Third World has been a spiritual one. If it appeared political, that is because true spirituality cannot be separated from politics. I come to Jerusalem as a pilgrim, and to continue the work of the Nazarene."

"You mean Jesus Christ?"

"Yes."

"Sheik Asghar, you seem to have tremendous appeal among the Arab people. Do the Israelis have any reason to be concerned by this visit?"

"Jews, Muslims and Christians all worship the same God. The conflict between Arab and Jew is not one of religion—it is cultural and primarily about land, and always has been. Islam, Judaism and Christianity form a holy trinity."

"Even so, our sources indicate that the Israeli government was hesitant about allowing you into the country. Isn't that true?"

"You will have to ask the Israeli government. I have never received any information that they objected to my visit."

"Do you intend to meet with Yasser Arafat?"

"Yes."

"Will you be speaking at the al-Aqsa Mosque?"

"Yes."

"Sheik Asghar, what will you say to the Muslims there?"

"What I have said to people everywhere: We must unite as a race if we are going to survive on this planet. Now, if you will excuse me, I must continue on." Abu hurried off, with the ever-growing parade of people following him and chanting his name.

Basmanti turned back to the camera, her face was flushed and her eyes bright. "Well, you heard him, David, and as you can see, both the man and his message are quite extraordinary. I believe he is now headed to the Via Dolorosa where he is going to walk the Stations of the Cross, the holy journey that took Jesus from the place where he was condemned by Pontius Pilate to his crucifixion."

With television cameras and a procession of followers in his wake, Abu walked the stations, oblivious now to the masses surrounding him. He entered the Chapel of the Condemnation to pray for a few minutes, then at the Third Station, where Christ fell for the first time, Abu knelt down and kissed the ground. At the Church of the Holy Sepulcher, the Coptic monastery that marked the Ninth Station of the Cross, where Jesus fell for the third time, Abu no longer merely looked solemn and reverent. His face had taken on a pained expression, as though he could feel Christ's suffering emanating from the cobbled stones he walked on.

Inside the church, Abu quietly visited the site where it was said that Jesus was nailed to the cross, where his mother wept as his body was taken down, and the tiny chamber cut from the rock of Calvary where his body was laid to rest.

Abu emerged from the Church of the Holy Sepulcher and guided his enormous procession through the narrow streets and bazaars toward the Temple Mount. On the way, he stopped and visited the merchants, carpet vendors, metalworkers, vegetable farmers, butchers. Every event was eagerly recorded by television cameras, although no further interviews took place. CNN had scooped the rest of the media.

One merchant, a maker of Arabic prayer beads was so overjoyed when Abu stopped at his display of beads—ivory, amber, precious gems, silver and gold—that he asked Abu to take any one he wanted, as a gift. When Abu picked a strand of plain tan beads made from olive wood, the merchant was disappointed. "Those are not worthy of you," he said and quickly lifted up a strand made of delicate gold filigree beads with tiny pieces of jade set in them. "These," he said with pride, "these are worthy of you. Those," he said, pointing to the wooden beads, "are for a poor man."

Abu shook his head. "Your kindness and generosity are what make them valuable," Abu said and returned the gold strand to its velvet display pad. He held the olive-wood prayer beads in his hand and said "Thank you," to the vendor.

The merchant bowed to Abu with "Salaam, Sheik Asghar. May Allah watch over you."

At the Temple Mount, Abu marveled at the intricate beauty of the colored tiles and pastel marble panels that supported the brilliant, gold Dome of the Rock. Inside, alone except for the guards who stood watch over the sacred artifact, Abu knelt before the rock and prayed. Television camera crews, newspaper photographers, reporters and assorted paparazzi, along with the hordes of people, waited impatiently outside. When Abu emerged, the media frenzy began anew. They followed him to al-Aqsa Mosque where Abu paused at the fountain to perform the ritual ablutions before prayer. He removed his shoes and entered the mosque. The multitudes trailed right behind him.

The opulent interior made al-Aqsa one of Islam's preeminent mosques. Abu walked over the rich, ornately woven rugs and between the massive marble colonnades. Overhead, huge beams supported arched joists and an elaborately carved ceiling. The prayer niche, or mirhab, was engraved with verses from the Koran. It also served as an acoustical 'dish' which echoed the speaker's voice to ensure that all would hear him. Curious Muslim holy men—mullahs—gathered along the walls of the mosque as all those who had followed Abu, now squeezed into al-Aqsa; more were crammed into the outer courtyard.

Absolute silence filled the mosque. Abu raised his hands high. "I have come to speak to you today of love." Quiet tears filled the eyes of hundreds of Abu's listeners. The media focused on him with rapt attention.

"Who among us has not felt some form of love in our lives? We all look upon love as necessary to our survival. Yet, we can live and succeed without it. We can build and conquer, exploit and destroy without it; we can acquire power and wealth without it. But love is essential to our well-being. No matter how great one's riches, or the power at one's command, without love we are bankrupt, alone, desolate.

"Why is this so? Because the need to love and be loved emanates from our very souls. And we are linked to God through our souls—they are but parts of God, individual cells of a greater body. And God is love."

Abu looked down, then paced back and forth before the mihrab. "And so, we cannot live without love, just as we cannot live without Allah." There were murmurs from the vast throng in the mosque; the mullahs nodded with approval.

"Without love, without God, there is only fear—it is all that remains in the absence of love. Fear will enable you to survive, to command the beasts of the earth, to build great monuments to the glory of your egos, but it will never provide you with the light that shines on the path to the true meaning of love. Just as God and love are one and the same, fear and the devil are one! The degree of love in your life will determine your closeness to God; the absence of it will show your alignment with Satan. Make no mistake: Fear will fill the void left by the absence of love."

Abu looked out over the sea of faces staring intently back at him. Everyone in the mosque waited hungrily for his next words. His voice, warning and chastising one minute, coaxing and compassionate the next minute, now became gentle and compliant. He was their servant, the answer to their prayers, the Mahdi.

"But, my friends," he said, "I am here for you. The time is rapidly approaching when God and Satan must confront one another. We have reached a point where the whole of humanity is in danger of losing its soul. We must not let that happen."

"How shall we fight the devil?" a man shouted out.

"Let in the light! The blazing light of God! Fear cannot exist in the light of love. And you can only find God and that light by looking inside yourselves. Each and every one of you."

"But Sheik Asghar," another man called out, "how shall we know if Satan is speaking to us? How can we know what is truth?"

"God is Truth!" Abu shouted back. "Satan can only speak to you in the language of fear! Satan will use blame, anger, hatred, jealousy—any device he can—to make you think you are better than your brother and convince you of your superiority. Or he will tell you that you are inferior to others, not worthy of love or of God's mercy. But God will not compare you to anyone or anything. To God you are a divine creation, to God you are all equal with your fellow human beings."

A mullah stepped out from his place along the wall. "But what of those who are evil, who cause pain and injustice? Do we love them as well?" he challenged.

"The greatest means of fighting injustice is through love. We must learn to love our enemies." Abu's voice resonated throughout the mosque.

"How do we love those who attempt to do us harm?"

"To love your enemy does not mean you must hold him dear or feel joy from his presence—it means only that you should regard him without fear, without anger, judgment or jealousy."

"You speak like a Christian," the mullah called out.

"So be it," Abu said. "The prophet Muhammad never repudiated the teachings of the prophet Jesus. The work of the prophets who came before me is not finished!"

"Are you a prophet of God?" a voice in the rear of mosque shouted.

"Yes," Abu responded.

"And what is your mission?" the man asked loudly.

"To help humanity create a world based on love and unity, and compassion. A world that recognizes our diversity and honors it. A world that does not rely upon superiority as a measure of power, or power as a measure of superiority. A world that provides choices and opportunities, equality and justice. A world without fear." Abu paused for a brief moment, then: "Will you join me and carry this message to every corner of the earth?"

"YES!" rang out; the mosque suddenly erupted with the booming chant of *"Allahu Akbar,* Abu 'Ali Asghar!"

Abu left the mosque and stood at the top of the stairs leading to the Mount of the Temple. He waved to tens of thousands of people, all trying to reach him, touch him, bow before him.

Israeli security officers surrounded Abu in an attempt to keep the crowds from crushing him.

As TV crews filmed, and cameras flashed and journalists frantically made notes, Abu stopped and placed a hand on the head of an aging woman. Suddenly a man stepped out from the crowd and raised his arm. He stood a foot or so from Abu and placed a pistol to Abu's head. Bhaiji saw what was happening and screamed: "Abuji!" as he reached to grab the gun.

"Blasphemer!" the assailant cried.

Shots pierced the air—*bam! bam! bam!* in staccato succession.

The crowd panicked; screams echoed off the walls of the ancient temples. Abu fell to the ground, blood soaked his turban and poured from his temple. The police grabbed the assassin and wrestled him to the ground, crushing the bones of his hand as they wrenched the gun from it.

Bhaiji dropped to the ground and cradled Abu's bleeding head in his arms. "I am sorry, Abuji," he cried.

Abu opened his eyes for a moment. His lips were slightly parted but he didn't utter a sound. Then his eyes closed and, like a rag doll, his head fell back and his arms went limp.

CHAPTER 36

Bennett Williams jogged along the narrow highway near Herschel Strunk's mountain cabin. He'd made a point of running every morning since arriving there; the clean, crisp air and the run itself helped him think and clear his mind for that day's writing. He missed Aimee terribly but they hadn't spoken yet. He knew she wouldn't phone him, that she would wait for him to call her—and he wanted to, but he also wanted to have his feelings better sorted out. He owed her that. He had to know what kind of commitment he was ready for; what kind of promises he could keep. Yet the thought of her, and how much he loved her, and the fact that she was carrying his child, had put him on an emotional roller coaster—making his nights especially hard to get through, and often his days, for despite his having immersed himself in his work, he'd also gotten used to her being there. She was not only his lover and friend, she was his editor, sometimes collaborator, critic and motivator. He had come to count on her opinions and reactions—their discussions and disagreements, their togetherness. He had no idea he would feel so bereft without her presence, and it added a conflicting layer of emotions that he didn't know how to deal with.

"Morning, Vern," Williams said to the proprietor of the local general store that served as the small town's market. It wasn't really a town—just a gas station, drugstore, the market and a hardware store. It was Williams' turnaround point after jogging a couple of miles down the two-lane state highway.

"Mornin', Ben," Vern said without even looking up from the newspaper he was reading.

Williams went to the cold-drink case and took out a small bottle of orange juice, opened it and took a swig. He took a folded dollar bill from inside the top of his sock and put it on the counter. "What's new in the world, Vern—?" Williams had started to say just as his glance fell on the front page of the newspaper Vern was reading.

ARAB LEADER SHOT DEAD IN JERUSALEM the headline screamed.

"Oh Jesus," Williams gasped. "Vern, can I see that please?" he asked and without waiting for the proprietor to give him the paper, Williams grabbed it and stared in shock at the front page.

> *JERUSALEM* . . . Nobel Peace Prize winner, Sheik Abu 'Ali Asghar, was gunned down on the streets of Jerusalem late yesterday. He was pronounced dead at the al-Maqasid al-Kharyriyah Hospital in the Muslim section of Jerusalem. Eyewitnesses said that a young Palestinian stepped from the crowd and pointed a pistol toward Sheik Asghar, firing three shots mere inches from his head. This event is eerily similar to the assassination of Prime Minister Yitzhak Rabin when he too, just minutes after finishing a speech that called for peace and reconciliation and mutual respect between Arabs and Jews, was shot and killed by one of his own people—an Israeli Jew.

"Oh God," Williams said as he dropped the paper on the counter and ran from the store.

"Hey, Ben, your change—" Vern called out as he opened the cash register, but Williams was already out of earshot.

He ran along the edge of the highway, his mind racing, his body struggling to keep up. He'd never run so fast in his life. He had to call Aimee. He had to check the television for more news. He had to hurry. He ran to the point of exhaustion. When he heard a car coming from behind, Williams frantically flagged it down. The driver of the Ford pickup stopped and Williams jumped in.

"Whaddya runnin' from?" he asked half-joking.

"Nothing. Could you drive faster?" Williams asked curtly. The man looked at him nervously and pressed the accelerator.

As soon as the cabin came into view Williams asked the driver to stop. He jumped out of the truck and ran the rest of the way to the cabin and bolted through the door. The phone was already ringing. He grabbed it. Aimee's anxious voice was on the other end.

"Ben? You've heard—"

"Yes, yes—I can't believe it." He was so glad she had called.

"How much do you know?" Aimee asked.

"Just that a Palestinian shot Abu and he was pronounced dead at the hospital."

"Ben, it's worse than that. His body is missing." Aimee's voice was shaky and breathless.

"WHA-A-T!?"

"The hospital claims it disappeared from the morgue. Jerusalem is in chaos. Arab Muslims are dousing themselves in blood and marching through the city. He's become a martyr. Riots have broken out all over Israel—all over the Middle East. Ben, thank God it was a Palestinian who killed him. If it'd been a Jew, we'd have World War Three! It's bad enough it happened under the eyes of the Israeli government. Practically the whole Third World has already accused Israel of having something to do with this."

"No, that's not possible. The Israelis are too smart for that."

"Anything is possible, Ben. They killed their own peacemaker years ago—"

Williams was adamant. "That's not what this is about. I think Abu is up to something."

"What? What do you mean?"

"Aimee, this isn't what it appears to be. Nothing with Abu ever is. I saw soldiers in Sri Lanka aim automatic rifles at him and pull the triggers. And nothing happened! He jammed their guns—he can do that! I saw it. I tell you he's up to something—that's why his body's missing—"

"Ben," Aimee shouted into the receiver, "he's *dead*! He was shot and killed in front of thousands of people—and television cameras—the whole world saw—"

"What about his missing body?"

"Some fanatics must have taken it—there's no other logical explanation."

"Abu is no ordinary man, Aimee," Williams shouted back. Then he stopped, realizing they were starting to fight about something that was not explainable or debatable in any rational way. It made no sense to discuss it another second. Williams could not begin to fathom the implications of what was happening; and if he, who had been at Abu's side for so many months, didn't have any answers, then no one else did either.

When Williams hadn't said anything for what seemed a long time, Aimee called, "Ben—are you there?"

He realized how desperately he wanted to see her, hold her, to tell her what he felt. "Aimee, I miss you," he said simply.

"I miss you too, Ben."

"How are you?"

"I'm okay."

"And the . . . ?" He didn't know what to call it. Baby? That made it too real, too human. He thought she might even have had an abortion by now.

"The baby's okay, too. The doctor says everything's fine."

Williams was instantly relieved. "Then . . . then you've decided to keep it?"

"Yes." Aimee's tone was firm. "I've thought about it a lot since you left. I'm not getting any younger and, well, you know, the biological clock and all that. I want this child, Ben. I truly do. But please understand, it doesn't have to involve you."

"How can it not?"

"You can just walk away, Ben. That's all. I mean it when I say I absolve you of any responsibility you might feel."

"How do you know I want to be absolved of responsibility? It's my child too—my son or daughter."

"Yes, of course. But—"

"Aimee, I need to talk to you, I need to see you."

"I'm not going to change my mind about—"

"I know. That's not what I'm suggesting. Would you . . . come up here?"

"Things are so hectic at the office—"

"Will you try—?"

There was a pause. "I'll do my best, I promise."

Williams hung up and plopped down on the sofa across from the television, grabbed the remote and clicked it. His heart was pounding.

CNN's Veronica Basmanti was describing the pandemonium that had broken out in and around Jerusalem. "It's well into the evening now and you can still see flames from fires set by Arab rioters. A state of emergency and martial law has been declared. Several hundred people have already been killed by Israeli soldiers. Troops have cordoned off the Temple Mount and the al-Aqsa mosque. Tanks and armored personnel carriers can barely maneuver through the narrow streets of Old Jerusalem. I've also received reports that heavy rioting is still occurring in cities on the West Bank, most notably in Nablus, the place that gave birth to the Intifada uprising by Palestinians."

"Is there any end in sight, Veronica?" the CNN anchorwoman, Elizabeth Woodall, asked.

"Not for a while, Liz. Anger and retaliation seem the order of the day at the moment. I don't think anyone truly appreciated the enormous popularity of the Sheik among the Arab people. Many Muslims had begun to consider him a new prophet of Allah. Now, as a martyr, he has taken on even greater stature—as great as any Islamic leader since the Prophet Muhammad himself."

Williams sat hunched forward, mesmerized by what was playing out in front of him on the TV screen. When Elizabeth Woodall announced that they were about to replay portions of Abu's speech at the al-Aqsa mosque, Williams turned the sound up so that Abu's voice filled the room, the whole cabin. He heard Abu's declaration that he was a prophet of God. Williams sat back. He couldn't remember Abu ever saying anything quite like that before.

Abu was moving around the mosque's prayer niche and making the same dramatic gestures that Williams had come to know so well. But his words went beyond what Williams remembered as typical of Abu's speeches. This one was decidedly different.

"We must change the existing order," Abu exhorted. ". . . fight injustice in the world . . . Will you join me? Will you fight in that cause?"

Williams watched as the crowd roared back "YES!" They were aroused and impassioned. It made Abu look like a raging fundamentalist.

Then, once outside the mosque, the televisions cameras had picked up filming Abu among the crowds. One cameraman must have been right behind Abu because he caught the act of assassination. The film showed the gunman step out and place the gun to Abu's head and fire three times. Williams saw Abu fall. He felt sick to his stomach. He saw Bhaiji covered in blood and cradling Abu's head in his arms.

Elizabeth Woodall was on camera again, one hand holding her earpiece more tightly against her ear. "Veronica, we've just received word that Syria and Jordan have begun amassing troops along their borders with Israel. Can you confirm that?"

The television screen split to accommodate both women. "I haven't received any information about that yet, but I wouldn't be surprised if that is actually happening. We've seen an increase in troop movements and fighter jets have been racing over the skies of Jerusalem."

Woodall interrupted. "I've also just gotten word that the President of the United States has placed U.S. forces on alert in the event hostilities should erupt."

"Jesus Christ," Williams groaned.

"Veronica, is there any word on Sheik Asghar's body?"

"Nothing official, Liz. That is the mystery of the moment. No one seems to know, or if they do, they're not saying. One rumor is that the Israelis have stolen it, another has it that a Palestinian organization has taken it."

"Why?" the anchorwoman asked.

"Your guess is as good as mine, Liz. All I know is that it has provided a bizarre twist to this horrible event."

"Thank you for that report, Veronica—" As Elizabeth Woodall continued talking, Williams clicked off the TV. He needed to think. He walked out the back door, letting the screen door bang shut behind him. He walked down to the lake, to the edge of Herschel's pier. He thought of Abu. Could he possibly be dead? It was inconceivable to him. Did he really think Abu was immortal? No, not immortal. Invulnerable maybe. Invincible even.

His mind went back to that day in Bangladesh when he sat on a river bank, convinced he was going to die from contaminated water. He remembered so many of his travels with Abu, and what he had learned from him—this mentor, this spiritual guide. Should he now mourn Abu? Williams just couldn't accept that he was gone.

His thoughts turned to Aimee. He knew his feelings went far deeper than chemistry. It was hard for him to imagine not having her in his life. He felt a desire he had never known before: To share everything with her. But with his feelings came the old fear of commitment—of an intimacy that he was afraid would ultimately hurt him—that was what made him push her away. The truth was he didn't know how to really love. He had to admit he was in uncharted waters. It was even harder to know how to be loved. To open up and receive it. Aimee knew how to love him—warts and all, he believed that much. But *he* needed an instruction manual.

"You're a piece of work, Williams," he said to himself as he got up and began slowly walking toward the cabin. Then, something he'd not defined, not given a name to, suddenly stopped him in his tracks. Aimee was going to have his baby. He was going to be a *father*. And it would be the child of the woman he loved. A wave of panic swept over him. If he and Aimee never married, never even continued their relationship, he'd still be a father. He realized Aimee would be a great mother, he was certain of that. But what kind of parent would he be? Would he do to his son or daughter what his father did to him? How would he prevent that from happening? How would he be different? What would it take? Then, from somewhere deep inside him, welling up, and finally emerging in a single word: 'Love,' he heard his own voice saying. 'Love.' There it was again. What he felt for his unborn child, growing in Aimee's womb, was total, unconditional *love*. With laser-beam clarity, he realized there was nothing more important in the world than this child. Not because it was *his*, but because this 'creation of God' as Abu would say, comes into the world in a perfect state of unconditional and pure love, devoid of the prejudices, fears and hatreds that it will one day be carefully taught. He vowed that he would not allow the doomsayers, the warmongers, the hate-filled bigots, to influence his child's beliefs. He would teach it love. And he would do anything to ensure its welfare and safety. He would even die for it. As he began to understand his feelings, he realized that his fear was beginning to subside.

He went back into the cabin and flipped on the TV set again. In Jerusalem, a hastily-devised press conference was being conducted by a spokesman for the Israeli government. He had just finished reading his prepared statement and was taking questions from the assembled reporters. "Is there any further word on the whereabouts of Sheik Asghar's body?" a journalist for one of the European newspapers shouted.

"No," the Israeli said abruptly.

A Middle-East TV correspondent called out, "There have been allegations by the Palestinians that Mossad—the Israeli secret intelligence—has confiscated his body. Do you have any response?"

"Those are absolutely false and irresponsible allegations. They are absurd," the spokesman said, anger creeping into his voice. "As a matter of fact, our investigation is looking into the possibility that radical Islamic factions may have stolen the body in order to embarrass the Israeli government and exploit the already-existing tensions in the Middle East."

Veronica Basmanti waved her arm and was acknowledged by the

spokesman. "Following up on that question, sir. Some Palestinians have gone so far as to claim that it was the Mossad that is actually responsible for the assassination of Sheik Asghar—"

The spokesman interrupted. "That is equally false and just as absurd. Sheik Asghar was not an enemy of Israel. He was on a mission of peace embraced by the Israeli people. May I remind you that it was a Muslim who shot Sheik Asghar—"

"Then have you been able to find any connection between the assassin and the Islamic Resistance movement?" Basmanti asked.

"Not at this time," was the abrupt reply.

Another reporter from an American news service jumped in. "We understand that, in a couple of days, tens of thousands of Muslims are planning to break the police cordon around the Temple Mount in order to enter the al-Aqsa mosque for evening prayers. Will Israeli troops allow them to pass?"

The spokesman hesitated uncertainly. "The situation is being reviewed. At present, security forces have been ordered to keep the Temple Mount area closed."

"Even if that means more bloodshed?" someone called out.

"It is our earnest desire that there be no more bloodshed. Sheik Asghar's mother, Satki Kaur, has arrived in Jerusalem and has agreed to appear before the marchers with a plea for peace."

"And if that fails?" a European reporter yelled.

There was no response.

"Syrian forces are massed on Israel's eastern border. Does this mean you are expecting an invasion?"

"The U.N. Secretary General is in Damascus attempting to diffuse the situation."

An American reporter in the front row stood up. "We have word that American aircraft carriers are moving into position in the Persian Gulf, and another task force is on duty in the Red Sea. Does Israel intend to ask for U.S. military assistance in the event of an Arab invasion?" The reporter sat down.

Again, the spokesman hesitated. "No request for American assistance has been made, nor is it anticipated. I assume the U.S. government has put its forces on alert to protect its own vital interests in the region. Thank you all very much." With that the spokesman quickly stepped down from the podium and disappeared from the room.

Three days had passed since Abu's assassination and while rumors ran rampant, there still were no real clues as to where his body was. Israel had refused to withdraw its troops from the Temple Mount, and as reported, tens of thousands of Muslims were preparing to march through the streets of Jerusalem and storm the Temple. The international media were in place for the great confrontation. Arab and Palestinian Muslims expected there to be thousands of new martyrs in the ongoing war against Israel. America and Russia publicly urged Israel to avoid bloodshed. The U.N. General Assembly denounced Israel through a series of resolutions.

It was nearly sunset, the time for evening prayers, at the Temple Mount. The marchers could be heard long before they could be seen. Israeli soldiers nervously gripped their rifles. The whole world watched and waited.

An automobile pulled up at the foot of the steps, and its back door flew open. Satki and Bhaiji emerged quickly and were escorted up the steps. She stopped and looked down at the dried pool of blood where Abu had fallen. The marching, chanting Muslims drew nearer. *"Allahu Akhbar,* Abu 'Ali Asghar," they shouted. Bhaiji urged Satki on.

At the top of the steps, Satki looked out over the masses of people moving toward them. She was handed a microphone and held it close to her mouth. "Please!" she shouted. "I am Satki Kaur, the mother of Sheik Abu 'Ali Asghar. I beg you all, please go home!" No one seemed to listen, or care. The Israeli soldiers donned tear gas masks. Satki implored the crowd: "Please, stop before any more are killed or hurt— go back, please!" Still the marchers moved forward, not heeding her pleas.

Then, suddenly, everyone stopped. Behind Satki, from inside the Dome of the Rock, a huge glow appeared. It grew brighter as it emanated through the stained glass windows. The ground rumbled simultaneously. The sun had already set and now, in the night sky, a bright star began to grow. The massive crowd of marchers and onlookers, the security forces, the world's media, all stared silently at the golden Dome as it reflected the star's light, the way it reflected the sun on a clear day. Like some celestial spotlight, the star illuminated everything around it. Then, just as quickly as it appeared, its brightness faded and it disappeared into the blackness of space.

At that moment, the entrance doors to Dome of the Rock flew open. A blinding light surged out. Instantly, the entire city experienced a power outage. There was no electricity anywhere for several seconds. Even the battery-run cameras and microphones of the international media suddenly went dead. A fierce wind blew across the Old City, swirling dust and debris and then it died down. As it did so, the blackout ended. And then, from inside the Dome of the Rock, out stepped Abu. He was dressed in clean white robes and a fresh blue turban. Tens of thousands of people gasped in unison.

Abu walked to his mother at the top of the Temple steps. Tears streamed down her cheeks; her eyes filled with joy. He touched her shoulder and smiled. Bhaiji stood there with adoration and awe, gazing unblinking at Abu who reached out to take his hand. Abu turned his attention to the massive crowd. "I am Abu 'Ali Asghar!" he shouted, his voice echoing off the ancient stones. "For what purpose have you come here?"

"To avenge you!" a man in front called out.

"But I am here. I am well. There is nothing to avenge." There were murmurs and shouts and confusion from the marchers, from the media, from everyone witnessing the sight of Sheik 'Abu Ali Asghar, healthy and whole, more imposing and powerful than ever before.

Abu spoke to the military commander of the security forces that surrounded the Temple Mount. "If these people go in peace, will you let them into the mosque to pray?" Abu asked.

The commander paused, then nodded. "Yes."

Abu called out to the crowd, "Will you pray with me for peace?" The unanimous response was a roaring "YESSSSS . . ."

Abu turned and began walking toward al-Aqsa. The cordon of troops parted and the thousands of faithful followed behind him, peacefully, without incident.

CHAPTER 37

"MIRACLE MAN A HOAX!" screamed the *National Inquirer* head-line, and then went on to say:

> Sheik Abu 'Ali Asghar has pulled off the greatest publicity stunt in history. While millions of people are still convinced that this Islamic prophet of Allah was actually resurrected after his assassination—an event seen by much of the world as a 'miracle'—the *National Inquirer*'s sources have learned that while Christ's resurrection was the real thing, this one by Asghar is a hoax. The Sheik himself staged the entire event. Everything from fake blood to the hiring of an actor to play the assassin was planned and rehearsed. Two doctors and a nurse at the hospital where Sheik Asghar was taken had been bribed with hundreds of thousands of dollars to pretend they tried to save him and then announced he was dead on arrival. After that, he was whisked away to a safe, secret hideaway to wait out the three days and prepare for his 'resurrection.' Even Hollywood can't come up with better entertainment than that! In fact, we'd like to nominate the Sheik for another Prize (he's got the Nobel): The Academy Award for Best Performance.

Bennett Williams laughed out loud as he sat reading the article, sitting alone at the kitchen table in the cabin. Guess it's as good a theory as any, he thought. *The Inquirer* was one of several newspapers and magazines that Herschel Strunk had sent to him via overnight mail. *Time* magazine announced it was voting Abu its "Man of the Year." *The New York Times* was circumspect, not wanting to portray Abu as the new messiah, at the same time, admitting they couldn't help but be impressed with the 'miraculous' occurrence. Newspapers across the country ran the gamut from condemning the Sheik for his Islamic beliefs—some called him a spiritual terrorist and a charlatan—to accepting and revering him as the 20th century's savior—the Mahdi.

The telephone rang. It was Strunk. "How you doin', Ben?"

"Fine. Thanks for the Fed Ex."

"It's incredible, eh? He's suddenly more famous than Elvis, Michael Jackson and O.J. Simpson put together!"

"Yeah. Guess I was lucky to have the inside track on him before he became Jesus Christ Superstar."

Herschel laughed. "Oh, were you ever. No one can get a one-on-one interview with him now. Not even Oprah or Peter Jennings. Barbara Walters flew over to Israel and pleaded with him personally—he said no. She was last seen wailing at the Wailing Wall!" Strunk let out a hearty laugh. Williams joined him. "Which reminds me," Strunk said, "the media's dying to interview you, too."

"Oh yeah? Like who?"

"Like everybody. From *Inside Edition* to *Sixty Minutes*. Oh, and Larry King called this morning. He says your take on what Abu has done would be the most respected opinion, bar none. I told him he was right, but he'll have to wait and read the book."

"Hersch, maybe I oughta do the interview. Tell the world what I think Abu is really up to; warn people."

"No. The only thing TV will do is sensationalize it—turn it into sound bytes. Not to mention how it will diminish the impact of the book. You start talking now, you'll piss the book away. Besides, you've got a publishing contract that says you can't talk about Abu until the book's published. Brandon House would sue your ass off if you went public now."

"But Hersch, this is bigger than just my career. Abu is capable of—"

"No, I said." Strunk's tone was adamant. "You went to the cabin to work in peace. Now finish the book. The hell with the media." There was a pause. "And Ben, you gotta realize something else—"

"What's that?"

"There are plenty of skeptics out there. A lotta people don't buy what this guy's selling. Which means, if you say he's really doing this stuff, they're gonna think *you're* nuts, that you're hallucinating. Or worse, that you're part of his little game plan. They'll twist your words, and misquote you, and your credibility is down the crapper. I'll keep the media at bay. You go back to work. You've got a deadline, remember?"

Williams sighed. "Hersch, what would I do without you?"

"I shudder to think, dear boy," Strunk said with a mock British accent, and hung up.

299

Williams put the phone down and picked up another tabloid. This one posed the provocative question: "If Sheik Asghar Is The New Christ, Is Satki Kaur The Virgin Mother?" Williams chuckled. He glanced at the *Wall Street Journal* which was trying to remain phlegmatic, assuring the world of business and industry that the stock market had not been affected by the so-called 'miracle in the Middle East.' But *Vogue* magazine felt quite the opposite. It was extremely impressed with Abu, and announced that the new fall fashion trend would have the catchy name: *Sheik Chic*, and that the world's top designers were rushing to create flowing robe outfits, and that turban-style hats, once so popular with women in the 1930s, would finally be making a "long overdue comeback." Williams laughed again and picked up a British tabloid whose headline screamed: "SHEIK THROWS WILD SEX PARTIES."

Williams shook his head, not surprised by the media madness, but unnerved and appalled by the omnipotent height it had reached in its dispensing of lies and deception, how it manipulated and distorted——and how, certainly in the last decade, it had become the Great Trivializer. Whether it was a supra-violent movie that glamorized brutality, or the fact that the commission of a heinous crime frequently led to media fame and financial fortune, or the plethora of sordid, vicious and sometimes violent daily TV and radio talk shows—they had succeeded in turning it all into tawdry, degenerate entertainment. And it was feeding the apparently insatiable appetites of countless millions of viewers and readers.

Williams wondered if this was, in fact, nothing more than the true reflection of what society had become, that the mirror doesn't lie. And this ugly sight was the majority view. It had become acknowledged, accepted, and finally, embraced. Williams wondered how much further the pendulum would swing in this direction.

He also pondered what Abu was making of the media circus that had suddenly sprung up around him. All the messages and images he had created in the world press were now forever fixed in people's minds. Was he using it—the frenzied attention—to create the polarities that his reappearance was now causing? He used me for his own end, Williams thought, why not use all the media? It must be part of his plan—making sure events, phenomena really, kept happening on a grander and grander scale. In fact, if it weren't all so ominous, Williams could have had a good long laugh over it. But a number of terrible natural disasters had occurred at the moment of Abu's reappearance. There were simultaneous earthquakes in Los Angeles, Tokyo and Mexico. Fortunately, they involved little loss of life but property damage was in the billions. And an Alaskan volcano erupted without warning, causing one of the Aleutian Islands to sink into the sea. A commercial 747 airliner, with 250 passengers, flying near the volcano, drew a vast amount of powdery ash into its engines; the plane lost control and plummeted into a mountain, bursting upon impact and killing all aboard. Another volcanic eruption in Ecuador melted its shawl of deep snow and created enormous floods that wiped out whole villages and killed thousands of people. At the moment of Abu's emergence from the Dome of the Rock, power outages were set off around the globe, causing the telecommunications systems throughout entire countries to crash. At the world's major airports, radar tracking went haywire and near-misses were rampant as planes tried to land and take off. Lights went out everywhere, emergency generators shut down, elevators stopped, electronic pagers began wildly beeping, and for a few moments, there was worldwide shock, confusion and chaos. None of it surprised Bennett Williams.

In Jerusalem, reactions to Abu's resurrection went from devout Muslims proclaiming it a miracle and decreeing Abu a divine prophet, to the Israeli authorities who denounced Abu's reappearance (they refused to use the word resurrection) and saw it as the work of Arab extremists. Abu offered no explanation at all.

Williams flipped on the small TV set on the kitchen shelf a few feet from the table. *Good Morning, America* was interviewing a respected astrophysicist from M.I.T. who was trying to explain the event that was on everyone's mind: The source of the so-called 'heavenly light' that had illuminated Abu as he walked out from the Dome. "We believe it was the sudden eruption of a quasar, which is a distant, star-like object about a million times brighter than our sun," the scientist said.

"A cosmic phenomena, in other words," the newscaster said.

"Yes, but one of unparalleled proportions. Mind you, there have been several other energy bursts in the universe which were reported recently by observatories in Los Angeles and other parts of the world, but this one has been the most dramatic. You must remember that there is quite a bit we still do not understand about our universe."

301

"And what of the earthquakes and volcanic eruptions that occurred at the same time?"

"I'm not a geophysicist—so I'd rather not speculate on the effect such a burst of radiation might have on the tectonic plate movement. But I think the sudden onset of solar activity it triggered caused the satellite failures and electronic—"

Williams clicked the remote. On the *Today* show, Williams was surprised to see a familiar face. A reporter was interviewing Dr. Philippe Bertone. They were seated in a television studio in Nairobi. The journalist introduced Bertone as the "highly-respected physician whose Third World disaster relief efforts were well known throughout Africa, indeed around the globe."

"Dr. Bertone," the reporter said, "you described yourself as a convert to the belief in miracles. How and when did this happen?"

Bertone looked composed as he spoke. He was dressed as Williams remembered him—in khakis and a plain cotton shirt with a bandana around his neck. "It happened last year," Bertone said, in his French-accented English, "at one of the refugee camps in Ethiopia. There were tens of thousands of people—all dying. They were starving to death, dying of diseases, of wounds inflicted during the horrible tribal massacres that were taking place. We had so many coming to the camp every day and never enough food or medical supplies to keep these people alive. They died by the thousands. Other disaster relief organizations tried to help us, but none were equipped to handle the starvation and dying on so massive a scale. Then, one day, Sheik Abu 'Ali Asghar arrived. Unannounced, unexpected. I had no idea who he was. He said that by dawn the following day, I would have all the food and medical supplies I needed. I scoffed at him, of course. I am a man of medicine, I believe in the scientific, the practical, in what can be proved. And then he showed me. I don't know what he did, or how, or when, but the next morning I discovered this 'mountain' of food supplies in sacks and drinking water and cartons of medicine and operating equipment and clothes and beds and blankets—it was amazing. He brought life back to the dying, he gave hope to the hopeless. I know now what I witnessed. It was a miracle."

Williams turned off the TV. The memories of Bertone's camp came flooding back. He remembered the horrible sights and smells, the children, the mothers holding dead babies, the boys without arms and legs, blind, forever maimed. Abu had done so much for so many suffering thousands. That was real—that was genuine.

Williams heard a car approaching the cabin. He felt his stomach tighten as he opened the screen door and went out onto the porch.

Aimee saw Williams before she brought her rented Jeep Cherokee to a stop. She smiled nervously. "Hello," she said as she stepped down out of the vehicle.

"Hi," Williams said. His heart raced at the sight of her. He wondered how long she would stay but was afraid to ask. "How was the drive?"

"Uneventful." Aimee walked toward him as Williams came down the porch steps. They kissed, in a tentative sort of way.

"I'm glad you came," Williams said.

Aimee nodded. "It was really hard to get away from the office—" Before Williams could respond, Aimee took a deep breath. "Ah, that's what it smells like."

"What smells like?" Williams asked as they went into the cabin.

"Clean air. The country."

"It's even better at night." Williams wanted to convince her to stay. "The stars are so bright, you can actually make out the Milky Way."

Aimee smiled and stared at Williams. "I'm glad I came, too."

Williams longed to take her in his arms and hold her, but still felt awkward, constrained. "Want something to drink—tea, coffee—?"

"Coffee's fine." Aimee followed Williams through the living room with its huge stone fireplace and dark green velvet couches and Persian rugs on the pegged hardwood floors. "Not exactly a rustic cabin," Aimee said as they walked into the well-appointed French country kitchen.

"Herschel's idea of roughing it is having to use paper napkins because he forgot to bring the linen ones." Williams filled the small copper tea kettle with water, put it on the stove and began to grind fresh coffee beans. "You'd never know it to look at him, but he does have elegant taste."

Aimee laughed. "I like Herschel. He reminds me of my father." She watched as Williams poured two large mugs of strong hot coffee.

"I was hoping we could go for a walk this afternoon, but there's a thunderstorm on its way."

"So we'll just light a fire and stay cozy inside."

Williams sat across from Aimee at the kitchen table and reached for her hand. He held it for a moment, then kissed it. "God, I missed you."

Aimee's smile was soft as a caress. Her hand gently touched his cheek. "Same here." She paused. "Ben, I need to ask you about Abu."

Williams took a large swallow of coffee. "Go ahead."

"Do you think it was a hoax?"

"No. That would be beneath Abu. Whatever it was, it was real."

"You mean you think he was actually . . . *resurrected*?"

"Maybe. Or maybe he was never dead. He can do things with his body that are incomprehensible to you and me."

Aimee sipped her coffee thoughtfully. "But what about his wounds? Did they just spontaneously heal?"

Williams shrugged. "Probably."

"But how'd he get out of the morgue, for God's sake?"

"I don't know. How did Christ get out of his tomb?"

"Come on, Ben—"

"Aimee," Williams said, getting up from the table. "Let's take a walk down to the lake before it starts to rain." As if to reinforce his prediction, there was a rumble of thunder, closer this time.

Aimee nodded and Williams took her hand as they walked out the back door and down the wide path that led to the lake and the small dock.

"Aimee, a lot of what Abu told me I never wrote about in my articles."

"Why?"

"Because people might not be ready to accept it. They'd just think that Abu was too weird. But some of it would help to explain what's been happening, what he's just done."

"Such as?" Aimee's curiosity was piqued. They went to the end of it and sat down, dangling their legs over the edge.

"Abu says that linear time doesn't exist."

"What exactly is linear—"

"It works only for something with a beginning and an end. But God—and the universe—and our souls, have no beginning or end—they're infinite. Therefore they exist beyond linear time. Abu is fond of saying that 'our souls are forever beings,' but that we live only in a

304

three-dimensional reality, and there are seven other dimensions beyond the physical world. So, if there is no linear time, the past, present and future all co-exist in a single moment."

Aimee nodded tentatively. "Okay, go on . . ."

Williams took a deep breath and put an arm around Aimee's shoulder. They were both staring straight ahead at the distant horizon and the gathering storm clouds. Williams spoke with quiet conviction as he gazed into the distance. "Maybe Abu just manipulated time. Maybe he focused his soul into another reality—one where he survived the assassination. Aimee, if there's one thing I learned from Abu it's that there is so much more to us—to our lives and our place in the universal scheme of things—than we are able to comprehend. We have so incredibly far to go before we can consider ourselves enlightened. Christ, we're still in the Stone Age. And all Abu is trying to do is get us to acknowledge that it is time for us to change, and grow, and go another step up on the evolutionary ladder."

Aimee nodded and took Williams' hand. She held it tightly. Neither spoke for a few minutes. Finally, Williams broke the silence.

"Aimee, I'm so sorry."

"For what, Ben?"

For how I behaved in New York—I didn't know where all that anger was coming from until I started wandering around the woods here— like a goddamn Thoreau—and sorted it out. Abu taught me more than I'll probably ever know, but it took meeting you for it to make any sense."

"You mean commitment? Relationships?"

Williams nodded. "Aimee, I was so scared of you."

"Why?"

"Because you got in . . . you got in where no one, not even Abu, had ever been."

"And you're not afraid anymore?"

Williams stroked her long wavy hair, and tilted her chin up to him. "You know, everything Abu talks about comes down to love—the art of loving, both ourselves and others. When we're connected to one another in love, then we are ultimately connected to our souls, and to . . . God . . . or the universal consciousness, or whatever you want to call it. I had never met anyone I ever wanted to be connected to, until I met you."

Williams paused, took a deep breath, then plunged in, as if diving into the cold lake. "Aimee, can we please be a family? Can we grow old together? Do you love me? Will you marry me?"

Aimee took Williams face between her hands and kissed him on the cheek. "Yes." On his forehead. "Yes." On his eyes. "Yes." On his mouth. "Yes."

Williams laughed with relief and joy. "Oh Aimee," he said, covering her face with kisses.

Aimee grinned. "It was easier than you thought it would be, huh?"

Williams held her tighter. "Aimee, I'm going to work like hell to be a good father, a good husband." He paused and let out a deep exhale. "Well, I feel like I just crossed the Rubicon." He stopped and his face suddenly clouded. "Aimee, there's so much ahead that's unknown—"

"We'll find our way together, Ben."

As they kissed, the wind whipped up and a loud clap of thunder pierced the stillness. "See," Aimee said, "Abu's not the only one who has a powerful effect on nature."

They ran for the cabin as huge droplets of rain began falling. "Ben, I want to get my suitcase out of the Jeep—"

"I'll do it—you go in the house."

Aimee went through the back door as Williams headed around the front. Just as he got to the Jeep, a black, four-door Buick sedan pulled onto the property. "What the—?" Williams said to himself as two men got out of the car. They were dressed casually but didn't look like vacationers or locals.

"Bennett Williams?" one of the men asked.

"Yes," Williams replied as he opened the back door of the Jeep and took out Aimee's suitcase. The rain was starting to come down harder. Both men reached into their shirt pockets, pulled out wallets and flashed photo I.D.'s at Williams.

"National Security Agency," one of the men said. "I'm Roger Turner." He gestured toward his colleague. "This is Jim Clark."

Williams shook both their hands. "Up here to do some fishing?" he asked.

"We'd like to ask you a few questions. Mind if we come in?"

"Of course not," Williams said. "No point in getting soaked out here."

Aimee had watched from the living room window and went to open the front porch door. Williams came in first and went into the bedroom with Aimee's suitcase while the two intelligence agents stood on the porch and smiled at Aimee. "Hope we're not intruding, Ms. Argent," Clark said.

Aimee was surprised they knew her name. She studied the two men as they came into the cabin, then glanced at Williams who had just entered the living room, wiping his hair with a towel. "These gentlemen are from the CIA, I mean, the NSA." he said to Aimee. She looked at him nervously. "Don't worry, honey, they're just on a . . . uh . . . fishing expedition."

Aimee understood what Williams meant but since he didn't look too concerned, she relaxed. "Would you like some coffee?" she said to both agents.

"I'd love some, thanks," Turner said. Clark shook his head.

Aimee went into the kitchen as Williams gestured to the living room couches. "Have a seat," he said without sounding the least bit hospitable.

Turner and Clark sat down opposite Williams. He eyed them with dislike, but wasn't surprised that they had managed to find him. "So, this isn't a social call—don't I feel foolish."

Clark came right to the point. "You are a friend of Sheik Asghar, isn't that correct?" He had used the word 'friend' as though it were some kind of euphemism.

Williams glared at him. "Yes, I suppose you could say that."

Aimee came into the room with a cup of coffee and handed it to Turner, then she sat down next to Williams. The agent nodded politely to Aimee as he took the coffee.

"What's Asghar's mission?" Turner asked.

Williams looked puzzled. "Mission—?"

"We'd like to know what he's about, Mr. Williams," Clark said more politely, trying to diffuse the tension.

"You mean you haven't bugged this place yet?"

Turner smiled. "No need to be paranoid. We just want you to cooperate with us, that's all."

"Why the hell should I?"

Aimee squeezed Williams' hand as if to keep him from getting too angry.

"Because we're on the same side," Clark said.

"And just what side is that?" Williams asked sarcastically. "Truth, justice, the American way, right?"

"Mr. Williams," Turner said, starting to bristle, "we're investigating a potential threat to our national security. Just where the hell is your allegiance?"

The question stopped Williams cold. Aimee looked at him.

When Williams said nothing, Clark got up from the couch. "Are you going to help us?" he asked.

Williams looked up at him. "Fuck off," he grumbled.

"I'll take that as a no," Clark said stonily.

Turner put his cup down on the coffee table and got up from the couch. He started walking toward the door. Clark followed him. "Oh, by the way, Mr. Williams, how's your book coming along?" Turner asked.

Williams got up from the couch, went to the front door, and opened it. "Fine."

"I'm looking forward to reading it. Maybe it will tell us what we need to know." He glared at Williams. "Only then it'll be too late, won't it?"

Turner opened the screen door and he and Clark stepped onto the porch. Ben watched as the agents made a dash for their car through the downpour. A bolt of lightning and a clap of thunder accompanied their departure as the car sped off Herschel Strunk's property.

"Ben—" Aimee called from the living room. When he came in and sat down beside her, she scanned his face, looking for an answer. "Is Abu really a threat?"

Williams shrugged. "Look, in some ways, Abu is just what he appears to be. He's a man of peace who believes in the sanctity of all life. He has dedicated his life to helping humanity. But remember, he will be the hammer."

"And what do you think this hammer will do?"

"Show us who we really are." Williams paused. "I don't know how else to explain it."

"How bad is it going to get?"

"I don't know. How bad does it have to get?" Williams asked.

"Before what?"

"People decide to change."

The two sat quietly for what seemed like a long time. The thunderstorm had turned the day dark and cold. Aimee shuddered. "Light a fire, Ben, it's so chilly in here."

Williams turned to Aimee and took her in his arms. He looked deeply into her eyes. "I've got a much better way to warm you—"

He lifted her off the couch and carried her into the bedroom. They undressed each other with a hungry urgency and were on the bed in seconds. Williams kissed Aimee's neck and breasts and his mouth moved down to her stomach. Aimee groaned with pleasure as she reached her hands toward his shoulders and lifted his head. "Ben, I want you inside me, right now, please . . ."

Williams moved up and pulled her under him. As he entered her, he cried out, "Oh Aimee, how I missed you."

"Welcome home, my love," Aimee said as they began moving rhythmically together.

They both knew that, for a little while anyway, their lovemaking could drown out the rest of the world and become the only thing that mattered.

CHAPTER 38

There was no denying it; Abu wasn't merely celebrated anymore, he was now worshiped. After all, he had defied death; he had transcended mortality.

He swept over Israel's West Bank to the roaring multitudes of Palestinians. Everywhere he went, the masses cheered and struggled to get near him, to feel the power of his divinity. He went to Jordan where he was given a royal reception by King Hussein. In Syria, President Hasef Assad, usually the most guarded, secretive and unresponsive of the Middle East's leaders, feted Abu with a state dinner. In Turkey, the most populous nation in the Middle East, and the only Muslim member of NATO, Abu met with Suleiman Kamaral, the Turkish president who personally escorted him to the Byzantine monuments of Istanbul. In Iraq, the cradle of modern civilization, Abu met the nation's nefarious leader and was invited to join him in a solemn memorial for the thousands of Arabs who died during the three-day Persian Gulf War.

In Iran, tens of thousands of fanatic Shiite Muslims turned out to chant his name, while at the same time, creating huge pyres of burning American flags. It filled the Iranian television news and led to an invitation to speak before the Iranian parliament.

When Abu entered the impoverished and war-torn country of Afghanistan, no matter how poor and oppressed the population was, they gathered new strength, new hope and faith, as they followed their savior wherever he spoke, in mosques or at stadium rallies, through city streets and rural villages.

Television and radio continued to broadcast Abu's travels and speeches so that the millions who could not get a glimpse of him in person, were at least able to see and hear this spiritual warrior as he moved ever closer to his goal.

In Pakistan, after a brief meeting with Prime Minister Zattar, Abu and Bhaiji loaded the Mercedes onto a freighter in Karachi and sailed to Oman. The Sultan of Oman rolled out the red carpet for Abu, as did several other leaders in the oil-rich sheikdoms of the United Arab Emirates. But when he arrived in Saudi Arabia, the Saudi king was somewhat less than enthusiastic about Abu's journey to his country. To help diffuse the speculation that his private meeting with the King, held in Riyadh, did not go well, Abu decided to hold a press conference. It was his first since leaving Jerusalem.

When a reporter asked Abu how his meeting went, Abu answered firmly, "Most productive." Forced to elaborate by another journalist, Abu explained that democratic reforms were long overdue in Saudi Arabia, and the people deserved a greater voice in their government. "Dictatorships, no matter how benevolent, are relics of the past," Abu sternly told his interviewer.

There were murmurs in the room. "How did the King respond?" someone shouted out.

Abu admitted the Saudi king was not in "complete agreement," but he told the roomful of reporters, "self-government is not a privilege; it is a right. Equality, justice and liberty are not simply ideals, they are the foundation for existence. They constitute God's mandate for all humanity."

"Sheik Asghar, do you claim to be divine?" The reporter's query brought the room to an immediate halt. Abu's eyes sought out the man who asked the question. Everyone in the room stared intently up at Abu.

"Yes," Abu said simply. Once again the room was abuzz. Abu waited patiently until it was quiet and then continued, speaking with a warmth not typical of him. "But as I have said many times, we are all divine—every human being, every animal, every plant and rock is divine."

"And do you consider yourself immortal?" the same reporter challenged.

"Yes. My soul is immortal. The same as yours. I am flesh and bone— the same as you."

"Not quite, Sheik Asghar," another journalist said, his tone clearly mocking. "Your flesh and bone withstood a point-blank bullet to your head. And you haven't so much as a scar."

"I suspect that is true," Abu responded. There was no anger or argument in his voice. "But I can tell you that everyone in this room has the same potential. I simply represent what is possible. Every human being carries within them the power of God. When you accept that God's divinity is within you, then, and only then, will you truly realize your own infinite potential. Anything will be possible. *Everything* will be possible."

Another reporter raised his hand, but Abu shook his head and smiled. "I would think that all of you, as members of the press, could most easily and readily accept your divine nature." Instant laughter filled the room. Abu raised his hand for silence.

"Nothing has ever been invented that was not already possible. God's gift to humanity is in having given us the ability to understand our universe, to be both the instrument of creation and the creator. Evolution is not a predestined path; it is a journey of choice—it is not achieved by accident, but is the consequence of cause and effect. The power of creation can also destroy. Therefore, the choice of how to use that power has always belonged to humanity. You need only to look at the world around you to see what choices have been made."

There was an uncomfortable silence in the room. Abu drank from a glass of water and waited. Finally, a journalist stood up. "Sheik Asghar, there are reports that you will be attending an upcoming OPEC meeting. Is that true?"

"Yes," Abu replied.

"Why?" the reporter asked.

"Because it is the centerpiece of regional cooperation among Arab nations. Oil is the one thing the Arab world has that the West needs."

"Many say OPEC is dead," the reporter baited Abu.

Abu smiled. "Many said I was dead. Yet, here I am." There was grudging acknowledgment and laughter from the audience.

"Sheik Asghar," another reporter demanded, "Do you intend to call for an Islamic revolution around the world?" An immediate hush fell over the room.

Abu hesitated and averted his eyes for a moment. When he spoke his voice was filled with compassion. "Those who perpetrate violence often simply want change. This may be an opportune time for those who are in a position to effect change to show the terrorists that they need not kill innocents in order to be heard."

A European reporter was on his feet. "Sheik Asghar, you speak so much of change—that it is a good thing—but look what change has done in the former Soviet Union, for example. Russia is now in chaos—all its political and economic restructuring has brought about more misery than ever before—"

Abu interrupted. "True. But that is because the extent to which a house must be rebuilt depends on the degree of dry rot. Sometimes the entire house must be razed and a whole new foundation must be built."

Abu's tone turned ominous. "Time is running out," he said with prophetic urgency. "Our system does not work; a new house must be constructed; Islam is one means of achieving that. Its supreme virtues are an insistence on equality and justice, protection of the weak, and a fair distribution of wealth. And it recognizes that there is no real separation between spiritual values and government. Please understand, I am not advocating a global theocracy; I believe, as Jesus did, that self-government in its purest form is the only means of establishing a kingdom of heaven on earth." Abu paused for a moment, placed his palms together and bowed. "Thank you, ladies and gentlemen."

As Abu began walking off the podium, a reporter shouted, "Sheik Asghar, where are you going next?"

Abu stopped and called out, "To Mecca!" He made it sound like a rallying cry. "I shall participate in the Hajj." He left the room accompanied by a flurry of clicking cameras and popping flashbulbs, and several reporters still calling out questions.

Abu's announcement rocked the Islamic world. The Hajj was the most sacred—and most political—event in Islam. It constituted one of the Five Pillars of Islam. To many Muslims there was also a Sixth Pillar: Jihad. It referred to the army of Muslims established by Muhammad, whose first loyalty was to Allah, and whose purpose was to fight against those who were non-believers or infidels.

But the Hajj itself was a journey to the heart. It brought together the many races and peoples of the Islamic world and was considered a sacred duty for every Muslim to participate in at least once in their lifetime. From around the world, Muslims made this annual pilgrimage to Mecca to visit the large, cubic-stone structure covered with a black cloth at the center of the Grand Mosque. Known as the Ka'ba, it represented Islam's spiritual center, the focus of concentration upon the Divine Presence. Muslims everywhere turned in the direction of the Ka'ba when they offered up their daily prayers.

In one corner of the Ka'ba sat the Black Stone. Legend has it that it was a fragment of a star that had crashed to earth many thousands of years ago. It was believed to have been placed in the original Ka'ba by Adam. The star had once shone so brightly that it illuminated everything from east to west but became blackened by contact with Earth and human sin.

The Ka'ba was considered the temple of Adam—thus, the first temple. Now, as a temple of Islam—the last religion—the Ka'ba has become the last temple.

Abu's participation in this holiest of holy occasions transformed it into a sensational event—not only would it be documented by the entire world's media, but it also brought a new wave of tourists and a record number of Muslims vying to be part of the pilgrimage led by Sheik Abu 'Ali Asghar as the Commander of the Faithful.

Alone once more in Herschel's cabin, Williams wrote feverishly. The words came cascading out of him, through his fingers and into the keyboard with relentless force. His eyes remained riveted on the screen in front of him. He knew he wasn't the creator; merely the conduit, the vessel through which the thoughts and words were meant to come. He felt like a typist simply transcribing a story that had already been written. It made Williams feel humble—an unfamiliar sentiment for him.

Aimee had returned to the city. Williams had objected; he wanted her to stay, not just for his own selfish reasons, but for her safety. "What about the baby?" he had asked.

"What about the baby?" Aimee had responded. She was touched by his naïve concern for her welfare. "Ben, I can't live in a bubble until our child is born. I'll be fine, darling. And I need to get back to work."

"I just don't like the idea of you being alone in the city."

"I was alone before you came along."

"That was different."

"How?"

"I didn't love you then. You weren't carrying our baby."

Aimee put her arms around Williams. "I promise that everything is going to be okay. Besides, I'll be a distraction sitting around here—you'll worry about me being bored. And I probably will be."

"I can't stand sleeping alone anymore. And I hate waking up without you beside me in the morning."

"I wouldn't be beside you in the morning," Aimee said with a laugh. "I'd be in the bathroom—throwing up."

So Aimee went back to the city and back to her work—Brandon House was getting ready to put its fall/winter catalogue to bed—and she plunged into the most demanding deadline schedule she'd ever had. It often left her quite fatigued at day's end, and Williams worried about this. But Aimee reassured him that it was a normal part of pregnancy. She saw an obstetrician on a regular basis, had begun a regimen of eating very healthy foods, and whenever she became too tired at the office, she went home and took a long afternoon nap. In fact, she had taken to the role of impending motherhood with surprising ease and grace—something Williams found so appealing. Aimee's long-dormant nurturing instincts surfaced as naturally as the life within her belly was growing.

"How do you feel?" Williams asked the moment he had reached her by phone one day.

"Like Mother Earth," Aimee replied with a chuckle. "You're going to love my boobs—they're getting huge."

"But I loved your boobs just the way they were," Williams said.

"Well, there's just more to love now."

"What about morning sickness?"

"It's gone, thank goodness. How's everything up there?"

"Good, but I'm lonely."

"Ben, I'm talking about the book—how's it coming?"

"Aimee, it's the strangest thing—it's . . . writing itself. That's the only way I can describe it. So much comes pouring out of me—and most of the time, I feel like I haven't even stopped to think about it before it ends up on paper."

"That's because you were more ready to write this book than even you imagined."

Williams nodded. Aimee was right. The outpouring of thought and inspiration—something he feared would not be there—had been unleashed. He felt free for the first time in his life. Free and calm. And with a sense of purpose.

315

He realized this as he stood on the shore of the lake one late afternoon. He watched the sunset—an orange and purple flame across the sky, as though giant brush strokes of primary colors had been painted on an endless canvas. Williams felt his heart swell; his eyes filled with tears. He knew what it was: He felt *connected*. Not just to himself but to everything. He felt a part of the whole. Separate and distinct, but integrally related. He was no longer the outsider looking in, the detached observer. For the first time in Williams' life, he felt at one with his world.

And he wanted people to understand what he now understood. Not for himself or his ego; not even for Abu. It was for his child; for all the children yet to be born. It was so they could know a better world. He now knew it could exist; he could see; he'd been shown. Moreover, he now had a stake in the outcome.

CHAPTER 39

"At thy service, God! At thy service!" Abu, in the white toga-like ceremonial garb of the Hajj, with his olive-wood prayer beads in hand, repeated the ancient words of Abraham, spoken by every pilgrim to Mecca, as he circled the Ka'ba.

Abu pressed himself against the Ka'ba and recited prayers from the Koran, occasionally touching his lips to the outer wall. He drank from the Well of ZamZam, a well dug by the son of Abraham, and from which sprang the oasis of Mecca.

On the second day of the Hajj, Abu made the long walk to Arafat and climbed the Mount of Mercy along with millions of white-robed pilgrims. The gathering was symbolic of the coming of the Day of Judgment when a Muslim would look upon his life and examine his conscience. As Abu stood beneath the scorching sun until twilight, a pilgrim called out to him: "Sheik Asghar, give us a sermon."

Abu shook his head. "I am here only to pay homage to God. If it is guidance you want, listen to the sermon of your heart. Look within; that is where God speaks to you."

He turned away from the thousands of Muslims who wanted to hear him speak and continued to pray in silence.

Abu's trip to Mecca was notable for another reason. There were now new faces among his entourage. They called themselves Ikhwan and were Abu's self-appointed bodyguards. In ancient times, the Ikhwan were Bedouin warriors, fanatical Muslims single-minded in their devotion to the establishment of an Islamic state. They were cunning, brave and ruthless. The Ikhwan had helped King Ibn Saud establish the nation of Saudi Arabia by defeating the king's enemies. But once Saud was in power, he quickly betrayed and disbanded the Ikhwan in favor of his worldly kingdom. Abu now resurrected them because they were the perfect symbol of a dream not yet realized.

During the last three days of the Hajj, Abu fasted, as was the tradition. His final visit of the pilgrimage was to the tomb of the prophet Muhammed and then prayers at Masjid at-Taqwa, the first mosque of Islam. It was there that a reporter—the press dogged him everywhere now—asked, "Where are you going next, Sheik Asghar?"

Abu smiled and answered without stopping. "If the mountain will not go to Muhammed, then Muhammed must go to the mountain."

"Which means—?" the journalist called out.

"I shall go to the West; I must take my message there before darkness falls upon us all."

Within twenty-four hours, in a Lear jet owned by the Saudi royal family, Abu and his Ikhwan guards landed in Geneva, Switzerland. It was here that Satki had started the World Peoples' Organization. She was currently on a brief fund-raising trip to Denmark and Sweden. But Bhaiji was waiting for Abu in the Geneva headquarters. He had not been allowed to make the trip to Mecca because he was not a Muslim.

"Bhaiji, you have done very well," Abu said, as he looked around the vast offices of the WPO with its state-of-the-art equipment and well-trained, dedicated staff.

"Your mother is the one to thank—"

"Yes, of course," Abu said. "She has made all this happen."

"Come, let me show you around." He took Abu into a board room where a large wall map was filled with small flags that dotted the nations of the southern hemisphere. Bhaiji pointed with pride to the map. "There are now over one thousand relief centers around the world, and more being planned."

Abu nodded and smiled. "Excellent."

He continued to smile when, a few hours later, a group of Swiss accountants and several financial consultants met with him in the board room and provided Abu with a detailed briefing—complete with slides and charts—of the extraordinary progress and financial stability of the WPO.

In the middle of the presentation, the conference room door opened and a secretary shyly announced that the man Sheik Asghar was waiting to meet with had just arrived. Abu thanked the secretary and asked her to show him in.

Heinrich Demmler was instantly and warmly greeted by Abu. The German-born Swiss citizen was impeccably dressed, from his

London-tailored suit to his Italian silk shirt and tie, to the butter-scotch cashmere coat and the ivory-handled walking stick. He strode over to Abu and offered a perfectly manicured hand. Demmler's un-smiling face was set off by his shock of snow-white hair which framed icy blue eyes and pale skin. His face was a study in winter.

During the second World War, Demmler's father had been a close friend of Albert Speer and had amassed a fortune manufacturing arms in Nazi Germany. But when, in 1944, it became apparent that Hitler's dream of a thousand-year Reich was the doomed and demented vision of an evil madman, Demmler's father moved the family and their wealth to the safety and security of Switzerland. It was here that the young Heinrich could hone his skills for banking, investment, and ultimately become the behind-the-scenes manipulator of global economies. Demmler presided over Europe's most prestigious investment bank, whose clients included the world's largest corporations and wealthi-est individuals. But Demmler himself shunned publicity and avoided any exposure—his power as a king maker was sustainable only in ob-scurity. Whenever there was a summit meeting of leaders and finance ministers of the world's largest industrialized nations, Heinrich Demmler was always there, but away from the scrutiny of either the press or those attending the meetings. With a cadre of close aides, Demmler would take over a suite of hotel rooms and temporarily turn them into his office headquarters—a bank of telephones and com-puter terminals would be hastily set up from which Demmler could operate. He would briefly attend the summit, then offer his well-placed advice. He was automatically involved in any significant economic decision—and if he didn't approve of a proposal by the summit lead-ers, it would not be implemented. As a result, Demmler was in control of billions of dollars and, like a demi-god watching over a mighty river, he could alter its course when he deemed necessary.

Demmler had long held an elusive dream—that of a global, unified economic system with a single fiscal policy, one currency, one central bank. Therefore, he was a man now critically important to Abu. But Demmler was getting old and his dream was all that kept him in-volved; all else was folly. And he was afraid his time was running out.

He saw in Sheik Asghar a possible means by which to revitalize, and perhaps even realize, his own fading dream. He knew that Abu was amassing enormous sums of money through his WPO enterprise and that substantial contributions had started to come in from OPEC. Demmler's bank was handling the multi-million dollar transactions that would, very soon, amount to billions of dollars.

Abu had politely asked his advisers to leave the conference room so he could meet with Demmler privately. Only Bhaiji remained.

Abu wasted no time. "Herr Demmler, would you not agree that money is power?"

A thin smile crossed Demmler's face and then quickly faded. "Sheik Asghar, it is the ultimate power—the source of all other power."

"Herr Demmler, I want your help—I want you to help me realize my vision, and by so doing, I promise that you will find your dream as well."

"I am at your service, Sheik Asghar."

"You agree too quickly. I shall require your absolute trust and allegiance. I will seek your advice, but you must carry out my instructions without question. You will have to resign your current position as head of your bank in order to commit all your time, energy and loyalty to me, and me alone. You shall have no other masters but me. Do you understand?"

Demmler's hard blue eyes stared unflinchingly back at Abu. "Yes, I quite understand," he said in a tone that was polite and non-committal. Then he squinted and said, "But why does it sound as though I'd be making a deal with the devil?"

Abu thought for a moment, then nodded to himself. "Because there are many who will think so, Herr Demmler. Some will call you the devil's disciple."

"I see." Demmler's eyes narrowed again. "And so, exactly what do I get for this Faustian pact?"

Abu's piercing dark eyes locked onto Demmler. "A new world order," Abu said with such humility that, for a second, Demmler thought he was joking.

Demmler leaned back in his chair. "What sort of new world order, Sheik Asghar?" he asked, trying not to sound cynical or, worse, disdainful. He did, after all, have enormous respect and admiration for Abu. He knew of Abu's astonishing, supernatural powers and the adulation and devotion of the millions who now worshiped him. Even the beloved Catholic Pope was not as revered as Abu these days. No, this man was no ordinary mortal.

"One which the world has never seen. A unified, integrated world order—a single organism, if you will, the sum of its parts acting in concert for the good of the whole. One based on cooperation rather than competition, compliance rather than control, need rather than greed."

"Can you truly create such a world order?" Demmler's tone was plaintive.

Abu nodded and spoke softly. "Yes. With your help, Herr Demmler."

"I have long held a similar vision, Sheik Asghar." Demmler nodded slowly. "I will join you."

"And I have your absolute allegiance?"

"You have my absolute allegiance," Demmler said. His tone was unequivocal.

"Good," Abu said firmly. "Here is what I need you to do." Abu described how he wanted Demmler to establish secret bank accounts that only he, Bhaiji Singh and of course, Abu, would have access to. With each account, Abu instructed Demmler to create other foundations for which the WPO would be the funding source. Demmler nodded in agreement.

Bhaiji was puzzled. "Abuji, what will be the purpose of these foundations?"

"Whatever you deem appropriate. It does not matter," Abu explained, then looked at Demmler. "I think you understand." His tone was chilling.

Demmler nodded. "Yes, I understand."

"With the money brought in through these 'channels,' I want you to purchase a shipping company with a large fleet of seaworthy vessels. Acquire shipyards in Algeria, Egypt, Libya, Turkey and Somalia to service them." Demmler and Bhaiji nodded. Abu got up from the table. "That is all for now. You must get started at once."

Demmler rose from his chair and gave a slight bow in Abu's direction. He leaned lightly on his ivory-handled walking stick and smiled at Abu. "Sheik Asghar, you have given this old man his dream back. For that I thank you."

Abu nodded and smiled, putting his hands together and bowing, almost imperceptibly, to Demmler. Bhaiji watched the two men with his usual mixture of awe and respect, but tinged this time with a strange sense of foreboding. It was nothing he could really put his finger on, let alone define—only the hint of a feeling that crept over him more and more often these days and then, like an apparition, floated away.

Abu's schedule included several brief but important stops in Europe; the first was a private tour of the Vatican conducted by the Pontiff himself. At Vatican Square, in front of St. Peter's Basilica, over a hundred thousand people had gathered to hear the Pope deliver a plea for world peace and a call for cooperation between Christians, Jews and Muslims throughout the world. When His Holiness had finished speaking, he brought Abu to the microphone and as the enormous audience recognized Sheik Asghar, a collective roar went up from the crowd, louder than anything ever afforded the Pope.

Abu bowed deeply and then raised his arms. When the noise and adulation had quieted down, he began speaking. What the listeners were about to hear was unexpected and disturbing. "I beg the Catholic church," Abu cried out, "to divest itself of all its worldly wealth and spend its immense fortune to help the homeless and feed the starving." Abu's words shocked the vast audience; the Pope showed visible discomfort. Abu's voice rose with passion. "The Holy Mother Church must return to true Christian values and principles—it must live the essence of Christ's teachings. His message told us that God does not require external glorification—the true glory of God can be seen in the eyes of starving children when they are given food to eat; in the gratefulness of mothers who know their children will live. What value are paintings and marble statues and gold altars to a child of the Third World whose belly swells with hunger and pain? How do you preach conversion to millions of diseased and dying refugees? The material wealth of the Church must help to overcome the suffering and squalor that afflicts more than half the world! Christ meant for humanity to create the 'kingdom of heaven' here on earth, to serve God not through worship and suffering but through God's greatest gift: Life itself. Life is what matters, not the afterlife. The way we live and the world we create determines our Godliness. All else is hypocrisy."

Abu's provocative challenge set off a political storm in Italy. The Pope did not take kindly to Abu's veiled accusations, and in a private audience the Pontiff pointed out to Abu the numerous and generous charitable works that the Church was continuously engaged in.

Abu smiled politely but was having none of it. "It is not enough, Your Holiness, not nearly enough. The scope is far too narrow. The Holy Roman See worries far too much about internal scandals, and issues of divorce and birth control, and how to preserve the patriarchal priesthood. It should be worried less about saving souls and do far more to save lives. To offer the Church's worldly treasures and priceless possessions to help humanity would be an act of true spirituality, the ultimate Christian morality."

The Pontiff curtly announced that it was not up to him to "pawn the Vatican's material wealth and vast holdings," and then motioned for one of his aides to escort Abu out of his private chambers.

While many Catholics around the world applauded Abu's message, others were angered and insulted by it. Italy's president had scheduled a meeting with Abu but now promptly canceled it. But Abu stayed on in Italy, touring with his own entourage of bodyguards, and the ever-present contingent of reporters and photographers. In the country's poorest rural areas and in the ghettos of its bigger cities, Abu spoke to the people who had taken to the streets to hear the man who, however momentarily, had understood their suffering and gave them a measure of hope. When Abu left Italy, riots broke out all over the country.

Abu arrived in France right in the middle of the nation's worst political and social crisis—a massive strike had literally shut the country down. It had begun in Paris with striking transportation workers and spread to the airlines, forcing Orly Airport to close. Without trains and busses, cars and bicycles created a constant state of gridlock; drivers were forced to ride on the sidewalks and pedestrians were killed in alarming numbers. Hospital employees went on strike. So did teachers. Garbage collectors and street sweepers stopped working. Restaurants, shops and cafes were closed. Supermarket shelves were empty due to a lack of food delivery; panic and hoarding had begun. Electricity and clean drinking water were in short and erratic supply. The country was crippled as it had never been before, thanks to a government that had created an economy its people could no longer live with. The French began marching, protesting, and fighting in the streets.

Abu could not have found a more receptive audience—he empathized with the plight of the people, he called for change; they called for revolution. The admiration was mutual.

After Abu left France, he made a brief visit to Germany, particularly the industrialized northern part of the country, where he marched with Turkish Muslims who had taken to the streets to demand that the government end the persecution of the thousands of Turks who had immigrated to Germany. Neo-Nazis, dressed like storm troopers and brandishing swastikas also marched, but they did so to protest Abu's visit. The resulting violent clashes in the streets of Hamburg and Dusseldorf—the gutters ran with Turkish blood—prompted Germany's Chancellor to call out his country's national guard to control the rioting. He also begged Abu to leave Germany, saying that it was up to the German people to solve their own problems and they would do so without Sheik Asghar's interference.

Abu left the Continent and flew to England. His visit to Great Britain had a dual purpose. He had been invited by the Prime Minister to address the House of Commons. And he had another, private, darker mission to accomplish.

The British government welcomed Abu and the members of Parliament listened with interest and respect as the Sheik spoke to them. Despite the fact that the London tabloids were blaring stories about Abu's conviction for murder over a decade earlier and his curious release from Dartmoor prison in the wake of riots there, the British royal family welcomed Sheik Asghar at Buckingham Palace for an informal late afternoon tea. They even commiserated with Abu about the relentless exploitation by the press—something they complained they'd had more than their share of.

But Abu had commanded tremendous admiration from the respectable British newspapers, as well as the venerable BBC. Both the *London Times* and the *Manchester Guardian* wrote glowingly of Abu's Nobel Peace Prize, and his tireless efforts to help humanity's suffering masses. And they only mentioned in passing the visit Sheik Asghar made to the home of a retired Sikh businessman and his wife. They were the parents of his beloved Nanaki.

After dinner with Nanaki's parents, Abu returned to his hotel. A short while later, he came back out again. No one saw him exit the elevator, walk through the lobby and step into a waiting taxi. It was as though he was invisible.

"Vauxhall," he said to the cabdriver.

Abu looked out the window as the taxi rode through the dark, deserted, winding streets, across the Thames and into the working-class neighborhood. Abu didn't say a word as he studied the passing scene with an intensity so fierce, so palpable, that the taxi driver became terrified of his passenger. He was greatly relieved when Abu finally ordered him to stop the cab "at the the next traffic light." Abu jumped out and handed the driver several bills, then watched as the cab drove off in a screeching hurry.

A misty rain had begun to fall as Abu walked down one dark street and then another, through an alley, then onto another street. He knew exactly where he was going. When he stopped, it was across the street from a neighborhood pub. Abu stood patiently in the shadows and never took his eyes off the oak wood, leaded-glass door of the pub. It opened and several pub regulars came out, noisily exchanging goodnights, then going off in separate directions. A few minutes later, the door opened again and a solitary, drunken man emerged. He cursed the cold rainy night and slippery streets.

As he staggered along, Abu followed him. Despite his drunkenness, the man sensed someone was tailing him. He walked faster and bumped into a tree when he turned for a moment to look over his shoulder. He saw Abu gaining on him and broke into a clumsy jog, frantically searching for somewhere to hide. He headed for a narrow alley behind two buildings. Abu followed. The man reached the end of the alley; it had no outlet. Panic gripped him as he realized he was trapped. And Abu was coming toward him. He stood with his back to the wall and called out to Abu. "What d'ya want?" he whined.

"Justice," Abu said from the shadows, his voice as cold and dark as the night.

"Who are you?" came the frightened question.

"Do you not remember?" Abu asked as he stepped closer. A street light illuminated his face. The man stared for a moment in horror. And then recognition.

He swallowed hard. "It wa'nt me what killed 'er," he pleaded.

"Oh but it was," Abu intoned. "You murdered her. You alone smashed her skull into a hundred pieces. And for that you must die."

"No!" the man cried up at Abu. He looked frantically around. "Someone help me!" he shouted in vain.

"No one can even hear you," Abu said moving closer to him. "Justice will be done. I have waited many years for this moment."

Abu's black eyes, menacing as a shark's, bore into the man's face and mesmerized him. Suddenly, he clutched at his head and pulled his hair. Excruciating pain coursed through his body. He screamed and fell to his knees. Then, as if struck by a powerful electric volt, he went reeling backwards. He writhed on the ground. A cracking sound emanated from his head; blood spewed out from his nose, eyes and ears, from every opening in his body. He went into convulsions, choking and gasping. His eyes bulged clear out of their sockets, his tongue fell back into his throat, his hands clawed at his head and face. Then just as suddenly, his death throes stopped, his body went limp. An ever-widening puddle of blood, mixed with urine, spread around him.

Abu looked down at the lifeless form at his feet. His face was expressionless, his voice hollow. "Nanaki, your death has been avenged. Rest now, in peace."

CHAPTER 40

The jet plane with the letters WPO painted on its huge silver body, made a wide swing around New York harbor in preparation for its landing at Kennedy Airport.

Abu turned to Bhaiji sitting beside him and motioned for his aide to look out the plane's window. Bhaiji's eyes widened, he grinned gleefully.

"The Statue of Liberty!" he exclaimed as he stared at the famous landmark. Abu nodded.

As they passed over the Manhattan skyline, Abu pointed out the Empire State Building, the Chrysler Building, The World Trade Center and other New York skyscrapers. "And there's Central Park," Abu said, looking down at the enormous expanse of trees and lake and meadow. "And over there is the East River and the Hudson's on the other side of Manhattan."

Bhaiji gazed in childlike wonder at the huge, graceful bridges, and the buildings whose towering spires pierced the clouds.

"What a beautiful city, Abuji."

"Yes," Abu sighed. "From up here."

Just as the jet touched down and taxied to the location reserved for Air Force One and planes carrying visiting presidents or reigning monarchs, a group of waiting dignitaries, including New York's governor and the city's mayor, moved into position, ready to greet the man whom they were according diplomatic status by waiving entry-visa requirements. A small group of spectators had been allowed to stand a short distance away, cordoned off from the politicians and official greeters. Their excitement mounted as the door to the plane opened and several Ikhwan emerged. Then Abu stepped off the plane and the crowd began screaming and cheering. He moved gracefully down the row of officials and shook everyone's hand, bowing slightly, smiling slightly. Someone in the crowd of onlookers began shouting racial epithets at

327

Abu; he ignored the angry protester, and instead nodded toward several Muslims in the group who bowed to him in deference. A few placards bobbed above the heads of the crowd; some proclaiming Abu as the new messiah, others accusing him of being the son of Satan.

As Abu was quickly ushered to a waiting limousine, the private phone line in Herschel Strunk's office rang loudly. He grabbed the receiver.

"Hersch, are you watching this?" Williams' voice was agitated.

The small TV set on the table behind Strunk's desk was tuned to CNN's broadcast of "breaking news."

"Sure am," Strunk said with a laugh. "I was just about to call you."

"I had no idea he was coming," Williams said.

"Your boy is a last-minute kinda guy. Even the White House was taken by surprise. But the government granted him diplomatic status—and I hear he's gonna make a speech at the United Nations. Christ, he'll probably get a ticker-tape parade down Fifth Avenue!"

"I'm coming back, Hersch, I've got to."

"Is the book finished?"

"Almost."

"Good." There was a pause, then Strunk said, "You gonna try to see him?"

"Yeah . . . I am."

"Okay. Be careful."

The moment Williams hung up the phone, it rang again.

"Ben, do you know what's going on?" Aimee's voice was excited.

"Yes, babe, I do. And I'm on my way back."

"Great. Because Fairlie wants to arrange a meeting between you and Abu—for the book—Brandon House thinks it will be a terrific promotional—"

"No, Aimee," Williams interrupted. "I don't think that's a good idea."

"Why not?"

"I'm not sure I want my meeting with him to be public."

"Oh Ben, Harry's not going to like that. He's really counting on—"

"Aimee, listen to me," Williams said with urgency. "I have to see Abu, but it has to be private. Something is going on—there's been a . . . a shift. Look, I'll talk to you more about it when I see you. Just stall Harry, okay? I know what I'm doing."

Aimee sighed on the other end of the line. "Okay," she said reluctantly.

"I can't wait to see you," Williams said.

"We can't wait either."

"We?"

"Yes. Me and junior."

"Oh God, how is he?"

"Darling, 'he' might be a 'she,' you know. Anyway, the little tyke's started kick-boxing in there. I think we're producing an Olympic athlete."

Williams laughed. "I love you. I'll see you tomorrow."

He hurried into the bedroom, pulled open the dresser drawers, grabbed his suitcase from the closet and began throwing clothes into it. His mother would have had a fit if she saw the way he was packing. When he was a kid going off to camp, she did his packing for him. But when he went off to college, she stood in the doorway and watched in shock as he threw clothes, shoes, and books into one suitcase. When she could stand it no longer, she pushed her son aside and emptied his suitcase. Then, slowly, methodically, she began folding every shirt and pair of pants, and carefully repacked the suitcase he had thrown onto the bed. Williams had protested that he was grown enough to pack his own bags. "Mom," Williams had said, irritated but trying not to get angry, "could you just not do that?"

"Ben, it's going to save you from having to iron all these things when you get to school."

"Mom, I wasn't planning to iron."

"And when you open the suitcase, what will your roommate think?"

"Who cares?! He's probably going to be a bigger slob than me—!"

Williams wondered what made him think of this now. He had long since forgotten his mother's penchant for neatness, except for that one terrible reminder when he first arrived at the hospital to visit his dying father, and she commented about his crumpled clothes.

Would he tell her about Aimee? And the baby? He didn't think so. Then it struck him that he *should* tell her. That maybe she would welcome his family, just maybe she would really like being a grandmother for the first time. His sister Margaret had no children despite two marriages. Which was just as well since she often said she wasn't cut out for motherhood; her career as a high school teacher had given her enough children to deal with, and the more she dealt with them, the less she wanted any of her own.

Williams zipped the heavy fabric suitcase and left it on the bed as he went into the bathroom, grabbed two handfuls of toiletries and dropped them into a separate flight bag. He went into the guest bedroom where he'd set up his laptop computer and printer. He took a pile of papers off the small desk, stuffed them into a briefcase and was just about to shut down the laptop when he stopped short and stared at the computer screen. On it was what he had written only an hour earlier.

> We live in a time in which nothing is more important than finally coming to terms with what is the essence of our soul: Love. But like so many things that we do not understand and cannot fathom, we pretend in our ignorance to know what we seek and how to satisfy the yearning of the heart. But Abu reminds us that we do not comprehend how to even begin the search. He has always said that humanity was in transition, living in that twilight period between the darkness and the light, when indigo fades to violet and night melts into dawn. Abu talked once of his vision for a world and all its people being governed only by the dictates of Love. He said that if we did not learn how to live in such a world, we would be "forever lost, strangers in a strange land."

That was the essence of it, Williams thought. That was *all* Abu was trying to say. He was trying to show us the path we needed to take, the overgrown brush we needed to clear away in order to see the sky. He merely wants us to plant the seeds of change—those that will bear the fruits of hope and promise, not the bitter harvest of strife and suffering. Abu wants to be the catalyst for the kingdom of heaven, on earth.

But were people truly listening and 'seeing' what Abu envisioned for them? The media was not paying attention, nor were most people. They were all fixated on the miracles—more enamored with the messenger than the message. Maybe that's exactly what happened to Jesus, William thought. Would it take another two thousand years for people to hear—to listen? Would there be anything left by then that was worth saving? And if they weren't listening to Abu, would they care about what Williams was trying to say in his book? Or would they read it only in anticipation of sensational details about Abu and his 'miraculous' powers?

New York received Abu as though he was the proverbial conquering hero. Herschel joked about a ticker-tape parade, but that's exactly what Abu got—right down Fifth Avenue. It recalled images of Lindbergh's tumultuous welcome, or the astronauts when they returned from the moon landing. There was a private, black-tie reception at the Gracie Mansion—the Mayor's home—and a benefit concert for the WPO at Carnegie Hall with celebrities from all over the country flying in to perform or attend. And every New Yorker of wealth, power and influence—the cream of New York society—sent invitations to lavish dinners and galas, all to be held in Abu's honor.

For the most part, he shunned the festivities and chose instead to go to the slums of Harlem and the Bronx, the AIDS hospices, the overcrowded and understaffed homeless shelters.

In Harlem's Marcus Garvey Park, the controversial, separatist leader of the Nation of Islam, Reverend Emanuel Shalam, introduced Abu to an enormous gathering. In a typically rambling and verbose speech, not unlike the one Shalam gave at the 'Million Man March' he had once organized and led in Washington, D.C., he told his followers that Sheik Abu 'Ali Asghar had come to deliver them from oppression and exploitation. "He will stand with us!" the bespectacled black leader shouted, "as we cry out with righteous indignation: NO MORE!" The crowd rose up as one and chanted Abu's name for almost ten minutes before he was finally able to quiet them down. He called for the start of the second American revolution, and by the time the speeches and the evening were over, Abu had left in his wake what looked like the beginning of that revolution. Riots broke out all over Harlem. Right-wing extremists and fundamentalist Christians denounced Abu and the aftermath of his appearances; all of which led to violent clashes between the city's diverse ethnic and religious groups.

ABC-TV's dependable evening news anchorman, Phillip Reardon, was the only TV journalist granted an exclusive interview with the man whom many city leaders now wished had never set foot on American soil.

The interview took place in the televison studio with Abu sitting in a chair opposite Reardon, who had a clipboard in his lap, and some papers attached to it that he occasionally referred to. "Sheik Asghar, what has brought you here?" was Reardon's opening question.

"If this was two thousand years ago, coming to New York would be like going to Rome," Abu said.

"How so?" Reardon asked.

"The disciples of Jesus went to Rome because they knew that to create a new world order, one must go to the center of power."

"Do you consider yourself a disciple of Christ?"

Abu shook his head. "We are simply part of the same plan. Two thousand years ago, Jesus began the process. I am here to complete it."

"And what process is that?" Reardon had a hint of irony in this voice.

"Profound change. A fundamental shift—a transition to a higher, more enlightened state of consciousness."

"Yet, in Harlem, yesterday, you preached a second American revolution—" Reardon challenged.

"Yes, in thinking, in being." Abu's eyes sparked, his voice became passionate. "And it is not truly revolution, but evolution. Humanity is at a crossroads; it is time to choose which path to take. One path remains with the injustice and suffering of the past, the other moves out into a glorious future of infinite possibilities. One is driven by our fear; the other transcends our fear. Whether this evolutionary shift is violent is entirely up to humanity. But I will tell you that I am not optimistic."

"Why is that?"

"Because fear does not let go without a struggle. Armageddon is at hand."

Reardon looked skeptically at his guest. "As in the Book of Revelations?"

Abu nodded. "The final confrontation between good and evil."

"Sheik Asghar, some people have come to see *you* as inherently evil—a political opportunist, a charlatan, an Antichrist—"

"People call me many things, each according to what they perceive."

"And what do you perceive, Sheik Asghar?"

"I see a champion of humanity, a humble servant of God."

"Is it your intention to bring the grievances of the Third World to America?" Again there was challenge in Reardon's tone.

Abu shook his head. "America has its own 'third world'—just look at your inner cities. Your starving and homeless, your violence and crime, your slums. They are no different from those in the so-called

Third World. That is part of America's delusion, and its hypocrisy."

Reardon persisted. "Do you not feel responsible for the chaos and turmoil that has just occurred here—and in other places around the world—as a result of your revolutionary speeches and call to arms?"

Abu smiled politely. "I incite no one. I merely articulate the anger and oppression that is in the hearts of the people—that is what incites them to act." Abu leaned toward Reardon. "I cannot compel anyone to act. Yet I am committed to action. Whatever must be done, will be done."

Williams clicked off the TV set in his apartment. Aimee was sitting beside him on the couch, rubbing her huge belly. She looked at him. "I'm scared, Ben. He means to be what he says, doesn't he?"

"Oh yes, I'm sure of it." Williams lowered his head and put his ear against Aimee's stomach. She smoothed Williams' brow and smiled.

The baby within her kicked and Williams suddenly sat up, a look of amazement on his face. "I heard him. I mean I felt him. He's *real*."

Aimee nodded, looking tenderly at Williams. "Of course, silly, what did you think—that I was just getting fat?"

Williams hugged her. "Aimee, don't worry about what Abu has been saying—I don't want you to get upset or frightened. I'm here. Nothing is going happen to us."

Aimee took Williams face between her hands. "Ah, my knight in shining armor—"

"Yeah . . . the armor's a little rusty though. But please, don't be afraid."

Aimee nodded tentatively. "Are you coming to bed?" she said as she pushed herself up from the sofa, using her hand to brace her back.

"Soon," he said. "I just want to stay up a bit longer."

"Okay," Aimee said, kissing the top of his head. Williams buried his face in her ample breasts for a moment. Then he watched as she walked out of the room.

"I love the way you waddle," he called after her.

"I'm going to roll over on you for that," she called back.

Williams went to the bar and poured himself a scotch. He took it to the window and looked out at the city's nightscape. The skyline, with lights strung across bridges like delicate diamond necklaces and flickering on the tops of buildings and from thousands of windows, competed with the stars to create a jewel-encrusted night sky. But in the streets below, riots had broken out, worse than anything since the 1960s. Williams remembered the terrifying encounter in Harlem the night he and Aimee had gone up there. He now looked down at the street and saw streams of police cars and ambulances heading uptown. It's escalating, he said to himself.

And then he thought of his unborn child—the perfect, beautiful, innocent creation growing inside Aimee's womb. A wave of anxiety swept over Williams. His heart quickened, his palms began to sweat. Abu's warnings and words began to swirl around him.

I shall be the hammer . . . To what will you give your allegiance, Ben Williams? . . . Humanity must choose which path it will take . . . I am here to serve—Time is running out . . . Allahu Akbar, Abu 'Ali Asghar.

Then the voices stopped, the chanting abated. Williams' panic subsided and his own inner voice spoke to him. He had to *do* something. He wasn't thinking about heroics or some egotistical desire for glory. He thought of his child, his new and future family. He thought of survival. Not Armageddon.

" 'When in the course of human events . . .' " Abu's voice cried out to the largest audience the United Nations Assembly chamber had ever had. Delegates and ambassadors, visiting dignitaries from around the world listened attentively. Vice President Stanley Gordon and Secretary of State Roger Campbell sat, side by side, and occasionally looked anxiously at one another as Abu spoke.

" '. . . it becomes necessary for one people to dissolve the political bands that have connected them with another, and to assume among the powers of the earth, the separate and equal station to which the laws of nature and of nature's God entitle them . . .' "

The Vice-President whispered to Campbell, "Jesus, why the hell is he quoting the Declaration of Independence?"

"Because," answered the Secretary of State, "he wants to show us just how far we've come from what our founding fathers had in mind. A brilliant ploy, I'd say."

The Vice President turned back to Abu as his voice intoned, " '. . . all men are created equal . . . endowed by their creator with certain inalienable rights . . . life, liberty and the pursuit of happiness. That to secure these rights, governments are instituted, deriving their powers from the consent of the governed, that whenever any form of government becomes destructive of these ends, it is the right of the people to alter or to abolish it, and to institute a new government . . .' "

Bennett Williams was seated in the gallery watching Abu with an intensity he had never experienced before. He had also not seen Abu looking quite this impressive either. A bejeweled dagger gleamed at his waist, his robes were made of the finest Egyptian cotton, his turban was pure silk. He no longer looked like a man of the people; he was now a mighty head of state, a demi-godlike figure. Williams had refused to applaud Abu's entrance to the Assembly—actually a standing ovation was accorded him when he strode into the vast, green marble chamber. Williams listened to what he knew was vintage Abu, but behind it, now, was the substance of something that Williams believed was profoundly ominous.

Abu went on. " When that small group of idealistic men created the United States over two hundred years ago, they embarked on an unprecedented path. Never before had the principles of equality, justice, freedom and liberty been the foundation for a government. Never before had government been charged with *protecting* those fundamental human rights. And to that noblest of ends, they pledged their lives, their fortunes and their sacred honor."

Abu paused and looked out over his audience. It was quiet in the great chamber, quiet and waiting. The Secretary of State looked over at the Vice President. He said nothing, but a small, enigmatic smile began forming at the corners of his mouth.

Abu stared fiercely at the members and guests, looking suddenly, Williams thought, much like a fire-and-brimstone preacher. "But what has become of your America? Your shining city on the hill; the land of hope and dreams! The land that offered refuge for the world's oppressed. What has become of it?! Now you turn away the poor, you ignore the homeless, you fear the huddled masses. You, who once stood for freedom, now use your superior military might to impose your will on the lesser nations of the world! Materialism is your opiate, power your ideology, competition your creed!"

Vice President Gordon looked at Secretary Campbell. "You were right," he said in an audible whisper. He got up from his chair. "And I've heard enough." Campbell nodded in agreement and the two men, much to Abu's irritation, walked up the long aisle to the exit and left the hall.

"My friends," Abu called out as he watched the Vice President and Secretary of State leave, "America has abdicated its leadership! And it has done so because, rather than hear the truth, rather than renew its commitment to the principles on which it was founded, America has grown corrupt, isolationist, and indifferent." Abu raised his arms and in tones never more passionate, cried out, "And so I call upon all of humanity to rise up and overthrow the existing order!"

Bennett Williams could hardly sit still in his seat; he wasn't as much surprised by Abu's words as he was by the audience Abu chose to say them to. "I call for a worldwide revolution! We must end the domination of tyrannical despots. We must create a world government. We must abandon national sovereignty. We must offer up all our weapons of mass destruction to a world government dedicated to the preservation of freedom, justice and equality. We must create a government order that truly is of the people, by the people and for the people. That is the cause I am dedicated to. And I promise you this: It shall be!"

The audience was stunned. Some people applauded, others sat in shocked silence, some called out words of praise and approval, many were confused and angry. Dozens of foreign delegates whispered excitedly among themselves as reporters and photographers scurried about—the reporters holding cellular phones to their ears, noisily relaying the Sheik's speech to a newspaper or magazine editor or a network news producer.

Abu was gone. The Ikhwan had ushered him out of the hall within seconds after his last words were still ringing in the air. Williams tried to leave but the crush of reporters and TV crews, and the Assembly's enormous audience, blocked his way, forcing him to move slowly to the exits along with the surging crowd of people. He made it out just in time to see Abu step into a long, black Mercedes-Benz limousine. "Not quite like the one Bhaiji used to drive," he said to no one in particular, as he stood watching the limo speed away from the United Nations building.

"ABU TO UN: U.S. BLEW IT! I'LL DO IT!" shrieked the *New York Post's* headline.

The *New York Times* ran a story that told of Abu as the emerging leader of the Third World and how he'd been brought to world attention by one of their own, Pulitzer Prize winner, H. Bennett Williams. The *Village Voice* ran an article describing Abu's secret meetings with black Islamic leaders and alluded to his having met with the heads of New York's powerful street gangs. A sidebar told of the billions of dollars being funneled through the WPO and claimed that Abu was organizing a secret army under the command of a Botswanan general.

Williams came back to his apartment. Aimee had moved into it at Williams' insistence as soon as he returned from Herschel's cabin. Williams didn't even object when the macaw, Napoleon, arrived with Aimee.

"He's going to have to get used to me sooner or later," Williams had said. "Hope his ego can stand the competition."

Fortunately, Napoleon had been, in Aimee's words, "an absolute brick" about the whole thing, even though the ubiquitous New York pigeons that landed on the window ledges sent him into angry screeches. Territory was territory, be it jungle or skyscraper.

"Aimee—!" Williams called out as he entered the apartment. He immediately found her note on the hallway table. "Gone to office for the afternoon. Fairlie needs some soothing since you don't want to get promotional with Abu. Dinner out tonight? My treat. Love, your goddess."

Williams picked up the phone and dialed the number of the Waldorf Towers. "Bhaiji," Williams exclaimed upon hearing the familiar voice.

"Ben!" Bhaiji responded. "My friend, Ben Williams! How are you?"

"Just fine, Bhaiji." Williams was surprised at how good it was to hear the Indian's voice. "I need to see him. Can you arrange it?" There was silence. "Bhaiji?"

"I am here, Ben."

"Well?"

"I will try, Ben. But I cannot promise."

The response irritated Williams. "Why?"

"He is very busy."

"Jesus Christ, Bhaiji, it's me!" Williams was angry and hurt. "What the fuck is going on?"

"I will see what I can do." Bhaiji hung up.

Williams stood for a few moments in frustrated silence, then his eye caught the previous day's copy of the *Village Voice* sitting on his desk. Its cover story was about Abu meeting with powerful gang leaders in New York. Christ, were they creating some kind of underground army? What if they *were* being organized under a single command, possibly led by General Mubambo? And linked with armies and terrorist groups around the globe, all with the one purpose of overthrowing the existing order? In a way, Williams somehow felt responsible—hadn't he been the vehicle for Abu to get his message to the world? At least in the beginning. Now the steamroller had its own momentum and was picking up speed. He had to stop it.

The ring of the phone startled Williams. It was Bhaiji. Williams hadn't expected him to call back so quickly.

"Abu will see you," Bhaiji said politely.

"I'll be right over."

"No, he wants it secret. No media."

"Where then?"

"The Malcolm Shabazz Mosque in Harlem. One hour. Come alone."

Bhaiji hung up without saying goodbye.

In exactly an hour, Williams entered the onion-domed Muslim sanctuary where Malcolm X had once preached. An Ikhwan was waiting for him and escorted Williams to a large meeting room within the mosque. It was empty. Williams stood alone, fidgeting for a few moments, then Abu seemed to have suddenly materialized from a dark corner of the room.

Despite the dim lighting, Williams could see how different Abu looked. His beard had more gray in it, his face seemed more weathered, his eyes showed fatigue. "Ah, Ben Williams, my old friend," Abu said. There was a vulnerability in his voice that Williams had never heard before. My God, was he becoming more . . . human?

"How is Aimee?" Abu asked.

"She's fine," Williams answered, wondering why he was even surprised that Abu knew about her.

"And your son?"

Williams nodded. "Maybe you should tell me."

Abu closed his eyes for a moment. When he opened them, a warm, gentle smile appeared. "He is well," Abu said, then looked at Williams with what amounted to genuine affection. "I envy you, Ben Williams. I would gladly trade all the fame and power I have acquired for what you have—"

"Abu, you must stop what you are doing," Williams said firmly, instantly dissipating the friendly air between the two men.

Abu's soft smile turned into a tight-lipped line as he glared at Williams. "I cannot. You of all people should understand that."

"No!" Williams was surprised by the defiance in his voice.

Abu shook his head. "You still see only what is in front of you, Ben Williams. Do not misunderstand—I am happy for you, happy that you have found what you want, and that you are able to make the welfare of two other human beings more important than your own. You have discovered something greater about love. But there is even more, my friend. Do you love all of humanity, or just your safe little niche in the rock of the world? Are you able to want for all of humanity what you now have? Or is protecting what *you* have all that matters?"

Williams had not expected to hear this. But, as usual, Abu said things to him that caught him off guard.

Abu stared into Williams' eyes. "This is not just about Bennett Williams and what he wants. Any more than it is about me and what I want. Can you not see that?"

"I see *you*," Williams said with mounting anger, "about to destroy the world!" He glared back at Abu and realized the man before him was both saint and Satan, savior and destroyer.

"Do you think you can stop it?"

"How can you do this? For what? Some perverted notion that something good will come from the destruction and suffering that you'll inflict?"

"Do you know another way? We have gone well past the point of no return. Look around, Ben Williams, fear is everywhere, in all its disguises. The devil has been loosed upon the world and is slowly killing life on this planet. Evil is winning. We do not have time to hope and wait. Humanity must act. Or perish."

"Abu, you know that this country, and other superpowers around the world, will not easily allow you to recreate things in your own image—they will oppose you and they'll use every means at their disposal—"

Abu put a large hand on Williams' shoulder. "And so I ask: To what will you give your allegiance, Ben Williams?" Abu's voice was eerily calm and gentle again. "Darkness is falling. You should go now."

CHAPTER 41

Aimee watched with anxiety as Williams hastily packed his suitcase in the bedroom. "Why do you have to go to Switzerland, Ben?"

"Because that's where the WPO is. That's where the money is."

"But why you?" There was genuine fear and concern in her voice.

"Aimee," Williams said with a touch of irritation as he stopped packing long enough to look at her. "I can't sit back and do nothing."

"Just what is it you think you *can* do?" she challenged.

Williams threw a pair of boots into his suitcase. "I can expose him."

"Ben, it's too late for that! He's become a god to half the world!"

"I have to try to stop him."

Aimee refused to give up. "Then if you think he's such a terrible threat, why not get the government—the FBI, the CIA—to help?"

"They're not going to do anything—they don't understand what's happening. Besides, they're not the solution, they're part of the problem."

"Ben, what about the baby? It's almost time."

"I'll be back soon, I promise." Williams shut the suitcase and zipped it.

Aimee gingerly lowered herself on the bed. She knew it was futile to try to stop him. She sighed, reached for the TV remote on the night table and clicked on the ABC News with Phillip Reardon.

The anchorman was in the middle of his lead story. ". . . Nobel Peace Prize recipient has been—ever since he stunned the world with his speech before the U.N.—on a whistle-stop tour of the United States. In city after city, Sheik Asghar has created controversy and debate, won tens of thousands of converts and made a few enemies . . ."

Williams put his suitcase on the floor and sat down on the bed next to Aimee. He absently stroked her belly as they sat, riveted by Abu's latest news making exploits.

". . . Brent Lawson reports from Philadelphia," Reardon said as the scene immediately switched to a reporter standing on the outskirts of an enormous park where, several hours earlier, Abu had spoken to thousands of people.

"Good evening, Phillip," Lawson said into the camera. "I'm here with the Sheik's entourage, and I must say that this afternoon's reception for Abu 'Ali Asghar was like a combination of the Pope's last visit and a Michael Jackson concert! Never saw anything like it before. Someone said it was like the 'second coming.' Maybe so. Let's look . . ."

An earlier videotape showed Abu arriving in a motorcade procession, then walking up onto a stage as deafening cheers greeted him.

"I speak to you today," Abu began, when the tumultuous throng had finally settled down, "of American indifference and injustice. Of how America can no longer cope with its rampant poverty and violent crime, its homeless crisis, its decaying cities and corrupt government, its overwhelming drug problem, its capitalistic greed. Its material wealth and spiritual bankruptcy . . ."

The scene switched briefly to Chicago, a day earlier, where Abu was seen walking through that city's poorest, blackest neighborhoods, flanked by leaders of the African-American community. They marched through Chicago's worst ghetto areas, and into the projects where the drug dealers were ten and twelve-year-olds who stood in front of their squalid, graffiti-covered, rat-infested apartment buildings selling crack cocaine.

Abu went inside a filthy apartment that had no heat and only sporadic electricity. No adults were in sight, but four children ran about naked, vying for space with cockroaches and mice. Abu stepped over human waste mixed with rotting food and used drug vials and syringes that littered the foul-smelling floors, and picked up a malnourished five-year-old boy. He was crying and sucking his grimy thumb, his saucer-like eyes stared at Abu in dazed confusion. Abu turned to face the cameras, holding the boy in his arms. "These are your children, America," he said. "Who will you blame when this pitiful child grows to manhood and turns his rage on you!?"

Brent Lawson was back on camera, microphone in hand. "Phillip, as you can see, the Sheik is not only charismatic, but he knows how to use the media to his best advantage."

Williams nodded cynically to himself. Aimee rose awkwardly from the bed. "Want anything to eat?" she asked as she headed toward the kitchen.

"No thanks, hon, I've got to leave."

As Williams put some papers and his laptop into his briefcase, in the background the television news now showed a press conference between rival Chicago gang leaders who had decided, because of their new-found allegiance to Abu, to call a truce amongst themselves, and to bring an end to drug dealing 'in the hoods.' Their mission, they said, was to restore dignity, equality and justice for all African-American people. The spokesman for the gang leaders ended the conference with: "Praise be to Allah and his servant, the great Sheik Abu 'Ali Asghar." He was flanked on one side by Abu and the other by Reverend Shalam.

Phillip Reardon appeared again. "When we come back, a look at the rise of Islam in this country as a powerful force in black politics, and the new alliance between the Nation of Islam and the World Peoples' Organization. What does it mean? And, later in our broadcast: Just what is that mysterious source of light in the Pleiades star system that has astronomers all over the world confused and concerned. We'll be right back." An upbeat commercial for Preparation H hemorrhoidal cream immediately followed.

Abu had saved Los Angeles for the final stop on his American tour. The city, whose four seasons were not so jokingly referred to as "earthquakes, fires, floods and riots," was now barely recovering from its most recent and devastating catastrophe: A 6.8 aftershock from a previous earthquake. The seismologists were stubbornly refusing to acknowledge that this was a brand new quake, rather than a tremor from the earlier one. Although they admitted that no aftershock had ever been this high on the Richter scale, to consider it another quake would have undoubtedly thrown the city's inhabitants into a panic that could lead to a mass exodus—and probably more people would be killed in the stampede to get out of Los Angeles than had ever been killed in an earthquake. Thus, the mayor, the police and fire department officials, and the scientific community decided to stonewall it.

But local residents knew they were being lied to; however, they did nothing. They were too busy sifting through debris.

Los Angeles was definitely the 'strangest' city in the country. New-Agers saw L.A. as a magnet for negative energy, Christian fundamentalists said it was a modern-day Sodom and Gomorrah. Eastern mystics said Los Angeles suffered from bad karma. The average Angeleno blamed the city's perverse troubles on freeway gridlock, smog, the gangs of the barrio and South Central L.A., and the burgeoning illegal alien population. Some even blamed the movie industry.

Abu toured the sprawling city that stretched from its downtown glass skyscrapers and decaying old buildings to the majestic canyons and beaches along the Pacific Ocean. Hanging over all of it was the perpetual mantle of smog which so completely destroyed the oxygen in the air that, according to a recent survey, 50% of all babies born in L.A. in the 1990s would develop emphysema by the time they were young adults.

Wherever Abu went, he was flanked by local, eminent black politicians, a few celebrities, and several Muslim leaders. In Watts, Compton and Inglewood he met with the gang leaders of the infamous Bloods and the Crips and privately enrolled the gangs into his growing army. They announced solidarity with their brothers in Chicago, Detroit, Philadelphia, and every other city where Abu had forged a similar alliance.

At the Los Angeles Coliseum, the enduring reminder of L.A.'s short-lived glory, Abu was scheduled to deliver an address on the last day of his whirlwind tour. Thirty-foot tall speakers were being positioned in the vast sports arena, music was blaring from every corner, and a colored light and laser-beam show was in rehearsal. If New York would give Abu a ticker-tape parade, Los Angeles would top it with a Disneyesque display fit for a rock star. In a private room, somewhere in the bowels of the stadium, Abu sat, meditating. The sound of the expectant crowd, chanting Abu's name in praise and glory, now seeped into the small, empty room where Abu sat in the middle of the floor, ignoring the growing distractions. There was a slight knock on the door. Bhaiji entered. Abu opened his eyes.

"It is time," Abu said. Bhaiji nodded. Abu looked down at the floor in front of him and took a deep breath. "Bhaiji, do you ever think of Kartarpur?"

The question took Bhaiji by surprise. "Yes, Abuji. I do, often." Abu took another deep breath, but this time it was more like a sigh. "As do I." Bhaiji felt the sadness in Abu's voice. His master sounded like a reluctant king, carrying the burdens of state but wishing for a simpler life, one more private and free of celebrity. "But alas," Abu said, "it is nearly over."

Bhaiji looked at Abu as he stood up, erect, more regal than ever, a king, of sorts; the Commander of the Faithful and, above and beyond everything else, the Mahdi—the Awaited One.

In the Coliseum's darkness, pillars of fire suddenly shot up fifty feet into the air from various points around the top of the wall on the stadium's perimeter. Then a single, dramatic spotlight illuminated the man whom thousands had come to hear.

In a voice filled with solemn dignity, he spoke. "America prides itself on being the richest nation on earth, yet here in the land of plenty, there are forty million of you—*forty million Americans*—living in poverty. And yet the United States spends a smaller percentage of its vast wealth on basic human services than any other industrialized country on the planet!

"The gap between rich and poor is greater now than it has been in fifty years. And it is easily illustrated: A rich drug addict goes to the Betty Ford Center; a poor drug addict goes to prison. The land of the free, the land of opportunity, imprisons more of its citizens than any other nation on earth. The land of opportunity spends twice as much money defending itself than taking care of its people. Billions are wasted every year to strengthen military power, to stockpile nuclear weapons. And all to protect the so-called American way of life. But what is that way of life? A way of life dominated by unemployment, poverty, crime, violence, prostitution, drug trafficking, AIDS, and inner cities filled with unspeakable horrors? Perhaps those in power do not even care about you. Perhaps the billions spent are only to protect the privileged few—those who own the politicians, sit in the corporate boardrooms and manipulate the world's economic markets. My friends, you have been lied to long enough. America is not the land of the free and the home of the brave—it is the land of the slave and the home of the hypocrite."

The Coliseum fairly shook with the angry agreement that went up from thousands of spectators—they chanted Abu's name in reverence and solidarity. Abu paced the stage, then called for quiet. "I am here to tell you that you are not without power! And you are not alone!" The audience began cheering wildly. Abu's voice rose above the din. "Your children shall not go hungry anymore! Your families shall not be torn apart by violence and disease and loss of dignity! You shall rise up against your oppressors and say: 'No More!' "

Abu's words echoed back to him in mass unison. "No More!" reverberated throughout the stadium. Rockets shot into the air and exploded in a fusillade of garish light and sound.

"Join with me," Abu cried out, "and God will send forth the might of the universe to help us! Join with me . . ." Abu paused. A sudden hush filled the stadium. ". . . AND WE WILL MAKE A NEW WORLD!" Instantly, music blared from the loudspeakers and thousands were on their feet, screaming, cheering, stomping, crying, worshiping.

As the Coliseum's light and laser show continued—now accompanied by an enormous fireworks display, and as Abu bowed and waved to his adoring audience—no one noticed that another bright flash filled the night sky, followed by several more in rapid succession, like a celestial strobe that had appeared out of nowhere.

In the aftermath of Abu's visit, rioting erupted in Los Angeles that far outdid the 1960s Watts' riots and those in 1994 that came on the heels of the Rodney King verdict. This time, the marching, protesting, burning and looting took place on the streets of Beverly Hills and the residential canyons of the Pacific Palisades. Rioting occurred all along Sunset Boulevard and Rodeo Drive and in the Wilshire 'corridor'—an enclave of million-dollar condominiums, housed in giant, luxury buildings that stretched for a dozen blocks on Wilshire Boulevard. This time it was the wealthy, white, privileged establishment that felt the fury of the wrath Abu had unleashed.

In Washington, D.C., members of Congress met with President Bob Stanton to tell him that although there was enormous risk in meeting with Abu, there was even greater risk in not meeting with him. It was time, said Stanton's critics—both in Congress and the media—for the President to 'stand up for America.' But there were many politicians in Washington and all around the country who also lambasted the President for failing to endorse the new champion of the poor and oppressed—the man who was, potentially, the most powerful of all the world's leaders simply because he owed allegiance to no one country and no one people. It was a fact that deeply worried President Stanton. He'd had a lot of sleepless nights in the last two weeks.

"Of course, I'm willing to meet with the Sheik," Stanton said in his folksy Midwestern accent to the small, elite group of Congressmen and women seated in the Oval Office. "But let's just keep it, well, like a 'business meeting.' No invited press, no photo ops, no speeches. Not even on the front portico."

"Excuse me, Mr. President," Stanton's Chief-of-Staff, Lee Cowles, interjected, "but I think it's going to be mighty hard to keep anything discreet when it comes to Sheik Asghar. Besides, his visit with you is probably the highlight event of—"

"Do the best you can, Lee." Stanton looked irritated. "I want as little fanfare for Asghar as possible. He already looks like he's a candidate for president!" The President grunted a laugh which was echoed by several senators in the room. "In fact, the party should hire the P.R. firm that's doing his American tour." There were some nervous titters and exchanged glances in the Oval Office. "I'm serious," Stanton said, gazing candidly at the group seated around him.

Forty-eight hours later, Abu's limousine pulled through the gates at the side of the White House and stopped. The Ikhwan emerged quickly from the vehicle, but when asked by the Secret Service to hand over their weapons before entering the White House, they refused. Abu interceded and a compromise was reached. The Ikhwan would remain on the lower floor, under the watchful gaze of well-armed Secret Service agents. The only person to greet Abu at the side entrance was Eleanor Cummings, the President's private secretary. She was a fifty-ish woman with short, graying hair and a cherubic face. She held the door open for Abu and offered him a friendly smile. She had been with the President since his days as a freshman senator some twenty years earlier. She was devoted to him, and the Stantons considered Eleanor 'family.'

Today, Eleanor was particularly protective of the President. She wished he didn't have to meet with the controversial Mr. Asghar. Her 'boss,' as she sometimes teasingly called him, had had enough of a bad day—and it was only ten-thirty in the morning. He'd already dispatched federal troops to Los Angeles where the rioting had required the national guard to restore order. And many of Stanton's wealthy Beverly Hills friends and fundraisers were now the direct victims of this latest California disaster. One billion dollars in damage was the estimate from FEMA that Eleanor had handed him an hour earlier.

There were also natural disasters plaguing the country as never before. Within a twenty-four hour period, two earthquakes had occurred, one in the northeast and one in the midwest, places that were never prone to any seismic activity. A hurricane had ripped across Florida, worse than any other in the last fifty years, several tornadoes had devastated Texas and Kansas (the President's home state) and unseasonal blizzards were raging in the northwest, breaking all records for snow, hail and wind chill. Stanton was dispensing disaster aid for half the country.

Politically, the Stanton White House was having a disaster of its own. Polls and ratings revealed the president's popularity was plummeting—there had been one scandal too many, a top aide had committed suicide, another was under congressional investigation for fraud, two influential congressmen had resigned in the wake of the government's budgetary fiascos, including the recent two-month-long shutdown of the whole bureaucracy itself. Then there was one of Stanton's sons, the eldest of his three, rather spoiled, children, who had just been expelled from the private high school he attended for underage driving while under the influence. One respected newspaper suggested it was a combination of drugs and alcohol, which was enough of an embarrassing ordeal for Stanton's wife, Joanne, to send her directly to her large, private cache of prescription pills. Her inability to cope with family crises—which she blamed on their 'fishbowl existence'—had, according to media pundits, rendered the First Lady a political liability.

Stanton's foreign policies weren't faring much better. He had sent tens of thousands of American soldiers to a miserable war-torn country with little hope of being able to maintain the fragile peace agreement that none of the warring ethnic parties wanted in the first place. "Let them all kill each other," one Administration official had said at Stanton's Cabinet meeting a few weeks earlier. "We can't be the world's policemen, anymore," another Cabinet member had said. "These people have been at it for centuries—they're never going to learn to live in peace—they'd rather die."

Stanton's Secretary of State, Campbell, had agreed. "Mr. President, too many of our young boys are going to come home in body bags," he said in his depressing monotone.

But Stanton, in a rare show of commitment, reacted defiantly. "We're going to give them a peace agreement, if we have to shove it down their throats!" The President often spoke in oxymorons.

On the morning that Abu came calling, Stanton had received several ominous faxes from the Middle East: Iran had just tested a nuclear device, and the CIA now confirmed that Libya had underground chemical and biological weapons facilities that were impervious to satellite detection or destruction. China had just sold long-range missiles to Syria and Iraq, and the CIA satellites had picked up massive military maneuvers in the North African desert. An American navy destroyer in the Pacific had actually been fired upon the day before by a Chinese warship—an event which would never be revealed to the public or the press. There was a sudden plague of terrorist bombings and Islamic fundamentalists were attacking and destroying buildings and bridges and embassies throughout the world. Riots and protests were undermining every government in Western Europe. Neo-fascists were threatening to overthrow Germany's Bonn government; the Italian parliament had collapsed and, in Britain, the conservatives went down in defeat. There was so much anger and unrest in the streets of London that the royal family—the symbol, many said, of what was 'wrong' with England had hastily scurried off to their northernmost castle in Scotland, fearful that they would either be assassinated or, at the very least, stripped of their monarchial wealth and regal powers.

No, this was definitely not a day that Eleanor Cummings found any comfort in as she escorted the formidable and forbidding man, who towered over her by a foot and half, to the Oval Office.

The moment she opened the door, President Stanton was on his feet, ready to greet Abu. Eleanor and the President exchanged knowing smiles, and then she closed the door quietly behind her.

"Sheik Asghar," Stanton said, mustering a disingenuous smile and extending his hand. "It's a pleasure to finally meet you."

Abu put his palms together, chest high and gave a slight bow. "Mr.

President," he said. Stanton awkwardly withdrew his hand.

As the President motioned for them to sit down opposite one another on the two sofas near the fireplace, Bob Stanton studied his guest for a moment, and found himself even more uncomfortable with Sheik Asghar than he thought he would be. He had been in the company of enough of the world's leaders—many of whom were despotic tyrants, even a few madmen—to be shaken by anyone, no matter how dangerous or meglomaniacal they might be. But Asghar was a breed apart, and Stanton, like his secretary Eleanor, wished this meeting never had to take place. He felt momentarily relieved when the door opened and the well-tailored and wily presence of Lee Cowles entered the Oval Office.

"My Chief of Staff, Lee Cowles," Stanton said, introducing him to Abu. The same, slightly embarrassing moment occurred when Cowles offered a handshake that went unreciprocated. Cowles, instead, nodded in perfunctory deference. He sat in a chair next to the sofa, put a large yellow pad on his lap and took out a Mont Blanc fountain pen from the pocket of his conservative charcoal-gray suit, immediately ready to start taking notes.

"I've heard some pretty extraordinary things about you, Sheik Asghar," Stanton began in a voice that was polite, if not friendly.

"I have no doubt," Abu responded. There was an awkward silence.

"Yes, well," the President said, "let's get down to business then, shall we?" Abu nodded. "What exactly is it you wanted to see me about, Sheik Asghar?"

Abu looked at the President, his penetrating gaze made Stanton want to turn away. "I am here to offer you an extraordinary opportunity."

"And what might that be?" Stanton looked over at Lee Cowles whose face wore an expressionless mask, but who was listening attentively as Abu spoke.

"For you to go down in history as the greatest president this nation has ever had, and one of the world's great leaders."

"Really?" Stanton said, almost bemused. He sat back on the sofa. "That's very generous of you." His voice belied sarcasm.

"But you will have to earn that place," Abu said. Cowles had been making some notes on his yellow pad, but now stopped to look at Abu.

"How do you foresee this happening, Sheik Asghar?" the Chief of Staff asked.

Abu continued to look directly at the President. "By your leadership in the creation of a world government—one that would have supreme authority over its constituent states. And by ceding this country's sovereignty and its weapons of mass destruction to that supreme authority."

President Stanton stared at Abu in disbelief, then smiled slightly, as if about to talk to a recalcitrant child. "Sheik Asghar, I'm afraid I can't do that."

"You must."

"I'm a busy man, Sheik Asghar, too busy to play games."

"So am I, Mr. President. Please allow me to elaborate."

Cowles instinctively looked at his watch. "I shall be brief," Abu said, smiling. The President nodded. "The United States is in a unique position to do what I have asked. This nation—your great country—was born of a divine mission. It was created to be a model for the world—a prototype, if you will. The genius of your founding fathers must now be realized on a global basis. Mind you, Mr. President, it is not the ultimate end, but only the next step in humanity's evolution."

"And you honestly think the creation of a world government is going to solve the world's problems?" Stanton asked.

Abu nodded. "The interdependence of every nation on the planet, no matter how large or small, rich or poor, has become a fact of life. America is not an invulnerable fortress—"

"I'm well aware of that, Sheik Asghar," the President said.

"Then you know that the nations of the Third World are breeding grounds for tyrants and despots, anxious to gain dominance over their neighbors. If united, the people of the Third World can become a force of enormous magnitude, capable of bringing total destruction upon the planet—"

"Ah," Cowles interrupted, "the Armageddon you're so fond of predicting. Am I right, Mr. Asghar?"

"Mr. Cowles," Abu said trying to restrain his frustration, "the poor of this world will no longer be denied. You see, they have nothing left to lose. The American people will soon realize that no one is safe until all are safe. All the nations of the world must participate in the solution. It will require unprecedented levels of cooperation and only the United States, and you, Mr. President," he said, glancing at Stanton, "as the leader of the free world, can initiate such a momentous undertaking."

"Let me ask you something, Sheik Asghar," the President said, almost deferentially, "what makes you think that a world government will solve the world's problems? How will you keep the leader of this new order from becoming just another dictator, another tyrant? You, above all people, know that power corrupts. And absolute power corrupts absolutely. Have you considered that you might be setting the world back two thousand years? Have you read your Roman history, Sheik Asghar?"

"I prefer American history to Roman, Mr. President. May I remind you that this country, after the American Revolution, existed for over a decade under a loose confederacy. Many feared and mistrusted central authority so they devised the Articles of Confederation and allowed individual nation-states to exist. But in less than ten years the system was not working. There was no regulation of commerce, no common currency, no authority to resolve state boundary disputes, and no army or navy for the common defense. Trade wars erupted, debts went unpaid, open hostilities broke out at state lines. And there was no central authority to define the rights of its citizens. This then became the reason for the Constitutional Convention where your great forefathers, Hamilton, Madison, Adams, and Franklin came together and combined their wisdom, experience and creativity—their noble regard for the decency of all humanity—to establish a new form of government based on the interdependence and cooperation between all the states. Perhaps your greatest leader, President Lincoln, said it best almost a century later: 'United we stand, divided we fall.' " Abu paused and looked from the President to the Chief of Staff and back again. "The world now requires such leadership again, on a global scale. A leader who shows the vision, courage and, yes, the way, to achieve this greatest of all achievements: A new world order. Perhaps it will be you, Mr. President."

"Or you," Stanton said, eying Abu cautiously.

"You misread me, President Stanton. It is not personal glory I seek, but the glory of all humanity. I have no aspirations for any office."

"But if drafted, you will run, won't you, Sheik Asghar?" Lee Cowles challenged.

"Only by default, sir, only by default."

The President shifted uncomfortably on the sofa. Eleanor Cummings knocked on the door and opened it. "Mr. President, you have a press conference in five minutes and the Secretary of State is waiting to brief you—"

"Thanks, Ellie, we were just finishing up here."

Eleanor Cummings nodded and closed the door. Stanton looked back to Abu. "Sheik Asghar, let me explain something to you. I love my country and I love its people. I have only their interests at heart. Without their approval and their elected choice, I would not be talking to you as the President. I know what the American people and their congressional representatives want. And it is *not* a world government, I assure you."

"We must be bold, Mr. President. We must take risks, and we must have faith," Abu urged, in a voice that entreated as it warned.

"Oh, I have faith, Sheik Asghar, in my God. As you do in yours," the President said.

"But it is all one and the same," Abu said. "As are the countries of the world, as are the people—all the people on this planet are merely the collective consciousness of the universe made manifest—"

"Sheik Asghar," the President said, standing up as if to signal the meeting was over, "I am a pragmatist—a man who deals in reality, practical and tangible reality. I have to concern myself with what is going on, here and abroad, on a daily basis—the cold hard facts of everyday life. Not your prophecies of doom, not your so-called 'miraculous' resurrection, or the fanatics that you seem to attract by the score; I have more pressing and urgent matters to attend to. I have—if you will permit me, Sheik Asghar—a country to run!"

Abu rose abruptly from the sofa and moved to the door of the Oval Office. "I will not waste any more of your time, Mr. President. Nor my own." Abu placed his palms together and bowed, then opened the door and hurried out.

Lee Cowles closed the Office door and turned to the man he had known since their days together as classmates at Yale Law School. He looked worried, almost fearful. "Bob—?"

"Yeah, Lee, I know." The President walked over to the huge picture window flanked by American flags and draped in beige damask silk. "He's trouble. Big, big trouble," Robert Franklin Stanton said, as he watched Abu's limousine driving out of the West Gate of the White House and onto Pennsylvania Avenue.

CHAPTER 42

On the day Abu left Washington, D.C., Bennett Williams returned from Europe. Right before he boarded his Swissair flight, he phoned Aimee to say he would be home in about twelve hours and would call her again from the airport as soon as he landed. Aimee was due to go into labor at any time—in fact, she was a few days late—and Williams wanted to be as accessible and reassuring as possible. Now, ten minutes before his flight landed at La Guardia Airport, he decided to phone Aimee again from the plane. A message on the answering machine clicked on after two rings. Aimee's voice came through, strong and almost cheerful. "Ben, this is the mother of all mothers-to-be speaking . . . please go straight to Mt. Sinai Hospital where our baby is about to enter the world . . . if you miss this deadline, the only exclusive you'll get for the next year is that of changing diapers!"

Williams went back to his seat, not knowing whether to laugh or cry. He had to be there when his son was born; it wasn't only a promise he had made to Aimee, he had made this one to himself. He intended to be at every milestone in his child's life, beginning with its birth. Williams made a private vow too: His son would know the love and encouragement and appreciation he had never received from H. Bennett Williams, Sr. He'd be a different kind of father—of that he was certain.

Williams ran through the airport apologetically bumping and pushing his way past the other disembarking passengers. He grabbed his luggage off the carousel, ran out into a cold, rainy New York night and jumped into one of the waiting taxis. Heavy traffic, slowed down by the inclement weather, caused Williams to curse and squirm uncomfortably in the back seat. The cabbie noticed his fare's agitation. "Going as fast as I can, mister."

"I know," Williams said, "but my—" he hesitated for a second "—

354

wife—" he couldn't think of anything else to call her at the moment "—is having a baby. It's our first and—"

"Ohhh, so that's who's at Mt. Sinai. Whyn'cha say so?" the cabbie scolded, grinning. He instantly pulled out from a middle lane on the Long Island Expressway and with his horn blaring, forced the cars in front of him to veer off in whatever direction they could as he wove his way to Manhattan with the speed and skill of a NASCAR driver. Williams leaned back in his seat, closed his eyes and smiled.

At the hospital, a nurse whisked Williams into the delivery room, put a mask on him and a white gown. When he reached Aimee, she was only moments away from giving birth; sweating, crying, yelling in pain and gasping her Lamaze breaths. Williams kissed Aimee's forehead and held one of her hands. "Guess we're sharing diaper patrol," he said, joking nervously. Aimee tried to smile; she was grateful that he was there, but all she could manage were groans and pained grimaces. Williams watched her helplessly. The obstetrician leaned toward him.

"Ben, are you going to be all right?" he said as Williams mopped his own brow. He looked a little faint.

"I'm fine, I'm fine," he said. But in fact, Williams had never felt more emotional upheaval than he did at that moment. It was not only that the woman he loved was about to give birth to his first child—perhaps his only child—it was that this extraordinarily spiritual and physical reaffirmation of the act of creation was coupled with the terrifying truths he had learned on his trip to Geneva. Could he protect his family, keep them out of harm's way? The responsibility seemed awesome given the chaos he now believed was imminent.

But there was no time to think about the future, or even tomorrow. This moment in Williams' life was all there was, and all that mattered. His son was born with a last, gut-wrenching shriek and exhausted push from Aimee. Williams watched the newborn's emergence in amazement, coupled with an inner happiness he'd never known before. The doctor handed him the surgical scissors. He shakily took it, and with the help of the nurse he cut the umbilical cord. Aimee smiled tears of joy through her exhaustion.

"Is he okay?" she said weakly.

"He's looking great," the doctor said, as he placed the infant on Aimee's chest for a few moments. She kissed his tiny hands.

Williams looked lovingly at Aimee and then at his son. He patted the infant's head with great tenderness. "Welcome to the world, Matthew Argent Williams," he said. In response, the baby let out a long, lusty howl.

Williams slept overnight in a hospital bed next to Aimee. In the morning, in the room now filled with congratulatory bouquets and balloons, and a teddy bear from Herschel Strunk that was three times the size of Matthew, Williams watched blissfully as Aimee took the baby in her arms and put his mouth to her breast. Matthew began to nurse greedily.

Williams went home that afternoon, showered and changed clothes. He was just about to leave the apartment for a meeting with Strunk, when he stopped at the front door and went back into the den. He picked up the telephone and dialed his mother's number in Milwaukee. A part of him—the part that bitterly remembered the past—hoped she wouldn't answer, but when she did, he took a deep breath and dove into the icy waters.

"Mom, I'm calling to let you know that Aimee has just had a baby—it's a boy—"

"—Ben, that's wonderful news." His mother's voice sounded sincere and happy. Williams couldn't believe it. "I only wish your father was alive to know this."

"Me too, mom, me too."

"How is Aimee?" Williams' mother had spoken to her only once when Aimee had answered the phone in his apartment. His mother had called to discuss some minor matter concerning his father's will—it was about four months after Bennett Sr. died—and she'd had a brief, polite exchange with Aimee.

"Great," Williams said. "She's nursing him and he's beautiful."

"Of course he is, he's your son. What did you name him?"

"Matthew. It's a name I've always loved."

"Yes, it's a good, strong name. Biblical too."

"Right," Williams said and then paused. "Well, listen, mom, I'm late for a meeting at the *Times*—"

"Ben, in a few months when the winter's over, will you bring Matthew here? I want to meet my new grandson."

Williams swallowed hard. "Of course. We'll come out to see you in the spring."

Williams hung up the phone and quickly left the apartment. His step was lighter than it had been in years. Perhaps the heaviest weight he had carried around for almost two decades had suddenly, effortlessly, been lifted from his shoulders.

But the feelings of relief, of ancient guilt unburdened and Williams' new-found familial happiness, began dissipating as soon as he sat across from Herschel Strunk in the editor's office. The fears and anxieties that had been gnawing at him during his trip to Europe now resurfaced.

"Exactly how much money do you think is flowing through the WPO?" Strunk asked, his eyes fixed intently on Williams.

"A couple billion so far, and more is coming. Security is very tight, but as best as I could determine, most of it's from Saudi Arabia, Libya, Iraq, Syria—you know, the OPEC crowd. And from places like Brunei, Pakistan, India, even Egypt. Hell, there's probably a chunk of U.S. aid money there. All the pipelines converge in Geneva."

"Then where does it go?"

"Hard to know exactly. There's an incredibly complex labyrinth of dummy foundations, each feeding money to another, back again and out another pipeline. Heinrich Demmler's the genius behind it all."

Strunk's eyes widened. He sucked in his breath. "Demmler—no kidding!" Strunk reached for the mug of coffee on his desk. "You need a refill?" he said, nodding toward the mug Williams held in his hand. Williams shook his head. "Ben, what's your boy, Abu, doing with all this dough?"

Williams let out a long exhale. "He's buying up a lot of our strategic stockpile—"

"What?!" Strunk's jaw suddenly dropped.

"Yeah. The Pentagon started selling it off ever since the Cold War more or less ended. All that stuff we were storing—magnesium, cobalt, nickel, aluminum—in case the Russians ever started World War Three."

"And Demmler made the Pentagon an offer they couldn't refuse."

Williams nodded. "He's also buying materials like industrial diamonds—the stuff used for high-tech weapons, aircraft, ships. Oh, and he's bought a slew of shipyards and whole shipping lines. All around the Mediterranean."

"Jesus Christ, what's he want ships for?"

"Officially? They're transports to carry relief supplies. But he's hired thousands of ship workers and they're refitting the vessels—"

Strunk's brow furrowed. "What the hell—?!"

"Hersch, I think he's building troop transports, that's what I think."

"Can you confirm it?"

"No, no one will talk. Security is tighter than Fort Knox."

"Ben, we need corroboration. I can't print it otherwise, you know that."

"Fuck corroboration! We both know what he's doing. Journalistic integrity isn't going to mean jack-shit if Abu is allowed to build some kind of goddamn international, monolithic army!"

"And do you think the *New York Times* can stop him?"

"Maybe not, but we sure can tell people what he's up to."

"Without corroboration, no one is going to listen, we won't print it. And if the tabloids print it, you can be certain no one will believe it."

"Then I'll have to go it alone," Williams said, getting up from his chair, but he knew Strunk was right.

Herschel Strunk watched Williams leave his office in a state of frustration and anger. He hurried to the door and called after him, "Ben, I don't want you pay for this trip out of your own pocket—put in a voucher for it—we'll pick up the tab."

"Yeah, right," Williams said, as he continued walking, without turning back to look at Strunk.

After his U.S. tour, Abu headed for Mexico and then South America. It didn't matter to him that most of those countries—Brazil, Argentina, Chile, Columbia, Venezuela—were predominantly Roman Catholic. The vast majority of their populations were desperately poor, and Abu had come to these people, not with the Holy Mother Church's blessings on them for their suffering and struggles, but with a genuine caring, and a promise that he would do something for them in *this* lifetime; they would not have to wait for the next one to see an end to their misery. By the time he left South America, Abu had garnered millions more to his cause.

He returned to India, to Malaysia and Bangladesh and Myanmar—the places he'd been before the world had come to know him as a prophet and a savior. This time his visits were triumphant and the masses that flocked to hear and see him now affirmed that Sheik Abu 'Ali Asghar was leading a global crusade for justice and equality. He had come full circle.

And then Abu disappeared. Not like when he went to Tamenghest. He just went into seclusion. Things got quiet in matters concerning the WPO and Abu himself. The world's attention was focused everywhere else.

And the picture one beheld was nothing less than grim, ominously frightening. Terrible events around the globe were escalating with alarming speed. Islamic fundamentalists swept the elections in Turkey and established a new government which immediately withdrew from NATO, establishing instead an Islamic Economic Union. The United States' burgeoning budget deficit caused it to announce more troop reductions in Europe, thus destabilizing military security in numerous countries in the Western world. The Sunni Muslim majority of Saudi Arabia called for an end to the royal family and demanded democratic reforms. Iran was found to have nuclear weapons in its arsenal, and this news resulted in widespread fear of a nuclear arms race in the Middle East. OPEC increased the price of crude oil to its highest level since the oil embargo of the 1970s. A news report that morning which had come across President Stanton's desk, confirmed that Nigerian drug cartels now moved half of the world's cocaine, stating that the lax security in South Africa's harbors and airports had allowed the countries of the region to become "the new gateway for global narcotics smuggling."

In Russia, the economic market reforms were finally declared a failure, Borovsky was proclaimed a pariah in his own country, and the conservative Nationalists gained control of the government. All of Washington was now expressing grave concerns over potential resumption of the Cold War. Stocks in New York, Tokyo, London, Bonn and Paris plunged dramatically for the second week in a row.

American treasury agents in the U.S. raided a cell of Islamic fundamentalists in New Jersey, seizing millions in counterfeit currency and the largest cache of illegal weapons ever confiscated, including 'plastik' explosives which the extremists had recently and successfully detonated in Paris, killing hundreds of people. The counterfeit currency had been used by terrorists in the Middle East to undermine American dollars abroad. It also signaled an expansion of terrorist objectives.

Street riots continued all across the United States and had reached an unprecedented level of violence. The same was true in cities throughout England and Italy. In China, troops swept across the western reaches of the country to stem a rising Muslim insurgency. NAFTA, the free trade agreement between Mexico and the United States had collapsed, brought down by bitter controversy, corruption and scandal. Its demise caused rioting and protests throughout Mexico and all along the borders of the two countries. Floods of refugees trying to cross into Texas and California could not be contained.

And then came the devastating news that Saudi Arabia, Kuwait, Bahrain and the United Arab Emirates were withdrawing their deposits from American banks, cashing in their treasury bills, liquidating stocks and selling real estate investments, even at huge losses. Japanese and European investors soon followed. Shock waves radiated all across the financial markets of the world. Banks began calling in loans to shore up deposits. Investors began a rush of panic selling. The SEC ordered a halt to all shareholder trading. The New York and Pacific Stock Exchanges closed down. As people stood in line at banks, demanding their money, President Stanton declared a national emergency and the banks were closed. Federal troops were immediately dispatched to all major cities to maintain order. Stanton went on national television, begging his fellow Americans to remain calm, that this was only a temporary predicament, that a functioning economy would soon be restored. It was a message few people believed.

Within one week, OPEC closed down its shipments of oil to the West. Massive layoffs of workers took place around the world as the price of gasoline, diesel and jet fuel skyrocketed. In cities across the United States, mile-long lines formed at gas stations; violent fighting broke out between angry motorists. The government finally stepped in and ordered mandatory rationing. Airfares suddenly tripled. Trucks, unable to get enough diesel fuel, were stranded on their way to city and suburban markets; their shipments of food rotting in their giant trucks. Supermarket shelves went unstocked causing food prices to soar. Hoarding became the order of the day. The dollar, the yen, deutschmark, pound, franc and lira all plummeted in international trading despite frantic efforts by the various governments to buy up their currencies in a futile effort to forestall their collapse.

Fear and panic swept the globe. People took to the streets, looting and burning. Some armed themselves, huddling their families around them in darkened cellars, as though waiting for a bombing raid. Some people went mad, withdrew inward, while others lashed out, shooting randomly in crowded stores and office buildings. Some jumped out of windows, some quietly placed revolvers to their heads and blew their brains out.

The dark night of Abu's prophecy was descending.

Williams sat with Aimee and their newborn son, watching the incomprehensible, worldwide nightmare that played out on television. All the networks' standard programming had been canceled—except for three soap operas and two popular talk shows. Television broadcasting now consisted exclusively of the global horrors that were occurring daily. They had gathered strength and momentum, these ghastly cataclysmic events, and like water raging through a burst dam, they flooded through city and country in every corner of the globe.

Aimee rocked Matthew in her arms, where he slept the peaceful and contented sleep of innocence. His mother leaned back against the sofa and sighed. "It's really happening, isn't it, Ben?" Aimee said in a small, frightened voice.

"It started a long time ago," Williams replied. "But I never thought it would get this far this fast."

"Ben, we have to do something, we have to leave here. I'm scared."

Williams put his arms around Aimee and his son. "We're going to be okay, I promise." But the conviction in his voice sounded hollow.

Aimee's maternity leave from Brandon House would be over in a few months, but the venerable old publishers had put a hold on all new book printings and weren't very certain about the state of the ones already published. These days people were buying only the basic necessities for survival; books were far too much of a luxury. Aimee didn't know if she'd have a job to go back to, if there'd even be a Brandon House by then.

This climate of fear and uncertainty caused Williams' book to be one of the casualties—it was put on hold, even though Williams had been writing the most comprehensive, albeit speculative, text on who Abu was and the madness he had unleashed.

A few weeks later, Williams decided one more time to try to convince Strunk to run the article he had written—the one he still could not corroborate. This time Williams' tone was pleading and conciliatory.

"Hersch, please, I'm asking you as a friend," he said as he paced Strunk's office.

The older man stared back at Williams with compassion. The last couple of weeks had changed him; he had aged ten years, his eyes were filled with a profound sadness. "No, Ben, I can't."

Williams continued to pace. "What the fuck am I going to do, Hersch?"

Strunk leaned back in his leather chair and looked up at Williams. His voice sounded faraway. "Everything is going to hell in a hand basket. Nothing will ever be the same again. I just pray this new world is going to be one we want to live in. But I doubt it. And I doubt this paper will survive."

Williams stopped short and went over to Strunk's desk. "Then run it, Hersch! If it's all going down the tubes anyway, what've you got to lose?"

Strunk gazed back at Williams. There was a hint of the old fire in his eyes. "You know, Ben, Sir Thomas More once wrote something I never forgot. He said that a man's integrity was like a vessel formed by two hands cupped together, holding within them one's very soul. Open your fingers just a little bit and you risk letting it all run out." Williams said nothing. Strunk shook his head. "Ben, you might be right. But all we ever have are our principles. Compromise that and we compromise our integrity; compromise our integrity and we lose our souls."

Williams walked to Strunk's interior window and looked out at the busy newsroom. "Yeah, what the hell."

Strunk took a bottle of scotch from his desk drawer. Williams was surprised to see Strunk having a drink in the middle of the afternoon. "Helps numb some of my anxiety these days," Strunk said by way of explanation. Williams nodded in commiseration.

"By the way, Ben, I heard that Henry Fairlie's taking an indefinite vacation somewhere in the Caribbean. Has this affected the book?"

Williams picked up an empty glass from a tray on Strunk's desk and gestured with it toward the bottle of scotch. "Mind if I join you?" Strunk nodded. Williams poured a shot and gulped it down. "Book's on hold. It isn't quite finished yet, but there's not much point in writing it anymore, is there?"

Strunk looked upset, disappointed. Like a father whose son has just told him he's dropping out of college. "You've got to finish it, Ben. You might have to be resigned to telling it after the event, rather than before. People might not give you as much credit for farsightedness, if that's what's important to you. But write the book, Ben. If you recall, that was the whole point, once upon a time. Remember: *For Whom The Bell Tolls?*"

Strunk's words hit Williams like a blow to the solar plexus. Everything Williams needed to hear, Strunk had just said. Williams' realized he'd been off track and now he felt his focus returning, he felt his purpose renewed.

"Thanks, Hersch," he said and nodded. "You're right. I do have to finish it. No matter what happens."

Herschel Strunk opened his desk drawer and took out a set of keys that looked familiar to Williams. "Here," he said, tossing the keys to him, "take Aimee and Matthew up to the cabin. Get 'em out of the city before the shit really hits the fan. And stay up there 'til you finish the fucking book."

"What about you, Hersch?" He knew Strunk's wife had died a few years ago and they'd never had children. "Come with us."

"Maybe later. Until they close us down, I'm still a senior editor and you're a worthless reporter. Now get the hell outta here."

Williams grinned at Hersch as he pocketed the keys. "Thanks old friend. I'll be touch."

On the street in front of the *Times* building, Williams tried in vain to hail a taxi. Williams shivered in the cold gray afternoon, cursing the fuel shortage that had put half of the city's taxicabs out of business. As he stood at the curb, two young men in a nondescript minivan passed with the rest of the traffic in front of Williams. No one paid any attention as the van rounded the corner and went into the building's subterranean garage. When a bus heading uptown stopped at the corner, Williams jumped on it. Unencumbered by the usual gridlock, the bus moved smoothly along Madison Avenue, an ironic side benefit of the oil crisis.

Just as Williams had found a vacant seat on the crowded bus and sat down, from somewhere not very far away, a terrible explosion was heard. It shook the bus and panicked the passengers. Some of them looked frantically out the windows while others dove to the floor and covered their heads with their arms. People in the streets were yelling and running in the direction of the explosion as giant grayish-black columns of smoke began rising from the one of the city's concrete canyons. Williams' heart was racing as he ran to the front of the bus. He asked the driver to stop so he could get off.

Williams jumped off the bus and ran alongside the swelling mob of people that looked like one of the city's marathon races as they headed toward the site of the explosion.

And then Williams saw it. Billowing, acrid black smoke was pouring from every window of the nearly-collapsed *New York Times* office building. It looked like a devastating earthquake had hit it. Or like a bomb had exploded in the bowels of the structure.

Williams stared in stunned horror as the siren-screaming fire engines and police cars and ambulances, and the ever-present television news crews, converged on the mass destruction that had just been wrought. He could not get close to the building but could see dozens of dazed people, bloody and smoke-blackened as they staggered out of the building, some dropping and dying of their injuries as they tried to escape. Hundreds more were buried in the rubble.

As the disaster's pandemonium continued to surround Williams, he sank to his knees on the sidewalk. His whole body shook with wracking sobs. "Oh God, no, no . . . God, no."

CHAPTER 43

Aimee had just hung up the telephone when she heard Williams' key in the front door. She ran into his arms, burying her head in his neck. Then she looked at him, holding his tear-stained face between her hands. "Oh God, Ben, I'm so sorry. I just saw it on the news—"

Williams stared back at Aimee. "Were there any survivors?"

"A few. Herschel wasn't among them."

Williams nodded. He walked numbly into their bedroom and over to the crib where his infant son slept peacefully. He stared absently around the room, then, as if shaking off some terrible vise that he'd been locked in, he took a deep breath and seemed to suddenly spring into decisive action. He turned to Aimee.

"Start packing. We're going up to the cabin. Hersch gave me the keys—he wanted me to take you and Matthew out of the city. I think he knew something terrible was going to happen. Hersch always had a sixth sense about things."

"Ben, I need to take care of some work at Brandon House—"

"No—! I think we should leave right away—tonight!"

"Ben, I can't just abandon my job."

"Aimee—listen to me," he said, grabbing her by the shoulders, "there may not be any job to come back to. Brandon House may go the way of the *New York Times*—!"

The TV set in the living room could be heard in the background. A CNN newscaster was updating the bombing story. Williams ran to the living room. Aimee was right behind him.

". . . Word has just come into the newsroom that a group of right-wing militia extremists are claiming responsibility for the terrorist bombing of the *New York Times* Building. In a phone call to CNN, the militia group has stated that because the *Times* was the newspaper that first began documenting the exploits and travels of Sheik Asghar, they helped to perpetuate the myth that sprung up around him and gave credence to his deeds and glorified his words. They hold the *Times* and other media partly responsible for Asghar's extraordinary rise to fame and power. They believe he is somehow directly connected to the worldwide catastrophic events that are occurring. Since the militia does not have access to the Sheik himself, they have targeted those people and organizations—"

Williams could not listen anymore. He clicked the remote and looked at Aimee. "That's it, we're leaving tonight. How much cash do you have?"

"A couple hundred, I think. Maybe more, if I count what's in the cookie jar. Why?" She looked genuinely terrified. Williams took her in his arms and held her tightly.

"I heard a rumor that most stores aren't accepting credit cards or checks anymore. At least not until the banks open for business again. Which I doubt they will."

Aimee was scared and confused. The world had finally gone mad. Nothing made sense anymore. She closed the bedroom door, sat down on the edge of the bed and began to cry.

Williams sat next to her and rocked her in his arms. "We're going to make it, babe. I'm never going to let any harm come to you and Matthew."

"But what about *you*, my love?" Aimee looked pleadingly into Williams' eyes. "Don't you think that the militia might must come after you? They know who wrote those articles."

"No. They want to put the whole media out of business—I'm just a cog in the wheel." But, in fact, he *was* afraid that they might come after him. Focus and purpose became crystal clear to Williams: All that mattered right now was protecting his family.

He and Aimee hurriedly began taking down suitcases and cartons from the every closet in the apartment. They would shop for food on the way. Aimee began packing Matthew's clothes and toys while Williams began folding the baby's carriage and stroller, then carefully took apart the crib. Matthew continued to sleep in the middle of his parents' king-size bed.

Williams knew the dominoes had started falling and there wasn't any stopping them. He thought of that Yeats poem again: *Things fall apart; the center cannot hold; mere anarchy is loosed upon the world* .... Sirens raced through the streets below. Flames still illuminated the sky uptown, but the glow was closer now, signaling that rioting was headed their way. Williams wondered how long it would take for the entire city to become engulfed in chaos and destruction. He thought about Herschel. He wondered if, in the world to come, there would be any good people left. Was the world on the verge of an age of enlightenment or headed for another Dark Ages? He silently prayed it would not be the latter. But at this moment he felt anything but optimism. Maybe Herschel saw something he didn't.

On television, all the stations were broadcasting President Stanton's latest address to the nation. He looked tired, but tried not to sound defeated. He wasn't succeeding. Williams stopped packing long enough to watch. ". . . and after conferring with the leaders of the world's industrialized nations, I am confident that we shall all cooperate to bring this current crisis under control. We expect a resumption of stability in the monetary markets very soon. I want all Americans to join together in the sure knowledge that we will endure. As Franklin Roosevelt once said during the worst days of World War Two, '. . . the only thing we have to fear is fear itself.' "

A network news anchorman appeared on the screen. "Despite President Stanton's assurances, international money markets continue to spiral out of control. Record losses have been reported on the New York, Tokyo, London, Paris and Bonn stock exchanges and trading has been suspended. Meanwhile, fear and panic has swept the globe. Rioting continues in nearly every major capitol as the collapsing American economy sends shock waves rippling around the world." As the anchorman continued talking, images of frenzied masses of people were seen on the TV screen. Tens of thousands had taken to the streets, looting and burning. The National Guard and riot police had been called out, but could do little to control the unruly mobs. There were scenes of high government officials racing into private chambers and conference rooms for emergency meetings, while in the streets anarchy reigned.

Williams swiftly brought the Land Cruiser up from the underground garage. He began loading it in front of the apartment building as several security guards and the doorman watched protectively. Williams used ropes and straps to secure all their belongings, then hurried back up to the apartment to get Aimee and Matthew.

"I'm afraid we're really throwing Matthew's schedule off," Aimee said as she tried to soothe the restless, cranky infant. They were riding down the elevator, perhaps for the last time, Williams realized sadly. He had come to love the apartment that Herschel had helped to find for him when he first returned to New York—my God, how could so much had happened since then?—and once Aimee had moved into it, the place had become a real home to Williams. Better than any he could remember.

Napoleon, the macaw, paced nervously in his cage as it was loaded into the jeep, but at least he wasn't squawking. He knew something was very wrong, but as long he saw Aimee and Williams, he felt a measure of security. Aimee spoke soothingly to the bird, and even though he hated being in a moving vehicle, he finally settled down and accepted the drive that would take them to a safer place.

Surface traffic was unusually heavy. Massive gridlock had gripped the city; traffic signals were out and everyone drove offensively. Williams slowed down as he neared a police officer trying desperately to direct traffic. "Why are all the signals out?" Williams called to the cop.

The officer looked at him with contempt. "Where you been—? There was an explosion an hour ago at Con Ed's main plant. Power's down nearly everywhere. Nuthin's workin'. Now get moving—"

"Was it an accident, or a bomb—?"

"What do I look like—the *Six O'clock News*?! Now get moving," he said, furiously gesturing with his right arm.

As they rode, Aimee stared out the window at market after market where huge lines of people, extending onto the sidewalks, waited impatiently to get inside. Business was brisk—everyone had started hoarding. Williams maneuvered out of traffic and double parked in front of a gun shop. "No, Ben, please—" Aimee said, tugging on his sleeve as he started to get out of the Land Cruiser. "Guns scare me."

He held her hand for a moment. "We may need it," he said as he jumped down and raced into the store.

The place was packed. He went over to the shotguns and selected a 12-gauge, pump action model. He quickly handed it to a salesman and then looked inside the counter display. "And I'll take one of those," he said, pointing to a 9-mm automatic. "And a couple dozen boxes of ammunition for each."

The salesman eyed Williams. "I'll need some I.D. and you gotta fill out a coupla forms—"

Williams controlled his mounting anger. He didn't want the man to think he was some deranged fool. The streets were full of those right now. "Look," he said in a steady voice, "I'm taking my wife and child out of the city and I want to be sure we make it." He reached into his pocket for the wad of cash and peeled off two one-hundred-dollar bills.

The salesman looked furtively around him for a second then took the money Williams was sliding toward him on the counter. "Fuck it," the salesman said. "It's all going to shit anyway." He quickly pocketed the money and bagged the weapons. "Good luck," he said as he handed them to Williams.

"Yeah, you too."

It had become every man for himself. Williams had a sick feeling in his stomach as he pushed his way out of the crowded store. He tossed the weapons into the back of the jeep and got behind the wheel. He leaned over to kiss Aimee and to pat Matthew's head. His son was sleeping peacefully again.

Williams turned on the radio. Instantly a newscaster's voice was heard. ". . . this now in to CBS radio news: We have unconfirmed reports that the French Finance Minister has apparently committed suicide. We reiterate that this is still an unconfirmed report. In other related developments, Indonesia, Malaysia, the Phillippines, Nigeria and other African nations have announced they will no longer honor their enormous debts to Western banks. The International Monetary Fund cites the current global economic crisis as the reason for the default by these countries—" Williams frantically turned the radio dial, hoping to find some music, but the stations were only airing accounts of mounting terror, destruction and havoc. He angrily switched off the radio.

"Ben, I think we have some tapes—" Aimee said as she opened the glove compartment and began rummaging through it. She pulled out a tape of the popular 1960s musical, *Hair*, a favorite of Williams'. Aimee popped it into the tape deck. Instantly the music and lyrics that reflected a bygone era floated around them. Songs that heralded the "dawning of the Age of Aquarius" and the dream for peace and harmony, for no more wars—the lyrics that exhorted everyone to "let the sun shine in . . ." How naïve the words sounded now, Williams thought. How far away the dream, how crushed the hope.

It took hours for them to get across town. Williams decided to take the Lincoln Tunnel into New Jersey, then head back into upstate New York once he was past the mass exodus from Manhattan. There was a long line of cars leading into the tunnel. Williams had a momentary flash of being trapped inside, beneath the Hudson River. He tried to hide his impatience and anxiety from Aimee. She was watching Matthew in his car seat—he gurgled and cooed as she put a small bottle of milk to his mouth, and he began sucking on the nipple.

As they sat behind the endless line that snaked its way into the tunnel, there was a sudden, deafening explosion. Aimee screamed. Williams thought they were going to die. *God, not now!*

The blast was immediately followed by an eruption of fire from deep within the tunnel, a fireball sent from hell's inferno began to engulf cars that were just outside the tunnel. Boom! Boom! Boom! went gas tank after gas tank as the chain explosion came closer to Williams' jeep. Aimee clutched Matthew and Williams at the same time. Cars were veering away and driving off in all directions to get as far from the tunnel as possible. Williams swerved the Land Cruiser onto the sidewalk, deftly maneuvering to avoid hitting injured and terrified pedestrians who had been hit by shards of jagged, flying glass and metallic debris.

He turned and headed north on 8th Avenue and then cut over to the Henry Hudson Parkway. He sped toward the George Washington Bridge, praying they'd get there before anything else happened.

As he drove through Harlem, Williams could see the bridge up ahead. "It's intact—!" he said excitedly to Aimee. Williams speeded up, weaving in and out of the slower-moving traffic. Matthew had been frightened by the explosions and hadn't stopped crying despite Aimee's holding and comforting him. She watched Williams' reckless driving with growing alarm. "Ben, slow down! You're going to get us killed!"

Williams paid no attention to her; he was too busy searching for openings between the cars ahead of him. "My guess is they've probably hit the Holland Tunnel too—and maybe the others—we've got to get out before they hit the bridges."

"They? Who are they?"

"Terrorists, part of Abu's secret army. They probably hit Con Ed. My guess is he wants to close off the city and isolate it."

"Why is he after New York?"

"It's a center of power, and he wants to decimate it."

Aimee looked with horror out the window of the Land Cruiser. What would it be like if all hell broke loose and no one could get out? "You'd better hurry," she said softly.

Williams turned on the radio. A news report was detailing the very catastrophe Williams had foreseen. The Queens Midtown, Brooklyn, Lincoln and Holland Tunnels had all been bombed. "There are reports of heavy casualties," the newscaster's shaky voice announced. "We don't know exactly what the death toll is. Although information is sketchy as to the possible cause of these disasters, one official has ruled out accidental causes. He said the orchestrated manner of the explosions would imply careful planning and preparation . . ."

The bridges were next; Williams was certain of that. He hit the accelerator and Aimee held Matthew tighter. When they got close to the George Washington Bridge, Williams looked at Aimee. She felt his hesitation. "Do it, Ben." Williams nodded and made the turn onto the bridge. There was no going back.

The Land Cruiser inched across the bridge. There were no sidewalks to climb up on, not a drop of space in any lane to maneuver through. He had to protect Aimee and Matthew but felt powerless. He scanned the bridge ahead looking for anything suspicious, like a truck or van that might contain a fertilizer bomb or TNT. He considered how little 'plastik' explosive it would take to collapse the bridge. Was it already in place, next to a crucial support beam? Was there a suicide bomber on the bridge at that moment, sitting behind the wheel of a van or truck, anticipating his union with Allah as he waited for just the right moment to become a martyr? Williams saw a dark-skinned, bearded man behind the wheel of a stalled delivery truck. The truck's panel doors advertised its wares: Rami's Middle Eastern Bakery. Was it him? Williams was relieved when the truck finally passed without incident and traffic started moving again.

Part of the irony of this whole terrible nightmare, and the life-threatening events it had unleashed, was that thousands of people were still coming into the city to go to work, commuting as they always did in the daily rush-hour traffic. Williams shook his head in amazement. Were they more afraid of getting fired than getting killed? He remembered Abu talking about the villagers who, like the ants, did what they had always done because it was the only way they knew how to survive. The thought made him shudder.

Reaching the opposite side was like being rescued from a collapsed building after an earthquake. The air smelled fresher, the sky looked bluer. Williams relaxed and noticed Aimee was breathing easier. Matthew slept again in her arms. Even Napoleon was quiet; the explosions had agitated him so badly, Aimee thought he might have a heart attack right there in his cage. But now he had stopped pacing and climbing around the bars. When they hit the Palisades Parkway, Williams gunned the engine and headed north.

When they were about a dozen miles into New Jersey, Williams pulled up to a supermarket. "I'm going with you," Aimee said, as she strapped Matthew into his papoose which she wore against her chest. They pushed a cart quickly through the aisles and grabbed cans of food, flour, powdered milk, eggs, butter, frozen dinners, sodas, coffee, baby foods, several loaves of bread—as much as they could fit into the Land Cruiser. Williams cleaned out a section of beef briskets. "We'll dry it. I hope you like beef jerky." Aimee grimaced.

As soon as they got back into the Land Cruiser, and began driving toward New York State and the Catskill Mountains, Williams said, "Aimee, there's good soil all around Herschel's cabin. We could probably grow what we need. And we can fish in the lake—"

"My God, Ben, you sound as if we're going to be there forever." She was looking for reassurance that the world they lived in, and the civilization they were a part of, wasn't coming to an end. Williams offered her none.

At the moment chaos had begun descending upon New York City, President Stanton had just finished a breakfast meeting with Vice-President Alvin Gordon. A butler brought a telephone to the table and said, "Mr. President, it's Mr. Cowles."

As Stanton listened to his Chief of Staff, he grew visibly distraught. "Get hold of Mike Del Vechio and Arthur Kleinholtz—"

He was referring to the Director of the FBI and his National Security Advisor. "The Vice President is with me. We'll meet in the Oval

Office." He hung up the phone. "Goddamn, sonofabitch," he said staring off toward the Jefferson Memorial. He looked back at Gordon. "New York's been hit by terrorists—they've bombed the tunnels—"

"My God," Alvin Gordon muttered.

In the Oval Office, Cowles had just turned on a wall panel revealing five television screens tuned to CNN, CBS, ABC, NBC and C-Span. Stanton and Gordon watched the scenes of burning cars and buildings, bloodied corpses, and injured screaming people desperately seeking safety through the smoke and debris that was everywhere.

Stanton shook his head in disbelief, his shocked eyes riveted to the screens. "This is the sort of thing that always happens somewhere else in the world. 'It can't happen here' we always say." He went to his desk and hit the intercom button. "Get me Governor Brady in Albany."

The Oval Office door opened and Michael Del Vechio, a short, wiry Italian—the son of poor immigrant parents—with thick hair, a large nose and steel-rimmed glasses, quickly entered the room. Following behind him was the portly and slower-moving national security advisor, Arthur Kleinholtz. The two men were a study in contrasts. Del Vechio, swift, volatile—"street-wise," the President had labeled him—was a tough decision maker. He admired the President but had limited interest in international politics. Kleinholtz, on the other hand, was born into a wealthy, political and intellectual Austrian family, sixty-three years before. He was the oldest member of Stanton's cabinet. And the most educated. He spoke seven languages fluently, and had already published two seminal books on national security affairs under previous administrations. Kleinholtz, very much a product of his European cultural heritage, often found himself uncomfortable in the presence of the all-American boys who ran the White House and the country.

Stanton motioned to both men to take a seat on the sofa as he picked up the buzzing phone on his desk. "Hello, Governor, how bad is it?" He listened for a moment. "I'll have FEMA and the FBI on this immediately. Anyone claim responsibility yet?" He listened again. "Yeah, I didn't think so. George, I want you to know that we are now doing everything possible to help—New York's been declared a disaster area on a magnitude never used before. Disaster relief is moving with all possible speed. If there's anything else you need, let me know." As Stanton hung up, he eyed Michael Del Vechio. "Mike, what does the FBI know about this?"

"Precious little at the moment, Mr. President. But we've got two dozen special agents and our top terrorist experts on their way to New York by military jet."

"Any suspects?" Stanton asked.

"Not yet."

Stanton turned to Kleinholtz. "Arthur, what do you think?"

"Mr. President, I think Sheik Asghar is behind it."

"So do I, Arthur."

Del Vechio looked surprised. "What makes you say that, Mr. President?"

"Because that sonofabitch stood here in this office and practically told me it was going to happen if I didn't do what he asked."

"But remember, Mr. President," Kleinholtz said cautiously, "we have no proof at this point."

"That's what I want you and Del Vechio to get for me. And use the CIA, use whatever it takes."

Alvin Gordon interjected. "This is domestic, Bob, the CIA lacks jurisdiction—"

Stanton looked impatient and agitated. "Gentlemen, this is not domestic. If I'm right, Asghar will strike again and again, all over the world, unless we provide an appropriate response!"

Lee Cowles had turned to the television screens. "Oh my God—" he said, and instantly everyone in the Oval Office stopped to look at the unfolding cataclysm. ABC aired live images from a helicopter as it circled around the demolished bridges of Manhattan. Hanging sections of gnarled steel and broken concrete, of twisted car wreckage and human bodies were all that the eye beheld. More bodies and debris floated in the East and Hudson rivers below the bridges. Smoke and concrete dust billowed up, rising from the gaping maw of death and destruction. Coast Guard vessels frantically searched for survivors from the black waters. "The Queensboro, Williamsburg and Brooklyn Bridges are completely down," the TV newsman intoned. "The Manhattan Bridge is severely damaged. A collapse is probably imminent . . ."

Del Vechio's eyes were both fierce and tear-filled. "Jesus Christ," he exclaimed.

The President's phone rang. Lee Cowles picked it up, listened for a minute and then put his hand over the mouthpiece. "Mr. President, lower and midtown Manhattan are virtually cut off. The only way in or out is through Harlem and the Bronx."

"Lee, get hold of General McClennan; get him here as fast as you can." McClennan was the Chairman of the Joint Chiefs of Staff. "We're going to have to mobilize the military."

As Cowles picked up one of the colored phones on the President's desk, the others in the room remained glued to the TV monitors. A battle was taking place at the George Washington Bridge between the New York police and an organized group of urban guerrillas armed with assault weapons, hand grenades and rocket launchers. Hundreds of citizens were abandoning their cars and fleeing on foot. Two fifty-caliber machine guns placed at the entrance to the bridge were spewing thousands of rounds a minute. Dozens of people were falling beneath the fusillade. The entire area looked like a World War Two battleground. The men in the Oval Office watched in stunned silence as a rocket-propelled grenade struck a police car, instantly creating a fiery inferno. Another grenade struck a squad car as it attempted a high-speed reverse. It collided with another police vehicle and the two exploded. Trucks filled with equipment and young men arrived on the scene. The moment the trucks stopped, the heavily-armed men jumped out and took positions. They fired their assault weapons in the direction of the retreating policemen. Two SWAT trucks arrived, but before the men could get out of the vehicles, a rocket shot out from a shoulder-launched weapon hit both trucks and detonated. It was over within minutes. Every officer at the scene was dead. The shooting stopped and the urban warriors celebrated their first victory.

Michael Del Vechio had received a phone call in the midst of all this. He listened silently, then hung up and turned to the others. His voice was low and urgent. "Mr. President, we have something unprecedented here. I just received a report that indicates this was an extremely well-organized and coordinated attack. There is more happening than what we're seeing here."

Stanton nodded. There was a knock on the Oval Office door and it opened. The tall, erect four-star general, Henry McClennan, stood there for a second before the President waved him in. "Hank, you've seen this—?" Stanton said pointing to the TV screens.

McClennan never looked more somber. "I'm afraid so, Mr. President."

The FBI Director hung up the phone and looked at the others. "This is a carefully planned operation. It's clearly a military action, not the work of a group of terrorists. The line of demarcation seems to be at 116th Street. They are well-armed and their defenses are layered. If one blockade is penetrated, there's another behind it, and another behind that."

Stanton and McClennan exchanged glances. "Hank, as your Commander-in-Chief, I'll order whatever military action you deem appropriate."

"Yes, Mr. President."

Kleinholtz looked worried. "Mr. President, I must caution you, brinkmanship may not be wise—we could be starting World War Three—"

Stanton stared at his trusted security advisor. "It's already started, Arthur. It's already started."

CHAPTER 44

Late that night, Williams, Aimee, baby Matthew and a very agitated macaw arrived at Herschel's cabin. It looked like El Dorado to Williams, the Emerald City, the Promised Land. Aimee got out of the jeep and hurried to the front door, protectively carrying Matthew in her arms. "It's okay, Aimee, relax honey, please," Williams said, trying to sound reassuring. The city was far behind them, the lake looked serene, the cabin was untouched. Williams took a deep breath, inhaling the clean mountain air. He looked up at the crescent moon and star-studded sky. "Thank you for getting us here safely," he said.

Once he and Aimee had set up Matthew's crib in the bedroom, changed his diaper, and given him a quick bottle, the baby went to sleep. His parents brought in the luggage and cartons, the food, and Napoleon, who had finally settled down again. They positioned his cage near the living room window that looked out onto the lake. "Nappy," she said, handing him some sunflower seeds and a piece of bread with peanut butter and jelly on it—his favorite food—"you're going to look out at trees and flowers and a few of your feathered friends." Napoleon began squawking at the sound of Aimee's voice.

At three in the morning, exhausted, Williams and Aimee fell into bed. As much as they wanted to make love, they were both too tired, too drained from the day's terrifying events. Instead, they clung to each other under a soft blanket, the full length of their bodies holding onto one another in an embrace that was as spiritual and emotional as it was physical in its totality.

The attack on New York City stunned the Western world. All eyes turned to Washington and waited for a response. In the planning rooms of the Pentagon, in secluded CIA offices in Langley, all available resources were being marshaled to gather and analyze information for President Stanton on a 'round-the-clock basis. At the State Department, a high-level task force remained in constant communication with all the American embassies abroad.

In the basement of the White House, the National Security Council frantically sought ways to maintain some semblance of security in the nation. It was a losing battle.

From Beirut to Jakarta, from Johannesburg to Algiers, from Mexico City to Santiago—throughout the entire Middle East, Asia, Africa, Central and South America—millions poured into the streets in spontaneous demonstrations, rejoicing over the severe blow dealt to American power, prestige and credibility. They proclaimed the end of American dominance and the dawn of a new era. Abu's likeness was everywhere, on huge posters and banners and flags—the Great Lion had struck with his mighty paw and wounded the lofty eagle. The forgotten masses now smelled blood; they sensed their hour was upon them.

And then came the second attack.

Hundreds of feet below New York City lay its jugular vein: Two tunnels that functioned like underground rivers. They delivered two billion gallons of water a day to the city's millions of inhabitants. They were New York's only source of drinkable water. Constructed in 1917, they'd never been inspected; and although a much-needed third line was under construction, it wasn't scheduled for completion until the year 2025.

Two massive explosions ruptured the aging tunnels, abruptly stopping all water coming into Manhattan from the Catskill Mountains. Such a calamity would normally lead to a massive evacuation, but under present conditions, an evacuation was impossible; Manhattan's 1.4 million people were trapped on their twenty-square mile island.

Faucets, toilets and fire hydrants went dry. Fires burned out of control. Human waste rotted in clogged sewers. A sickening stench filled the air, assaulting the senses and assuming its own hellish incarnation.

Two large oil tankers sailed into New York harbor and then took separate routes, one moving up the Hudson, the other the East River. Just north of Manhattan they dropped anchor. The tankers' skeleton crews went quickly to work; they scuttled the vessels, blocking the riverways, and began releasing the largest oil-slick the world had ever known. And then they set it ablaze. The island of Manhattan was surrounded by a moat of fire. Both rivers became raging infernos, belching up a blanket of thick, black smoke. It merged with the city's already flaming buildings to create Hiroshima-like clouds that rained down suffocating, deadly fumes, killing tens of thousands of people. Those who survived would be facing massive outbreaks of diseases that still plagued Third World countries—cholera, dysentery and typhus—but were unheard of anywhere in the United States, let alone New York City. Attempts to escape the doomsday scenario that was unfolding were futile. The devil had been loosed. Death, destruction and anarchy reigned.

"Goddamn it!" President Stanton shouted. Lee Cowles was the only one in the room. "The whole world is looking at this office and we're caught with our dicks in our hands while that sonofabitch hits us again!"

"The Joint Chiefs are working on it, Mr. President," Cowles said trying to pacify Stanton. He'd never seen him so angry, apoplectic really. "Chairman McClennan says it going to take a week to—"

"A week's going to be too late!" The president pointed to the television screens and the images of a city in flames. "Lee, it'll be all over in a week. There'll be nothing but rubble! The streets will be littered with corpses! Jesus, we can't even get drinking water to them. Unless we can put troops in there soon—"

"Sir, restoring order is going to be a 'mission impossible,' " Cowles cautioned. "What's going to happen when American soldiers start shooting their own people?"

"For Chrissakes, Lee, we can't let the city be destroyed." Cowles didn't reply. Stanton stared at him, incredulous. "Is that what you're . . . actually suggesting?"

"It is an option, Mr. President," Cowles said with disturbing coldness.

"Not one I will even consider. Lee, what the hell are you thinking—?"

"That perhaps this is exactly what Sheik Asghar wants." Lee Cowles took a deep breath and grew introspective. He chose his words carefully. "Perhaps he wants America distracted; divert our attention, cause us to start warring on our own people."

"Divert our attention from what?"

"Whatever his master plan is. You and I know it isn't just about this country, or any one particular city—"

"What I know, Lee, is that I'm not going to sit back and watch one and a half million people go berserk and kill each other!"

The intercom buzzed and Cowles answered it. "Send him in."

He knew the president was expecting Arthur Kleinholtz.

The moment the National Security Advisor entered the Oval Office, Stanton said, "Arthur, what have you got for us?"

Kleinholtz looked tired, there were dark circles under his eyes and his forehead was set in a frown that seemed permanently embedded. "Some very troubling developments abroad that may require a prompt U.S. response," he said in his perfect English diction with a hint of an Austrian accent.

"Christ, Arthur, we can't be everywhere at once!" he exploded. "I'm sorry. Go on—"

"Greece and Turkey have put their military forces on alert. The dispute is over oil located on islands between the two countries."

"What else?"

"The Phillippines are on the brink of collapse. Muslim insurgents are poised to capture Manila."

An ironic half-smile crossed Stanton's face. "Good thing we don't have Subic Bay or Clark Air Force Base anymore." Kleinholtz nodded in agreement. "Let's order an immediate evacuation of all American personnel."

"Mr. President, we mustn't destroy our relationship with the Phillippines altogether. They have always been an ally—"

"And with an Islamic government in place, they will be an enemy," Stanton said adamantly. He glared at his national security advisor. Kleinholtz didn't pursue the issue. "Arthur, I hope that there's no worse news—"

Kleinholtz looked at the president for a moment, then, "There is, I'm afraid. And it's much worse. An Iranian submarine fired on a U.S. Navy destroyer—"

"What!?" the president exclaimed. "And I'm just now hearing about it—?"

"Communication problems, Mr. President. Apparently there have been highly unusual solar flares on the sun. They emit huge bursts of electromagnetic energy. It has affected satellite surveillance all over the world."

Stanton nodded, not understanding any of the scientific or astronomical aspects of Kleinholtz's explanation. "Where did they hit us?"

"In the Strait of Hormuz. The Iranian sub fired a torpedo but it missed. We're not sure if it was intended as an attack or a warning. The destroyer held its fire, the naval captain chose not to pursue."

"Have State demand an immediate apology from the Iranian government, and issue a warning that any American vessel fired upon will, henceforth, return fire." He paused. "I was briefed yesterday about troop mobilization along the southern Mediterranean—Morocco, Libya, Algeria—is there an update on that?"

Kleinholtz nodded. "It's escalating—nearly a half million troops, a thousand tanks, personnel carriers, mobile missile launchers from Egypt and the Sudan, and a substantial number of ships—"

"Damn!" the President interrupted. "The Egyptian government has assured me that it was nothing more than a military exercise to promote cooperation between friendly Arab nations. I was under the impression this was being done to ensure greater preparedness in case Iran or Iraq decided to invade another Persian Gulf state. Has the Pentagon changed its mind about these maneuvers?"

"They're seeing a disturbing pattern—"

"Oh?"

"I'm afraid ever since our former allies in the Persian Gulf have started withdrawing their Western bank deposits, the United States has become *persona non grata* in the Middle East. No one is talking to us except Israel. And the Israeli attitude is now one of: 'We told you so.'"

The president gave a disgruntled snort. "How does all this interrelate? The disturbing pattern you mentioned—"

"Ah, yes. We may have found the connection between what happened in New York and Sheik Asghar."

Lee Cowles shot Kleinholtz a look of astonishment. The president's eyes were instantly locked on his security advisor. "Let's hear it," he said between clenched teeth.

"General Muhammed Mubambo," Kleinholtz said, reading from his notes. "Supreme Commander of the Botswanan army and close aide to the Sheik."

"What's he got to do with all this?" the president snapped.

"According to CIA files, information from British Intelligence reveals that General Mubambo was once a man named Gerald Morton. He met Sheik Asghar when they were both inmates at Dartmoor Prison. In fact, they instigated prison riots that eventually got them both deported. Asghar went on his now-famous trek through the Third World and Mubambo became a military hero in southern Africa. He's been one of the primary orchestrators of those joint exercises in northern Africa. And he was with Asghar when he came to the States. Under a false passport, you can be sure. He was with him here in Washington and New York—"

"Goddamn it! We've got the sonofabitch!" Stanton said, gesturing with his fist. He turned to Cowles. "Call a press conference immediately. Get all the information you can on his imprisonment. We're going to debunk the myth of Sheik Asghar and show him for the monster he really is. Give the American people an enemy with a face and they'll demand his head!"

Kleinholtz and Cowles nodded, but the national security advisor looked far less confident than the President. "As I said, this disturbing pattern I mentioned has led me to only one conclusion." The president looked quizzically at Kleinholtz. "It is something you yourself have inferred, Mr. President. Asghar, in all probability, intends to invade Europe."

Stanton turned dead serious and nodded in agreement. "Is this the consensus of the National Security Council?"

"Yes, Mr. President."

"Let's go downstairs," was all Stanton said as he hurried to the Oval Office door. Kleinholtz and Cowles followed close behind him.

A uniformed officer barked "Ten hut!" as the president entered the NSC chamber in the basement of the White House. Council members and aides were in the large room, as well as Stanton's entire cabinet, along with the Director of the CIA, Elliot Wycroft, a man whom the president had never liked and tried once, unsuccessfully, to get fired, and the Secretary of Defense, Kyle Anderson, a man Stanton did like, but whom he thought was a bit too much of a hawk. In private, to his cronies, Stanton often referred to Anderson as "trigger happy." Even the Chairman of the Joint Chiefs was far more inclined to use negotiation as a weapon of choice, often to the frustration and exasperation of the Secretary of Defense. But obviously, Anderson was just what the president needed right now—someone who would declare an all-out war on Sheik Abu 'Ali Asghar.

"If Ashgar planned to invade Europe," Stanton said to the group now assembled around the large conference table for the meeting they had known for several days was inevitable, "what countries would he attack first?"

General McClellan looked thoughtfully at the president. "That is difficult to say. But if *I* were planning such an invasion, I'd go through Eastern Europe, the continent's soft underbelly."

"The same route Hitler took," said Kyle Anderson, making no attempt to conceal his anger. "And it didn't take him very long at all, did it?" he asked rhetorically.

The Chairman of the Joint Chiefs continued. "Another invasion point could be through the Strait of Gibraltar into Spain. That's how the Arabs swept into Europe a thousand years ago. He also has the manpower and the fire power to launch missile attacks on Italy, France and England."

"And how the hell did he get so powerful right under our noses and we didn't see it coming?"

"Many people asked that question about Hitler," Arthur Kleinholtz volunteered almost matter-of-factly.

"Mr. President," Elliot Wycroft interjected, his thick dark moustache and bald head adding to his already sinister look, "Our informed sources now agree that our buddy, Asghar—" he deliberately emphasized the first two letters of the name so that it sounded like Ass-ghar, "went on much more than a rock star tour of the Third World. Everywhere he went, he formed a complex chain of command, drawing from each country's military echelon; then his boy Mubambo handpicked the generals, but the Sheik masterminded the whole operation. The economic and military foundation for this alliance is the whole goddamn fucking Arab world." Wycroft's public profanity was always irritating to Stanton, but today he couldn't have cared less. Everyone ignored it. "Plus a lot of black gold is going into this one," he said, referring to Arab oil resources.

"Let's face it," Secretary Anderson reasoned, "he's done what no other Arab leader has ever done: Established a Pan-Arab world, and he's going to use it to take over the rest of the world." Wycroft nodded in agreement.

"Mr. President," Kleinholtz said, "there is something of great historical significance here which we must not overlook." Kleinholtz spoke like the Harvard University professor he once was. All eyes around the table turned to him. "Centuries of anger and resentment have been building among the Arab nations—they were once an enlightened civilization back when the Western world was still locked in the Dark Ages. Then political and economic stagnation caused the Arab empire to disintegrate; eventually the world came to look upon them as the backward, poor underclass of the planet. But now, in this century, they have begun, shall we say, their renaissance, due mainly to the discovery of oil. They are awakening from a long sleep. And there are over a billion Muslims who think Sheik Asghar will restore justice to the world. As well as the political power of Islam, for you must remember, first and foremost, their allegiance is to Allah. We're not up against one man, Mr. President; we are up against a much greater force—"

The president interrupted. "I'm sure you're right, Arthur. But don't you agree that if we bring down Asghar, we are at least stopping the great force in its tracks? You've said it yourself, he's the divine leader—"

"The Mahdi, yes," Kleinholtz responded.

The president nodded. "Right. And if we render him powerless, we create a void in this Arab movement's leadership—an unfillable void—which could just give us the window of opportunity we need to mount a counter offensive that will stop his bloody march around the globe!"

There were nods and verbal assents from everyone around the conference table. But General McClellan looked skeptical and extremely concerned. "What is it, Hank?" the president asked.

"A counter-offensive move is less possible than a defensive one. Asghar has amassed a formidable arsenal of men and machinery—"

"I know that, Hank. We have to believe that we can match him and overpower him. For Chrissakes, we are the world's preeminent superpower!" Stanton paused and looked at the men who, with him, were about to decide the fate of the world. His gaze came to rest on Secretary Anderson. "Put our military forces on worldwide alert. I want contingency plans. What about the Russians? And the Chinese? Where will they likely come down in all of this?" The Secretary of Defense nodded emphatically and made copious notes on the yellow legal pad in front of him. Stanton turned to his CIA director. "Elliot, step up intelligence gathering. We need a plan to take Asghar out, don't you agree?"

"Absolutely, Mr. President." Wycroft replied enthusiastically; the president was saying exactly what he wanted to hear.

"Only no ludicrous suggestions or aborted attempts like we did with Saddam and Kadafi, not to mention Castro for over twenty years," Stanton said with a warning glance at Wycroft.

The CIA director cleared his throat. "With all due respect, Mr. President, none of those were on my watch, sir."

Stanton nodded. "Sorry, Elliot. I didn't mean to offend you." But that's just what he meant to do.

There was a moment of embarrassed silence at the table. "There's one more thing—" the president said, this time addressing everyone. "What's the nuclear scenario in all of this?"

Kleinholtz slowly closed his eyes. McClellan stared grimly. Others looked down at their notepads. Wycroft reached for his glass of water. Anderson was fiercely tight-lipped.

Stanton's tone was solemn and certain as he searched the faces around the table. "Asghar must have one, don't you think?" It was a statement, not a question.

CHAPTER 45

Minutes after the historic White House meeting in the security council chambers, President Robert Stanton issued an order for military troops to be on the streets of New York City within twenty-four hours. "Send in the 82nd Airborne, the Rangers, the Green Berets, the whole damn Marine Corps, if you have to, but I want New York back!" he demanded of General McClellan.

The following morning, under cover of darkness, the unprecedented edict was carried out. A mechanized battalion of infantrymen was dispatched to retake Manhattan behind Abrams M-1 battle tanks. Apache attack helicopters circled overhead. To the relief and surprise of the military, there was little or no resistance as they crossed the George Washington Bridge; the enemy had apparently abandoned their positions. The city, however, was in state of total ruin, and it took the combined armed forces just to maintain law and order.

The rest of the country was now going the way of New York City. Carefully orchestrated attacks were taking place from Houston to Chicago to Los Angeles. Power plants were being blown up, freeway overpasses demolished, aqueducts destroyed, reservoirs contaminated. Oil refineries were set ablaze in Los Angeles, Houston and New Orleans, causing massive explosions that reverberated across the cities and closed their ports.

The southern tip of the L.A. basin was hardest hit. Oil refineries from El Segundo to Long Beach were blown up by terrorist bombs that had been planted next to the two tall cylindrical tanks that normally mixed oxygen and fuel through a highly controlled refining process which turned it into gasoline. The bombs that set off the explosions were, according to several FBI and local police reports, undoubtedly brought into the refineries by any one of the dozen independent contractors who regularly did work for the plants.

The spontaneous fires that the explosions caused—even at the area's gas stations—erupted with alarming speed; there were over a thousand separate blasts. Shock waves from the explosions created a series of sonic booms, several of which collided with such force and intensity that they knocked commercial jet planes out of the sky and left most people on the ground believing that a nuclear bomb had been detonated. All of southern California's fire departments were no match for the devastation that was being wreaked upon the state. Tens of thousands died as the deadly hydrofluoric acid from the exploding refineries spread out for miles, turning everywhere it touched into American Bhopals.

Mortar attacks on the country's major airports destroyed the runways and shut down Chicago, New York, Denver, Atlanta and Los Angeles; all air traffic had to be aborted. In San Francisco, the Golden Gate and Oakland bridges were simultaneously exploded. Twisted bits of mangled steel and loose cable sent cars nose-diving into the freezing waters of the once beautiful Bay. Huge chunks of concrete went flying in every direction, like a giant meteor shower, raining down on the hapless inhabitants who tried in vain to survive this latest catastrophe.

The following day, a worldwide trinity of devastating earthquakes struck. The first two were in Tokyo and Rome, nearly leveling both cities. The third convulsive jolt occurred in the most unexpected place: The heartland of America. An 8.2 on the Richter scale had its epicenter in Missouri and radiated out as far east as Virginia, west through Nebraska, south to Louisiana and north to Minnesota. It caused the Mississippi River to flow backwards in some places and make new tributaries in others, just as it had once done in 1811. Roads were ripped apart, railroad tracks burst at their seams, skyscrapers swayed and collapsed in Chicago, St. Louis and Kansas City. Ruptured gas lines set off countless fires. Tens of thousands of homes were reduced to ash and rubble, the dead and dying lay buried or strewn about. Fires raged out of control, creating—in several cities—the most dreaded of all incendiary horrors: Firestorms. This 'hurricane' of fire was caused by the intensity of heat and the magnitude of the area that was ablaze. The fire, spurred by the immense drafts of rising hot air, generated its own prodigious wind currents with hurricane-force velocity. In no time at all, everything in its path was incinerated.

Beneath the vast mushroom clouds that covered the sky and turned day into endless night, hundreds of thousands of people became wandering, wounded refugees. While cities burned, farmlands were destroyed by floods and earthquakes. Panic and hysteria broke out, along with virulent, contagious diseases—all of it spreading across the country like the tentacles of some cosmic beast that could only have been created in the mind of a madman. Chaos and violence permeated every city, suburb and town. Vigilante groups sprang up overnight. Police were open targets. National Guardsmen fired into mobs of rampaging looters, desperate to maintain some measure of control. But there was little anyone could do. People had gone mad. The whole world, it seemed, had gone stark raving mad. Those who sought refuge in places of worship were convinced the Day of Judgment had arrived, as the frightened clergy cried, "The Antichrist is loose and the devil is among us!" Most everyone agreed it was the beginning of the end.

In the days that followed, long dormant volcanoes, with amazing synchronicity, vomited up their mud and glowing lava in Bolivia, Peru, Indonesia, New Zealand, in Iceland and Italy. Sulfuric acid, sulfur dioxide and dangerous levels of carbon monoxide, along with volcanic ash and dust, formed a wind-borne shroud that penetrated the upper atmosphere. Global temperatures fell, dropping to near freezing at the Equator. Violent thunderstorms—producing baseball-size hailstones—occurred in desert regions where they had never been before, while in places where rainfall was traditionally heavy, droughts and dust storms prevailed. Blizzards and tornadoes reached every corner of the globe. Cyclones caused massive tidal waves which inundated island nations and, in many instances, completely obliterated them.

The daily bombardment of planetary disasters had left many of the world's leaders, whether president, prime minister, monarch or military dictator, in a state of fear and bewilderment, coupled with a feeling of helplessness and an inability to cope with the overwhelming events. In Washington, a pale and pessimistic Bob Stanton hovered on the brink of nervous exhaustion. He hadn't slept in a week; every time he closed his eyes, images of burning cities and a collapsing civilization tormented him. There was no respite from the unfolding nightmare. Stanton's administration and the directors of the various agencies and bureaucracies within the government were also concerned about another aspect of the president's behavior: The man who had always been so outgoing and accessible, was now becoming increasingly isolated. Only his closest aides and cronies were able to talk to him these days. Lee Cowles was one of them.

"Mr. President," the Chief of Staff said upon entering the Oval Office and closing the door, "we've just received word that Sheik Asghar has signed a non-aggression pact with the Russians and the Chinese." Cowles sat on a chair opposite the President's dark walnut desk and placed a Top Secret file folder in front of Stanton.

"In whose name?" the president said, incredulous. "How can he sign treaties with anyone? He doesn't even have a fucking country!"

"Right now he has something more powerful, sir." Stanton looked up at Cowles. It pained the Chief of Staff to see the president's condition. There were pouchy bags under his bloodshot eyes, his hair had turned gray almost overnight, he needed a shave.

"And what is that?" the president asked with intense curiosity.

"A League of Allied Nations, over which he is the sovereign leader. They have placed their combined armies under his command. He has appointed a panel of ministers."

"Who the hell are the members of this League?"

"Arab nations mostly, but also Iran and Iraq, Pakistan, India, Turkey and South Africa."

"And I suppose General Mubambo is his Chairman of the Joint Chiefs of Staff, right?"

"Exactly."

Stanton groaned. For a moment his gaze wandered off. He was remembering another, happier time, before the decline and fall had begun. He had grown up believing in the American ideal and the promise that it held. He remembered the pride of his Irish immigrant grandparents when they became American citizens, giving their allegiance to what his grandmother called, "the best country on earth." Stanton recalled his love of American history, of what he considered the visionary wisdom of the founding fathers, the simple genius of the words they wrote in the Constitution, encompassing all that is just and fair, ennobling and enlightened. How, in God's name, thought Stanton, could it all have come to this? When did it begin to unravel? What were the warning signs, if any? Could some one person have prevented what was now happening? Or were we all, in one way or another, responsible?

". . . total anarchy is a very real and present danger to the nation," Cowles was saying. His words brought Stanton out of his reverie. "The Chairman of the Joint Chiefs is urging you to suspend the Constitution, declare martial law, and seize key sectors of industry. If Asghar invades Europe, we will need to act quickly. There will be no time for congressional debate over a declaration of war—"

Stanton stared out at the Rose Garden and the snow that blanketed the rose bushes and cherry blossom trees. He loved the garden, he loved the elegant premises that were home to him and his family. And he could not deny that the power and prestige the presidency afforded him was a potent aphrodisiac. But above all, and often in very sentimental ways, Stanton had a deep and abiding love for his country. He was, after all, the personification of the American dream come true.

And now, someone had killed that dream.

"Lee, do you realize what you're asking? That I declare a police state—a military dictatorship!"

"Not me, Mr. President. The Joint Chiefs. They want you to declare a state of national emergency for security reasons." Cowles paused. "If you don't, Mr. President, they will."

"How? Are they going to mount a *coup d'etat?!*"

Cowles nodded. "In effect, yes. They'll declare you unfit to lead and remove you from office."

"Can I stop it?"

"I'm afraid not, Mr. President. It would only cause further chaos, even a civil war. The country would be leaderless and Sheik Asghar would have no opposition—"

"And the Congress?"

"Most members have returned home. There would not be enough support."

Stanton got up from his desk and sighed. He glanced over at the painting of George Washington. "It began with him and ends with me," he said.

"If you issue the order, you will at least remain the head of state." He paused. "When the time comes, you can restore the republic."

"If there is anything left to restore," he said in voice that conveyed an ineffable sadness. He looked at Cowles. "Lee, do you ever long for our halcyon days—?"

"You mean when we were Yalies?" Cowles asked. Stanton nodded.

"And when you were a freshman senator and I ran your first campaign?" Cowles again asked rhetorically. Stanton smiled wanly. Cowles smiled back. "All the time, sir, all the time."

Stanton took a deep breath and straightened his back, as if shucking some invisible restraint. He sat down at his desk, and for the first time in days, he suddenly looked focused and in control. His voice became strong and steady. "Issue the order. I'll inform the nation. Set up a live telecast from this office. I want the people to hear it from their president."

Herschel Strunk's cabin was still a safe haven for Williams, Aimee and Matthew. They had stocked the place with kerosene lamps and candles in case of a power shortage. A gas-powered generator on the property had several spare drums of gasoline sitting next to it. Williams had placed floodlights outside the house. He built a chicken coop and stocked it so that they would have fresh eggs, and chickens if necessary. At the town store he bought a good supply of wheat, oats and cornmeal. Aimee dried the beef and stored it. She canned fruits and vegetables the way her mother and grandmother had taught her when she was growing up in Iowa.

But Williams knew that time was short. He chopped firewood and stacked it outside the cabin. Aimee boarded up the windows. The ash cloud made television and radio transmission unreliable, but not impossible. Scientists were now describing the highly unusual solar activity that continued to cause havoc with satellite transmissions. They wondered if the huge sun spots and solar flares were connected to the earthquakes and volcanic eruptions. And they asked: Was the mysterious bright light in the night sky somehow related? No one seemed to know, but astronomers agreed that it was getting larger and brighter.

Williams was often glued to Strunk's short-wave radio since it was the most dependable source of information. He was becoming obsessed with needing to know what was going on in the world. Aimee would tear him away when it was time for bed, but he frequently got up in the middle of the night, put on the headphones and listened to the horrifying tales of civilizations crumbling all over the globe.

The night that Williams heard the president's speech, he came away from the radio and went into the bedroom where Aimee was nursing a chubby and contented Matthew. She looked up at him and sensed his distress. "What's wrong?" she asked.

"The president has suspended the Constitution. He's declared martial law. He's suspended the goddamn Bill of Rights."

"Oh God, no."

"This means the government can now arrest anyone, anytime, for any goddamn reason it wants! And there will be no trials. He's turned the country into a military dictatorship."

"But it must be for national security reasons—"

"So he says. But maybe he's gone off the deep end like almost everyone else." Williams sat beside Aimee on the wicker settee and looked at her and his beautiful son. They were more precious to him than his own life. Yet at the moment, he felt powerless, afraid that he might not live up to his promise of keeping them safe from harm. He thought of Abu and a conversation they had had around a campfire in Uganda, not so very long ago.

"Maybe we were given a gift," he said to Aimee, "and we squandered it. We forgot that we were no different or better than anyone else on earth. Just luckier perhaps."

"Are we in danger here?" Aimee asked.

"No," Williams said reassuringly. Not yet, he thought.

CHAPTER 46

Operation Reclaim was the official name the Pentagon had given to its mobilization of the U.S. armed forces. In every major city across the country, massive detention facilities were hastily erected, at first to accommodate the legions of looters, rioters and vigilantes that were arrested in the sweeps, but later to detain the countless people arrested for a myriad of reasons, or for no reason at all, other than that they were merely in the way. The president was given daily briefings on the progress, but the Joint Chiefs made the decisions.

A second plan was set in motion, this one dubbed Operation Lionheart. It was created as the American response to an anticipated invasion by the League of Allied Nations.

General McClellan sat in Bob Stanton's office and brought the president up to date. "Italy has just signed a non-aggression treaty with Asghar, and one of his apparent conditions was the immediate removal of all U.S. and NATO forces. In exchange, he's pledged over a billion in emergency aid to stabilize their economy. Unfortunately, he has, in effect, bought Italy and in so doing, has neutralized our southern flank."

Stanton nodded in grim understanding. "What's the status of Lionheart?"

"We're still not up and running yet—not in a position to launch a counter-offensive. Operation Reclaim has been a priority—there simply aren't enough resources for both. Reclaim must repair and rebuild our ports, bridges, power plants, all our communication systems, our infrastructures. And, there are significant pockets of resistance."

Stanton seemed genuinely surprised. "Hank, are you telling me there are still people out there in armed opposition to our own troops?"

"Yes, Mr. President."

"Asghar's forces?"

"In part. But there's a considerable number of our citizens who've formed their own militias. And they're well-armed."

"Oh, I'm sure they are." He thought of the years of congressional hearings and watered-down legislation he was forced to agree to in his attempts to reign in the national gun lobby. How desperately he had wanted to pass anti-gun laws that once and for all prevented the runaway sales of firearms. At least he had managed to put some bans on certain assault weapons. But it wasn't enough. Not nearly enough.

"We're also having major glitches in our Pentagon computer systems."

"What sort of glitches?"

"Malfunctions, lost data, crashes. Our systems analysts believe it's a virus. Unfortunately, it's immune to all our anti-virus programs. And it mutates as it moves through the system. It's damned sophisticated."

"Has it gotten into our weapons' systems?"

"We're checking on that right now. What we do know is that foreign intelligence operations are reporting similar problems. It cannot be a coincidence. This must be a prelude to an invasion."

"And the first phase is to undermine the West's technological superiority," Stanton speculated.

"Looks that way," the General conceded.

The phone buzzed and Stanton grabbed it. He listened in somber silence for a minute, then said, "Thank you, Kyle. I'll relay this to General McClellan; he's here with me now."

Stanton stared at the Chairman of the Joint Chiefs. "Asghar's forces have moved into Greece and Bulgaria. He's launched an amphibious and air attack on the southern coast of Spain, across the Strait of Gibraltar. Which carrier do we have in the Mediterranean?"

"The *U.S.S. Kitty Hawk*, Mr. President. But as you know, I've tried to keep the Sixth Fleet clear of—"

"Hank, I'm ordering you to put our nuclear forces on alert. And no matter what limited manpower we have, we must launch a counterattack. Don't you see—? Asghar's assuming we won't do anything because he's devastated us so completely at home. He wants a clean sweep through Europe. And we're all that's preventing him from achieving it! If we can just slow him up long enough for our allies to regroup and launch a combined offensive, we've accomplished a small victory.

Can't you see the importance of just one setback for Asghar? We've got to make the world see that he is not omnipotent!"

General McClellan couldn't help but agree. From a purely military standpoint he knew that Stanton made great sense. "I will do whatever is possible, Mr. President," the Chairman said.

Stanton nodded. "Thank you." He paused. "Hank—?"

"Yes, sir?"

"Do you believe in God?"

"Yes, I do."

"So do I . . . very much." Stanton sighed deeply. "I hope He hasn't forsaken us."

It was two in the morning when Williams heard something outside the cabin. First a rustling sound, then a disturbance by the chicken coop, followed by footsteps near the front of the cabin. Williams looked over at Aimee, asleep beside him in the bed. He quickly slipped out from under the comforter, and pulled his shotgun out from under the bed.

Aimee woke up. "Ben, what is it—?"

He put his finger up to his lips. Williams went to the front door, listening. There was no sound. His hands nervously readjusted their grip on the shotgun. Aimee came into the room, holding Matthew in her arms. He silently motioned to her to get back into the bedroom.

There were more footsteps. Williams squatted down, aiming the shotgun at the door. The only light in the room came from the fireplace where embers continued to burn from a fire they had lit earlier that night.

It was quiet again. Williams readied himself. There was a knock on the door. He didn't move. Another knock. He stood and stepped slowly toward the door, the shotgun held tightly across his torso. He listened. There was another knock. "Yeah," he called out, "what d'ya want?"

"Some food, man," a male voice called back. "We're hungry and cold."

"How many of you are there?" Williams asked suspiciously.

"Three," the man answered.

"Are you armed?" Williams asked.

There was a pause. "Yes," the man answered.

"So am I," Williams said. "So leave 'em outside. If there's any trouble, I'll kill you. Understand?"

"Understood," the man answered.

Williams carefully unlatched the door and stepped back into a shadow. "Open it," he said, "slowly. Keep your hands where I can see them."

The door opened and three hooded figures in heavy parkas walked in. The last one in closed the door, then the three stood motionless, their hands in the air. Williams stepped out of the shadow. "Who are you?" he asked.

The first man slowly moved his hand toward his head. "May I?" he said, indicated he wanted to remove his hood. Williams nodded. The other two did the same. Williams was surprised to see the smallest of the three was a woman, in her thirties, and rather pretty. The two other men were also about the same age as the woman, both of them had a week's growth of beard. One of them said, "My name's Frank Dryer, this is Gerry Gellman and Maria Rodriguez." They nodded toward Williams. He nodded back but chose not to introduce himself. He wasn't sure he could trust them.

"Look," Frank Dryer said, "we're not renegades, if that's what you think." He was referring to the people who roamed the cities and countryside, looting and killing for food or whatever they could lay their hands on.

"And we're not members of Asghar's forces," Maria said. The mention of Abu's name startled Williams. At that moment Aimee came into the room.

"Who are they?" she asked Williams, but before he could respond, Gerry Gellman spoke up.

"We're part of a people's militia. There aren't many of us just yet. We're heading south to join up with another militia group. Ours was destroyed in a firefight with government troops. We're the only three who made it out."

Williams bristled at the word "militia." It brought back the horrible memory of Herschel Strunk's death at the hands of the right-wing group that took responsibility for blowing up the *New York Times* building, convinced that Abu was the Antichrist. Maria noticed Williams' look of contempt. "Sir, we're trying to help people," she said; "we're not terrorists. My husband was arrested by the army and I don't even know where he is now.

"What do you do?" Williams asked her.

"I'm a data processor. Was."

Frank smiled slightly. "I'm a structural engineer."

"I owned a gas station, until it blew up," Gerry said.

Aimee looked sympathetically at the threesome. She sensed they were decent people, and harmless. "I'll get you all some sandwiches, and some tea, will that be okay?"

Maria looked at her gratefully. "That'd be wonderful." Aimee went into the kitchen while Williams finally started to relax. He put his shotgun down.

"Why did they arrest your husband?" he asked Maria.

"After Stanton declared martial law, Carlos joined in a protest and got beaten with a rifle butt. The army just took him away. You know they turned all the baseball and football stadiums into detention centers. He could've been taken to any one of them." She paused. "I don't even know if he's alive," she said with more anger in her voice than heartbreak.

"The army's out of control," Gerry said. "They're shooting and arresting for no reason. They're doing summary executions, they're making war on their own people! That's why our group formed. We're gonna take back this country."

Aimee came into the living room with a tray of hastily-made sandwiches and hot tea. The three hungry guests immediately pounced on the food.

"God, this is good," Frank said, his mouth full of a bologna sandwich. "We haven't eaten in a day and a half."

"I'm sorry this has happened to you," Williams said. "Guess we've been pretty lucky." Aimee nodded in silent agreement as she poured three mugs of tea. "By the way," Williams said, reaching out to shake each of their hands, "my name's Bennett Williams, and this is Aimee—"

"Bennett Williams—?!" Gerry Gellman said, utterly surprised.

"Yeah . . ."

"You wrote about him! You won the damn Pulitzer Prize—"

"'fraid so." Williams wished they didn't know who he was.

"I heard you were doing a book about Asghar," Gellman said, clearly impressed by his host.

"Yes . . . yes, I am," Williams said slowly.

"Mr. Williams—" Maria said.

"Call me, Ben, please."

"Ben," she continued, "do you know about Operation Lionheart?" Williams shook his head. "It's the government's plan to stop Asghar's invasion of Europe."

"They'd better hurry," Frank said. "He moves fast, and he's not inclined to take prisoners."

"They can't stop him," Williams said ominously. "It's too late."

"Don't say that," Maria cried out. "He can't destroy the whole world. He's got to be stopped!"

"Maybe Ben here knows something about Asghar that we don't," Gerry said to Maria, but stared at Williams.

Williams shook his head. "No, not really. Just that it's no longer *about* Asghar anymore."

"Who is it about?" Frank asked.

"All of us," Williams said enigmatically. Then he turned silent, unwilling to pursue any further explanation.

Frank, Maria and Gerry finished eating. Aimee had put a few logs on the fire and the room glowed with renewed warmth.

"Look, if you need a place to stay for the night, you can use these couches," Aimee offered. "Maybe put a couple of pillows on the rug—"

"No," Frank said, getting up. "We've imposed on your hospitality enough—" Aimee started to protest but Frank interjected, "We really need to get going. We'll be able to hitch a ride on the main highway."

"Are you sure?" Williams said with genuine concern.

"We'll be fine," Gerry reassured him.

As the three put their parkas on, Aimee filled a paper bag with a few canned goods, a loaf of bread and some dried beef, then handed it to Gerry. They thanked Aimee for the food, said goodbye and walked to the front door. As they opened the door and went out, Maria turned back to Williams. Her eyes burned with a fierce conviction. "You're wrong, Ben. Asghar *will* be stopped. You'll see."

Williams said nothing but watched as the three went down the front porch steps, walked along the path he had floodlit, and off onto the road that was about a half mile from the highway. He watched until they disappeared from view. He knew they would have no trouble finding their way to the main highway, for despite the volcanic shroud that blocked the heavens, the stars had never shone brighter.

CHAPTER 47

The skies above southern Europe swarmed with Abu's fighters and bombers. Spain's navy, with its small fleet of World War II vintage destroyers and frigates, was quickly decimated when Mirage jets out of Morocco and Algeria fired Exocet missiles.

In the Pyrenees of northern Spain and southern France, Basque separatists—who had trained long and hard in Algeria and were equipped with state-of-the-art weaponry—had joined with Abu's forces to launch a full-scale offensive from the north. What remained of Spain's two-hundred-thousand-man army and its land-based defenses was no match for Abu's massive ground troops and air attacks. In rapid succession, the great cities of Spain—Madrid, Toledo, Seville, Granada, Barcelona—all fell under the crushing blow of Abu's armies.

Portugal, with its limited military resources, offered little resistance, surrendering quickly in hopes of avoiding total annihilation.

By capturing the island of Majorca, Abu's troops gained easy access to northern Spain and the French Riviera. The Basques launched a second front from their base in the southeast. Cadres of Muslim militants from France's enormous immigrant population had been organized and trained by General Mubambo. Selectively recruited, they now joined under a single command with local terrorist groups. The result was underground attacks on Paris, Lyon, Bordeaux, Le Havre, Dijon, Nice and Marseilles. Power plants and telephone systems were sabotaged. The French infrastructure was quickly crippled. France's defense computers started to crash and their missiles began missing all their intended targets. Outnumbered three to one, French fighter planes were blown from the sky.

The large Arab and African populations of France's southern cities held no allegiance to the country they had once emigrated to; they welcomed the invading armies as heroes and liberators. In the streets, thousands cheered Abu's convoys of tanks and troops.

Greece succumbed soon after France, but not before bloody combat had destroyed a third of its people. When Bulgaria's desperate cries for help went unanswered, the country surrendered as ground troops, tanks and artillery poured from Turkey through Europe's back door. Romania, Hungary, and the Czech Republic soon fell like dominoes as Abu's relentless march continued.

Italy, which had allowed Abu into the tent, soon realized its mistake. Sicily, and most of southern Italy, came under heavy air attack. American naval ships stationed there had long since fled to open sea. Once Italy had signed its non-aggression pact with Abu, the U.S. Sixth Fleet abandoned its headquarters in Naples. In the north, American airfields were deserted and now became bases for Abu's advancing forces.

When the League of Allied Nations' tanks moved into Rome, they encircled the ancient city and unleashed missile attacks, artillery and tank fire. The Pope, having fled the Vatican, issued futile pleas for peace as the Sistine Chapel became rubble.

With the entire Mediterranean a churning cauldron of armed conflict and destruction, Operation Lionheart finally went forward. Troops were airlifted in commercial jetliners commandeered by the military. Ships carried tanks, weapons, food and medical supplies across the Atlantic. Fighter bombers, AWACS, cargo planes and air refuellers were redeployed to the European continent. The U.S. Second Fleet joined with British, Dutch, Norwegian, French and German navies outside the Strait of Gibraltar. A joint U.S.-European command hammered out the final plans for a counteroffensive.

The U.S. carrier *Kitty Hawk* stayed close to the Israeli coast. Like drones protecting their queen, the remainder of the U.S. Sixth Fleet surrounded the carrier as a heavy canopy of U.S. and Israeli fighter jets kept the dogs of war at bay. There was no way in or out of the Mediterranean; Abu had sealed off the Suez Canal and the Strait of Gibraltar. The U.S. Sixth Fleet was trapped. Everyone wondered: When would America step into the fray?

But Abu wouldn't allow the United States to choose the opportune moment. The timetable was all his.

When the U.S. Seventh Fleet, stationed in the Pacific to safeguard American interests in Japan and South Korea, set sail to rendezvous with European naval forces in the Indian Ocean, Abu's military might lay in wait. An armada of over fifty frigates and destroyers from the combined navies of India, Indonesia and Malaysia had their Exocet, Sea Killer and Harpoon missiles ready. As the Seventh Fleet passed into the South China Sea, its multi-billion dollar Aegis defense system gave confusing and contradictory information; electronic countermeasures failed and the defensive missiles never hit their targets. In less than fifteen minutes, almost the entire U.S. Seventh Fleet was lost or destroyed.

Abu's strategy worked with the precision of a Swiss timepiece. The demise of the Seventh Fleet left 40,000 American troops in South Korea without support or protection. It allowed North Korea to send its one-million-man army to recapture South Korea, then to launch its invasion of Japan. The U.S. Third Fleet was dispatched from Hawaii to aid in the defense of Japan.

At the same time, in the Mediterranean, seven squadrons of Russian-made MiGS and French-made Mirage fighters zeroed in on the *U.S.S. Kitty Hawk*. The early-warning radar systems didn't pick them up. The Aegis-equipped cruisers couldn't distinguish friend or foe. Onboard computers fed false data to the Tactical Action Officer—who was on the command ship, *U.S.S. Belnap*—causing him to instruct his F-14s to "Splash the sonsabitches!" Within minutes, the voices of panicked pilots radioed back their horror and confusion. "Christ! We're shooting down our own aircraft!" shouted one pilot. And then there was only static.

The attackers had slipped through the net. Exocet and Maverick missiles from Abu's navy skimmed across the surface of the sea at near supersonic speed. Electronic countermeasures and jamming signals on the U.S. warships had little effect. Anti-missile Phalanx systems on the *Kitty Hawk* and her escorts began firing 3,000 rounds of depleted uranium per minute at the incoming destruction. While several missiles were destroyed, enough of them had hit their mark; the *Kitty Hawk* was mortally wounded. Explosions ripped across her flight deck. A frigate, two cruisers and two destroyers, along with the *U.S.S. Kitty Hawk* were sent to the bottom of the Mediterranean with all hands on board.

Incoming Harpoons and ASM-1s continued to bombard the refuellers and ammunition ships, exploding them like gigantic fireballs. Several more destroyers and frigates were demolished. On the *Belnap*, the Tactical Officer looked at one of his aides and said simply,

"May God have mercy on us." In less than thirty-five minutes, the U.S. Sixth Fleet was destroyed.

It was three in the morning when President Stanton was finally able to reach the Russian president, Vladimir Borovsky, by telephone. Stanton did not like his Russian counterpart. He was an obstinate man, unwilling to admit that the problems his country faced were real, let alone a prelude to economic disaster. He was also somewhat vulgar and obstreperous. And he drank too much vodka. He had made a public display of it once too often which caused great embarrassment among his ministers and aides. It had even been the subject of parliamentary discussion. Those closest to him begged him to enter a treatment center, but Borovsky had laughed in their faces.

After a brief and superficial exchange of amenities, Stanton asked Borovsky, "If Europe falls, Mr. President, do you honestly think Asghar won't invade Russia?" Stanton waited impatiently while the interpreter translated. "There isn't time to wait and see!" The president would not hide his irritation. "Your non-aggression pact isn't worth the paper it's written on. Look at Italy! President Borovsky, if Russia enters the war right now, we can turn him back," Stanton pleaded. "If we wait, he'll only gain strength."

There was a pause. "We need time, President Stanton," the Russian bear, whose benign looks masked a fierce temper, said through his translator. "We must ready our forces."

"There isn't time! I've met Sheik Asghar—he'll accomplish what he sets out to do faster than you can possibly imagine. We'll be over there to help, but it takes four days for our ships to cross the Atlantic. You are already there."

"It is ironic, is it not?" Borovsky said, "that when the Soviet Union was under attack by Hitler, and we pleaded for immediate help from Britain and America, we were told to wait, and we did, while our cities were bombed and millions died."

"That was a very long time ago, President Borovsky. It has no bearing on the present situation."

"Perhaps. But the Russian people have a memory like the elephant.

Do you know there are many Russians who still believe that America and Britain simply *wanted* Hitler to further weaken the Soviet Union."

"That wasn't true then, and it's not true now."

"And when the Russian people asked to become part of NATO, America and its allies turned us away like poor relatives." Borovsky whined on as if not fully aware of the enormous and imminent danger that Stanton was trying to prevent. "Now you want us to do your fighting and then you can step in for the kill—"

Stanton was exasperated. His voice turned hard and demanding. "Mr. President, I must know: Will Russia attack?"

"Nyet," Borovsky said flatly. Stanton hung up.

"What did he say?" Lee Cowles asked. He'd been standing nervously next to the president's desk during the conversation.

"Nyet, he said *'nyet.'* That damn fat fool wants to wait!"

"Wait for what?!" Cowles was dumbfounded.

"It's the Russian version of payback. I think they want to see just how far Asghar can go."

"But he must know that the Chinese are amassing troops on their borders—they're going to be brought in eventually."

"Not unless Asghar attacks them, and he won't make the same mistake as Hitler or Napoleon did. If it appears that the West is winning, then the Russians will jump in and claim victory. If it looks like we're going to lose, they'll wait for Asghar to dare an invasion, then let the Russian winter destroy them. And as for the Chinese—they think they're destined to rule the planet anyway."

"Bob, he can't be crazy enough to take on over a *billion* people."

"Wanna bet? He will—not because he's insane but because it's logical. Don't you see? It's got to be part of his plan. The Chinese could never be allowed to exist in Asghar's vision of the future. He'd have to share half the world and he knows that would never work." Stanton paused reflectively. "Lee, I underestimated him when we met. He's not going to stop until the entire world is his. And I shudder to think what kind of a world it will be, without this country, without Europe . . ."

"Jesus Christ . . ." Cowles said slowly as he sat down on the sofa, leaned forward and put his head in his heads. The president watched his longtime friend for a moment, then turned away. When he had won his landslide presidential victory, the country was ready for a young, vigorous, hardworking leader. He'd run on a platform of change—it didn't matter that generations of complacency and greed had molded the system into an intractable foe of change. He was convinced he would succeed where so many had failed.

The honeymoon was brief. Public impatience and media intolerance no longer allowed for on-the-job-training. The microscopic scrutiny—which even a saint could not have withstood—exploited Stanton's foibles until they became political handicaps. His sometimes youthful naïveté translated into inexperienced blunders. America's obsession with debunking its heroes was never more in evidence, never more damaging. The puritanical religious right went after Stanton with a vengeance, perhaps to make up for all the other presidents or congressional leaders that they'd never bothered to hold accountable for their unsavory actions.

And now this unspeakable nightmare. The thought that he would go down in history—assuming there would be anyone left to record it—as the president who presided over the demise of the United States, was the bitterest, the most incomprehensibly terrible legacy to leave behind. He would not be remembered for this, not while he held the highest office in the land.

"What's the status of our nuclear forces?" the president asked, breaking the long silence.

Cowles looked up. His cheeks were wet with the quiet tears he had shed. "The Joint Chiefs don't know how far the weapons systems' virus has gone. They're afraid of blowing up our own cities."

Stanton stood up and looked out the window behind his desk.

"Lee, we've got to do something. We cannot sit by and wait for Asghar to attack."

"I don't know what there is to be done, Mr. President."

Stanton remained thoughtful for a few minutes. Then he looked at Cowles. "Suppose we got somebody in?"

"What do you mean?"

The president's mouth was tense, his eyes narrowed almost to a squint. "Suppose we were able to get someone inside to Asghar. Someone who could take him out." Cowles stared at the president in stunned silence. "Lee, I think we've been going about this all wrong. We've been attacking the tail, when we should have been going for the head.

Kill the head and you'll automatically get the tail. Without Asghar it would all fall apart—he's what holds it together."

Cowles shook his head. "My God, Bob, we don't know where the hell he is! He's probably like Sadaam or Khadafi; y'know, never sleeps in the same tent two nights in a row. How're we going to find him?"

Robert Stanton picked up the phone. "Ellie," he said to his secretary, "get Arthur Kleinholtz in here right away. Thanks."

The battle for Paris was costly and bloody. Like Rome, the "city of lights" was bombed. Unlike Hitler's famous edict not to destroy the glorious French capital and its beloved landmarks, Abu's forces brought the city to its knees, in rubble. A triumphant parade down the Champs Elysées recalled horrible images of German troops and tanks doing the same thing over five decades ago. Only this time there was no Arc de Triomph left to march toward, no tree-lined boulevards, no Notre Dame or Sacré Coeur, no Louvre, no fountains, no sidewalk cafes or Eiffel Tower—it was all gone.

Abu's expanding empire now included Austria and Poland. He had bypassed Switzerland, perhaps because of its long-standing neutrality, or perhaps because it was the headquarters of the WPO. All that remained still untouched on the continent were Germany, Belgium, the Netherlands and Denmark.

But hope was rekindled when U.S. troops began assembling in England. Operation Lionheart was ready. Abu had fortified the coastlines of France, Spain, Portugal and Morocco in anticipation of a counteroffensive. But everyone wondered: Was it too late?

Bennett Williams stood on the cabin's front porch, drinking a cup of steaming coffee and watching a heavy snowfall blanket the surrounding Catskill mountains. He thought back to his childhood and remembered snowfalls that looked like immense ermine carpets covering the ground, soft and white and sparkling under a bright sun. This snow was dirty and gray from the volcanic ash that hovered despite rain and snowfall, making everything look dingy and depressing. A large German shepherd appeared from around the back of the house. He had wandered onto the property one night, looking for food and shelter. He sat whining on the porch until Aimee got up at three in the morning and, despite Williams' protests, went to the front door. She opened the door and the dog just walked right in. He was friendly and gentle; Aimee took an immediate liking to the dog and insisted on keeping him. Williams didn't object, the shepherd would be protection if nothing else. But then he too, grew fond of the animal; he was extremely intelligent, alert, and protective. They named him Hersch and, in less than a week, Williams and Aimee considered him one of the family.

Hersch's ears perked up and he emitted a soft growl as he stood on the porch alongside Williams. "What is it, boy?" Williams asked, his eyes searching through the snowy night, but he couldn't see anything. Hersch growled again, louder, and his hackles raised as he, too, looked around and sniffed the air. Just then, Williams heard a deep pounding sound, muffled at first, then growing louder and sharper. As if out of nowhere, an Army helicopter approached the cabin at tree-top level, slowed, and maneuvered into a landing position. Hersch barked ferociously, but the thunderous sound of the helicopter's engines drowned him out. Aimee, wearing a heavy long coat over her nightgown, rushed onto the porch, staring in shocked disbelief as the olive-green helicopter landed in a snowy whirlpool created by its rotors. It came down in the middle of the large front yard and the moment it was on the ground, the pilot cut the engine. As soon the blades slowed, it was quiet again. All except for the agitated chickens and Hersch's angry barking. Williams had grabbed his shotgun and now aimed it at the helicopter. As the craft's door opened, a man jumped out and began walking toward the cabin. Two Marines in battle gear were right behind him.

"Hersch, shhh," Aimee commanded. "It's okay, boy, shhh." The dog obeyed.

"Bennett Williams—?" the man called out.

"Who are you? What do you want?" Williams lifted the rifle.

"May I come in?"

"First tell me who you are?"

"Name's Sanford Martin, I'm with the CIA."

"Oh Jesus, not again," Williams groaned. "Don't you guys ever give up?"

"Pardon—?" Martin stood at the foot of the porch steps and looked up at Williams.

"A couple of your colleagues were here earlier this year—but then, you wouldn't know that—in your line of work, the right hand never tells the left hand what it's doing—"

"Look, Mr. Williams, I don't know what you're talking about but I need to discuss something with you. And it's urgent."

"Urgent—?"

"I'm here at the personal request of the president of the United States," Martin said.

"Let him in, Ben," Aimee urged. "We're all going to freeze out here."

Inside the cabin, Martin stared solemnly at Williams. "The president has asked me to bring you to Washington, to meet with him at the White House."

"No fucking way," Williams shot back.

"I'm afraid it's not a matter of choice. My orders are clear."

Williams started to raise the shotgun. Aimee stopped him.

"What does the president want with Ben?" she asked Martin as she put her hand on Williams' arm.

"I'm not at liberty to discuss any of this. Merely to escort you back to Washington. Tonight."

There were a few awkward moments of silence. Then Williams took a deep breath and nodded in resignation. He motioned toward the Marine stationed at the front door. "One of them stays here until I get back."

"I don't think—" Martin said.

"Look, there are renegades running all around these mountains." Williams was adamant. "I'm not leaving my family alone—"

Martin acquiesced. "Fair enough. I've got a wife and kid myself. Sergeant Dickson will stay. Now please, Mr. Williams, we've got to get going."

Williams grabbed his parka and turned to Aimee. She appeared to be on the verge of tears. "Everything's going to be fine, sweetheart. You'll be safe here."

"I'm not worried about me or Matthew, I'm worried about you!" she said in a loud whisper.

"He'll be okay, Mrs. Williams," Martin said.

Williams smiled softly at Aimee. He walked her to the far end of the living room, and whispered low enough so only she could hear. "Hey, I like the sound of that . . . 'Mrs. Williams.' "

"Ben, for God's sake, stop acting like this is some kind of lark!"

"Oh, I'm not, believe me, I'm not. I love you, Aimee. And I'll be back."

They embraced quickly but passionately. Williams hurried into the bedroom and looked down at his son who had awakened. As soon as he saw his father, he began gurgling and cooing. Williams picked Matthew up and held him for a moment, kissed the delicate head that now was covered with tiny dark curls and put him back in his crib. "Listen, sport, take care of your mom. I'll be home before you know it." The moment Williams left the room, Matthew began crying. With one last look at Aimee, Williams rushed out of the house and climbed quickly into the helicopter. Aimee watched it take off in its own self-made blizzard, and roar out of sight.

CHAPTER 48

It was still dark when the Huey helicopter set down on the south lawn of the White House. There were no exterior lights and the windows were completely shaded. Williams jumped out of the aircraft, crouched down and followed Martin to the south portico. When he was able to stand upright he looked around. He could make out Marines in full battle gear hunkered behind machine guns in sandbag bunkers that lined the balconies and rooftop. Anti-aircraft guns, surface-to-air missiles, Patriot anti-missile batteries and Abrams tanks dotted the grounds of the White House. Soldiers with M-16s and attack dogs patrolled the entire area. The symbol of American power and freedom had become an armed fortress.

President Stanton greeted Williams hastily but cordially inside the Oval Office. Williams felt somewhat strange standing face-to-face with the president. He realized that Stanton was no more than ten years his senior, but he now looked twenty-five years older. The last six months had irrevocably aged him. Williams had always rather liked Stanton—he voted for him and, on the whole, believed he'd done an extremely competent job for the last three and a half years. Now he felt sorry for him. But still, he wished he hadn't been summoned. As Williams waited nervously, he wondered what this middle-of-the-night invitation was about.

"Have a seat, Mr. Williams," the president said, gesturing to the sofa. At that moment the Oval Office door opened and Arthur Kleinholtz entered, followed by Lee Cowles.

When he was introduced to Kleinholtz, Williams, in an uncharacteristic gesture, complimented the National Security Advisor. "I've read both your books, sir. I thought they were brilliant. Their historical significance will never be dated."

"Thank you," Kleinholtz said. "I've no doubt I'll say the same thing about your book someday."

Yes, someday. Williams felt a tinge of embarrassment. He would have to finish it. He remembered Strunk's words, that even if he were writing it after the fact—in retrospect—it would still be enlightening. After all, he had been the only 'outsider' who had been with Abu from the beginning, who witnessed firsthand the genesis of events that had led to this terrible point in time.

The president gave Williams the merest hint of a smile. "Let me thank you for coming, Mr. Williams."

"I didn't have much choice."

"Yes, well, I suppose that's so," Stanton said, "but it was critical that we meet and talk." His eyes had an intensity that reminded Williams of Abu. It made him extremely uncomfortable. "Mr. Williams, I need your help; the country needs your help." He paused, his voice deepened, combining both the sadness and magnitude of what he was about to say. "In fact, so does the entire world." There was another pause. Cowles watched the president as he spoke; Arthur Kleinholtz stared at Williams with compassion.

"Western civilization, as we know it," Stanton said, "is on the verge of total collapse. Three thousand years of history, of greatness and vision, of extraordinary potential and promise, of hope and glory—" Stanton sounded like he was making a campaign speech, Williams thought, but decided not to interrupt. "—all of it, Mr. Williams, is going up in smoke and we've been powerless to stop it. Half the world has already been destroyed by this barbarian 'friend' of yours."

There it was. The lines were drawn. Not by Williams, but by those who had already decided where his allegiance lay. Still, Williams couldn't deny that despite everything that had happened, Abu was his friend. Ironically, it was at this very moment that Williams realized he loved Abu. He wouldn't defend him, and he certainly wouldn't defend what Abu was doing, but that didn't change what Abu meant to him. He remained silent.

"I'm appealing to you as an American, Mr. Williams," the president said, sounding somewhat more conciliatory. "I'm appealing to whatever sense of loyalty and patriotism you feel toward your country."

"With all due respect, Mr. President, this isn't about patriotism," Williams said. "If that's what you think, then I'm afraid you're missing the point of what's really happening."

Kleinholtz cleared his throat and spoke in his usual sonorous tones.

411

"Mr. Williams, what's important is that we bring an end to the destruction and the global war that is being waged. Don't you agree?"

Williams nodded.

"And time is running out," Cowles added.

Williams looked at the three men opposite him. "What is it you want from me?"

Stanton chose his words carefully. "You're the only man in the Western world who stands any chance of getting close to Sheik Asghar."

"What makes you think that?" Williams asked. He remembered the last time he and Abu met in New York; it was not a friendly parting.

"Because of your special relationship with him," Stanton said simply.

"And because," Kleinholtz added, "he's asked for you."

Williams was shocked. The three men in the Oval Office waited for this stunning piece of news to sink in. "What—!?" was all Williams could say.

"While we were considering how we might arrange to get someone close to Sheik Asghar," Kleinholtz explained, "we received word through the Swiss that he would be willing to discuss terms for peace, but would only do so through you."

"We were as surprised as you, Mr. Williams," the president said.

"You want me to negotiate peace with Abu?" Williams was incredulous.

The president looked at Williams with an ironic half-smile. "No," he said firmly. "Mr. Asghar is hardly someone we can trust. We don't believe for a second he's serious about peace."

"Then why send me?" Williams asked.

There was a long moment of silence as the three men appeared to be deciding amongst themselves who would tell Williams. Cowles was the first to speak. "We believe our best chance might be to terminate Sheik Asghar's leadership in the League of Allied Nations."

Williams got up from the sofa and began pacing the Oval Office. He looked at Cowles and Kleinholtz and then at the president. "You want me to kill Abu?" Williams asked.

"Yes," President Stanton said without emotion.

"With Asghar gone, the League would collapse," Kleinholtz said. "He's the glue that holds it together."

"We want you to dissolve the glue," Cowles said, as though trying to remove the human element from the equation.

Williams stopped pacing and looked down at the carpet. The bald eagle, clasping arrows in one set of talons and an olive branch in the other, stared back as if mocking him. The irony of it all, he thought. "No," Williams said slowly. "I can't do what you ask."

"Goddamn it!" the president suddenly exploded. "Where's your allegiance, Williams?" Before Bennett Williams could respond, the president angrily bellowed, "Good God man, millions of people are suffering and dying because of that monster! You know he's destroying the goddamn world! If you won't fight for your own country, then fight for whatever it is you hold dear and sacred!"

The president's passionate outburst struck every nerve in Williams' being. It was all finally being put on the line—it was about involvement and commitment, about love and loyalty, about what he believed in, what he would live and die for, what it would take to make his life truly stand for something. Overcoming his personal demons and fears through his love for Aimee and his son—that had been only the beginning; this was his real moment of truth. There were no more spectators in the world, only participants. Abu had made certain of that.

Williams sat down on one of the elegant Chippendale chairs next to the sofas. "All right, I'll do it."

The president, his Chief of Staff and his national security advisor heaved a collective sigh of relief. "Good," the president said, visibly pleased. The tension in the room evaporated.

"I'll go. I'll see Abu," Williams added. "But I won't promise anything beyond that."

"What do you mean, Mr. Williams?" the president said, his voice had turned instantly cold.

"I won't be your assassin." Williams looked down again. "Besides, I don't know that he can be killed."

"He's just a man, for Chrissakes," Cowles said. "Of course he can be killed."

Williams glared at Cowles. "Mr. Cowles, Abu is no ordinary man. You don't know who you're dealing with."

Kleinholtz, who had been carefully studying Williams during this entire conversation, said, "Mr. Williams, would you agree to do whatever you can to end the suffering and destruction?"

"Dr. Kleinholtz," Williams said, using the security advisor's Ph.D. title, "Abu said he wanted to talk about peace. I know you and the president don't trust him or believe him. But I do—I know him to be a man of his word. I'll talk to him about—"

Just then there was a knock on the door. It was 6:00 a.m. and daylight was beginning to creep through the closed draperies of the huge picture windows. An aide to Kleinholtz hurried in and handed him a piece of paper. Kleinholtz read it quickly, then looked at Stanton. "Asghar has invaded Russia on three fronts. Casualties are heavy and the Russians are in retreat. He's also begun his move on China across the Indian border."

"Mr. Williams," Lee Cowles fairly sneered, "would you like to tell us again how much you trust Sheik Asghar? I think your friend has made his first crucial mistake."

"Operation Lionheart is going to begin tomorrow," the president said and turned to Williams. "The Pentagon estimates that we have less than a twenty-five percent chance of winning this war. If defeat appears likely, we will launch our nuclear weapons, as will Russia, France, Britain and China. Many may not reach their targets since our computerized weapons' systems have been severely compromised. We may just end up incinerating our own cities. But some will reach their targets—of that the Joint Chiefs have assured me. What will be left after we bring on a nuclear holocaust, God only knows. This is secret information. There's nothing I can do to prevent you from telling Asghar. I just wanted you to know how much the fate of the world is in your hands . . ."

The president's words still echoed in Williams' head as his Swissair 747 landed on the runway in Riyadh, Saudi Arabia. His heart pounded and his hands were damp. He took several deep breaths to quell the wave of nausea that swept over him. He thought of Aimee and Matthew back at the cabin. "Please God," he whispered, "watch over them." He unbuckled his seat belt and stood up. As he approached the door of the plane where two weary flight attendants stood, he felt that he was stepping to the precipice; although a vast unknown awaited Williams, there was no turning back—the bell had tolled for him.

It was past noon, but the dim sunlight was strange and eerie, mixed as it now was with the perpetual planetary shroud of dust and volcanic ash, of fires and gaseous clouds, and the endless residue of destruction, both natural and man-made.

"Ben Williams," a familiar voice said from the bottom of the plane's steps. Williams peered through the semi-darkness and saw Bhaiji waving to him. It wasn't the wave of an old friend, but rather a brusque motion to simply make contact. There were armed soldiers standing by his side. Williams hurried down the steps.

"Bhaiji, it's good to see you." Williams meant it with all his heart.

Bhaiji gestured with his head toward the soldiers. "Please do not be offended, Ben, they are for my protection. Abu insists."

But Williams was offended. "Protection from *me*?"

"Enemies—there are some among us who would wish us harm. Trust is a precious commodity. The closer to the center of power, the rarer it becomes." One of the guards stepped forward to frisk Williams. Bhaiji looked slightly apologetic.

"Am I the enemy?" Williams said as he raised his hands and allowed the guard to pat him down.

"I do not know, Ben. It has been a long time." Then he quickly escorted Williams to a waiting limousine, and the two climbed into the back seat. An armored personnel carrier followed them.

"Strange you not being behind the wheel," Williams said, trying to rekindle their old friendship.

Bhaiji gave a slight smile. "We traveled many miles together, Ben. I hold those memories very dear."

"And how are you these days?"

"I am well," Bhaiji said politely.

"And Satki?"

Bhaiji sighed. "She is dead, Ben. She died just before the war began."

Williams felt his heart constrict. Shock mixed with sudden grief. "How did she—" his voice trailed off.

"She died quickly, it was a stroke. God was merciful."

Williams leaned back and stared vacantly out the car window at the undulating, monotonous desert that fanned out in all directions from the two-lane highway. In a leaden voice Williams finally said, "My God, Bhaiji, why is all this happening?"

"Is it really a surprise, Ben? We all knew this hour would come."

Bhaiji was right. Williams folded his hands in his lap and the two sat in silence as the car sped toward their destination.

It wasn't too long before Williams spotted the first of several Bedouin tents and a group of camels lying in the sand nearby. A small boy in Bedouin clothes was feeding them. As the car neared one tent, the entrance opened and the driver maneuvered the vehicle inside. Just beyond the entrance Williams saw a structure with a ramp leading down into the ground. The personnel carrier followed. The ramp became a tunnel that spiraled downward. It finally leveled out and they drove along a straight tunnel for another half mile. At the end of it was an immense steel door. Troops stood guard outside. When the car approached, they snapped to attention and one of them pushed a button on the wall. The door opened into two halves. The car moved into a cavernous room encased in heavy concrete. Williams marveled at the underground fortress. The car stopped and Williams continued to stare out the window, almost in childlike wonder, as if they'd driven onto the movie set of some fantastic, futuristic thriller.

The immense room was brightly lit, and Williams could see hundreds of soldiers scurrying about. Trucks and armored personnel carriers were parked in neat rows. Bhaiji looked at Williams. "Courtesy of the United States Army Corps of Engineers," he said. "And this is not the only one. There are others. And there were enough munitions and supplies stored by the Americans beneath the Arabian desert to fight three wars."

"Jesus . . ." Williams said, staring in disbelief.

"Come with me," Bhaiji said, opening the car door.

They walked across the concrete floor that was the size of three football fields. At a far wall Bhaiji stopped and pushed a button. A door opened and he and Williams entered a room no bigger than a closet. Bhaiji pushed another button and they began to descend.

"How deep does this go?" Williams asked.

"Quite deep," was all Bhaiji would say.

The tiny elevator came to a stop and the door opened. Williams followed Bhaiji into a room that was smaller than the one above, dimly lit, and filled with consoles lined with computer screens and video displays. A large electronic image occupied one entire wall. It changed between maps of different regions of the world, depicting troop and vessel movements on both sides of the war.

"Our command center," Bhaiji said dispassionately.

The electronic map was now showing the progress of the invasion of Russia. As he watched, Williams saw the lines that indicated three attack fronts moving deeper into Russian territory. Bhaiji looked at Williams. "We are winning," he said, almost in a monotone.

"You don't sound at all pleased," Williams said.

"I have seen enough death and suffering in this world," Bhaiji said. Williams studied him for a moment and realized Bhaiji looked extremely tired and world-weary. "Come, I will take you to your quarters," Bhaiji said as he headed out of the command center, expecting Williams to follow him.

"Quarters!?" Williams was confused and angry. "What the hell's going on? You know I came to see Abu. Take me to him!"

"Abu is very busy. He knows you are here and why you have come."

"Bhaiji, for the sake of our friendship, please, take me to him. I don't need hospitality, I need to talk to Abu." Bhaiji said nothing. "He asked for me, didn't he?" Williams' voice conveyed his insecurity. "Abu does want to talk peace, doesn't he?"

"Is that what they told you?" Bhaiji asked. "Does your president want peace? Is that why he sent you?" Now it was Williams' turn to be silent. He didn't know what to say.

"Please come with me," Bhaiji said, and began walking down a corridor. Williams had no choice but to go with him. Bhaiji stopped and opened a door. The room looked like a suite at the Ramada Inn. There were even curtains on one of the windowless walls. "I would advise you to remain here until you are sent for—it would be dangerous for you to be walking around without an escort." Bhaiji pressed his hands together in front of him and bowed. "*Sat Sri Akal*, Ben Williams." He turned and left.

Williams plopped down on one of the padded chairs in the sitting area just off the bedroom. But he couldn't stay still for more than a minute. He hadn't slept in twenty-four hours, but he was too nervous and too pumped up to do anything but pace the room, waiting to be sent for. He went to the bathroom and splashed cold water on his face. His stomach growled, reminding him he hadn't eaten since yesterday.

But despite the hunger pangs, he had no appetite. He continued his adrenaline-induced pacing.

From what he had just seen, it was obvious that a giant war machine had been unleashed on the world. Even if Abu wanted peace, could he stop the machine? Could he reverse the doomsday scenario?

The more Williams thought about his mission, the more agitated he became. Abu was probably all too aware of what the president was expecting Williams to do. And he himself was afraid of seeing Abu. The very real prospect that, if he killed Abu, he would also end up dead, was not very far from his thoughts. In fact, he couldn't imagine he'd get out alive. Then the irony struck him—the idea of the two of them dying together was somehow poetically fitting, perhaps even just.

But could he kill Abu? Look him in the eye and kill him? He had seen hundreds of men die in battle in the wars and uprisings that he'd covered for the *New York Times* over the last decade. Still, he'd never pulled a trigger or plunged a knife into another man's belly. The sour taste in his mouth made him want to vomit. He raced to the bathroom and leaned over the toilet. All he could produce were dry heaves. He splashed more water on his face. The anxiety continued. Just when Williams thought he was going to snap, there was a knock on the door. Before he could respond, it opened.

Two tall Ikhwan stared at him with black, menacing eyes. "Come," one of them said.

The two men quickly escorted Williams down a corridor, then turned, then down another corridor. Williams felt like a laboratory rat scurrying through a maze. The Ikhwan stopped abruptly at an elevator; its doors opened and they ushered him inside. They began moving up, which surprised Williams, and stopped when they had reached the surface. The doors opened and they were again inside a tent. Williams couldn't tell whether it was one of the three he had seen upon his arrival or another one some distance away. The immensity of this complex deep within the bowels of the earth was as astonishing as it was confusing.

And then Williams saw him. He was at the far end of the large tent, leaning over a table covered with maps. Another man was with him. Williams instantly recognized General Mubambo.

"Well, well. Bennett Williams," Mubambo said.

"General," Williams acknowledged.

Abu straightened and turned. Williams felt a jolt as their eyes met. The profound emotional and spiritual effect that Abu had on him was as powerful as ever. Abu always managed to reach that core place so deep within Williams that, for most of his life, he didn't even know it existed. Abu had given him that awareness, finally put Williams on a direct path to himself. 'If you don't know where you're going, any road will do,' had been pretty much the way Williams had gone through life. Abu changed all that—it was the beginning of his transformation, his true rebirth. He owed so much to this man, he owed *everything* to him.

"It is good to see you, Ben," Abu said. There was affection in his voice, and it was the first time Williams could recall Abu ever using only his first name.

"Hello, Abu." Williams offered a deferential smile. He noted how Abu had aged, how tired he looked, as though the life force within him was being used up very quickly.

General Mubambo looked from Abu to Williams. "You two have things to discuss. I will leave you." Abu nodded as Mubambo gave him a sharp salute and left the room.

Williams looked at Abu and suddenly saw images of Bhopal and Bangladesh, of Myanmar and Banda Aceh, of Somalia and the Ethiopia of Dr. Bertone and the refugee camps, Tipilet Ole Simel and the lion hunt, of sleeping under starry African skies, of dialogues with Abu that had challenged every perception he had, that forced him to face himself and his fears, to comprehend, with humility, his own place in the grand design of things.

Abu invited Williams to sit down across from him in a straight-back leather chair. They sat in silence for a long moment. Finally, Williams said, "I'm so sorry about Satki. She was a great lady."

Abu nodded. "Yes. She helped many."

"She was like a mother to me, you know." Abu nodded again but said nothing. Williams took a deep breath, his mouth was dry and his voice unsteady. He hoped Abu wouldn't notice. "President Stanton asked me to come," Williams offered. Abu nodded solemnly. "He said you wanted to talk peace."

"Is that so? What else did he say?"

"That the war must end."

"Anything else?"

"He said you asked for me." More silence. "Is that true?"

Abu looked at him for a moment. "Yes." Williams felt relieved but wasn't sure why. "I never wanted this war, Ben Williams," Abu said.

"But you started it."

Abu shook his head. "I was merely the hammer. That is all I was ever meant to be." He stared into Williams' eyes. "None of this would have happened without human beings choosing to make it happen. How many prophets must come forth before humanity will listen?"

"Abu, you can end it. You're the only one who can!" Williams' voice pleaded urgency.

"Not yet," Abu said quietly.

"Why?! Give the order! Disengage your forces—"

"It is beyond my control now; the tide of history is prevailing. If this is Armageddon, it is your Armageddon—"

"Abu, millions of people have died—millions more will die if you don't stop—"

"Ben Williams, do you remember the killing fields of Africa? Do you remember the children? What if they were your children? What if Matthew lay dying on bare earth because there was no food, no medicine? What if Aimee was being raped and beaten while your child died? Would you feel the same about this war? Might you not feel righteous in your anger and demand for retribution and justice?"

"This isn't about me, Abu—"

"Oh, but it is, Ben Williams, it is all about you. If you want this war to end, you must take the steps to end it. You choose not to see your impact on the world and, therefore, choose not to take responsibility for what has happened. But you must! Or I promise you, it will go on until the day of Judgment."

"Why me?"

"Because I am making it so!"

"I don't understand—"

"Ben Williams, someone must tell the world why this has happened. And that person is you. It is what you asked for. My task is almost finished; yours is not. That is why I sent for you. This war cannot end until you commit yourself to ensuring that it will never happen again!" Abu paused. "Now do you understand?" Williams swallowed hard. He understood. Abu sat forward. He spoke as if imparting instructions.

"Humanity will need to see me as evil, Ben Williams; he who nearly destroyed the world. It will have to be so for some time."

"How long?"

"Until humanity learns what my true purpose was. You must help them to understand this."

"Abu, why don't you make sure people understand?" Williams suggested. "Sue for peace now and begin the rebuilding. Remember Akhbar? Be a wise and enlightened leader."

"No, Ben Williams," Abu said emphatically, "that is not what I seek to teach. Humanity must learn to lead itself. The pyramid must be inverted. The power must remain with the people. Whoever governs must be the servant, no one must rest until all are rested, no one must eat until all have eaten. Such people will appear in the new order, Ben Williams—if you do your part; if humanity will allow them."

"And what of those you have invested with terrible power—those so-called leaders—the generals and despots you've made into your henchmen in this monstrous conflict? What if they become the new order?"

"Without me, Ben Williams, they will try to devour one another in an effort to become the One. It is what each had in mind to begin with. They do not care about the people; they never have. To them I was the path to their greater power, their ultimate glory. Without me, they will self-destruct." Abu paused. He looked at Williams in a way that he never had before. "Thus, I can no longer remain. I have always known it would end this way."

"I won't do it, Abu."

"But you agreed the war must stop, the suffering must end."

Abu stepped to the desk and opened the drawer. He took out a pistol. "I am the war, Ben Williams. For it to end, I must end."

"I can't." He extended the pistol to Williams. "You can't even be killed," Williams said ironically. "You proved that in Jerusalem."

"Unless I allow it. Unless it will serve a purpose."

"Why must I be the one?"

"Why should you not be the one?" Abu stepped toward him. "Take the gun, Ben," he insisted. Williams looked down at the weapon and extended his trembling hand. Abu turned around so that his back was to Williams. He knelt down. Williams stared at the gun. "It is right,

421

Ben," Abu said in a reassuring voice. "Above all, it is time. The new world order is waiting."

Williams knew Abu was right, about everything. And he knew he had to do it. He held the gun with both hands. He extended the barrel and placed it against the back of Abu's head. Abu remained motionless. He braced himself for the recoil.

Williams felt as though his heart had stopped. Time was suspended. There was stillness all around. They were no longer in a massive military bunker beneath the Saudi Arabian sands, they were no longer anywhere on earth. Nothing felt real and yet everything was more real, more focused than ever before—blazing with a clarity and purpose greater than anything Williams had ever experienced or imagined.

Williams eyes brimmed with tears. His hands steadied around the pistol. "Goodbye, my friend . . . until we meet again," he whispered. Then he pulled the trigger.

CHAPTER 49

The blast from the gun shattered the tranquility of the surrounding desert and rolled unimpeded across the silent sands as if carrying a message for all the world to hear. It wasn't an ordinary gunshot; it was far louder than Williams had expected—an angry explosion, almost human, like the poignant, bitter wail of a parent witnessing the death of a beloved child. Yet, it was beyond human; Williams felt that some preternatural force had been unleashed in the fiery discharge that blew smoke from the barrel and burst Abu's skull. At that moment Williams knew that he was merely the instrument—like the gun itself—its mission: To end Abu's life on earth.

As he gazed down at Abu's corpse, the entrance to the tent flew open and several Ikhwan guards rushed in. They stared in shock at the man who lay face down in an expanding pool of blood. Instantly they drew their swords and charged at Williams. He was about to raise his gun, then stopped. Let them kill me, he thought for a second—perhaps it is only right. They are demanding a just retribution. At that moment, a voice rang out from behind the Ikhwan. "Stop—!" Bhaiji Singh commanded. The guards reluctantly withdrew.

Bhaiji kneeled down and placed a hand on Abu's back and then gently stroked his cheek. He slowly stood up and turned to Williams. The journalist expected his old friend to look at him with condemnation and hatred, but instead all he saw in Bhaiji's eyes were deep sadness and loss. Williams couldn't speak; there were no words to convey apology or guilt or grief. He wanted to embrace Bhaiji; to share the consuming sorrow, take consolation in their mutual anguish. But Bhaiji simply extended his hand for the gun. Williams dropped his eyes and gave it to him.

The tent's entrance flap flew open again. General Mubambo, his pistol drawn, ran in, followed by a small squad of soldiers with automatic rifles. Mubambo looked down at Abu's body, then at Williams.

The soldiers took positions facing the Ikhwan with their backs to Williams. It was then he realized the general's soldiers were there for his protection, not to harm him.

"Come," Bhaiji said, "you must leave now."

To Williams' surprise, a car was already waiting outside and two armored personnel carriers sat idling in front and behind the vehicle.

Bhaiji opened the rear door of the car and motioned for Williams to get in. He climbed into the back seat next to Williams and ordered the driver to go. The car and its escorts swiftly made their way onto the main highway.

After several minutes of pained silence, Bhaiji finally said, "I am sorry, Ben Williams, that you had to be the one."

Williams looked shocked but said nothing. "It was necessary," Bhaiji continued. "There is a chance for peace now." Williams nodded in numbed agreement. "The West will not launch its nuclear weapons— total destruction will not be brought upon the world. The alliance will collapse; the center will not hold. It will become clear that no one can win this war, or any war."

Williams gazed at Bhaiji with tears in his eyes. "And what will happen to you, Bhaiji?"

"It is over for me. My life has served its purpose."

"No—!" Williams said in a pleading voice. "Come with me—carry on the work."

Bhaiji shook his head and smiled. "That was never my task, Ben. This is the way it must be and I accept it. I have no regrets. I have done what I was supposed to do." Bhaiji paused and stared directly into Williams' eyes. "It was Abu's final order that the General and I protect your life. Do you understand?"

At the airport in Riyadh, the waiting Swissair 747 sat on the tarmac. Bhaiji escorted Williams to the foot of the plane's staircase. He would say a final goodbye on the spot where he had greeted Williams less than eight hours ago. To Williams it seemed a lifetime ago.

Bhaiji hastily embraced Williams. "We have each done what we were meant to do. The rest is up to you, Ben, but you must choose to do it."

Williams nodded. "Farewell, my friend," His voice was choked with emotion.

"*Sat Sri Akal*, my brother," Bhaiji responded. His dark eyes were moist, but a smile appeared on his lips.

The moment Williams entered the plane and took a seat, its engines roared to life. The seats next to Williams were empty, and he could have stretched out on them and slept. But despite his exhaustion, he knew he couldn't sleep. He felt a surge of relief as the plane broke free of the earth and climbed into the cloudless sky.

He was going home. Home to Aimee and Matthew.

He let his head fall back against the seat and took a deep breath. Then from somewhere inside him, an intense sadness grew. He thought of those he had loved and lost in such a short period of time—his father, Herschel Strunk, Satki, Bhaiji.

And Abu.

He started to weep; tears poured out of him as never before. Like some great cathartic cleansing of soul and mind and body, they flowed down his cheeks in steady streams, washing away the anguish that was a mixture of grief and pain and fear, of all that had happened, and all that was yet to be.

When he was spent—drained of every ounce of emotion and energy—when the spasms of sorrow and angst finally stopped, Williams felt sleep tugging at him. He reached out for it, but whatever had kept him going for the last two days wouldn't give up. It fought, jerking him back from the edges of unconsciousness. Eventually, exhaustion won—the gentle, steady movement of the plane had rocked him into a fitful slumber.

He began to dream.

A great beast appeared before him, with the body of a lion and ten heads. Except one of the heads had been severed, the one in the center. Broken, twisted arteries extended from the headless neck, pouring out blood with enormous force, blanketing the earth as far as the eye could see. Impassioned masses were no longer praising the beast; they had turned on it. The fearsome creature was impaled with spears until it stumbled and finally fell to the ground, trembling and dying. The masses roared in jubilation. Williams looked up to see a solitary falcon spiraling its way toward the heavens. When Williams looked down again, the beast was gone. He saw crops beginning to grow where its blood had saturated the earth. The spears hurled by the masses were now rakes and plows. He saw the people working the land in peace, in purposeful cooperation.

Then, suddenly, the scene changed. Williams was standing alone in a room. But it had no walls, no floor or ceiling. A bright radiance filled the space. It felt good to be there. Then Satki and Bhaiji stepped out of the light and came, smiling, toward Williams. He looked around. "Am I dead?" he asked.

"No," Satki replied in her sweet, reassuring voice.

"Then where am I?"

"You are where we all live." Williams looked at her quizzically. Satki placed her hand on his heart. "Here," she told him.

Williams felt suffused with a sublime joy. He wanted to cry and thought it was from sadness. But then he realized the fine line between sadness and joy, and the richness that formed the bridge between them.

"None of us are truly separate, my dear Ben," Satki said. "Love fills the void—it is what joins us all. If we choose to see it."

With that, Satki and Bhaiji melted back into the radiance. Williams was content to remain in that place for all eternity. It held neither the emptiness of want nor the compulsion of desire. It was where he felt the peace that comes from simply being. He wanted to savor this contentment, this blissfulness, forever.

"It is time to go, Ben Williams," a familiar voice said.

Williams looked around in all directions trying to find Abu. Want turned to need. The perfect serenity he had just experienced became an overwhelming and urgent yearning. Abu appeared from somewhere in the vast brightness and came toward Williams. He looked remarkably younger, ruggedly handsome, strong and smiling.

"You're still alive," Williams said with surprised relief.

"Yes," Abu said gently. "In this place. Inside you, Ben Williams. It's where I've always lived." Williams looked confused. "I am you, Ben. I have always been you."

Williams nodded with understanding. Abu smiled in that extraordinary way that always filled Williams with an embracing warmth. And then Abu was gone.

A slight turbulence shook the plane and woke Williams up. They were flying through a night sky. Williams looked out the window. The stars never looked closer, brighter, or more reachable. But, Williams wondered, what kind of world are they shining down on right now? At this very moment. A hellish brew of death and destruction, of fear and hatred. Williams sighed. Then something struck him: This was Abu's plan all along. To make all the evil hatch out. To hold the mirror up to humanity; it could either continue on its path of savage madness, of ignorance and violence, or it could choose to change. What choice would humanity make?

Williams thought of the horrors that had recently occurred. Was there enough left standing to begin building on? Millions of people had died. Millions more were homeless and jobless. The world's economies had been toppled. Cataclysmic earthquakes and volcanic eruptions had devastated the landscape. The infrastructures of countless cities, along with roads, bridges, tunnels, and all manner of transportation had been severely damaged or completely destroyed. Farm lands were frozen, flooded or burned. Contaminated air hovered over continents like massive cloud formations. The armies of the West, including the United States, had been decimated. Who would be left to ensure the peace?

Then, another very real, tangible fear suddenly gripped him as though a vise had tightened around his head. What if the world were plunged into another period of feudalism, plague and barbarism, of violent conquest—another Dark Ages? He shuddered at the thought. Then he heard the voice again—the one he had heard in Yangon— 'see how easy it is?' How easy to see through a glass darkly. Williams had to acknowledge that fear would always be there, lurking, just as it had been for him after Bangladesh. From now on though, it wouldn't be the master, merely a servant who bore watching. His anxiety started to abate, almost fade away.

But could there be the 'new order' that Abu had spoken of; that he had lived and died for? Realistically, it was *possible,* Williams reasoned. Abu hadn't destroyed the entire world; he had left just enough. Knowledge had survived. Technology still existed. Industries, schools, hospitals, libraries, universities, centers of art and culture—many remained standing or could be rebuilt. True it would be an enormous, almost daunting task. One that would require a leap of faith for its achievement. Could the human spirit rally? Or had its indomitability been forever vanquished? Williams prayed and hoped—and somewhere deep in his heart, believed—it had not. If people were not completely shattered, were not hopeless and despairing, then they could see the possibilities.

And it was all possible, Williams thought. Abu had made it so. Love is what holds us together, Satki had told him. And now it was up to him, Williams realized. He'd been given a task, he'd been given a life. And so had humanity. He knew he had to rededicate himself to whatever it would take to begin the rebuilding, to begin the healing. He didn't have a plan; he didn't need to know what it would look like—his allegiance would govern his participation in the creation of a better tomorrow. He now knew that was what he had been given to do. It was why he was sent to Bhopal; it was why Abu 'Ali Asghar had come.

Williams looked out at the stars. He was going home. Home to Aimee and Matthew.

And to a new millennium.